MIDNIGHT MAGIC

Chase's fingertips grazed the small shell of her ear and he felt her delicate shiver. "Do you like that?"

"Aye," Marea sighed, before realizing what she'd said.

"And this?" he asked huskily as his lips neared hers. He gave her a first feathery kiss. "Do you like this?"

Her answer was lost in his next, deeper kiss.

Her faint gasp brushed against his lips. Her large amethyst eyes stared up at him, their depths darkened with a passion that tugged at his heart. " 'Tis a powerful spell you've cast on me, temptress," he whispered. He rested his forehead against hers. Her flesh felt like raw silk. "Never have I dreamt anything as sweet as you. I want you. Do you know that?"

They were forehead to forehead, nose to nose. His breath rushed over her face, warming her lips, her cheeks. It felt wonderful, more wonderful than the moonlight playing over their bodies, more wonderful than the cool breeze caressing her aching hot flesh.

"Aye," she whispered back. "Aye, I—I know it."

FIERY ROMANCE

CALIFORNIA CARESS   (2771, $3.75)
by Rebecca Sinclair

Hope Bennett was determined to save her brother's life. And if that meant paying notorious gunslinger Drake Frazier to take his place in a fight, she'd barter her last gold nugget. But Hope soon discovered she'd have to give the handsome rattlesnake more than riches if she wanted his help. His improper demands infuriated her; even as she luxuriated in the tantalizing heat of his embrace, she refused to yield to her desires.

ARIZONA CAPTIVE   (2718, $3.75)
by Laree Bryant

Logan Powers had always taken his role as a lady-killer very seriously and no woman was going to change that. Not even the breathtakingly beautiful Callie Nolan with her luxuriant black hair and startling blue eyes. Logan might have considered a lusty romp with her but it was apparent she was a lady, through and through. Hard as he tried, Logan couldn't resist wanting to take her warm slender body in his arms and hold her close to his heart forever.

DECEPTION'S EMBRACE   (2720, $3.75)
by Jeanne Hansen

Terrified heiress Katrina Montgomery fled Memphis with what little she could carry and headed west, hiding in a freight car. By the time she reached Kansas City, she was feeling almost safe . . . until the handsomest man she'd ever seen entered the car and swept her into his embrace. She didn't know who he was or why he refused to let her go, but when she gazed into his eyes, she somehow knew she could trust him with her life . . . and her heart.

Rebecca Sinclair
Wild Scottish Embrace

ZEBRA BOOKS
KENSINGTON PUBLISHING CORP.

To Hannah Howell, for showing me the way . . .

ZEBRA BOOKS

are published by

Kensington Publishing Corp.
475 Park Avenue South
New York, NY 10016

Copyright © 1991 by Rebecca Sinclair

First printing: July, 1991

Printed in the United States of America

Prologue

Scottish Middle Marches
Kinclearnon Castle in the Scottish Borders. 1571.

They came.

The girl pressed her nose against the glass, fogging it with her rapid breath, but still she could see them clearly. What she saw made her blood run cold.

Her father led them, no doubt to subdue resistance. Her fifteen-year-old chest tightened at the sight of his tall, brawny form. The large arms that had cradled and carried her sleeping body were now secured behind him. His coarse red beard was smeared crimson with dried blood. His left eye was swollen shut. Gashes on his cheeks, brow, and arms bled freely.

Even defeated, as he was trailed by his victorious enemies, Connor MacKenzie's proud stance could not be humbled. His shoulders were squared, his chin held high.

Conquering shouts and laughter melded with agonized screams of those in the keep who resisted and fell.

As the girl watched, a boy of not more than eight summers skidded to a stop in front of the first rider. A broadsword, heavy and unwieldy, was brandished in his untrained hands. His lips were drawn back in a feral snarl. Deadly intent shimmered in his eyes.

A disembodied voice drifted to her, as cold as the glass pressing against her face. The English twang struck fear. "He thinks to fight you, m'lord."

"He's but a pup," another, deeper voice replied.

"Ah, but the pup has fangs."

"I'll tear you apart wi' me bare hands!" the boy shouted, his brogue thick and clear. His cheeks, still bairnishly round, reddened with anger.

Her father turned, and muttered something that made the boy furious. Young muscles strained as he lifted the heavy sword, and arranged his stance in a way that elicited a glint of pride in his defeated laird's eyes.

"Nay! He's English scum! I'll not spare the bastard," the boy argued, shaking his head. The ragged crop of jet black hair scraped his slender shoulders. "Do no' ask it, m'lord."

The derogation had its proper impact on the English leader. Though issued from a mere boy, the insult was nonetheless grave.

The man on horseback slipped his sword from its scabbard. Though the girl could not hear the hiss of it in the air through the glass, she thought she did. Flickering torchlight played off the cold steel blade. Again, her breath fogged the pane. She quickly wiped the vapor to a smudge.

"Come away from the window, Marea," a hushed voice beckoned, as a hand tugged her arm.

Marea turned to see her mother, her waist thick with child, crouching at her side. Alice MacKenzie's nor-

6

mally placid eyes were bright with fear. It was an emotion Marea rarely saw there, and the sight of it frightened her more than that of her father — bruised and beaten, but not subdued.

Her long fingers trembled as she placed her hand in her mother's and let herself be hurried down a dimly lit corridor. The stones beneath her bare feet vibrated with the many footsteps rushing over it. A door slammed at the end of the corridor. At the other end came an anguished scream.

The boy had fallen. Marea knew it without being told. A sob lodged in her throat when she thought of his bravery to country and laird. Would the same fate await her? And if so, would she be as brave as the scrappy lad had been?

A tremble rippled through her as her feet padded to keep step with her mother's heavily burdened strides. As they reached the kitchen at the back of the great hall, she heard the front door crash open.

"Mother?" Marea gasped, turning large eyes on the woman who gripped her hand so tightly she thought it would snap off.

But Alice MacKenzie wasn't looking, she hadn't heard. Her mother's delicately molded face had drained to ash white. Her free hand covered her enlarged waist, and she winced when another bolt of pain tore through her body.

Determined footsteps echoed in the hall, down the corridor. Laughing voices and ribald jesting seemed to shake her mother back to life. She tugged on Marea's hand. "Come, lass. Be quick and silent. They maun not follow."

The door might have been reached had it not been for the gripping pain that made Alice double at the waist.

7

She dropped her daughter's hand and clutched her stomach as an anguished moan slipped past her lips. Her legs buckled, and she slipped limply to the floor, like a rag doll.

Marea had been afraid before. She was terrified now. Kneeling on the stone, she cradled her mother's head in her lap. Her fingers shook when she smoothed back the damp silver curls from her mother's brow. Her frightened gaze darted between the door leading outside, and the door that led from the kitchen back into the keep.

The men were getting closer. Already she could hear their footfalls clomping down the corridor. There was no help for it. Try though she did, Marea was unable to draw her mother to stand. And she would never be able to carry the woman's unconscious body to the safety of the hills.

"What else? We'll skewer him like the pig he is, then set his head high as a warning to the rest. The sight of their defeated laird should humble these bastard Scots—"

"Well, well, well. What have we here?"

A demonic chuckle made Marea's head snap up. She swallowed hard as her gaze fixed on the two men. One she recognized by face. The other by voice. Both were of an age just past her father's and both struck terror in her heart.

One was tall, broad, and light, with the headiness of victory etched in his not unpleasant features. His green eyes were sharp, bespeaking intelligence and cunning. He held a sword drawn and at the ready. The blade was slick with blood.

The other man was everything the first was not. Dark haired, short, and lanky. Bloodthirst sparkled in his black eyes. Like the sword of the other, the dagger in his fist dripped blood on the stones. More splattered over his doublet and hose, matching that which was smeared and caked in his hair, caused by a gash close to his temple.

Seeing the girl gave the men pause. Obviously, they'd thought the keep's inhabitants had escaped long since. Most had. Those who'd not been slaughtered had fled in panic, presuming their mistress and the child had already done so. But her mother had labored hard through the night, and Marea, not knowing what to do, hadn't dared move her. Even now a bright stain of crimson spread with alarming speed across her mother's skirt.

For the length of a heartbeat, her gaze met and held the dark-haired man's. Courage she did not feel sparkled a cold challenge in her gaze, even as his eyes raked her head to toe.

A smile that could only have been cast by the devil himself twisted the dark one's thin lips. "We've made this night's profits all the sweeter," he said, his voice a nasally purr.

"She's but a girl," the blond man scoffed. His green eyes narrowed, his callous gaze picking out the small breasts, newly formed, beneath the splash of the limp white nightdress.

Marea's attention shifted back to the dark-haired one—the devil. An emotion sparked in his eyes. She gulped. She'd seen that look enough times in her father's eyes, when he looked at her mother, but where her father's gaze had always been warm, the one she looked into now was hard, with not a shred of compassion to soften it. And it was punishing.

He spared his blond companion a quick glance. "The boy you just ran through was young. That hardly

9

stopped you."

"The boy deserved what he got. The little cur insulted me. I'll not be insulted before my men. Boy or no boy."

The devil's gaze strayed back to the girl, and his black eyes burned. "Given the chance I'm sure the girl will insult me as well, David. 'Tis a chance I fully intend to give her. Do I have your permission to deal with her as I will?" It wasn't a question. It was clear from his tone he cared not a whit for the answer. His devil's eyes said he would do what he pleased. And what he pleased frightened Marea to death.

"Of course," the one named David said with a shrug. His golden brows arched and an amused grin tugged his lips. His attention diverted by a commotion in the corridor, he turned away. "Do as you please, Reubin. With her and the other," he said over his shoulder, his fingers tightening around the hilt of his sword. "Haven't you always?"

"That I have." He laughed. It was a cold, brittle sound. He was talking to dead air, for his companion had already left. His gaze shifted and pierced the girl as he repeated softly, meaningfully, "That I have. And always will."

Her mother's body tightened with another contraction. Marea stroked her mother's hair with one hand, while the other smoothed over the enlarged abdomen. Both hands shook uncontrollably.

From the corner of her eye, she saw the man approach and felt a shiver of fear. In her mind's eye, she remembered the boy. His fierce loyalty and courage, combined with her own determination to emulate him, kept her chin high.

The devil's boots slapped the floor, crunching over stone and rush. There was no need for caution and he

10

exhibited none. Instead, he stalked toward her like a panther, each footfall sure and precise.

Glancing down, Marea's gaze filled with the sight of his boots as they came to rest near her knee. His feet were two-thirds the length of her thigh, his calves muscled and strong beneath the hose. Swallowing hard, she prayed she'd find the courage to endure what she knew would come next.

"Stand up, bitch!" He sheathed the dagger and crossed lanky arms over his lankier chest. His sharp gaze noted the way her cheeks paled. With a grin, he waited for her to cower and plead before him.

Her MacKenzie pride ran strong; it left no room for begging. She eased her mother's head from her lap, and carefully lowered it to the cold stone floor. Then she did as she was bid. Nothing in her movements suggested reluctance, yet reluctance and hatred were wordlessly implied.

"What's this? No resistance? Hmph! I'd thought all you bloody Scots were filled to the eyeballs with it. Women and children alike. Are you so different from your kinfolk, girl?" He had only to look at her for his answer, for her striking beauty was rare. Rarer still for an age when gangliness was the norm. There was no gangliness in this lovely creature, only a fluid grace and a compelling beauty that could eat a man alive.

A menacing chuckle rumbled in his throat when he felt himself harden. She would not be so lovely, nor so haughty, when he was finished with her. And as for pride . . . he'd not leave her with a scrap of it.

His eyelids thickened when he raked her body. His black eyes fired. The girl's body held great promise. In a few years she would sport a figure to rival her comely face. A figure men for which would have died, had he

11

not stumbled upon her when he did. Now, they would never get the chance.

"Bonnie. You're a bonnie lass," he said in a mock brogue. He felt no regret when his hand snaked out and snatched a fistful of red-gold hair so close to her scalp it made her eyes water. Their gazes clashed. For a brief second, Reubin let himself drown in her large, liquid eyes. Amethyst, a color he'd never seen before, and most likely never would again.

With great force, he tore himself from that gaze. "Are you mute?" he sneered, giving her hair a vicious tug. His teeth were yellowed, his breath foul as it ravaged her upturned cheek. "Is it that you can't talk . . . or won't? Understand, it matters not to me. Your beauty is too fair to ignore. Not that I am gentleman enough to entertain such a notion."

With a flick of his wrist, he yanked her against him. Her soft body was a delight as it rubbed against his hardness. She was trying to free herself, but her struggles were weakened by her size and age. Like that of a doe caught in the steel teeth of a trap, her flailing fists did no damage.

The odor of horse and leather, sweat and blood, clogged in her nostril. The smell was pungent. And terrifying. No less frightening were the greedy hands that pinned her to his chest, snatching her breath away. Gauntleted fingers roamed over her body, the harsh material chaffing sensitive flesh as he invaded places no man had dared to touch before.

Marea was quickly losing control of her panic. In the end, it wasn't the devil's touch that proved her undoing, it was her mother. An agonized groan filled the air. She saw the murderous glint in the man's eyes a split second before she felt the twitch of his arm as he released

12

her hair and went for his dagger.

She reacted instantly. In a move her father had taught her to dampen the ardor of lovesick swains, she yanked her knee up hard into his groin. The softness that met bone was as repugnant as the stale breath that whooshed from his abruptly pale lips.

With childish ease, she broke free of his arms. Her breath came harsh and ragged as she watched him double over, his black eyes bulging and glazed. One gloved hand grasped his aching manhood, while the other continued to reach for the dagger.

Her eyes widened. He wasn't supposed to recover so quickly! She froze, torn between the urge to flee, and the stronger urge to rush to her mother's side. Her shock lost her what little advantage she'd gained. Like a starved wolf in the presence of raw meat, the man pounced on the indecision shimmering in her eyes.

He was on her in an instant, toppling them both with the momentum of his body. Cold stone rushed up to meet her back in a teeth-jarring crash. Pain exploded in her head. Her arms were trapped between them, her fingers numb from the weight of his chest.

She couldn't breathe. Couldn't even struggle.

His demonic chuckle seared her ear. It was swiftly replaced by his mouth. His lips were too warm and too moist. They moved hungrily over the side of her face. Her skin crawled. Though she knew it was useless, she struggled. His gloved hand lifted, cupping a fledgling breast, squeezing hard. She started to cry out, but fierce MacKenzie pride wilted the sound in her throat.

She was naked within seconds, her porcelain body laid out on the stone that froze her tender skin. His dark, lusty gaze scoured her greedily. He ran his tongue over his lips, as though he could already taste her sweetness. The sinister glint in his eyes said he thought the taste sweet enough to savor.

She pinched her eyes closed and bit her tongue. Her blood was warm and salty, the flavor a needed distraction. A scream echoed from the hall, followed by goading voices and harsh male laughter. The noise was muffled by the pounding of her heart.

Her thighs were wrenched apart. She felt him grind his hips into position. She tensed, waiting in dread for the piercing thrust. Her mother had told her the first time would be painful and not pleasant. That was when she'd informed her daughter of the MacKenzie's choice of a husband for her. There would be no husband now, Marea thought, and realized how foolish the notion was. At a time like this her thoughts should *not* be focused on—

The devil was still. For seconds now he hadn't moved, Marea realized foggily. The hardness between her thighs dwindled. His rhythmic breaths faded from ragged and harsh to slowly uneven. Confused, she pried open her eyes to discern the cause.

Her gaze rounded and fixed on a man standing not three feet away. The sounds pouring down the corridor from the hall receded until all she could hear was the rush of her own breath in her ears.

His bearing was every bit as proud as that of the clan he'd just conquered. That was Marea's first thought. Her second was not so generous.

He was much younger than the other two and English to the core. His stance was straight and tall, his build solid enough to cast an imposing shadow over the limp body pressing her to the floor. The light of a dozen sconces flashed over his hair, making it shimmer a rich shade of gold-worked blond. The ragged fringe kissed

14

the broad shelf of his shoulders.

He stepped forward, his heels clicking ominously over cold, hard stone. He hefted a foot on the buttocks of the man atop her and yanked a bloodied dagger from the devil's side. He wiped the blade clean on the uncon-scious man's sleeve, then slipped it into its sheath. Only once that was done did his gaze slide up and mesh with hers. His eyes were emerald green and narrow. In the sconce light, they reminded her of a hawk's. His expres-sion was taut and fathomless.

Marea's mind raced. She wanted desperately to get her mother and see them safely to the hills, then seek help for the babe, but none of that could be done until she'd gained her freedom. There was a problem there, and this third man was it. He was English, and he'd sub-dued her attacker. That could mean but one thing: he meant to take the dark-haired devil's place.

Marea's throat constricted. Frantically, she pushed at the weight pinning her down. The devil rolled off, his body thudding onto the floor beside her. A groan es-caped his lips, but he remained unconscious. Good. She hadn't the strength to fight off one attacker, let alone two.

Panting, she scrambled to her feet and faced her op-ponent. He made no move to lunge for her and Marea wondered why. And then her gaze dropped, her thoughts shifting to the devil's dagger. It protruded from its sheath at his waist, the jeweled hilt was lit by the flick-ering orange shadows like a talisman.

Her decision was sealed by the knowledge of what her fate would be should she not act. She lunged for the dag-ger, hoping to get to it before the man could guess her intent and stop her.

Using the momentum of her body, she rolled to a

squat and came up brandishing the bloody blade. A scowl furrowed her brow when she saw the man was still standing in the same spot, like a human tree sprouting up through stone and mortar. His eyes were still dark and probing, his expression unreadable. He was watching her as though she were a caged, wild beastie.

He stepped toward her.

She cringed.

The dagger sliced through the air, a threatening gesture meant to warn. He wasn't close enough for her to sink the blade into his flesh — yet — but he was close enough to smell. His scent was the same as the two men who'd come before him. Almost. Blood, sweat, leather, horse. Yet on him, the scent had a vague, spicy undertone that made it not quite as repulsive.

He bent and retrieved her nightdress, tossing it to her. The garment billowed and fluttered to the stone floor at her feet. He straightened, nodded briskly, then turned away.

It was a stupid thing to do, she thought, her gaze piercing the broad wedge of his back. How easy it would be for her to plunge the dagger between his shoulder blades. Her fingers twitched when she considered doing just that.

She would always wonder why she didn't. Why, instead, she slipped the nightdress over her head and tied the ribboned sash around her waist. When she was covered, she clutched the dagger to her breast, the sharp tip pointed toward the floor.

Her gaze searched him out. He was kneeling beside her mother. The sound of her bare feet slapping the stones made him glance up. Something flickered behind his eyes, but whatever it was, the emotion was gone before she could decipher it. Her gaze snagged on his hand

16

when he shifted it to his lap. His fingers were thick and stained dark red. Blood caked beneath his short, bluntly cut nails.

Her gaze shifted to her mother. The dear, familiar face was tinged a deathly shade of blue. Marea froze. A sob clogged in her throat and in her heart. She dashed hot tears from her eyes with her fist. The pain that knifed through her was overridden by a surge of fear when the man uncurled his body and stood.

Their gazes clashed. She saw pity swimming in his eyes. She hated that almost as much as she hated the tears that burned in her own.

Without warning, he stepped toward her, his hand extended.

To offer sympathy, or to battle for right of possession? Marea didn't know. Nor did she intend to find out. With trembling fingers, she lifted the dagger and turned it inward, pressing the sharp point against the white linen covering her heart. The jeweled hilt bit into her tender palm, while the tip pricked her flesh. She used that sting to keep her thoughts on an even keel. She had only herself to think of now, and she prayed to God her wisdom was sound.

"I'll not submit to a feckless *Sasunach* dog like you," she spat. Her thick brogue quivered with each panting breath.

His head tipped slowly to the side. A thick gold eyebrow rose respectfully. He studied her hard, as though committing her to memory. Then he cut a deep, mocking bow, spun sharply about, and strode from the room.

He left so abruptly, so unexpectedly, that Marea could do nothing for the space of four throbbing heartbeats but stare in astonishment at the empty archway. Would he realize his error and come back for her?

17

And was she foolish enough to stand there, waiting for such a thing to happen? Nay!

Stifling a sob, she lifted the skirt of her nightdress and filled her eyes, mind, and breaking heart with the last sight she would ever have of her mother. Then, she wrenched open the door leading outside, and, on legs that trembled and threatened to buckle, fled headlong into the night.

Chapter One

Scottish Middle Marches, 1581.

Kinclearnon Castle squatted like a giant stone shadow on a small island hugged by the jutting shores of Solway Firth. The curtain wall surrounding the stone keep and tower was thick and sturdy, weathered from more than two centuries of hard use. A long, narrow bridge of timber and earth ribboned from island to shore. The wood was torn away in places, the earth pitched — unhealed scars inflicted by Lord David Graham, the man whose son was now laird of the castle and its surrounding villages. It had not always been so.

The keep had originally been passed down through generations of Douglases — until Rory the Wretched let it fall into MacKenzie hands. It was Angus MacKenzie, an arrogant, displaced Highlander who, after years of effort, saw the last Douglas sit at the dais in Kinclearnon's great hall.

As tradition insisted, a fierce blood feud between the two clans had erupted, running strong down through the years. By the time Mary's infant son had been made King of Scotland in 1567 — and the Borders were glorying in their violent heyday, men living by the letters of fire and sword — a Douglas had not roamed Kinclearnon's corridors for well over one hundred years. Though not for lack of effort.

Now, to everyone's surprise and no one's pleasure, the castle was thick in the bosom of one of the most hated families on both sides of the Border. Kinclearnon, by way of the young King's regent, Moray, had been gifted to David Graham half a score of years ago in a half-hearted attempt to settle the feud between MacKenzie and Graham. Like similar attempts made by the Wardens of both Scottish and English Middle Marches, the ploy hadn't worked. The keep remained in possession of the Graham — a bold testament to both sides that Border violence did not always go unrewarded.

That, Marea MacKenzie thought as she gazed at the castle from the side of a hill flanking the bank, would soon change.

The history of the keep trickled through her mind as she lifted the gauzy pitch black veil from her face. Pushing the fabric over her head, she let it sag down her back to her shoulder blades. A few wisps of red-gold hair escaped the tight knot at her nape, and a soft breeze lifted the stands, tossing them against her cheeks. The black cloak billowed around her ankles like a blanket being fluffed in the air.

A horn blared inside the castle bailey, signaling the meal hour. The sound echoed off the hill, bounced off the water lapping at the bank, and curled with familiar ease up Marea's spine. A shiver worked over her shoulders as she hugged the woolen cloak tightly about her body to ward off a sudden chill.

In the ten years since she'd been driven from her ancestral home, she'd been within the castle's walls a mere handful of times, and within the keep but once. Yet she returned to gaze at the beloved stone from this spot on mid-hill time and again.

And she remembered. Her mind conjured up the image of her father, Conner, seated at the dais in the great hall, his frail Alice by his side. The image faded, twisting into the haggard Agatha, the witch who'd found her crying her young heart out on the forest floor hours after the Graham's attack.

The old woman had grudgingly welcomed Marea into her shack by the mist-strewn bog those many years ago. Dear, sweet Agatha. Of them all, Marea missed her odd, cackling friend the most.

Her heart constricted as she jerked the veil into place. She turned from the castle, abruptly finding it too painful to look upon, and entered the woods at the top of the hill. Her movements were slowed by the padding stuffed beneath her clothes; padding that gave her naturally slender figure an artificially plump, hunched appearance. Her feet crunched over a carpet of bright autumn leaves and moss. The sound was rivaled by the call of a hawk circling above.

The glen was set ablaze by the flickering orange fingers of dusk. She passed through it with only a glance at its fiery beauty and reentered the woods on the other side.

The bog was rich with its customary, salty scent. Wafts of mist swirled low on the ground. Like a living thing, it curled around her ankles. Had she looked down, she would have seen the wispy vapors had swallowed the lower part of her skirt and boots. But her vision was too blurred with unshed tears to see past the

21

shadowy tree trunks and gnarled brush she skirted around.

She hesitated when the deteriorated shack came into view. Except for tendrils of smoke curling up from the single chimney, the place looked deserted. But Marea knew better, for this shack was now her home.

The aroma of tattie bree, her own peculiar version of the spicy potato soup, thickened the air. Marea smiled. Long ago she'd grown accustomed to fare beggars would sneer at. The welcoming scent settled around her like a familiar blanket and made her stomach grumble in response. Her footsteps quickened as she approached the shack. In her rush to appease her hunger and seek the comforts of her meager home, she didn't see the man until she was upon him. Literally.

He was lying on his side, covered for the most part in mist. Only a broad shoulder and lean hip protruded from the foggy vapors. It was the latter that caught her attention. And her foot. With a stifled gasp, she tripped over the prone body and stumbled into the prickly needles of a pine tree.

The man groaned when her toe sank into his side. Rolling onto his back, he was immediately swallowed up by the mist. His breathing was not. It echoed through the bog in ragged, uneven gasps. It was an ominous sound, made even more alarming by the shadowy fingers of a darkening sky.

Marea's eyes widened as pine needles pricked through her coarse cloak and dress. Her mind was too preoccupied to feel them scratch her skin. Only in times of extreme need did anyone dare the bog. Fewer still braved the shack that housed Agatha, Witch of the Mist. And those who did were usually conscious.

Her hand had the dagger unsheathed from her waist

before she'd given thought to pulling it free. Gripping the metal hilt in her fist, she approached the place where she'd seen the man disappear. Her steps were guarded, the sharp blade ready to plunge. But the man did not spring at her. Indeed, he didn't move at all.

She found him by searching with her hand and what her fingers touched was warm and sticky. A soft moan punctuated the air. The smell of blood was strong here and it made her stomach turn as it fueled her memories. Her hunger evaporated.

Her breath caught as she fanned the mist clinging to his face. It parted like wisps of steam, awarding her her first true look at the intruder. What she saw made her blood run cold and the dagger slip from suddenly slackened fingers.

"Marea?"

Her chin jerked up. Was it the mist that hissed her name . . . or the man? She couldn't tell over the pulse throbbing in her ears.

Frowning, she pulled her hand back, only to find it red with blood. She wiped the stain off on the dried leaves concealed beneath the blanket of mist. Her fingers brushed the cold hilt of the dagger. She snatched it up, sheathing it with trembling fingers.

"Marea? Where are ye, lass?"

The voice, as gritty and masculine as its owner, came from behind. She stiffened when she heard determined footsteps crunch over dry leaves and twigs, drawing closer.

Recognition was instantaneous. Quickly, she scooted back against the nearest birch trunk. She was leaning against the rough bark, bent over one ankle and probing it with inquisitive fingers, when Raonull MacKenzie found her.

"Ah, there ye be." A broad smile cut across her cousin's craggy features, separating the upper portion of his thick red beard from the lower. "What are ye doing down there? And where the devil have ye been?"

Marea glanced up with a smile, which, of course, could not be seen though the thick black veil. Still, her gaze met and held the hazel green eyes of the man known throughout the High and Lowlands as The Randy MacKenzie.

Tall and broad, Raonull MacKenzie was the epitome of the fierce Highland laird's son. His weathered face seemed to sport a scar for every skirmish in which he had been involved. Marea did not doubt his clothes concealed more. His hair was a wild crop of untamed red. The unkempt beard was a shade darker, a tad coarser. In size and stature he had the appearance of a sorely disgruntled bear.

"I tripped over a log and pulled my ankle," she explained, brushing the hem of her skirt into place. She didn't miss the way his gaze darkened appreciatively as it grazed her slender calf and ankle.

Randy's bushy brows furrowed as he regarded her oddly. " 'Tis not like you to be so clumsy, lass. Be there something on your mind?"

"Nay, the padding makes walking awkward," she lied, patting her exaggerated waist. "There be nothing on me mind, Randy." Unfortunately, the "nothing" that was on her mind chose that moment to moan.

Marea's heart stopped, then skipped to life as she sent her cousin a quick glance. Had he noticed? His deepened scowl said he had. She sought immediate distraction.

Brushing the veil back from her face, she sent him a smile that was cast from heaven, and watched all earthly thoughts flee his mind. In a gesture she hoped looked frail and weak, she extended a hand in his direction, forcing a tremble to quiver over her shoulders. "Stop your gawking, Randy and help me up. I could use a pair of good, strong shoulders to lean on," the amethyst gaze twinkled as she perfected a sigh, "and since the Douglas is not here, I suppose you will have to do."

"The Douglas is it now?" he asked with a rumbling chuckle as he encased her fingers in his own. His skin was calloused from years spent wielding a battle axe and broadsword. She thought the feel not entirely unpleasant. "And since when do you harbor a fondness for the likes of that piece of scum . . ." his hazel eyes sparkled wickedly, "Agatha, Witch o' the Mist?"

All humor left her as she raked him head to toe. Her height was unimpressive; she barely reached the clan brooch pinned to his shoulder. Her gaze, however, could be intimidating. It was that which she turned on him now. " 'Tis Marea MacKenzie to you, you great oaf. Do not forget it. Now help me inside. My tattie bree will be burnt to sludge if I do not stir it soon." She smiled up at him, feeling not a twinge of guilt at using the MacKenzie's unnaturally hearty appetite to hasten him away from the wounded man in the mist. "Are ye hungry, Randy? I made enough for us both."

"For your tattie bree?" he asked. He circled her padded waist with his arm and guided her through the trees. "Aye, lass, I'm always hungry for that. Especially if you throw in some of your baps. A softer roll than yours I've never tasted."

Marea kept her gait to a slow hobble as she let herself be led into the small, cluttered, one-room shack. She ladled out their supper, while filling the void of silence by procuring bits of Highland gossip, a rarity in this part of the Borders. It wasn't until after she'd cleared away the pottery dishes that she turned the conversation to the reason she'd summoned Randy to Kinclearnon.

"I have the men," she informed him as her fingers played with a sprig of rosemary she'd left atop the table. "One hundred in all. Has Thomas changed his mind or will he still be matching their number?"

Randy sent her a shrewd glance as he tore off a piece of the bap he cradled in his calloused palm. He popped the chunk of bread into his mouth. A few crumbs scattered his beard as he said around the mouthful, "My father's no liar. If he said he'd match your number, then match it he will. He'll not be happy to do it, though. He's never agreed with your yearning to get Kinclearnon back. And he likes your posing as Agatha even less."

"He does not have to agree, nor to like it, so long as he honors his word. How soon before he sends the men?"

Randy shrugged and finished the rest of his bap. "A fortnight. Two at most." His gaze narrowed. "Do ye know what you're doing, cousin? Usurping the English is not a safe hobby these days. Not with young Jamie eager to test his mettle by settling the Borders. Mayhaps you should let the matter rest."

Marea's fist slammed down on the table. The sprig of rosemary bounced over the edge and fluttered to the floor. "Rest?" she cried, her cheeks crimson. "I've not rested since the bastard Graham slaughtered me family, Randy. Nor should Thomas. Or does he not care 'twas his brother's land they pillaged? His brother's family they *murdered?*"

"O'course he cares," Randy growled. "But these be unsettled, times, lass. More so down here than in the

26

Highlands. 'Tis not a rarity to lose a family to English reivers."

Her chin rose as she met his stare unflinchingly. "Aye. And 'tis not a rarity to want vengeance, either."

"Your time for blood vengeance passed years ago. If you get caught doing this now, the King will not go light on ye. Jamie's clamping down on the Border reivers with an iron hand. Three were beheaded in Sterling last week for pilfering cattle from the English clan Fenwick. I'd hate to see your life end so."

"I'm not pilfering beasties," she scoffed, "and just how *would* you see my life end, Randy? As Agatha, Witch o' the Mist? Would you see me live out my days here in this shack rather than laird Kinclearnon, as a MacKenzie should by right of birth?"

"A *Douglas* should by right of birth," he corrected, and won himself a very hot glare. His lips twisted in a mock smile. "In a man that courage would be admired, cousin. But I do not think you've planned this through. Highland or Low, the MacKenzies have never had a woman laird. I do not think the men would follow a skirt."

"I have gathered one hundred already who are not opposed to the idea."

"Yet," he added.

As she'd done often since Randy's arrival, Marea's thoughts shifted to the man who lay bleeding in the mist. She decided not to pursue the subject. It wasn't uncommon for her and Randy to disagree. They'd been doing so since they were bairns. "I thank you for the concern, Randy, but you canna change my mind. Kinclearnon will be MacKenzie again," she paused for the length of a heartbeat, "with or without your help."

Randy nodded as he reached over the chipped table

top and patted her tightly laced hands. *"With* my help, lass," he assured her. "And to prove it, I've started helping already. You'll find the keep easier to take without the new laird."

"Without—? But the Graham's sons live in Brackenhill. Did they come to attend their father's funeral?"

"The oldest." Randy smiled craftily and boasted, "Come . . . and gone, so to speak. He'll not be giving ye trouble, lass. I've seen to it."

"You went to Kinclearnon?" she asked, incredulous.

"Nay, I did not have to. I met the pup outside your very door, cousin. And ran him through with my broadsword."

Marea's face paled. Her fingers gripped the edge of the table until her knuckles ached. The face in the mist rose to haunt her. Could the man who had saved her life so many years ago be the new laird of Kinclearnon? She swallowed hard.

"Do not look so shocked," Randy scoffed, stroking the coarse length of his beard. " 'Tis the least I could do for your cause."

"Aye, well, I thank you, Randy. Really, I do. As ye say, 'twill make the raid easier. Wh-what did you do with the body?"

He sent her a lazy shrug and gestured to the window. " 'Tis out there . . . somewhere. The pup stumbled into that infernal mist of yours. But do not worry, the wound I gave him was fierce enough. He must have died by now. I'll look for the carcass on my way back."

"Nay," she said quickly. Too quickly, if the look Randy shot her meant anything. She willed her voice steady, and wished it was as easy to will her pounding heart to do the same. "Nay," she repeated, her voice softly controlled now. "I'll do it. 'Twill"—she cleared her throat

28

shakily—"bring me pleasure to bury the *Sasunach* scum myself. Do not deny me the honor."

Randy sighed long and hard. Apparently, the thought of her traipsing through the mist in search of a bloody corpse did not sit well with him. That was a pity, for she needed to tend to the deed herself—for reasons she would not disclose. Marea set about convincing her stubborn cousin of this as quickly as she could, and breathed a sigh of relief when he finally agreed.

She waited until Randy was far gone before gathering up her cloak and flinging it around her shoulders. The wool was warm from where it had been tossed over the rocking chair near the fire, a sharp contrast to the brisk air that stung her cheeks as she threw open the creaking door. Pulling the veil over her face, she stepped into the night.

There was no moon to guide her steps and Marea needed none. She'd traveled the path between shack and wounded man enough times in her mind while sitting with Randy to know it by heart.

The mist had thickened. It now swirled around her knees. In the dark, the rustle of leaves was eerily loud against the chirping and scurrying of night creatures.

Marea knelt at the spot where she remembered the man to be. Her breath fogged the crisp air as she pushed her hand through the mist. The steamy vapors wisped around her forearms and felt oddly clammy against her flesh.

Her fingers encountered bare dirt and crushed leaves. The tip of a broken branch scraped her palm. She snatched her hand back with a gasp, shivering when she felt a slimy creature squiggle across her knuckles.

Where did he go?! her mind screamed as she began pushing to her feet. She had only a second to wait for her answer.

A fist-sized rock whipped past her head, close enough for her to hear the whistle of its passing. It crashed into a tree trunk, then clattered to the forest floor. She stiffened. Her attention snapped over her shoulder.

"Looking for me, mistress? Come to finish the job your devil's spawn started?"

He was sitting on the cold ground, his back leaning heavily against the trunk of a crooked birch. From the waist down, he was obscured by mist. A crimson splotch stained his doublet, the hand clutching his left shoulder was smeared with blood. His broad chest heaved with each ragged breath that tore through his lungs. His cheeks were ashen, his eyes sunken and etched in unnatural shadows. Though his eyelids drooped, his emerald gaze was sharp and clear. Like a wary hawk, he watched her.

"I've not come to kill ye." Her soft voice was distorted by her "Agatha" cackle. Cautiously, she finished pushing to her feet. It was then she noticed the dag gripped tightly in his hand. The barrel of the small pistol was aimed at her heart.

"Then what have you come for, Agatha, Witch o' the Mist? To *watch* me die?"

The black veil rustled around her shoulders when she shook her head, the gauzy material obscuring her scowl. Lacing her fingers tightly at her padded waist, she returned his gaze, though she knew he couldn't see it. "Nay. I came to help, nothing more."

He shifted against the tree and grimaced at the bolt of pain that ripped through his shoulder. A muscle in his strong jaw worked as he waited for the agonizing wave to

30

subside. When it did, he sucked in a ragged breath and said, "Help me, witch? The way you helped my father? Are you not the one they called in to treat David Graham when he took sick? Are you not the witch who *poisoned* him?"

Marea swallowed hard, and was glad he couldn't see her face through the veil; couldn't see her falter. "Aye, 'twas I."

His lips curled into a sneer. "Forgive me then, but I'd rather take my chances and hope someone a bit more 'helpful' stumbles by before I die."

"They'll not find you. No one dares this bog but me." Good God, she was offering to save the man's life — *and he was refusing!* Leaving him here to die would be no more than his stubbornness deserved, she reasoned, while knowing full well she wouldn't do it.

"My men know where I've gone. They'll search for me."

"Eventually," she conceded. "After they get over their terror. They've spent too many years cultivating a fine fear of Agatha. By the time they conquer it, you'll have spilled the last of your lifesblood into the dirt. 'Tis a foolish way to die, even for a *Sasunach* dog."

His finely chiseled mouth drew down; his emerald eyes shot daggers. But he was weak, and growing weaker. Had he been at full strength, Marea would have feared for her life, his anger was that strong.

"Maybe," he said. "But 'tis a far cry better than perishing the way my father did, wouldn't you say? I've heard his death was long and painful. Tortured."

She feigned a careless shrug, proud that the quivering within her didn't show. "Aye, and I'm sure bleeding to death would be painless, and muckle quicker."

She spun on her heel with the intent of stalking away,

31

then stopped abruptly. Years ago, this man had saved her life. A weakness she abhorred demanded she not leave him here to bleed to death. The skirt settled in inky folds around her ankles as she glared at him from over an equally dark, padded shoulder. "Tell me the customs of English burial, *Sasunach*. If ye'll not let me heal ye, I can at least see ye set in the ground proper."

In the few seconds it had taken her to complete the motion, his face had drained to a deathly shade of gray. His body now slumped weakly against the bark. The emerald eyes, thickened by weary lids, had lost their spark, though he looked like he was fighting hard to hold on to it.

"I said," he shifted against the rough cushion of tree trunk ". . . my men . . ." the dag disappeared in the mist as it fell from limp fingers ". . . will come . . ." He blinked, and it seemed to take forever for his eyelids to swoop back up. The second time, they never did, but fluttered in a thick golden fringe against his cheek. His chin sagged until it was pillowed atop his rugged chest. His labored breaths scorched the air.

"Aye, Laird of the Kinclearnon," Marea replied, her voice stripped bare of its Agatha harshness. Swallowing her fear, she approached the unconscious man. Her hem rustled over the leaves and twigs crunching beneath her feet as a soft wind tossed the skirt around her legs. "And come they shall. But they'll not find you. Not whilst Agatha has you."

Chapter Two

Marea sighed and continued bruising the petals and leaves strewn over the flat wooden block. The pestel moved up and down in rhythmic motions that did nothing to belie her annoyance. The veil hid the glare she cast on the man who sat at her table. "I've told ye, Sir Godfrey, six times if my memory does me proud, I've not a clue where your laird went after he left me."

The softness of her voice was muffled by the veil, and obscured by the cackle that was with her always. Shrill and high, the nasal twang had the power to send shivers through the most stalwart of souls.

Robert Godfrey, tall, dark, and lank, was not as immune to the ominous sound as he pretended to be. Already he'd proclaimed his restless discomfort stemmed from the hard bench on which he sat. Marea knew better, for Agatha's reputation preceded her.

"So you've said, hag," he replied, his gaze drifting to the closed door. Outside, a half-dozen armed men waited, ready to charge to his aid if need be. He seemed to gain no comfort from the knowledge. "And so I still do not believe. Where else would Lord Graham go after leaving here? He was expected for the evening meal two days ago." Resting his elbows atop the table, he leaned forward threateningly. "A meal he never arrived for."

A red-tinged brow arched, and she was glad the veil masked her mischievous grin. "Think you his meal was taken here, sir?" Her grin broadened. "Mayhaps as the main course?"

Her cackle ripped up the man's spine. His lean cheeks flushed as the old woman voiced his thoughts to perfection. " 'T-twas not what I said," he blustered. The old wood groaned beneath him as he shifted his weight uncomfortably.

"Nay?"

"Nay! I said he had nowhere else to go. He's not been in Kinclearnon long. He could easily have gotten lost in the woods. 'Tis simple enough to do, even for those born and raised in this wretched place."

Marea shrugged. The fringe of veil brushed her padded shoulders as she turned back to her chore of grinding petals and leaves into a pulpy mash. Her humor took a sharp turn upward as she thought of this salve, when done, resting against the flesh of the man Sir Godfrey so eagerly sought. "Mayhaps you should turn your attention to combing the woods, mon. If your laird be lost, I'd think him anxious to be found by now."

His fist slammed the table. The assorted herbs, berries, and choice pieces of shrub bounced at the force of the blow. " 'Twas done days ago, witch, for all the good it did! His tracks lead to your door, and no farther." Placing balled fists atop the scarred wood, and supporting his weight on a pillow of knuckles, he arched menacingly over the cluttered table top. "I'll know what you've done with him or I'll have your head for the effort it will take me to find out. The punishment for witchcraft is severe in these parts, as you well know."

"Aye," Marea cackled. Raising the board, she pushed the watery pulp into a pottery bowl with her hands. The tips of her fingers were stained a soft lavender. "I know the penalty, were I a witch. I am not. What I be is a *healer*. Ask any who dare the bog. They come for my poultices and salves, not potions of love and vengeance. Ask them. They'll tell ye the way of it."

"They will tell me whatever I've paid them to say, hag. Do not doubt it."

Marea set the board aside and turned to face him. She met his threat head on, like any good MacKenzie would, without so much as a flinch. "I be not a witch," she repeated. The gritty precision of her shrill voice gave the man pause, and after a second's hesitation he collapsed back on the bench. It groaned in protest of his sudden weight.

She wiped the sticky juice from her fingers onto a scrap of soiled cloth, her voice lowering to a lulling pitch. *"Were* I a witch, though, I'd feel inclined to tell you that the grave only aides a sorceress's potency. If 'tis vengeance she seeks, the soil you cover her corpse with will not stop her powers, 'twill enhance them." She shrugged. " 'Tis only rumor I be repeating, o'course, but do you catch my meaning, *Sasunach?*"

His face flooded a furious shade of crimson, but he didn't stand again. "Aye," he growled. "I catch your *threat*."

" 'Tis good enough."

With a crisp nod, she scooped a handful of crossworts from the table, then settled in one of the creaking rocking chairs flanking the hearth. They sat in silence, the man watching as she plucked away the shiny leaves, casting them aside with the dainty, bright yellow flowers in favor of the stringy stems.

"Should you not be out searching for your laird?" she cackled. "Your daylight hours grow scarce, whilst you dawdle your time on a feeble old woman who knows naught."

"You are anything but feeble, hag," Sir Godfrey growled as he stood. The tip of the scabbard, hanging ever ready at his side, clattered against the bench.

"True," she agreed with a smile he couldn't see, and a lazy shrug that he could, "but old I be. Two thousand years, marked this summer past. Mayhaps more. 'Twas a count I lost after one hundred sixty-seven."

The man snorted with disgust, and moved to the door. The sound of his hand on the latch brought the men outside springing to life. He turned and regarded her coldly. "I'll not believe a word, hag. Nor do I believe you've no idea where Lord Graham is. Obviously," his gauntleted hand swept the room, "he is not here. Short of skewering you, there's little to be done about it to-night." His blue eyes shimmered and his black brows knitted severely. "However, let it be known here and now that should I ever find out you lied to me, I shall return to this filthy hovel and run you through myself. And take great pleasure doing it."

Marea's chin tipped up. Even with the gauzy veil hiding her features, anyone could see it for the proud gesture it was. "You can try. I'll not give you an easy time of it, though. Witches are not known for going to their graves complacently. And 'tis rumored that Scots witches are the worst of the lot. Not that *I* would know, mind you. But 'tis the rumor."

"Old bitch," he spat. Wrenching open the door, he stomped into the dwindling light of day, then slammed the door behind his back. Since the portal was not made for melodramatic exits, it made only a soft *whoosh* and *thunk*.

A smile tugged at Marea's lips when she turned back to her work of plucking and shredding. It broadened at the sound of his voice shouting angry commands to his men. The ground trembled with the masculine footsteps that stomped over it, then receded.

Thoughtfully, Marea listened to them go. Unless she missed her guess, Sir Godfrey would leave at least one man to guard her door. At all costs, he would secure her honesty, or, at the very least, exact punishment for her very real lack of it. Were the situation reversed, such would have been her own move.

She sighed and thought of the wounded man she'd concealed beneath the shrubs, a good distance behind the shack. He would need attention soon, before the effects of her drugging potion wore off.

Gathering the shredded mess of plucked stems in her skirt, she rose from the chair. A glance out the curtainless window confirmed her suspicions. A young man with wind-tossed reddish gold hair stood near the line of birch and pine, not close enough to be concealed by it. He was armed to the teeth and eyeing the shack intently. The way he shifted from foot to foot said he was not pleased with his lot.

Smiling and humming an old Scottish hunting tune beneath her breath, Marea set about dispensing herself of her young guard. And she took great delight in doing it.

Blessed is the darkness.

Or so Chase Graham thought every time his body felt

ripped asunder by the deep slash in his flesh. It was at those times, when the pain was at its peak, that he felt ready to surrender to the blessed velvet blackness that reached out like the warm arms of a loving mother.

At other times, he felt less inclined. Like the times he felt cool fingers brush his brow, or the tickle of satiny hair against his bare chest and arms. At those times he would sniff the air and smell the thick tang of spices, finely interwoven with the scent of blossoming heather. There was something exquisitely velvet to be had in those things as well, but it was of quite a different nature, a sweeter nature. The sort usually brought on by harmless flirtations across a crowded dance floor, or the sight of a gently turned ankle. The type was of the carnal variety, much easier for him to relate to.

And at the moment it was horrible absent.

Pain seared him from shoulder to waist, so intense it was almost unbearable. It cut through his mind with alarming regularity, obscuring his thoughts until Chase was positive he envisioned for himself a nurse with flowing hair — satin-soft and fragrant — and eyes the color of heather wet with crystalline droplets of dew.

It was only his imagination, of course. The vision was just that: a vision. A product of the fever raging through his body. What other explanation could there be? A woman of such beauty did not exist. Chase knew, for he'd made it his life's ambition to seek her out if she did. He'd yet to find her, which surprised him not at all.

Still, it was pleasant to imagine she did exist, here and now. And if it occupied his mind trying to name the color of each silky strand of her hair, if distracting thoughts of her took even a small edge off the pain slicing through his body, then what harm could there be in it?

The moist, cool cloth was back to swab his brow and, unconsciously, Chase turned his cheek into the gentle touch. The cloth hesitated for the space of a heartbeat, then continued down his throat. Swallowing proved to be a hard-won lesson in self-control, he found. Especially when the healing ministrations slipped lower.

The coolness of the cloth as it grazed his fevered skin reminded him of the wonderful softness of his vision's fingertips against his brow. The rough cloth did not bring about the same intoxicating sensations those fingers inspired, but he found he could abide the cool, soothing feel of it with little persuasion.

When the cloth slipped away, Chase's hand automatically came up. White-hot pain stabbed through his shoulder, made worse by the abruptness of the movement.

A soft gasp whispered in his ear. The sound tickled the nape of his neck, like the threat of a thunderstorm when the smell of it crackled in the air. The pain was made tolerable by the sweetness of the reward — a slender wrist ensnared within the circle of his fingers.

The flesh he held trapped felt like satin as it wiggled in his calloused palm. Too soft to be real, he thought fleetingly. A pulse throbbed against the heel of his hand, its beat sharp and erratic. The breath rushing in his ear — definitely not his own — turned ragged. When he sucked a gulp of air, he was touched with the scent of heather.

His "vision" was back and Chase couldn't be happier.

The focus of his being was drawn to the sensitive tips of his fingers. The pain in his side faded enough for semirational thought to return. Yet the thoughts plaguing his mind were far from rational and right now he was having the devil's own time trying to pry his eyelids open so he could feast his gaze on what he had, until now, considered only a pleasant dream.

"Rest," a soft, seductive voice murmured. Her sweet breath stirred the hairs on his brow. It stirred other things as well, things Chase was not pleased to find he was too incapacitated to act upon. "Ye'll not get back your strength if ye continue to fight your healer, *Sasunach*. Now, rest."

Like an obedient child, his fingers loosened and his hand dropped back to the straw-filled mat. Why, he wondered, did his palm feel suddenly cold and empty? 'Twas the fever, he told himself, knowing in his heart there was more to it, yet at the same time reluctant to search himself for the answer.

Sasunach, she'd called him in a healthy Scottish brogue. It was a name he'd been saddled with before, often. As always, it conjured up images of a feisty woman-child with a dagger pointed at her breasts. Marea MacKenzie, he'd learned was her name. She, like his vision, possessed hair the color of which he'd yet to name, and a husky voice that promised a man passion, and a body that would, in years to come, promise a man much more.

For the first time, Chase did not slip greedily into the black cavern that brought freedom from pain. His mind was too busy savoring the delicious beauty of his vision, and the sensations that vision evoked. Odd, that he should think of Marea MacKenzie now. Not so odd, he thought, since he'd dreamed of her often since that night in Kinclearnon Castle.

Ah, so 'twas a vision, he told himself as he petered on the edge of white-hot agony and soothing blackness. It *had* to be. No other woman possessed that hair, that voice, that body. It was a dream, a product of an imagination striving for any distraction to keep his mind off the pain.

Pity take it, Chase thought. If he was going to die — and there was never a doubt of that — then he should have had the good sense to choose a better memory than this to savor as his last. He'd yet to put the shame of what his father and Reubin had done the night they'd taken Kinclearnon behind him. And if he lived a thousand years, he probably never would.

So why did he keep thinking of it? And why now? Better he should be remembering the arms of a willing maiden, or the whisper of slaked passion in his ear. Better to remember the tortured days of his childhood in Brackenhill. Better to think of *anything,* even the agonies of battle, than to tease himself with a living, breathing version of his hotly inquisitive mind!

A vision, he told himself as he felt the darkness enfold him once more. This time, unlike the others, the black fingers of oblivion felt oppressive and unwelcome.

A vision, his mind repeated. The words echoing in his mind slurred. He was tired, his energy spent, but his mind refused to hush. *A vision, nothing more. A welcome distraction from pain. A trick of thought to occupy an overtaxed mind. She isn't real. Not to anyone but me, of course.*

Chase's last lucid thought before he began to doze was that he would have dearly liked to meet the spirited girl of his memory, if only to see whether or not she had fulfilled her promise of great beauty. Somehow, he knew she had.

A smile curved his lips as, with a sigh, he slept.

Chapter Three

The fever raged for the better part of a week. At dawn, two days previously, it had broken. Still, the man slept on.

For the life of her, Marea did not know why. He should be awake by now. She'd forgone adding the five-finger grass to his nightly potion the first time she'd touched his brow and felt it cool. Last night she'd omitted the heavy dose of lady's slipper, settling instead for the calming effects of warm chamomile tea spiced with cinnamon.

For two nights she'd lain on her bed of hardpacked earth, listening for sounds of the man's awakening — sounds that never came. She'd tossed restlessly atop the uncomfortable dirt. The few times she'd allowed herself to doze, her ears remained perked. She began to worry.

It was midday now, a week to the day since she'd found him bleeding in the mist. The sun outside was drying the rain that had fallen for the previous two days.

Marea was only half aware of mixing the herb-laced salve she would use when she changed the dressings on her patient's wound. Her mind was not on the task; she was too busy wondering what kept the man sheltered inside his cocoon of peaceful sleep. Without the drugs she'd forced down his throat, he should be alert. He was not. That he *should* be, seemed not to matter.

Sighing, she scratched her chin on her padded shoulder and wondered what else to do for him. The real Agatha's teaching of herbs and their healing powers hadn't extended far enough to cover this type of peculiarity. Not for the first time did she wish her old friend was here to instruct her. Surely there was some concoction the witch could have mashed or boiled to make the man awaken. If so, Marea had no idea what those herbs were, and she feared pumping his body full of more drugs; the effects of might be minimal at best—overtaxing at worst.

Six more hours, she decided as she covered the crockery bowl with a scrap of cloth and set it aside on the counter. She would give him six hours and not a second more. If his eyes had not opened by dusk, she would load him into the cart she'd used to tote the guard Sir Godfrey had left for her. And, not unlike what she had done to that young man, she'd leave her patient on the bridge leading to Kinclearnon Castle for his kinsmen to find. Let *them* aid him in the rest of his recovery, if they could. She had done all she knew how to do.

A wry grin played over her lips when her thoughts touched on the young guard. There had been a price to pay for what she had done to him. She'd barely had time to hide her patient in the thick brush out back before the clan captain was again banging on her door.

To say Sir Godfrey was upset to find his guard trussed and gagged like a pig ready for slaughter would have been an understatement. The man had been enraged,

43

his previous threats spiced by indignation. Only by playing on her well-earned reputation saved Marea from retribution. It would seem that even a man as powerful as Robert Godfrey hesitated to exact punishment from the most feared witch in all of Liddesdale.

Still, the temptation to do just that had simmered in his crisp blue eyes. She thought it was only her threat to slip a more lethal potion than the one she'd fed her guard into Sir Godfrey's own tankard that had finally quelled his ire.

No further guards had been posted, possibly for fear Agatha would murder the next one, and she was grateful for the reprieve. She was not, however, oblivious to the eyes that peered at her shack from the thick covering of trees and brush. The watch on her had grown lax these past three days. She was now spied upon once at midday, and not again until the next. Sir Godfrey kept a respectful distance from the bog.

Marea crossed the room and settled in the rocking chair. The wood creaked and groaned as she adjusted her weight and set it pushing to and fro. The air was chilled with the promise of the coming winter, and even through the thick padding, she welcomed the warmth of the fire.

Six more hours, she reminded herself as she glanced at her still sleeping patient. Six more hours and then she would return Chase Graham to his clansmen and be rid of him for good. Her duty to this man was over. She'd repaid the saving of her own life so many years ago with the saving of his. Surely she owed him no more than that!

The fever had broken two days before. Chase remembered the day well, for it was the same day his angel of mercy had evaporated like the mist that floated about the small shack's door at night, then fled with the first fingers of dawn.

His new nurse was gruff, in possession of the screech-voice of a shrew and a softly plump, shapeless figure that made a man not want to glance beneath the dark veil covering her face to discern what was beneath.

As yet he'd only glimpsed her from beneath a cloak of lashes, but the time for confrontation crackled in the air. Reasonably, he could feign sleep for only so long. When the fever had first broken, he'd needed heavy doses of rest. Today he found he did not need so much. His healing body craved activity. Anything to relieve the soreness immobility had brought to muscles and tendons used to long hours of labor. It rankled to lay here like the invalid he was, but until now there'd been no help for it. But today was different. Chase could feel the change of currents in the air as though it were a palpable thing, and he surmised that Agatha felt it as well.

Throughout the morning he'd often caught the witch regarding him oddly, as though waiting for his eyes to flutter open. The few times he'd risked an outright study of her, he'd found her movements to be awkwardly self-conscious, as though she instinctively knew she was being watched. Now, as she sat rocking in front of the hearth, with the firelight dancing over her darkly clad figure, he thought he saw her stiffen. Thought, but was unsure. Days ago he'd given up trying to guess the witch's actions or motives, for, in truth, he had never expected her to risk so much by saving his life.

Marea felt his gaze rake her. She stiffened, and after the first wave of shock passed, found she did not like at all the tingling sensations his careful perusal evoked.

45

Under the pressure of his gaze, the padding she had grown accustomed to felt heavy and awkward. A fine coat of perspiration dotted her brow and she knew it was the result of more than the aromatic bree she'd leaned over in the chair to stir.

The ladle splashed in the cauldron of bubbling soup. She was glad she was not standing, for her knees felt weaker than the watery broth. The feeling was unwelcome and unnerving, for only now did she realize the man had been feigning sleep, while using the opportunity to watch her. She had a feeling he'd been doing it for quite some time.

"Will you stare at me all day?" she cackled over her shoulder when she could no longer stand the silent inspection.

Slowly, she pushed from the creaking chair, unaware of how her awkward movements looked like the pains of age to the man who lay on the cot. She turned toward him, her hand straying to the base of her spine. Her fingers kneaded the knot of soreness there. Though the gesture suggested a weathered old body, truly the ache stemmed from sleeping on the hardpacked floor while the comfort of her cot was surrendered to her patient.

"I've been thinking of how to repay you for saving my life," Chase lied. The words were purposely slurred, as though the effort it took to utter them tapped what little strength he had.

"Aye, is that the way of it?" she scoffed doubtfully. The thick veil concealed a finely arched brow. Crossing her arms over her chest, she regarded him thoughtfully. "Humph! I'd think words of thanks to be the last to spring to your lips. Or did you forget how adamant you were on my leaving you to die?"

Chase shifted against the lumpy mattress, then

sucked in a quick breath. A wince furrowed his golden brow. Ah, now that was genuine enough, for the pain that had eased in his shoulder throbbed immediately to life. "I didn't forget. My body may be pained, but my memory is sharp. As I recall, my sole interest at the time was living through the night. You'll understand that I was *concerned* about accomplishing that in your care."

"Because of your father?" she asked, unable to resist. Wiping her palms down her padded thighs, she looked at him oddly. "Are you still pointing an accusing finger at me?"

His expression grew guarded. "Is there another place where it belongs?" he countered with forced sweetness.

Marea turned abruptly. Her footsteps were muffled by the dirt floor as she retrieved the pottery bowl of salve from the counter. If she gripped the chipped bowl a bit too tightly, she was the only one to notice.

"Your shoulder needs tending," she said, her tone strained. A smile twitched over her lips when she saw his gaze travel from the bowl to her veiled face. The last time she had seen such skepticism was when she had made her offering to his clansman. Where her young guard had a very real right to his suspicions—she'd liberally drugged his broth—this man did not.

Chase lifted his nose and sniffed. He grimaced at the unsavory smell emanating from the bowl. "What the devil is it?"

Marea found the concern in his eyes amusing. Swallowing her laughter, she cackled in her best witch's voice, " 'Tis poison, *Sasunach*." She waved a hand over the bowl as though a magical spell radiated from the tips of her fingers down into the horrid-smelling mash. "Not the kind one ingests, mind you. 'Tis much better, much slower, to be absorbed through the flesh. 'Tis also more

47

painful. The paste eats through the skin afore settling in the blood, you see. There's naught can be done to stop it. The agony is fierce. Many go insane from it before the first seizures grip."

"I take it there is no antidote?" Chase asked, his voice thick with laughter. His emerald eyes sparkled with delight as one corner of his mouth turned up in a reckless half-smile.

For a woman accustomed to evoking fear, his laughter was unexpected. Still, the sound of it was rich and pleasant, and before she could stop herself, Marea had joined him. "Aye, there is, but only if you be Scot. The cure is said not to work on Englishmen, though 'tis unproven since 'tis never been given to one. Who's to say whether or not it would take?"

Marea's good humor faded the nearer she eased to the cot. For the last week, whenever she'd approached her patient he'd been asleep. This was the first time she had his mocking green gaze with which to contend. And his newly awakened body. She was suddenly very much aware that tending his wound while he lay fevered and unconscious would be much different than doing it while he was vibrantly awake. Muscle and tendon that had lain weakly dormant now bunched and rippled with renewed life. The thought of touching that flesh, shimmering a deep shade of bronze in the soft glow of firelight, unnerved her.

Her sudden restlessness did not go unnoticed by a certain hawkish gaze. Chase watched the witch carefully and thought that for a woman of her considerable age she moved with uncommon grace. The straw filling sagged and crunched beneath her as she perched on the edge of the cot. The shift caused a fresh bolt of pain in Chase's shoulder, but the throbbing was pacified when his gaze drifted to the place where woman and cot met. He scowled, and the pain faded.

The woman, for all appearance, was heavily set. Yet, though the cot dipped, it didn't sway beneath her weight as much as he believed it should have. Either the cot was of a sturdier build than he'd initially given it credit for being, or Agatha was not. As she unbandaged his wound with featherlight fingers, he wondered which it was.

" 'Twill sting," Marea murmured, distracted. It was taking all her concentration just to keep her fingers from trembling. " 'Tis just the poison nibbling through your flesh. Do not spare it a thought. If you'd like we can try the cure in a bit—mind you, just to see if the rumor holds weight. In my calling, 'twould be helpful to know."

She dipped her finger into the bowl and brought it back with a glob of wretched-smelling, thick gray gel on the tip. She smeared the stuff into the nearly healed gash while glancing at him through the curtain of veil. Though his lips were grimly set, he did manage a tight smile at her words. Whatever thought had brought on the dark scowl of a moment ago was gone.

"There." Finished, she sat back to survey her handiwork. She thought that, had the real Agatha been alive, she would have been proud of her pupil's hard-learned skills. " 'Twill be a while afore the first seizures grip you. Care for a bit of bree while you wait? 'Tis scarce, with nary a vegetable, but hearty enough for a sick mon."

Marea set the bowl beneath the cot and started to rise, only to find her wrist ensnared by a surprisingly strong hand. She gasped when she was dragged to sit on the cot once more. His fingers were powerful and tight. She tried to pull away but his grip held fast, with more strength than she thought he should have at this stage of his recovery.

Scowling, she glanced down in time to catch a look of guarded confusion cloud his eyes. His gaze pierced the veil obscuring her face, as though trying to look through the gauzy fabric to the features beneath.

A ripple of fear tingled up her spine, but she pushed it aside. Not so easily overlooked was the rush of sensations surging up her arm. Or the feel of his warm, calloused thumb caressing the sensitive hollow of her wrist. Of a sudden, his naked waist lay much too close to her padded thigh, and the nearness of it fogged her mind with confusion.

"You saved my life, Agatha, Witch o' the Mist," he said. Whether his voice was husky with the pain his unexpected actions brought or with some hidden emotion, Marea was unsure.

"Aye, m'lord." Her clipped nod made the fringe of veil rustle around her padded shoulders. She fixed him with a curious look, wondering where his words were leading. " 'Tis glad I am you finally be noticing it."

"A puzzle, that," he continued as though she hadn't spoken, "since 'tis rumored you harbor no love for the Graham — as my father's death attests." A frown furrowed his golden brow. Marea tensed. "Yet you rescued his son from certain death. You risked all in bringing me to your shack and nursing my wounds." The fingers around her slender wrist tightened as, again, a confusion of emotion flickered in his eyes. Enhanced by the crackling firelight, it was quickly masked by indifference. His voice came low and hard. "I'll have your reasons, old woman, and I'll have them now."

"Do not flatter yerself, mon. I risked naught in bringing you here and playing the nursemaid. Who was there to question or forbid it? Few dare the bog. The fear

50

they have for me is muckle greater than their loyalty to a laird they do not know."

A flicker of pain — inward, not physical — lit his eyes. It was quickly concealed by a scowl. "Then no one came? No one?"

"Aye, they came," she said, and wondered why she bothered taking the time to reassure him. "It just took them a wee bit. I was not lying when I said they'd not search here until their fear was conquered. It took them two days. Would ye rather I'd left ye clinging to the hope your men would find their courage before ye found your maker?"

He glared at her for the space of a heartbeat. His voice, when it came, was as hard and as cold as a slab of granite. "Fine words, witch, but there's nary a reason in the lot. 'Tis your *motive* for saving my life I'm after, not the circumstances surrounding it. Those I remember well enough."

Marea didn't realize his grip had stopped the circulation to her hand until she felt it loosen, and felt the blood rushing back to her fingers. She flexed to aid the return of prickly warmth, and noticed the way the softness of her skin was countered by the calloused ring of his fingers.

" 'Twas entirely selfish, I assure you," she answered breathlessly. This much was true. The rest of what she said was not. Unconsciously, her accent thickened. " 'Twould not bode well for me if the carcass o' Lord Graham were found amidst me bushes, mon. 'Tis bad enough ye accuse me o' murder. 'Twould go doubly hard tae hae me accuser found dead on me doorstoop."

His gaze darkened and instinct told Marea he wanted the concealing veil gone so he might glimpse her eyes and judge for himself if she spoke the truth. "And that is

51

your only reason?"

"Aye," she lied as the image of this man, half a score younger, and a good deal thinner, flashed through her mind. "It be the only one." *I'll tell you of,* she finished silently.

A sigh hissed through his teeth. He dropped her wrist as though he no longer had the strength to hold it. His eyelids swooped shut as he tossed his good arm over his eyes.

His brawny forearm concealed his brow, and the bridge of a strong, straight nose. The lower portion of his face was cast in shadows that made his tanned cheekbones seem higher, the hollow beneath deeper. A muscle in the hard U of his jaw jerked beneath a stubble of golden whiskers. Marea's gaze strayed lower and she realized she had been so caught up in their conversation she'd forgotten to replace his bandages. The thought of touching his warm flesh again made her shiver and swiftly abandon the idea.

She was on her feet in an instant, and across the room in half that. She wanted as much distance between herself and this man as she could get. Not only didn't she want him reopening the wound she'd taken pains to seal should he try to grab her again, but she was also not pleased with the way her body was reacting to him. It was disconcerting, this wild throbbing of the heart, this inability to smell anything but a musky male scent. Nor did she like the way her legs turned to porridge, or the way her skin tingled as though it had been stung by a thousand honeybees in the very spot their flesh had touched.

"Agatha?" His husky voice startled Marea into turning her back on the warmth of the fire. It was clear from his raspy tone that his strength was tapped. So much so that he did not bother to remove the arm from his face as he spoke. "Be you the only one to nurse me through? I've memory of another."

Like a sliver of rope being firmly snapped, she stiffened. How much did he remember? Dear Lord, did he even now remember that night half a score ago as clearly as she did? Did he remember *her?*

Through the thickness that tightened her chest she said, "Nay, *Sasunach,* 'twas only those who danced in your mind. The potion I fed you for the fever is wont to bring on images that seem real enough to touch. But they be only images. Visions. Products of the mind." She swallowed hard, and before she could stop herself asked, "Who be the other you thought to see?"

" 'Twas a"—he stifled a yawn—"woman."

"Do you know her?"

His reckless grin had the power to stop her heart. Had his eyes not been shielded, Marea thought they would have been as dreamy as his voice.

"Nay," he whispered raggedly, "though many's the time I wish I did. As your kinsmen would say, a bonnier lass you'll ne'er set eyes to. Full of face and figure, with hair the color of . . . aye, a harvest sun touched with fire. And eyes to rival the richest field of Scottish heather."

"S-she sounds bonnie."

"Aye, she is." His voice thickened as the hand over his face clenched into a fist. "I met her when she was a child defending her honor. Many's the night I've dreamed of her since. The comely witch haunts me."

Marea collapsed onto the rocking chair. The hard seat groaned beneath her, but she barely heard the creaking wood or the crackle of flames in the hearth, over the pounding of her heart. The heat of the fire engulfed her, but it wasn't enough to warm the chill in her bones, the bitter cold of memories best left buried. "Have ye ne'er seen the lass again?" she asked, her voice shaking.

He was silent for so long she thought he'd fallen asleep. Then, suddenly, he shook his head. The fringe of shaggy blond hair kissed his wounded shoulder. "I thought to once, from a distance, on the streets of London." He smiled sleepily at a memory only he could see. "Chased her across the city before I realized 'twas not the same girl. It took years to live the jest down, for I was with friends who thought my curious behavior that of an insane man. Could be they were right. My emotions when I think of this girl are quite strong . . . quite unreasonable."

"What emotions are those, mon?" she queried weakly, holding her breath until the answer passed his lips, an answer which tied their memories together in an unbreakable silken web.

"Damned if I know, though not for lack of effort. Whatever they are, they are fierce." Sighing tiredly, he nuzzled his head against the meager pillow. " 'Twould seem a potent combination of protectiveness, admiration, and . . . aye, a small bit of lust."

Marea sucked in a shaky breath, trying to ignore the way his words made her heart stutter. "I-I do not understand, *Sasunach*. Why would you think to see the lass here? In a witch's hovel?" It was a dangerous question, one she already knew the answer to. Still, the need to hear the words surpassed her yearning not to.

" 'Twould be appropriate, since Kinclearnon is . . . where I saw her first," he confessed sleepily, already starting to doze. "Pity . . . she was nothing more than a vision." He fell silent, and again Marea thought he was asleep, until she heard him murmur, "Ah, so very beautiful."

His arm slumped to the pillow. His breathing slowed to a rhythmic pace. The thick fringe of honey-tipped lashes fluttered against his cheek, where healthy color was beginning to return.

Marea sucked in a breath and rose on shaky legs. She crossed to the cot and stood looking down upon the brawny figure encased in flickering shadows. With featherlight fingers she surrendered to temptation and reached out. His brow felt cool and smooth under her fingertips as she brushed a silky blond curl back. The tip of his hair tickled her palm, the feel of his flesh gliding beneath her hand was softer than it had a right to be. She snatched her hand back, her fingers oddly cold.

" 'Tis dead the lass is," Marea whispered. The Agatha shrillness was gone from her voice, but her tone was no less ragged, no less strained. "She has been for near half a score. I know. I buried her myself. 'Tis glad I am to see her gone, mon, for were she here you might have touched her heart with your gentle words. They might have made a difference."

Spinning on her heel, she snatched her cloak from where it hung on a peg by the door. She flung the threadbare scrap of wool about her shoulders and hugged it close, clinging to its warmth as she stepped into the mist that had come early this eve.

Come dawn she would see this man returned to the keep. He was well enough to survive without her now, and the sooner he was gone from her shack, the sooner she could focus her thoughts on gathering more forces and wrestling Kinclearnon from the clutches of the Graham. From him.

She filled her lungs with the crisp scent of salt rising

from the bog and thought that, in a short while, Kin-clearnon would be restored to the MacKenzie, where it should have passed by right of birth. Gone forever would be the Grahams, God rot their filthy souls. Every last one of them!

Chapter Four

"I do not like it. Not at all." The force of Lord Reubin's words were echoed in the fist he slammed on the top of the dais. More than one overfilled tankard rattled with the blow, sloshing their foamy contents over their sides. "And should I ask how much longer you suggest we postpone the funeral? 'Tis been over a week. Soon enough the rotting corpse will rise up and *demand* we bury it. Already the stench in the tower room grows thick."

Sir Godfrey's eyes narrowed, the thickened lids served as a shield to mask his disgust. His fingers played with his empty tankard. He'd been considering waving the buxom serving wench over to refill it when Lord Reubin's words rang through the hall. Now, he found a sudden distaste for the brew. The two tankards he'd already drunk churned in his gut when he raised his eyes to meet the dark, evil glare of the speaker.

'Twas rumored Lord Carl Reubin was a friend of long standing to the Grahams. But his sharp words and callous opinions denied it. Sir Godfrey wondered which it was for the man, friend or foe. And he wondered if a man such as Lord Reubin would even know what the difference was.

Sir Godfrey pushed the tankard aside and noticed the silence that engulfed the hall as those present awaited his answer. With the old laird laid out in an upstairs chamber, and the new laird glaringly absent, the weight of running the keep fell to his lean shoulders. It was a burden for which he had no taste. "Sir," he said finally, his voice laced with suppressed intolerance, "I understand your concern, but there's naught to be done. The keep has been searched thoroughly on the chance the new laird returned without being seen. The holdings have been combed. Peasants have been questioned, and caverns turned asunder. I know not what else you'd have us do."

Balancing his weight on clenched knuckles, Lord Reubin leaned across the table. His black eyes glinted like diamonds cast from the devil's own mold. "I'll have you find him, Godfrey," he growled, "or I'll have your head. The funeral will be set for dawn, day after tomorrow. Dead or alive, I expect the young laird to be in attendance." His smile was cold, quick, and devoid of feeling. "Do we understand each other?"

Slowly, Sir Godfrey's gaze lifted from where it was fixed on a minuscule chip in the rim of his tankard. His blue gaze clashed with stygian, black and his blood turned to ice.

Tension rippled through the men gathered in the hall. From the corner of his eye, Sir Godfrey saw more than one hardened hand drift to his broadsword. Unfortunately, too many of those skilled hands were under the control of Lord Reubin.

They were fighting men, the lot of them, all ruthlessly cunning, and as filled with bloodlust as the bastard to which they pledged their allegiance. All were itching for a battle too many days postponed. That they could, with ease, overtake the castle went without question. Whether or not they'd dare was not apparent. Only one thing was obvious: Reubin's forces far outweighed Graham's, in or out of the old castle walls. The sum of Graham had been sorely depleted by the many who'd drifted off during the last days of the old laird's illness.

" 'Twill be arranged," Sir Godfrey grumbled. He lost no love for Carl Reubin; the more the man raged and demanded, the more Sir Godfrey's respect for him dwindled. Now, it was nonexistent. Still, his position as captain was well earned, and it was one that demanded he protect Kinclearnon in the absence of its laird. As tempting as it was, it went against Sir Godfrey's grain to betray the trust placed in him. "I'll have the women prepare the burial feast and fetch the clergy. Dawn, day after next."

With a clipped nod, Lord Reubin pushed to his feet. Another nod, this one barely perceptible, brought his retainers to his back as he moved toward the stone archway. More than one grumble that there'd be no bloodshed this day rumbled through the men.

The hall was near empty when Reubin turned back, fixing Sir Godfrey with an imperial glare. Looking down his long nose, he sneered, "I'll not be disappointed in this. Many's the man, or woman, who has regretted disappointing me," he said, his eyes bright with demonic promise.

Sir Godfrey watched the man spin on his heel and

stalk from the hall. When the thunder of footsteps had receded, he seized his empty tankard and hurled it across the room. It shattered on contact, raining pottery slivers to the rush-covered floor. A mousey servant girl scurried to sweep the mess.

"Do ye think he has the nerve?" a craggy voice asked as a veritable sliver of a man slid onto the bench. Sir Godfrey didn't need to look to know who it was, though he looked anyway.

Zander MacVin was an odd man, in personality and appearance. Smaller than most, he had a crop of orange curls that framed his baby-round face. Of his body, only his hands were the size of a normal man's; all else looked like it had been shrunk to size.

For the most part, MacVin kept to himself—and the comely kitchen help when he could get away with it. He was one of the few retainers whose time within the keep dated to the MacKenzie—something about which the Grahams still taunted him. His loyalty to the Graham had always been in question—for obvious reasons—though his *dis*loyalty had never been proven. For the life of him, Sir Godfrey could not understand what kept MacVin there. Were the situation reversed, he would have sought the company of those who enjoyed his presence, not resented it.

"Aye," Sir Godfrey grumbled finally and waved a woman to bring him another tankard. "Reubin has all that nerve and more. Methinks he looks for an excuse to take control of Kinclearnon. 'Tis rumored he desires this keep for himself."

"He's had plenty of chances to take it, be that his wish," Zander mumbled thoughtfully, scratching the patchy, gray-red stubble that covered his chin. He sent a toothy smile to the wench who set twin mugs of foamy ale before them. "What makes ye think he'd try it now?"

Sir Godfrey drained a healthy swallow from his tankard and wiped the foam from his lips onto the sleeve of his tunic. "For the first time the lairdship of Kinclearnon is in dispute. Though his methods lean more toward trickery, I doubt Reubin could pass over such an opportunity. He will, no doubt, take advantage of the turmoil breaking in a new laird will entail. 'Tis the type of man he is."

"He's no mon by my standards," Zander grumbled.

Sir Godfrey agreed absently as he fingered his mug. "You may stand only as tall as a woman's shoulder, if she be short, but you're twice the man he is." He spared a gruff chuckle when the small man's chest puffed. "Not a compliment, MacVin. Yonder wench is as well."

"Ah, but the lass is woman enough to warm my bed anytime she pleases." The small man sent a sly wink to the woman in question who, having heard this remark, muttered something unintelligible, but unkind in tone, to a man at a nearby table. The hall rang with their laughter. Zander's lanky chest deflated as he snuck a shrewd glance at his thoughtful companion. "What be your plan to stop Reubin?" he asked, raising the tankard to his lips.

" 'Tis simple enough." He drained the tankard, then shoved it across the table and motioned for the wench to refill it. "I'll find the young laird in time for the burial. Reubin will see he'll not have an easy time wrestling Kinclearnon from a man like Chase Graham, though I do look forward to seeing him try."

Zander came very close to choking on his ale. His tankard slammed atop the dais and ale sloshed over the sides. His eyes grew wide. " 'Tis a large task you're about, sir. The new laird's not been seen for eight days. 'Tis rumored he's dead."

Sir Godfrey shrugged. "Since dead men usually leave corpses in their wake and since we've found none of Chase, I prefer to think he lives." He fixed Zander with a reproachful glance. "You'd do well to think the same, since I can only imagine what Reubin would do with the likes of you. 'Tis rumored there's not much he dislikes more than a Scot."

"Women," Zander spat vehemently. "He likes the lassies as much as us."

Sir Godfrey nodded as another tankard of ale was placed in front of him. He nodded a curt thanks, but did not pick it up. Rather, he stared thoughtfully into the foamy contents. "And speaking of women, I can think of one in particular I'd like to get my hands on." He sent his companion an assessing glance. "Agatha, the dreaded Witch of the Mist. Tell me what you know of her, MacVin and be precise. I've spoken to the villagers, but they won't talk of her."

"Are ye surprised? The witch is well known. Respected, if not well liked. 'Tis rumored she's lived in that bog since the first stone was set to this keep. 'Tis also rumored she placed a curse on the Graham the day he stormed it and took it as his own. O'course, 'tis only rumor. The people of Kinclearnon are wont to make up tales of Agatha. None know whether or not they be true."

"Then she really is a witch? 'Tis not just a rumor?"

Zander set his empty mug on the table and scratched his patchy beard with nails that were cracked and ragged. "Nay, she be no witch. Ask her yourself. She'll tell you she's a healer, not a devil's

62

aide."

Sir Godfrey smiled grimly. The same words, in Agatha's shrewish voice, echoed in his ears. "What she says as opposed to what she *is* could well be two different things."

" 'Tis possible. Who wouldn't fear being branded a witch? Mayhaps that be why she denies the charge so vehemently. Still . . ." The small shoulders rose and fell. "Be she truly a witch, methinks she would have been brought to call by now. Many's the chance they've had and not used."

"Could be fear that holds them back," Sir Godfrey mused. "If the rumors hold weight and her powers are strong, surely there would be few willing to speak against her. Lord knows what she'd do to them if they tried."

"Loony she be, sir, I'll not argue there, but the witch has never hurt anyone." His staunch tone caused Sir Godfrey to cast him a look just shy of astonishment. The subject of the old laird's death hung in silence between them. " 'Tis true. Most stay away from the bog, fear being as good a reason as any, but she's never hurt any who dared it. 'Tis many the life old Agatha's been *known* to save." He sent Sir Godfrey a sly wink. "*Known,* sir. That be fact, not a rumor like the rest."

"Aye," Sir Godfrey replied through tightened lips. "A fact, you say? As the dead man upstairs will attest to?"

Zander whitened, but held firm. "I'll not pretend to know the hows and whys of that. I've heard the rumor she killed the laird. Mayhaps 'tis true, but I do not ken it. She had no reason to do him harm."

"Her flagrant loyalty to the dead MacKenzie all

these years is good enough reason for me."

Zander frowned and shook his head. "If 'tis vengeance she seeks, it comes a wee bit late, sir. The MacKenzie's been dead many years now. And what purpose would killing the Graham serve? 'Twould not bring back her—" He gulped hard and snapped his mouth shut.

Sir Godfrey's demand that Zander finish his statement was, thankfully, cut off by the thunder of hooves in the bailey. Before either man could rise from his bench, a young page burst into the hall.

" 'Tis the Douglas, Captain," the young man panted, his face flushed from exertion. "His troops have been spotted near Malain. He appears to be riding this way."

Swearing under his breath, Sir Godfrey sprang to his feet. His fingers unconsciously caressed the hilt of his broadsword as he gathered what few men remained and strode from the hall. All but the castle's safety was gone from his mind.

No one noticed when Zander remained seated. By the time the serving wench who'd rationed the ale slid onto the bench at his side, there was no one left in the hall to see.

"Ye maun get word to her," she hissed.

"What will you have me say? That the Douglas attacks? What of it? I'd think her already aware of the fact by now."

The girl sneered when she felt Zander's fingers fondle her knee. Gritting her teeth, she slapped the offending hand away. "Nay, ye foolish mon. Ye maun tell her o' Godfrey's suspicions. Ye maun tell her to give the *Sasunach* back."

Zander shrugged. Though he agreed, he had his

own reasons for arguing. "She'll not listen, Sally. Nothing I say would make her give him back afore she's ready. O'course, there's a chance there's nothing left to *give*. Could be the young laird's already dead. You've heard the rumors about his father."

"Aye, and I'll not believe a word. She'd never do such a thing. But she'll die being accused of it if ye do not get to her in time." Sally nibbled her lower lip when Zander seemed in no hurry to leave the hall. Swallowing hard, she used the only other means of persuasion she knew. "Please, Zander," she murmured, and sidled up to him, nuzzling his small, wrinkled neck. She fingered the laces of his tunic. "I'd be most happy if you'd do this wee thing for me." Her tongue trailed up to his ear. "Most happy."

"And grateful?" he asked breathlessly. "Just how grateful would ye be, lass?"

She giggled, and her hand strayed lower. Zander sucked in a ragged breath when her fingers brushed against him.

"Very grateful, Zander," she sighed.

Zander grasped her wrist and pulled her away. He stood up, and looked down at her. Well, across really, for they were on eye level even when he stood at his full, unimposing height. "Then leave me be, lass, so I can be on me way." He winked, and the tip of his tongue darted out to moisten suddenly parched lips. "The sooner I be off, the sooner I be back . . . so you can show me how grateful you'd truly be."

Chapter Five

It was a fine day for a funeral.

The sky was dark and overcast, the air brisk with the promise of winter. Branches swayed in the soft wind. The ceiling of dry red, orange, and gold leaves rustled as they clung to their branches, defying the rapidly changing season to pluck them from their summer perch.

The mourners began returning to the castle walls. Soon the darkly clad figures began to scatter. Only a stalwart few lingered over the freshly filled grave. A light drizzle trickled through their hair, eventually convincing all but one to seek the dryness of the hall.

It was on the one remaining figure that Marea trained her vision. The clock was just shy four-and-twenty hours since the last time she'd seen him. Just shy of four-and-twenty hours since she'd given into Zander's insistent urging and lowered Chase Graham's rugged body onto the chipped stone bridge leading to the castle.

He looked none the worse for wear. Indeed, he looked quite good. Swathed in black from head to toe, the dark attire accentuated his appealing lightness. Black satin stretched over his torso, glistened with the rain that moistened it, enhancing the breadth of his shoulders and chest. The tightness of his sleeves called unnecessary attention to the strength lying dormant beneath. His head was bowed, his hands clasped tightly behind his back. His jaw grazed the silver braid at his collar, while his thick blond hair scratched his shoulders and brow. She saw enough of his face to know that his color was good and healthy. That he was on his feet attested to his swiftly regained strength.

Marea shifted amidst the concealing cloak of forest, but her gaze never strayed from Chase Graham. The hem of her pitch black cloak fluttered around her ankles. Her feet crunched over the blanket of dry leaves as the moist breeze tugged at the folds of her hood. Though the thick veil obscured her face, she felt the crisp October air sting her cheeks.

She was taking a risk coming here this morn. It was a risk made greater when one considered the crime Chase Graham accused her of, and the crime she'd every intention of committing against him. But Marea couldn't stay away. She was drawn to the wrought-iron encased burial ground bordering the forest like the vapors of mist were drawn to her bog. The need to see her father's murderer laid to rest was too overwhelming to deny.

As she watched, Chase Graham's broad shoulders tensed, and his blond head snapped up. A sharp gaze swept the clearing.

Marea stepped back, melting against a thick tree trunk. The bark bit through her cloak, scratching her back. She took a sharp breath, and held it until her lungs burned.

It was, of course, impossible for Chase Graham to see

her. The murkiness of the day concealed her darkly clad, rigid form in the shadows of the forest. Yet, even as she thought this, Marea felt an intense gaze fix on her and hold.

He stood for the space of two heartbeats, then took a step around his father's freshly filled grave. The breath left her lungs in a rush when she saw each sure footfall carry him closer to the trees that hid her. His direction never wavered.

Swallowing a lump of apprehension, she lifted her chin with MacKenzie pride and waited until he'd reached the line of trees. The sound of his boots crunching over moist leaves was deafening.

She slipped her hands behind her back, and gripped the rough bark until she felt the bite of it against her fingertips. "Good aft, *Sasunach*. Ye seemed to have healed well enough."

Chase stopped. Spreading his legs apart, he clasped his hands behind his back and let his gaze rake the old hag from head to toe. With her high, shrill voice, and the shadows playing around her veil, he could see why the villagers had such a deep fear of this woman. "My good health is all thanks to your handiwork, Agatha. 'Twould appear I owe you my life."

She waved the suggestion away and cackled shrilly. A genuine laugh almost escaped her when she saw him wince at the sound. "You owe me naught. 'Twould take a wee sum to replace the herbs and roots I forced down you." When his eyes narrowed at her glibness, she lowered her voice and added, "I did what any other would have done. 'Tis not heroics I was after, nor your thanks, merely the tending of another in need."

Dismissing the subject, she nodded over his shoulder

to the murky silhouette of Kinclearnon Castle. "Ye should be inside with your kin, *Sasunach*. Go, afore you catch your death." Her gaze narrowed on the moist droplets clinging to his golden hair. "I'd not be happy to think I saved you only to have you die of fever. And I'll not play nursemaid to you again."

"There'll be no need." His golden brows furrowed when he noticed her diverted attention. Chase glanced over his shoulder at the castle, and his frown deepened. "Since you have so bravely attended my father's funeral, Agatha, why not complete the task?" In a gesture that was exquisitely cut and gallant, he offered her a crooked elbow and sketched a bow. "Do me the honor of accompanying me inside. The second service will commence soon, and I'd think the meat and ale Reubin's supplied in surplus to be a welcome treat for you, if not the company itself."

Marea glanced at his arm, but refused to accept either it or his offer. Eventually, his arm dropped back to his increasingly rain-dampened side.

"Aye, *Sasunach*," she said with a cold chuckle, "would that not be a fine sight? I've no doubt your guards would clap me in irons the second I stepped past the portcullis." Her eyes clouded over as she fixed him with a meaningful stare through the veil. " 'Few's the time I've been in yonder keep, and then 'twas only through the servant's door they led me."

Chase flashed her a wry grin that belied the day and the grimness of events that had thrust them together. His arm rose in a second offer. "Then 'tis past time you were escorted into the castle proper. Wouldn't you agree?"

He took a step toward her. Marea felt the heat of his

body crackle through the thick padding and cloth. Her voice hardened. "Nay, *Sasunach,* I do not. 'Tis not welcome I'd be, and 'tis not an outcast I *feel* like being." She jerked her chin in the direction of the castle. "Go to your kin and leave me to my bog. 'Tis happy I am there."

His expression darkened, and his hand snaked out to wrap around her forearm when she turned to leave. A scowl marred his brow when he felt the unnatural softness of her limb crushed beneath his fingers. "You saved my life, witch. 'Tis the least I can do to repay your kindness."

"You still think 'tis my fault the old Graham gets buried this morn," she reminded him coldly. "How shall you repay me for *that?* Chop off my head and spike it like your father did to me—to the MacKenzie? Keep your thanks, *Sasunach,* I've no need of it." She glared at the calloused hand holding her arm until he was forced to let her go. "I saved your life, aye, but I do not own it. Nor do I want your thanks."

Her feet crunched over the blanket of leaves and twigs. The full skirt billowed like a cloud of mist around her ankles when she skirted the tree and began to melt into the forest. His next words stopped her cold.

"Don't you wonder why I've sent no guards to fetch you, Agatha? As your new laird, 'twould be my right."

Slowly, Marea turned back to face him. She kept her voice calm, in no way belying the caution that, but for the veil, etched her delicate features. Her amethyst eyes flashed with skepticism. "Nay, *Sasunach,*" she lied. "Your reasoning escapes me, true enough, but I've lost no sleep over it."

"Your pastime could lose you more than a night's rest," he growled, "it could lose you your *life!* The penalty

70

for witchcraft's severe now that James has come to the throne. Or did you forget that?"

"How could I when so many are wont to remind me of it?" She crossed her arms and glared at him as she leaned a shoulder against a sturdy birch trunk. "I've told you before, and I'll tell you again: 'tis not the black arts I practice, 'tis *healing*. There be nothing evil about it."

He cleared the distance between them in two steps. She gasped when rough fingers grasped her upper arms. The thick wad of padding was no protection from the force of his grip.

"There is a lot evil about murder," he sneered. His face was so close to hers the warmth of his breath rushed through the veil to caress her cheek. He shook her plump shoulders roughly, and Marea's head snapped back with the force of it. " 'Tis *that* we speak of, witch, *not* your kinship with the devil."

"You've proof to back up these accusations?"

"Nay." He shook his head and his fingers loosened — a bit. The breeze gusted, sending thick blond tendrils of hair dancing over his rugged cheeks and brow. The veil blew around her shoulders, the hem of her skirt flickered around her ankles as leaves rustled overhead. "If 'twas proof I had, you'd be feeling the bite of the irons you spoke of earlier."

"You accuse me of murder, yet invite me to my *victim's* services," she mused cautiously, continuing as though he hadn't spoken. "You'd dare escort me into your hall, even knowing what sort of reception would be waiting for the both of us." Shaking her head, she clucked her tongue. The sound was overridden by the mournful cry of the pipes sounding from the castle bailey. "Och! 'tis a fine mess of contradictions you be, *Sasunach*. One min-

71

ute grateful, the next eager to see me chained." Her gaze narrowed, raking him. "Methinks 'tis better off Kinclearnon is with a dead laird than with one who knows naught his own mind. Mayhaps I acted too rashly the night I found you bleeding in the forest. Mayhaps 'twould have been best for all concerned if I'd left you the way you asked me to."

"Mayhaps," Chase agreed with deceptive smoothness. "But 'tis past time for second thoughts, witch. You saved my life, now you suffer the consequences. Rash, or otherwise, I live."

"Aye," she nodded solemnly, thinking that the warmth of his body as it slowly invaded the thickness of her clothes was testament enough to his vital lifeforce. " 'Tis the burden I maun bear. And bear it, I shall." Tilting her head to the moist breeze, she let the haunting strains of the pipes flow over her. How long had it been since she'd heard it so close? Och! and what memories it stirred within her!

" 'Tis calling you, *Sasunach*," she said softly. Her attention was divided between the mournful cry of the pipe, and the rhythmic breathing of the man who stood too close. "Go. You've already tarried too long, and I've no wish for them to search you out again." She let go a soft cackle. "Your Lord Godfrey is a persistent mon. He never believed I knew naught about where you were, though methinks 'twas his fear of me that kept him at bay. Now that he's fostered his courage once, 'twill not take so much for him to return to the bog again."

They lapsed into silence. The sound of the rain, which was coming down harder now, was the only intrusion. In the distance, a clap of thunder rumbled. Rain puddled on the leaves above, and scattered to the ground in great, dewy droplets. A few pattered atop Marea's hood and shoulders. She was tempted to free the veil, push back her hood, and let the cool, refreshing moisture caress her cheeks.

Chase took a step back, as though he'd read her thoughts and feared she might give into them. Judging from the glint in his eyes, he'd had heard the rumors of Agatha's hideously burned face. A smile tugged at Marea's lips when she wondered what his reaction would be if he ever found out what lay behind her veil.

Chase dragged a palm down his chin, his gaze straying to the shadows of the keep. His eyes narrowed, and Marea felt his reluctance to return there. " 'Tis not over between us, Agatha. I'll make restitution to you whether you feel there's a need for it or not. My conscience won't allow me to do otherwise."

"Nay," she corrected, her voice light with the thoughts that tempted her mind. What kept him from enjoying the funeral feast with his kin? she wondered. What memories sparked the flash of disgust she saw in his eyes? She'd thought it before, and now thought it again: *Och! 'twas a fine mess of contradictions the man be.* " 'Tis over and done. You canna repay me for a deed I sorely regret having done. Instead, you should be concentrating on finding the proof you'd need to see me burned . . . worse than I am. 'Twould be more productive, would it not?"

What little light there was filtered down through the branches and danced over his uncommonly handsome features. His eyelids thickened, shading his vibrant green eyes and making the emotion in them unreadable. "If burning was what I wanted for you, witch, 'tis fried you'd be, not standing here exchanging pleasantries."

" 'Tis not pleasantries we exchange, *Sasunach,*" she corrected with a dry cackle, " 'tis barbs. Sharp, pointed ones." Ah, now that shimmer of the devil in his eyes was what she was more used to seeing! "They're not deadly yet, but I've no doubt we'll get to that end soon. 'Twould be best I take my leave afore we do." Again she nodded to the castle, waving her hand in that direction as well. The hem of her cloak rustled in the damp, leaves; the voluminous sleeves floated over her arms like a ghost. "Go enjoy your father's funeral, if ye can."

Chase grabbed her without thinking. His fingers coiled around her hand before it fell to her side. Her skin felt cool and soft, the bones in her wrist dainty and small, a protest to her girth. A sense of amazement lodged in his gut when he lifted her hand to his face. The scent of lavender clung to her wrist, piercing him through the heart like a sharply honed dagger. The fleeting image of amethyst eyes and red-gold hair swam before him, then burned away like the vapors of a thick mist beneath a hot summer sun.

His thumb stroked the sensitive hollow of her wrist, noting the quickening of her pulse. Chase would have needed to be blind to miss the tremble that rustled over her thick shoulders. "You have a delicate hand, Agatha," he said, watching her closely. Not for the first time, he cursed the veil that hid her reactions from him. Lightly, the palm of his other hand slipped from her forearm to her elbow. "And a soft arm. Too soft, methinks."

She gasped, and snatched her hand away, slipping it beneath the billowing folds of her cloak as she turned away. But not before Chase saw that her long, thin fingers had set to shaking.

Silently, he watched her large, darkly clad form pick

its way surely and stealthily through the forest. He made no move to stop her, in words or in deed, but let her go, content to watch.

Again he was struck with the fluid grace of her motions, such a contrast to her size. The receding crunch of leaves reached his ears over the drizzle of rain and rush of wind. He heard no *thump* of footsteps, as he would have expected from a woman so heavily set. Nor was there awkwardness of movement to confirm the advanced age her shrewish crackle suggested.

"A tryst with the infamous witch, brat?" a caustic voice snarled from behind. "So soon after your father's funeral? Your taste disappoints me. As does your lack of discretion."

The words shattered Chase's thoughts as surely as a tankard would smash a looking glass when thrown at it. He spun on his heel to find Carl Reubin pushing away from the tree trunk he was lazily leaning against. The gray strands of hair at his temple glistened with rain, as did his sharply pointed features. From the bored expression on his face, Chase guessed the man had been eavesdropping for some time.

It was pointless to keep the distaste Chase felt for this man, his father's friend, from showing. He didn't try. "My discretion, or lack thereof, is none of your concern."

Reubin's face hardened when he glanced in the direction the witch had disappeared. "It most certainly *is* my concern," he snarled, nostrils flaring. His black eyes snapped with fury as his gaze swept back to Chase. " 'Tis my concern when your choice of companions is my friend's murderer. I'll not have you disgracing David's memory by cavorting with his killer."

Chase settled balled fists on his hips. His jaw hardened as he returned Reubin's glare. "And I'll not tolerate *your* interference in my life. You may have been my father's friend — such has yet to be disproved — but you've never been mine."

"I don't intend to be." He jerkily fluffed the lace peeking from the cuff of his doublet. "My feelings for you have never been a secret, brat. Your father knew how I felt. He felt the same way. Though it was cause for great speculation — and a healthy bit of wagering — neither of us expected you to amount to much. 'Tis a pleasure to see you weren't a disappointment . . . in *that* respect."

Those who knew Chase Graham well would have recognized the emotion that flashed in his eyes for what it was: raw fury. But Carl Reubin had made it his business to ignore the boy at all cost, and was oblivious to it. Not that it would have mattered. He'd hardly have wasted his time worrying over Chase Graham's wrath, even had he known it was a concern.

" 'Tis a pity your brother couldn't be here for the funeral," Reubin said with a bored sigh. His shrewd eyes softened a bit at the mention of the boy for which he'd always harbored a weakness. "Perhaps you'd care to tell me why Henry wasn't sent for?"

"The Scottish side of the Border is hardly the place for an English boy," Chase growled, his hands clenching into tight fists at his sides. " 'Tis late in the year, Reubin. The reivers are out in quantity. I'll not pay ransom for the boy if it can be avoided. He can mourn his beloved father in Brackenhill as easily as he can here."

Reubin's gaze sharpened. "Is that your only reason, brat? If so, it rings hollow. Especially when one has only to consider the type of boy Henry is. He may be scarcely eighteen, but his wisdom surpasses his years. As does

76

his penchant for bloodlust. Remarkable quality, that. I can see why David took such a shine to his son."

His derisive tone grated on Chase's already raw nerves. "Your insults are wearing thin, Reubin. If you've sought me out for a reason, state it and be done with it."

Tipping his chin back, Reubin let out a cold laugh. "Thank you, my boy. You've supplied yet another reason for me to despise you. While most men would have driven me through by now, you tolerate my insults with amazing ease. Only a weakling would do so. A weakling, or a fool. Methinks you harbor a good bit of both in your wretched Scottish blood."

"*Half* Scottish," Chase corrected dryly. "You mustn't forget your dear friend David pumped his share of good English stock into me."

"A mistake," Reubin snarled. "One David, unfortunately, realized too late."

Chase shrugged and leaned his shoulder against a nearby tree trunk. "Mayhaps, but you can't alter the fact that I *am* David Graham's son. No matter how hard you try to ignore it, my parentage speaks for itself."

"Aye. But I can't help wondering how much better off David would have been had he allowed me to strangle you in infancy, as I'd wanted to do. 'Twas only his paternal urge that allowed you to live. Paternal urging that died quickly, I might add." With a heavy sigh, he scanned his surroundings, until his black gaze lit on the sketchy shadows of the castle. His hand swept a semicircle around him. "This should be Henry's, you know. The castle. The lands. Everything. They should be calling *him* laird, not you. And a fine laird the boy would make. He has a calling in him for it."

"Aye," Chase nodded, his features drawn and guarded. The dampness had started the pain in his shoulder throbbing anew, but the tightness of his lips was due to more than the annoying ache. "Many's the time I've glimpsed the serving wenches in Brackenhill boasting the marks of my brother's 'calling.' And more than one family pet was laid to rest because of it. Had I not known my father so well, I'd wonder if perhaps Henry shared a smattering of *your* blood, Reubin."

The gaunt face clouded over, and he looked ready to strike Chase for the insult. For his own reasons, Reubin resisted. "David was quite proud of Henry's nature. He wouldn't care to hear you, of all people, ridiculing it."

"I've no doubt," Chase conceded with a brisk nod, "since it was inherited from his father. Of course, possessing such a nature, the violence of the Borders will hold great interest for Henry in later years. Much the way it did his father. The distraction, however, must wait. Henry won't be allowed near Kinclearnon until the people here accept me as their laird."

"Your proclamation is harsh, brat. Henry would benefit from this place and all it has to offer. For certain he would learn more from studying warfare firsthand than to be taught it from a trainer. If he's ever to rule this keep, he should be schooled in it from the first. You do him disservice in denying him."

"The only disservice done is yours in presuming Henry will *ever* laird this place," Chase snarled as he pushed away from the tree. His anger snapped like the branch beneath his boot. A twinge ripped through his partially healed shoulder as he neared Reubin's suddenly stiff form. Up close, the older man's shortened height was not nearly as imposing. "Kinclearnon is

78

mine," Chase spat, his words clipped and precise. Angling his head, he brought himself nose to nose with Reubin. The stench of the other's uncleansed body gnawed at Chase's gut. "I'll allow neither brother, reiver, nor betrayer to snatch it from me."

Reubin did not back away, as most men were wont to do in the face of Chase's anger. A feral snarl curled his lips. "Aye, but the choice won't always be yours. There's not much control you will have over Kinclearnon from the grave, nor does a ghost have any say in the laird who follows him. Henry may yet rule this keep — and the time may come sooner than you think."

"Don't make the mistake of threatening me, Reubin, or you'll find those words crammed down your throat. 'Twas only your friendship with my father that's held me from it. But David isn't here to stop me now."

"Aye," Reubin agreed shrewdly, "but his ghost is. You wouldn't dare accost me so close to your own father's grave, freshly dug as it is."

"You think not? I held precious little respect for the man in life. I doubt his death will make a difference."

That said, Chase spun on his heel and stalked past the trees, into the downpour of rain. In less than a minute he was soaked through. The dampness didn't stop him from turning back for a parting shot. All the hatred Chase felt welled in his chest, sparking an emerald flame in his eyes. "A party of men was spied two days ago heading for Kinclearnon. They'll arrive by morning. You and your men are to be gone from Kinclearnon by then. If you aren't, I'll see you forcibly removed. Am I making myself clear, Reubin?"

When there was no answer, Chase turned back to the castle. Thunder rumbled as the storm gained distance.

His boots squished in the mud as he picked his way over broken tree limbs, wet leaves, and puddles. He did not look back.

Reubin's smile was pure evil, urged on by the black hatred that coursed through his soul. "Aye, brat, quite clear," he mumbled as he watched the retreating back. "Go, I shall, but you can wager your last shilling I'll return—in force. I'll see Henry take his rightful place here if it takes my last breath to do it."

Chapter Six

He was drunk. Very drunk. Marea needn't smell the liquor on Chase Graham's breath to know he was intoxicated. His ungraceful gait spoke volumes.

Five funeral services had been held throughout the day, with each serving liquor as its primary staple — ale, followed by whiskey, followed by wine, followed by rum, followed by brandy. Since he was the only immediate kin in attendance, Chase Graham had undoubtedly been expected to partake of it all. Aye, he was drunk, all right. He'd need to be built of stone *not* to be.

She watched the way he stumbled loudly through the forest, a bawdy tune slurred on his lips, and shivered, crouching closer behind the bush. For the first time in years she felt completely naked. Perchance, it was because she quite nearly was. Her red-gold hair was water darkened, and dripping as it tumbled down her back. Her only covering was the threadbare sheet she'd secured around her to soak up the moisture of her bath. This she now clutched tightly to her chest. Her shivering increased when the brisk night air dried the moisture clinging to her exposed flesh—of which there was a great deal.

She'd first heard him as she'd been picking her way over the well-worn path connecting her shack to the small, sheltered inlet at the southernmost tip of the firth. Of course, she would have to be deaf *not* to have heard his clumsy feet slamming over leaves and twigs that were still moist from the afternoon storm. At first she'd thought it was a large animal maneuvering through the forest. His bawdy tune had quickly dispelled that notion.

Marea had hidden behind a bush. Scant protection perhaps, but all that was at hand. What the man was doing here on this, the night of his father's funeral, was beyond her. Nor did Marea waste time wondering about it. Right now she was trying to decide how to reach the safety of her shack, and her Agatha garb, without attracting a drunken Chase Graham's attention.

His ungainly footsteps were in direct line with the ones she would have taken had she not spotted him. And his were about to lead him directly in front of the bush behind which she now crouched.

Since it was too late to change hiding places, Marea balled herself up tight and scrunched her eyes closed, afraid the heat of her gaze would draw him. Her ears were perked to the sound of his approaching footsteps, and a blush warmed her cheeks when she unconsciously pieced together the slurred phrases of his song.

She was never sure what gave her away, unless it was nothing more than the intuitively sharp instincts

82

of a roaring drunk. All she knew was that one moment her heart was racing and she was praying, *praying* that he'd pass her by. The next, she'd pried her eyes open and was staring at the muddied leather toe of an intimidatingly large boot.

A gasp lodged in her throat as her fingers fisted the sheet. She blinked hard, more to dispel the drips of water falling from her lashes and into her eyes, than from disbelief. Aye, she *could* believe her damnable luck at having Chase Graham find her without her veil, for 'twas the awful streak her luck had been taking of late. But need he have found her half naked as well?

Chase, on the other hand, was having the devil's own time trying to figure out why he'd stopped. He didn't spot the woman crouched near his feet. She was cloaked in murky shadows, and even if she hadn't been, his eyes had long since refused to focus on command. At the moment he was placing a silent wager with himself as to how long his feet would take his orders. He wasn't even sure how he'd managed to get this far without falling flat on his face — but, of course, there was still plenty of time for that.

And why was he paying the witch a call, anyway? Lord, but he couldn't remember. It had something to do with her arm, he thought, and scowled sloppily. For the life of him, Chase couldn't remember what it was about the pudgy arm of a woman who far exceeded him in age that had fueled his curiosity.

A twig snapped, drawing his attention downward. He had to concentrate to squint. Then, when he'd finally focused, he had to concentrate to *breathe*.

Marea glanced up. She would have been hard

pressed to say which of them was the most surprised. His emerald eyes widened, and his cheeks paled, as though he'd seen a ghost. She flushed to her toes, and her heart clamored beneath her breasts. The shock pulsing through her body felt no less tumultuous than his expression looked.

Because he was standing, and she crouching, she had to crane her neck to look at him. Her gaze widened as it strayed up over heavily muscled thighs, a taut stomach, a broad wedge of black-satin chest and shoulders to a face whose lines were sculpted to perfection in the flickering shadows of night.

Silvery moonlight danced over his rumpled blond hair, turning it to molten silver. The soft glow sparked emerald fire in the eyes that captured her gaze, and refused to relinquish it.

"Am I dreaming?" he asked huskily, wistfully.

Marea felt a tingle in her spine, a warming in her blood. Her own voice was no less hoarse. "Aye," she whispered, unable to summon a nod to enforce her words. " 'Tis a dream, mon."

He smiled then, as though he'd expected her to say that, and was glad to hear it. Her heart skipped a beat when, without warning, he reached down for her. With hands that were as gentle as they were insistent, he dragged her to her feet.

The sheet started to slip. Marea gasped, and caught it in the nick of time. His grip tightened, she felt him pulling her forward. She tried to pull back, but didn't have the strength for it. He drew her up hard against his chest, and she felt a surge of white heat slam through her body.

"Wh-what be ye doing?" she asked breathlessly.

She tipped her chin up when she felt warm fingers brush the damp hair from her brow. The gesture pressed her chest more firmly against his, until she could feel his heart drumming erratically against her breasts. He must have felt it too, for she heard him suck in a ragged breath. "Let me go. Y-you do not know what you're about."

"Aye, mistress," he slurred. His hand turned inward and down, until his fingers cupped her jaw. Her skin felt like moist silk against his palm. Ah, so nice. "I know exactly what I'm about. 'Tis my dream, after all, is it not? Aye, 'tis. My dream, to do with as I please. And it would please me greatly to keep you thus until I awaken."

Marea's eyes widened when his head dipped. His lips paused a hairsbreadth from her own. She could feel the heat of him against her sensitive lips, and smell the liquor on his breath.

Sweet Lord, *what have I done?* she thought frantically. And then she felt the first hesitant touch of his mouth, felt the first devastating wave of desire, and thought was beyond her.

His free hand slipped around her waist. The palm slid down to cup the round curve of her bottom. Her upper body was already pressed tightly against him, but her hips were not. It was that part of her he now tugged closer.

Chase's passion was overruled only by his intoxication. Both made him unprepared for the small, tightly balled fists that flailed his shoulders, dislodging his mouth from the heaven he had so very briefly tasted. She didn't dislodge his hand, however; that remained firmly curled around her slender arm

85

as she slipped from his embrace.

Marea stumbled back a step, her feet crunching over the leaves as her back slammed hard against a tree trunk. The rough bark nipped her flesh, but she was too consumed by the emotions raging through her body to feel it. She gripped the sheet to her breasts as though it was a babe in dire need of protection. "Let me go, mon," she demanded breathlessly. She spared a brief glance at the warm fingers curled around her upper arm. "I'll tell you again—you do *not* want to do this."

"Nay, mistress, you are wrong there." One hand over the other, he worked his way up her arm, tugging her toward him. "I've never wanted anything so badly in my life." He'd reached her upper arm now—ah, so slender!—and the feel of her breast brushing the back of his hand made his breath catch. With a flick of his wrist, Chase tugged her against him once more. "Aye, 'tis a dream too delicious to see end just yet."

Marea's fingers splayed his chest. Her palms came alive to the feel of firmly worked muscle rippling under the satiny cloth. She looked at her hands now as though they belonged to another woman—surely not herself, for they seemed to enjoy the feel of him most readily. The smell of liquor increased each time his warm breath fanned her cheeks and brow. Confused, she glanced up, only to be captured by his piercing stare.

His fingers slipped over the long taper of her neck, grazed her cheek, then buried themselves in the tangled wetness of her hair. He tried to pull her lips to his, but her neck had turned to iron, and she refused to budge.

Chase scowled down at her, but his intoxication made the sloppy expression less than threatening. Then too, there was the tenderness of his touch to contradict his sternness. And the slur in his voice. "Do you have a name, vision?"

" 'Tis your dream, m'lord. You tell me." She had been hoping the answer would touch a spark of awareness in him. Something to suggest this was *not* the dream he thought it to be. Instead, he surprised her by tipping his head back and laughing. It was a full, rich sound that made the blood tingle in her veins.

"Naming you has been the very last thing on my mind." His gaze darkened, suddenly serious as his thoughts took a passionate turn. His fingertips grazed the small shell of her ear, and he explored it thoroughly. A grin turned his lips when he felt her delicate shiver. "Do you like that?"

"Aye," Marea sighed before realizing what she'd said.

"And this?" he asked huskily as the hand gripping her arm loosened, and turned inward. "Do you like this?"

Marea gasped when she felt his fingers close around her breast. The sound, as well as her shallow protest, was swallowed by his mouth.

"Don't fight me, vision," he whispered against her lips when she started to push him away. His thumb flicked at the nipple beneath the sheet. A low groan rumbled in his throat when he felt it harden against his fingertips. His tongue licked her full lower lip. He savored the taste of her on his tongue for a full minute before pulling his head back to gaze down at her. " 'Tis only a dream, mistress. In dreams there is no fear . . . only pleasure."

His breath seared her face. For a split second, she wished she could believe him, wished it *was* nothing more than a dream. Never had she felt sensations to match the ones he fired in her blood with the slightest touch. Curiosity bade her to explore these feelings. Common sense bade her to come to her senses. The latter, eventually, won out—though not without a fight.

She glanced up at him, and again found herself captured by his gaze. It was his eyes, dark with passion and so very close, that told her Chase Graham was not going to let her go. His words confirmed it.

" 'Tis my dream, vision. One I've waited much too long for. I'll see it through." His gaze fixed hungrily on her lips. "I must." This last was a tortured moan.

His mouth crashed down on hers, deeply insistent. One hand held her head steady when she would have turned away, while the other left her breast to circle her waist. He crushed her to him as though trying to melt her slender softness into his hard, firm length. Shifting, he maneuvered her back a step, until she was again pressed against the tree. This time he used his chest and hips to pin her there.

Her hands had come up to ward him off. His movements now trapped them uselessly between their bodies. It was a delicious feeling. On the one side, she could feel his heart pounding against her palms. On the other, her own drummed frantically against her knuckles. Each beat tore down another brick of her defenses.

She was never sure when her struggles ceased, and her caresses began. The peculiar feeling that had begun tickling at her with the first touch of his lips bloomed into a white-hot demand. The intensity of it left her weak. She was no longer pushing against the solid wall of his chest, but stroking it, luxuriating in the feel of it. The warm flesh beneath the satin was alive with rippling motions that sent waves of exquisite heat up her arms. When the tip of his tongue darted out to tease her lips apart, Marea allowed herself to be coaxed.

He tasted of brandy and wine, a fiery combination that awakened a burgeoning thirst deep inside her. His tongue played teasing games with her own, until her heart quickened and her hands yearned to wrap around the thick cord of his neck. Her fingers itched to bury themselves in the thatch of golden hair at his nape.

Chase didn't want to move away, didn't want to free her, for fear she'd use his shift of weight to her own advantage. Capitulation was the last thing his liquor-fogged mind expected, so he did not look for it. Nor did he feel it when it was freely given. Instead, he put his time and what little control he had over his mind and body to better use.

He felt the warm flesh pressing into him tremble. The feeling ignited a fire of unknown proportions in his blood. A groan rumbled through the night, echoing over the soft, cool breeze. His or his vision's? He didn't know, didn't care. His body was growing more alive with the feel of her in his arms. Her small hands, splayed over his chest, felt warm as they seared the skin beneath the satin doublet. Her breath fanned his face, sweeter than a cool wind on a hot summer day.

His need to possess this beautiful creature was a tangible thing gnawing at his gut and loins. It had been years since he'd wanted a woman as badly as he wanted this one.

Her kiss had grown bold, her tongue darting past the barrier of his teeth to explore the honeyed recess within. He parried, teased, then retreated. He thwarted her hesitant investigation, and launched a persistent one of his own. She made no protest. He eased back far enough for her small hands to slip slowly up his chest. They hesitated over the breadth of his shoulders for a heartbeat, then curled around his neck. Her fingers tangled in his hair and drew him closer.

Her faint gasp brushed against his lips. It was almost his undoing. In order to prolong what would be a very short encounter if he kept his current pace, Chase tore his lips from hers and lifted his head to gaze into her eyes. Her large, amethyst eyes stared up at him, their depths darkened with a passion that tugged at his heart, and his gut.

" 'Tis a powerful spell you've cast on me, temptress," he whispered huskily, and rested his forehead against hers. Her damp flesh felt warm, like raw silk. His gaze dipped. The sight of her heaving breasts, covered by the sheet, did his composure little good. "Never have I dreamt anything as sweet as you."

"Nor I," Marea replied raggedly. A blush warmed

her cheeks as the words slipped past her lips. But she didn't take them back. How could she? She'd spoken the truth.

The arms entwined about his neck loosened, then slipped away. Chase made a grab for them. Though she looked at him oddly, she made no protest when he returned her hands to the perch of his shoulders.

"I want you," he said. "Desperately. Do you know that?" His hands roamed over her back, her waist, her hips.

They were forehead to forehead, nose to nose. His breath rushed over her face, warming her lips, cheeks, and jaw. It felt wonderful, more wonderful than the moonlight playing over their bodies, more wonderful than the cool breeze caressing her achingly hot flesh. "Aye, I-I know it."

"If so, then you also know I *will* have you. Nothing can stop me from it now that I've had a taste of heaven, a taste of you." His gaze darkened as he searched her face, his nose nuzzling hers. "Will you fight me, vision?"

"Would it matter?"

A slow, breathtaking smile turned his lips. Marea sucked in a sharp breath. Her heart throbbed. Smiling, the man's appeal was truly devastating.

"Nay," he answered softly, his voice thickly slurred. One hand reached up to stroke her cheek, as though his fingers were drawn to her satiny flesh and he hadn't the control to stop them. His eyes said he hadn't the desire to. " 'Tis the wonderful thing about dreams, wouldn't you say?" To her scowl, he added, "I've never taken a woman to my bed unwilling. I doubt I could even do it in a dream."

His hand stroked down, over the delicate line of her jaw. His battle-roughened fingertips tickled the taper of her neck, and the sensitive hollow between shoulder and throat. He didn't miss the way she shivered at his touch.

Fostering what little control remained, Marea looked at him levelly and said, "If I were to fight you, mon, then you'd hardly be able to call me willing."

His eyelids lowered, his gaze flashed assessively. He took his time in feasting on the sight of her delicately molded face before replying. By that time her cheeks were stained with a blush. "Your kiss was not unwilling, vision. The hands that pulled me close were not unwilling. To say so would be to brand yourself a liar. Do you want to do that?" He gave her no time to answer. His hand clamped around her jaw, his grip tight but not painful. He held her firmly when she would have looked away. "How long do you think it would last if you did fight me? A minute? Two? I wager you couldn't hold back on your own needs for much longer than that."

Marea stiffened, and lifted her chin from his grasp. For his own reasons, he allowed her that much. "You be a strutting peacock to say such things, mon. A lass could take those words to be a challenge, don't you know?"

Like a hawk, he swooped down for the kill. "Then consider yourself challenged, mistress."

Before she could retaliate, he pulled her hard against him. The breath left her lips in a raspy whisper that made him groan as the warmth of it tickled his face. Dipping his head, he ravaged her mouth with a punishing kiss that told her just how weak her defenses were.

He pulled back slightly, though his hips still ground her against the tree. " 'Tis not unwilling you are, mistress. 'Tis *not!*"

"Aye," Marea agreed with a gulp. Her body tingled where she pressed against him. She also tingled where she did not. " 'Twould seem that way."

For a split second their gazes clashed. The challenge was issued, and accepted. Marea couldn't deny the fire raging in her blood, nor did she know how to quench it. But she knew the feel of his arms around her was so good, and the sweetness of his lips made all rational thought leave her mind.

Surrender sparkled in the amethyst depths. Chase swallowed hard at the sight of it. This was more than he'd bargained for, more than he'd expected. Even drunk, his spirits sang.

His hands slipped down, over the gentle curve of her hips, tickling the back of shapely upper thighs. He felt her quiver. A slow ascent brought his palms up to sear her waist. His fingers spanned the circumference easily, with room to spare. He marveled at its smallness, reveled in the fragility of one so tiny. Lord, but he had no desire to hurt her!

Marea marveled at hands that were large enough to accomplish such a thing, and thought the power in his fingers was a startling contrast to the gentle reverence of his touch.

Chase moved away, clumsily lowering himself to the bed of pine needles and leaves. The ground rustled beneath his rugged body as he extended a shaky hand to his beautiful vision. "Come to me willingly, temptress," he rasped. "If only for this night, let me taste heaven."

"Aye." Her voice was as husky as his when she placed her trembling fingers in his hand. " 'Tis a place I've long wanted to go."

In a second he eased her down, so that she lay atop him, his arms surrounding her. Her sweet scent engulfed him, teased him, set him on fire. She squirmed and maneuvered herself into a comfortable position; it was the sweetest torture Chase had ever known. His body cried out in need, and he responded to that need without thought.

His lips found hers, his teeth nibbled her. He closed his eyes when he felt her moist tongue dart over his teeth. The hands that worshipped his chest and shoulders were almost more than he could bear. His control was already shortly leashed. In a scant few seconds her inquisitiveness would snap it.

That was not the way Chase intended things to be between them. He was no young boy to let passion rule over all else. His days for that were past, and he refused to revert back to such a base level. He wanted his vision, God yes! But he wanted her slowly, fully. He wanted to savor each second, to nurture this dream for all it was worth; it may not come again. Though the power of that thought terrified him, it fueled his resolve not to rush. Not his own body, and especially not hers.

Marea found much to appreciate in the muscles rippling under her fingertips. She also found a lot to appreciate in the magic of his lips, in the warmth of his breath against her flesh, and in the gentle caresses that drove her to distraction. Her breathing was heavy by the time he pressed her back against the cool, hard ground.

Her resistance was gone by the time she felt the sheet separate, then fall away. The thin cloth cushioned her naked back from the prickle of pine needles and leaves.

The sweet night air wafted over her exposed flesh. Marea shivered, but not from the cold. Nay, it was from the tingle of his penetrating green eyes roving hungrily over her body. And the matching hunger that coursed through her own.

Her hands refused to be still. She stroked firm biceps — so hard, so powerful! — then slipped her ultrasensitive palms up. The silver braid at his collar scraped her knuckles. Marea sighed and let her gaze flicker closed. Oh, how much more wonderful the ragged tips of his hair felt beneath her fingertips when it was the sole focus of her concentration.

It did not stay the sole focus of her concentration for long. His hand flattened over her stomach, tickled the indentation of her navel, then ascended slowly to her breasts.

She moaned when his warm fingers closed around her, exciting her beyond reason. Her own fingers closed in response, digging into the silky flesh of his shoulders, burrowing deep as a wave of desire washed over her. She surrendered herself to that wave, rode with it and let it carry her higher when the tips of his thumbs teased each breast to aching awareness.

Her fingers worked free the laces closing his doublet, then slipped beneath the opening. The ornamental braid scratched the back of her hand. It was a sharp contrast to the silk and steel feel of the chest that filled her palm as surely as it filled her heart. The muscle beneath her fingertips quivered, and a throaty chuckle rumbled in the back of her throat. The sound was stolen away by the lips that dipped to claim hers.

His kiss started slowly, tenderly, then gradually built in proportion to the growing boldness of his caress.

Her back arched up. His bowed down. She was crushed between hard ground and his hard male body. It was Marea's turn to think this a dream, for surely nothing could feel this heavenly!

Her hands stroked his back frantically, as though begging him to put an end to her torment. What sort of end she desired, she didn't know. But desire it she did. Most desperately.

He shifted. Marea whimpered a protest when his firmness left her. Her eyes snapped open, and locked plaintively with emerald green. His gaze never left hers as he quickly divested himself of doublet, hose, and boots. Then with a rumbled groan, he covered her quivering body with his.

It was a possessive gesture, one that Marea had no time to contemplate. His lips covered hers, firmly insistent—as were his hands. The fingers of one hand were buried in the moist softness of her hair, curling into a fist as he crushed her beneath him. His mouth moved to the sensitive hollow between her shoulder and neck. His breath came in hot, ragged waves, searing her flesh. His other palm seared her side as it roved impatiently between her hips and shoulder, then back again.

"Open, vision," he rasped against her neck. As he spoke, his big hands splayed over her creamy inner thighs, nudging them apart. "Open for me. Let me in."

She did. Marea knew a moment of panic when he settled between her legs. She felt something warm pushing against her core. Of a sudden, she was reminded of another time, another man. Her body stiffened. A moan of protest escaped her lips. Her hands, splayed against his shoulders, curled into fists. She pummeled his firmness as she twisted her head to the side.

Chase scowled when he felt her sudden, unexpected struggle. Resting his weight on elbows that flanked her side, he lifted his head to look down at her. Her eyes were tightly closed, her skin tinged a deathly pale. A grimace of panic lined her delicate features.

Holding himself in check was no easy feat, but he did it. He reached up and cupped her cheek. Her golden lashes flickered up, her confused amethyst eyes focused on his face. " 'Tis my dream, vision," he slurred raggedly. "I'll not have you a virgin."

Marea took a deep, steadying breath, and answered shakily, "Th-then you'll not have me, m'lord, for 'tis innocent I be."

"Nay!" His expression tightened. A flash of anger crossed his features. "Nay," he repeated, shaking his head insistently. Then, slightly confused, added, "But . . . 'tis my dream."

It was then he saw her fear, for it was plainly etched upon her fragile features, and mirrored in her wide eyes. His intoxication had allowed him to miss it before. But he did not miss it now. Her fright ate at his already churning gut. He had no way of knowing what had put the fear in her eyes, but there was one thing he did know—he could not leave her now, like this, with nothing. And not only because his body cried out for sweet release. Oh, no.

With a ragged sigh, he lowered himself and kissed both her eyes shut. To Marea, the touch was like the fragile wings of a butterfly pulsing against her flesh.

"I can't leave you with fear. 'Twould not be right," he whispered. His voice was as gentle as the hand that cupped her face. "Dream or no, I'll have you know there is naught to fear of what happens between a man and a woman." He lowered his mouth for a brief, tender kiss. When he lifted his head, her eyes glimmered with a mixture of burgeoning passion and trepidation.

"Open wider, temptress," he instructed. He thrust his hips against her, leaving no doubt to his meaning. "Wrap your legs around me. Invite me inside."

Hesitantly, Marea lifted her legs and wrapped them around his thighs. His firm flesh pressed against her—everywhere!—and brought an immediate, breathless response. She shivered, more so when she felt something else pressing hotly against a very different part of her.

Chase watched the fear melt from her eyes, replaced by a tiny spark of curious desire. Satisfied, he buried his face in her neck and allowed himself a brief taste of her salty flesh. Then he shifted his hips, and plunged deeply inside her.

Two groans ripped the air. Though he tried,

Chase's mouth wasn't quick enough to catch them. One was a guttural sound, a mixture of the pure delight and utter amazement. The other a gasp of pain and betrayal.

He didn't look into her eyes, but only because he was afraid any movement on his part would drive his body past the point of gentleness. Her warm sheath hugged him. Her hot, wet, tight feel was quickly eating away his good intentions.

The first wave of pain was beginning to subside when Marea bucked, trying to dislodge the bittersweet weight that pressed her hard against leaves and ground. It didn't work. Instead of pushing him off, she only drove him deeper within her. Again she gasped. The painful barrier had already been breached. It wasn't pain that made the breath rush from her lungs, but the tidal wave of stunning sensations that lapped through her blood. Her fingers curled into the flesh of his back, and her nails dug into the satiny steel of his skin.

Chase's first thrusts were gentle, and he found it a pleasing torture to make it so. He wanted to bury himself deep in her moist softness; to lose himself to the exquisite sensations her small body brought. But the fear he'd glimpsed so briefly in her eyes made him hesitate. Again he was struck—impaled sharply through the heart—with the urge not to bring her any more pain than he had to. Pleasure was what he wanted her to feel, enough pleasure to drive her mad.

Slowly, he began to withdraw from her. He smiled when her body rippled with the movement. A moan left her lips, and her legs tightened around his thighs. Her back arched up as she tried to pull him back, but Chase would have none of it. His teeth nibbled the shell of her ear and his tongue flicked out to moisten the curl of her earlobe as he let his body remain paused on the very threshold of her. He had not left her completely, but only made her think he would.

It was more than Marea could stand. The curling blond hairs which covered his legs tickled her thighs, and set a fire burning there. His chest rubbed her aching nipples, until they were alive with vibrant sensations. His breath was a hot rush in her ear. His hands, no matter where they touched her, burned.

A throbbing had begun in her thighs, seeping to her stomach in pulsating waves. Her heart hammered, and her breathing grew softly ragged. Her fingers curled inward, digging into his back, trying to drag him back. When that didn't work, she let her body speak of her need, arching up, demanding he end the sweet, sweet torture he'd begun.

The second time she arched, he met her with a powerful thrust. There was no time to recapture her breath as he rose and plunged again. Then a third time, all in quick succession.

The fire in her blood built. She met his thrusts, and demanded more. He was quick to comply. He filled her time and again. His mouth lowered to the delicate line of her shoulder, where he sucked and nibbled the satiny flesh. He pushed deeply into her, grinding his hips against her at the same time his hand closed around an aching breast. Her nipples were tight, yet the insistent play of his thumb and forefinger made them more so.

Marea groaned. She tossed her head wildly to the side as a veritable tidal wave burst and crashed around her in rhythmic, pulsating waves. She lifted, pressed into him, then pulled him down atop her as her legs rose and her ankles locked around his hips. She accepted him fully, her body stretching to accommodate.

The world shattered. The feelings that had been gathering inside her body suddenly pooled together and exploded into a thousand shards of brilliant, all-consuming sensation. His every plunge spiraled her higher, higher, carrying her to a place she'd never been before, a place she never wanted to leave.

Chase watched her ecstasy, and thought he had never seen so beautiful a sight in his life. He savored it, even as he felt his own release pumping through him, fast and swift, hard and demanding. Her tiny shudders quivered around him, and sent him over the edge. With three long, sure strokes, he flung his head back, and spilled his seed inside her. When the last exquisite surge of release had coursed through his body, Chase collapsed weakly atop her.

Marea accepted the crushing weight, basked in it, *luxuriated* in it. Her hands roved the hardness of his back as though she'd never feel it again and was memorizing each solid line. Her lips tasted the salt of his flesh as she buried her face in his neck and clung to him.

"Ah, vision," he slurred huskily against her ear, his warm breath making her tremble where it brushed her hot flesh. " 'Twas sweeter than I'd dared imagine. Sweeter than heaven."

He closed his eyes, nuzzled her neck, and then

grew still. His hand, which cupped her cheek, fell to the ground beside her head. The dry leaves crunched beneath it.

It was some time before Marea realized he'd slipped into a deep, liquor-induced sleep. And longer still before she sighed contentedly, and joined him in slumber.

Chapter Seven

Marea awoke to the most wonderful sensations she'd ever known. The fact that she was tired and sore and cold mattered not at all. The fact that she was curled securely into something warm and strong and hard mattered a great deal.

Her body tingled, even as a memory tickled the back of her slowly waking mind. Something heavy— though not uncomfortable—draped her waist and legs. A cool breeze rushed over her brow and cheek, stirring the wispy curls. A beat, strong and rhythmic, thudded in her ears.

She sighed contentedly as her fingers curled inward. The tips grazed something soft, something that felt like the frayed ends of a scrap of silk. She savored the feeling for one delicious heartbeat, then surrendered to the urge to stretch. Ah, now this movement brought a whole new wave of sensations.

Her body was pressed against a solid rock of warmth of which she'd been only partially aware.

She was aware of it now. Intensely aware of it. Her breasts and thighs burned where they rested against a cushion of satin and steel. A rush of breathless excitement surged through her, warming her to the core. A hushed moan passed her softly parted lips. A need built quickly within her.

Marea opened her eyes to discern its cause.

Her arms, stretched high above her head, lowered slowly. She watched, mesmerized, as her right hand grazed a rumpled crop of streaked, brown-blond hair.

The first fingers of dawn lit the treetops. The fragile rays flickered through the leaves, and glistened over a profile that was imbedded in her mind. The gentle light danced over his silky hair, setting the golden highlights on fire.

She brushed back a curl from Chase Graham's brow. Aye, his hair was soft indeed. His skin felt smooth beneath the palm she cupped to his temple, smooth and cool. In sleep, his forehead looked softly innocent.

Shifting her weight, she lifted up on one elbow to study him better. One arm was flung over his head and looked as though it had, at one time, shielded his eyes. It now rested limply atop pine needles, twigs, and dry leaves. The other was stretched at his side, the fingers buried in the scrappy shadows of a bush.

His profile was strong, his complexion held the hint of a fading tan, with a ruddy undertone from being kissed once too often by the hot summer sun. The same sun had lightly streaked his dark-blond hair so that the outer strands were bleached a shade lighter than the locks beneath them. His neck was thick and short, melding into broad shoulders which, in turn, tapered into muscular biceps. She spared only a glance at the wound that had healed nicely on his shoulder, before focusing on the dense thatch of dark gold curls covering his chest. The color did not match his hair, but was a wheaty hue all its own.

Her gaze dipped lower. Her breath caught. Blushing deeply, she skipped the part of him where chest hair ribboned down and narrowed, focusing instead on the powerful circumference of his thighs. These were not tanned, nor did they look as though they had ever been. A coating of coarse hair rippled over thighs and calves, the same color as that which covered his chest and arms.

Her gaze drifted up, and lit on his hands. They were large, those hands, the fingers thick. She thought that in his small finger—which did not appear so small in the crystal light of dawn—he possessed more strength than she harbored in her entire body. The thought made her heart race, for she remembered the feel of those fingers on her flesh. Though she had to give him credit for being exceedingly gentle with her, the power of his grip said that gentleness had been his choice.

Raw strength. They were the first words to cross Marea's mind as she gazed at him, and the impression held fast. The muscles that sculpted his body were dormant now, but it didn't overtax her to picture a time when they would not be. His rugged figure conformed easily to life on the wild Borders, as though the violent lifestyle had been born to him, and not the opposite.

Swathed in a padded leather and steel jack, trews, and boots, with a sword dangling dangerously from his side and a dagger tucked into his boot, he would cut quite the imposing figure. More than one reiver would think twice about meeting up with the likes of *this* man on a moonlit ride!

That thought eased Marea's mind, if not her fears. If a seasoned reiver took pause upon seeing Chase Graham from across a swordpoint, did she not have every right to fear him too? His hands looked strong enough to tear her apart, his body powerful enough to have her beneath him whether she wanted to be there or not. His finely chiseled face, his piercing emerald green eyes, were an intimidation unto themselves.

Aye, she had legitimate right to her fear. Marea clung to that fear desperately when she heard his soft sigh carry to her on the salty breeze. Her body went rigid, her gaze snapped to his face. Though he was still deeply ensnared in his liquor-induced sleep, he wouldn't remain so forever.

The time to leave was now, she decided abruptly, before he awakened. What she'd done last night had been done in a moment of rash impetuousness. Unwisely, she'd surrendered to white-hot sensations. She felt no remorse at appeasing her curiosity — 'twas something she'd always wanted to know, what transpired between a man and a woman. But she was smart enough to see the foolishness of her brazen ways. Her actions brought risk. She didn't dare push fate by having Chase awaken to find her lying naked at his side.

Her hand dropped from his brow to the dry leaves and she pushed to her feet. A cool breeze wafted over her, tossing her hair and making her shiver. She crossed an arm over her chest, and crouched to recover the sheet. The cotton felt warm from her body as she gripped it in her fist and tugged. She heard a slight tearing sound, but that was all. She scowled when she saw that the majority of the sheet was pinned under Chase Graham's rugged body.

The only way to retrieve it was to roll him to the side, and she dared not do that. No, the sheet would have to stay with the man. She'd have to make her way back to the shack without it. Of the two—waking him or running naked through the woods—the latter seemed the lesser, the *safer* evil.

The sharp points of pine needles pricked her bare soles as she picked her way home. Yet, even long after she'd found the safety of her shack, her thoughts lagged behind, returning time and again to the man concealed in the underbrush.

His teeth hurt. His mouth had the taste and texture of cotton. That was Chase's first conscious thought.

His second was that his head was surely going to explode if his temples didn't cease their rhythmic hammering. His head felt as though it had been crushed beneath a boulder. The rest of him fared no better. Worse still, he was chilled to the bone, and shivering.

A small bird rattled the ceiling of leaves above, letting out a shrill chirp. Was it his imagination, or was the tiny creature laughing at him?

Grumbling a heated curse, Chase attempted to close his doublet, then realized he was naked. His eyelids snapped open.

He groaned when white shards of light sliced through his eyes and cut clear through to the back of his throbbing head. He thrust one arm over his eyes, and his curses took an imaginative turn. The scent of heather clung to his flesh, tickling his nostrils, making his gut churn. Scowling, he concentrated on it.

The fragments of a dream nipped at his memory. His heartbeat quickened. The pain in his temples accelerated when he concentrated on piecing the images in his fogged brain together.

Realization dawned lightning fast. His lashes automatically swept up. He damned the pain sunlight brought.

In a flash he was sitting upright. Squinting, his gaze swept the clearing thrice. His head throbbed from the suddenness of the movement; the healed wound in his shoulder twinged. Chase was beyond feeling any of it. His ears pricked for the sound of footsteps, while his mind's eye desperately searched behind every scrap of brush and tree.

"Vision?" His voice sounded liquor-hoarse and raspy. The memory of her remained only in his mind, for as much as he wished his temptress to materialize from behind a rock or tree, it didn't happen. Chase quickly gave up hoping for it.

His shoulders sagged as he bent one knee and pillowed his elbow atop it. Of a sudden he was no longer cold, merely destitute. His gaze refused to waver from the shadow of trees, although it pained his head to keep his eyes so rigidly focused.

" 'Twas only a dream," he told himself harshly. His palm scraped down his bristle-coated jaw. "Just a dream."

His fingers curled tight fists in the sheet beneath him. A surge of injustice swelled within his chest, of love gained and lost, of betrayal, and, finally, of raw unadulterated passion. He'd had his vision once, in a dream. Sweet Lord how he wanted her again!

His palm itched to feel the satiny softness of her skin — *now*, when he had all his senses intact. He wanted to taste the honeyed sweetness of lips too soft, too perfectly formed to be real. He had a burning need to bury his fingers in the silkiness of her hair. Desire was a tangible thing, eating him from the inside out. The soft cloth he wrinkled within his grasp was poor compensation.

With a feral growl, Chase thrust the sheet away. Since most of it was pinned beneath him, it didn't go far. From a corner of his eye he saw the frayed hem catch on the breeze, then flutter to the ground. The sight drew his bleary gaze. He stared, dazed, at the scrap of cloth, and the stain of blood that marred it.

"Nay," he whispered throatily. He shook his head, even as his hand reached out to snatch up the cloth.

He closed his eyes and rubbed a corner of the sheet against his jaw. A waft of heather wisped through his nostrils, and fired in his blood.

Chase's eyes flickered open. With trembling fingers he searched for the stain. It was blood, there was no doubt, but it was too red to be old. A quick glance told him that his wound had not reopened.

A grin of pure delight tugged his lips as he reached for his doublet and hose, lying in a crumpled ball beneath the bush. The blood was not his, which meant . . .

Ah, aye, he felt better. Much better. Better than he had in years. And his day was about to improve, for he now had every intention of finding his vision—and what's more, he knew where to look. He would have her in his bed come midnight, and in his home, by benefit of the kirk, before another fortnight was past.

This, he most solemnly swore.

Fate had other things in store.

For Chase, it was planning revenge on the Douglas, the sneaky bastard who'd rousted near one hundred prime Graham beasties and four prisoners on their latest raid three days prior. A retaliatory raid, a legalized cold trod, had been planned for the next full moon and scheduled, unfortunately, for that very night. He had forgotten.

At the time of the trod's inception, Chase had no idea he'd have other pursuits in mind for the day. Unfortunately, personal pursuits need be put on hold. If the ride was not made now, the trail of thieves would grow too cold to follow.

Lord knew what would happen should the neighboring reivers think Kinclearnon had grown lax due to a shift of lairds. David Graham had been a force to reckon with; only the heartiest reivers dared invade and steal his property for fear of violent retribution. They did not, however, know what to expect from the son. This, no doubt, was their way of finding out.

To this end, Chase was obligated to appease their curiosity: by insuring his neighbors that he was every bit the reiver his father had been, though his methods were different, lacking the cruel, vengeful twist of his predecessor — as yet.

Chase had lived on the Borders long enough to know the ways. If he was to secure Kinclearnon, and provide protection to its people, he needed to show a strong hand at the start. He had to show neighboring families that he wasn't to be trifled with. Since there was only one course these reivers understood — swift, sure action — his way was mapped out for him. His retaliation was already planned, he'd only to see it through to its bitter end.

Much to his consternation, Chase was kept deeply embroiled in preparations for the trod for the better part of what might have been a very profitable afternoon. The only thing that helped improve his rather nasty mood was the realization that one of the people he sought to protect was none other than his lovely midnight vision. Aye, that helped a lot, and made the taste of the coming victory all the sweeter.

* * *

For Marea, distraction took the form of Thomas, the MacKenzie of Kintail. He was now sitting on the bench in her shack, his large fingers sifting through the various limp herbs and roots scattered over the scarred tabletop. A deep scowl marred his brow.

"How do ye tell all these shrubs apart, lass? They look one and the same to me."

" 'Tis because you're not a witch," she replied flippantly. Marea scraped the last of their supper plates, then set them atop the counter and turned toward him. She wiped the grease coating her palms off on the front of her black skirt as she cast him a warm smile. "I've heard the same thing said about the Highland chiefs, Uncle. You all look one and the same to me as well. 'Tis a hard time I have telling you apart from the Campbell. Or the MacGregor. Or the MacDougal. And how do you tell each other apart? 'Tis something I've oft wondered."

To this irony, Thomas tipped back his head and let go a pleasant laugh. For a man of his tall, lanky stature, the sound was deep and rich. Wiping a tear of mirth from his eye, he fixed his niece with a smiling glance. "Aye, lass, I can see how you would, what with the Campbell being so large and round, and me so tall and gangly. 'Tis twins we could well be. And the MacGregor! Ha! A squatter man there never was, except for your own Zander, mayhaps. But Zander is not so round."

Marea's eyes twinkled with mischief as she slipped

onto the bench across from him. He was right, of course. Thomas, the MacKenzie, was not what one expected when one thought of a tribal chief, Highland or Low.

Thin as a limb and taller than most, his stature was less than menacing. His face was round and youthful, which didn't aid the air of intimidation he constantly strove to attain, neither did his crop of straight reddish brown hair, nor the wisps of a beard that clung to his rounded chin. But his eyes were sharp and clear, and what he lacked in brawn, he made up for in craft. He had a shrewd mind that was rarely matched, and because of his quick thinking and shrewd tactics he'd earned himself a reputation of a man to be feared.

Marea snatched up a sprig of crosswart. Her fingers played idly with the stringy stem as she asked, "So what be your plans for the Graham, Uncle? Have you thought on it?"

"My plans?" Thomas said, suddenly serious. "Nay, wench, 'tis *your* raid. The plans be yours to make. I come only to help you with whatever you decide to do." He sent her a crooked grin and added, "And mayhaps add to me herd in the bargain. 'Tis coming up on winter, we can use all the beasties we can find."

"Find?" Randy exclaimed as he stepped through the door. He'd only caught the last of his father's words, but it was enough to set him to chuckling. "Is that the way of it?" He winked at Marea and told her slyly, "Already he's sent near fifty men trailing back to Kintail with the beasties he's 'found.' If he keeps the numbers flowing he'll not have the land to feed them all. And the Borders will have no beasties left come winter."

"Bah! I canna help it if these people let their herds roam free," Thomas defended good-naturedly. "What's a mon to do when he stumbles on herds just as you please in the open meadow? Keep the pace and ride past them? Nay. The poor beasties need a home, and I provide them with one. 'Tis as simple as that."

"A home?" Randy chided as he poured himself a mug of cider and slipped onto the bench beside Marea. "A home, he says! 'Tis not that way, I tell you, cousin." He sent a challenging look to his father, who looked less than chagrined. "What about that town near Crawford? 'Tis me memory failing me or did you—?"

Thomas cleared his throat and cut his son's words short. He sent Marea a silencing glare when she started chuckling. "Shush now. The lass does not want to hear about that."

Marea tossed the crosswart aside. "Aye, but I *do*."

"Nay, you do not," Thomas corrected, in a tone of voice that left no room for argument.

Marea sighed. The conversation had been as good an excuse as any to avoid the problem at hand. But the problem could not be avoided forever. The time had come for her to stop stalling. "What be your ideas about dealing with the Graham, Randy? Since me uncle here will not help, 'tis open I am to suggestions."

"Now, I did not say *that*, lass."

114

"You did not have to." Marea brushed her uncle's words aside and fixed her glance on her cousin. "Randy?

Randy's gaze flickered between his half-drained mug of cider and his father. His calloused fingers played with the chipped pottery handle. " 'Tis not me decision, lass, 'tis yours. I'll go along with whatever you decide — so long as 'tis reasonable."

Her eyes flashed, and the soft lines of her face hardened when she gritted her teeth together. By making her plan the raid, they were trying to force her hand, trying to make her back out of it in a way that would save her dignity. She knew it, but couldn't call either her uncle or Randy on it. They'd been too cagey, and she'd fallen into their trap too readily.

She divided an accusing glare between the two men. "I thought you said you'd be giving me help. If so, you should know this is not my idea of it."

Thomas reached across the table and snatched up her hand. He gave her long fingers a gentle squeeze. It was not returned. "And this is not our battle to fight, lass, but we be here anyway. Do not get angry, because you'll get no more help than what we've offered. I've no quarrel with the Graham, as yet, and 'tis long you've known how I feel about all of this."

"Aye," she snapped, pulling her hand away and placing it in a tight fist in her lap. "But I thought you'd help despite it. Mayhaps I was wrong."

" 'Tis help he brought," Randy reminded her coldly. It went against his grain to defend his father,

115

but defend him he did. "In the force of two hundred horses strong."

"One hundred fifty," Marea corrected absently, her gaze straying to the cluttered table top. Her fight drained a bit when she realized they were right. She couldn't ask more of them than what they'd reluctantly provided. It would be selfish. She looked up to find both men regarding her oddly. "One hundred fifty," she repeated, the hint of a smile playing at her lips. "Did Randy not say you've sent fifty men back with beasties?"

"Randy says entirely too much," Thomas replied with a crooked grin. As the tension in the room eased he again reached over and grasped his niece's hand. This time she did not pull away, but squeezed back. "So what be your call, wench? When do we get your castle back? Say it be soon. I'm itching to get back to me mountains."

Marea scowled. "I'm not sure. 'Tis not something I'd thought much on, since 'twas so sure I was you'd have a plan in mind."

"And now?" Randy asked.

"And now I'll have to think on it." Her eyes locked with her uncle's. "Give me a few days to decide. 'Tis not something I dare take lightly. When I strike, I want only to strike once. Anything more than that will mean defeat."

"Two days," Thomas agreed with a curt nod. He gave her fingers a tight squeeze, then let them go to run the palm of his hand down his chin. His eyes narrowed thoughtfully. "I'll not risk more than that. 'Tis open season on the MacKenzie to be caught

116

camped by the Sark twiddling our thumbs. And 'tis only a matter of time before me Highland foes discover us gone. I'll aide ye all I can, but I'll not return to Kintail only to find that damn MacGregor, God rot 'im, has raided me nice plump herd."

"Two days," Marea agreed, sealing the bargain with her own, hesitant nod. Reaching across the table she snatched her uncle's mug of cider and raised it to her lips. The tankard concealed her thoughtfully pursed lips. Two days was not so long to plan. Already she could feel the hours closing in.

Chapter Eight

All in all, it had been a wretched day for Chase Graham. The Douglas, on the other hand, had a fine day.

The cold trod Chase had carefully planned and executed had been decidedly unsuccessful. The Douglas, expecting pursuit, had left two ambushes. Only one found its mark — one too many. After a brief and, thankfully, bloodless encounter, five more of Kinclearnon's men had been taken prisoner. One of whom was Sir Godfrey. Only quick reflexes had spared Chase the same fate.

This defeat, by far not his first, ate at him. He was in a foul mood by the time he slammed through the trees and underbrush on his way to Agatha's shack. Determination mixed with moonlight — both etched his features hard as he set out to see at least *one* thing go right that day.

The mist curled around his knees as he stood on the doorstep. Through the thin portal he heard a fire crackling, felt its warmth seep through the slats in the door. The sound of muffled footsteps could be heard, as well as the swish of skirts. The smell of something hot and spicy wafted on the salty air, nibbling at his empty stomach.

He didn't knock. In truth, he didn't feel the need to since the shack was on Kinclearnon land, and he was the keeper of Kinclearnon. When the iron skillet crashed into his shoulder the second he set foot over the threshold, he damn well wished he'd looked past his immediate anger and taken time for courtesy.

"Ouch! What the devil—?"

"Are your fingers broken, mon, that ye canna knock?" the witch demanded shrilly. The skillet's large handle was gripped tightly in her hands. She wielded it like a deadly claymore.

"Hit me with that again and I'll show you just how well my fingers *do* work," he growled, and spun on his heel to face her.

Marea's breath caught as her gaze fixed on his rugged form. She'd been right in her guess earlier. He did cut quite the imposing figure clothed in his reiver's garb. Not a shred of the finely dressed man of last night remained. Gone was the doublet and hose, replaced by a nicely cut leather and steel jack. The laces of a soft yellow tunic were tied loose, leaving the gaping cloth to expose a good deal of his firmly worked chest. Tightly knit trews covered his legs, the bottoms of which were encased in knee-high boots, rolled over at the top. The hilt of a dagger protruded from the right boot. The long broadsword hanging from his lean hip spoke for itself.

Slowly, Marea's gaze rose. The firelight crackled over his wind-rumpled hair, warming the wheaty texture of it, and igniting an array of golden highlights. The dancing shadows played over the lines of his face, sculpting each hard angle and plane to vivid perfection. His strong chin was firm beneath the tight line of his mouth. A muscle ticked in the place where earlobe met hard granite jaw. His eyes sparkled with anger, but Marea had the feeling she wasn't the one who'd put it there; hitting him with the skillet had merely added fuel to it.

Aye, there was a most deadly air about the man, and she was suddenly leery about testing his patience. She had reason to believe he had reached the end of it. She lowered the skillet, although she didn't set it aside just yet.

" 'Tis a powerful arm you have, Agatha." His gaze never left her as he lifted a hand to investigate this, his newest bruise. He winced. Already he could feel a lump forming beneath the quilted padding of his jack. "I should have brought you with us on the trod. Mayhaps we wouldn't have been defeated."

"You were not victorious?" Marea asked, surprised. She'd heard about the cold trod, of course, and like everyone else she'd assumed it would be successful. "Why not? Is the Douglas too clever for you?" She shook her head and clicked her tongue. "Tell me you were not foolish enough to walk into one of his ambushes, mon."

"How did you know that?" His emerald eyes narrowed to glistening slits. That the witch could so easily guess the course his day had taken rankled Chase's already raw nerves.

"Why, the Douglas is reputed for them."

"And did you not think to *tell me* what he's reputed

120

for?! My day would have gone much easier if you had."

"I thought you knew. Everyone does. But . . . not you, eh?"

Chase dragged rigid fingers through his hair, and glared at the veil that scraped the witch's fatty shoulders. "Nay, I did not," he barked mockingly. "If I had, do you think his victory would have been so easy?"

Marea pursed her lips and she tossed the skillet to the table. It landed with a clatter amidst the array of herbs. "The Douglas be a clever mon," she replied cautiously. "Not so clever as—er—*others*, but clever nonetheless. I'm not too surprised to hear he bested you."

"And I'm less than pleased." Chase whipped about and stalked to the hearth in long, angry strides. The warmth of the fire caressed his cheek, softening the lines of his face and easing his anger—a bit. "Tell me something, Agatha," he said as he leaned an elbow atop the timbered mantel and regarded the witch from over his shoulder. "How did you learn of the trod? 'Twas not I who told you."

"Nor did you have to," she scoffed. She smiled as she eased her padded body onto the bench. "They may be old, but me ears are still intact. I can hear the sounds from within the bailey as clear as any. 'Tis often enough I've heard the preparation being made for a trod to recognize them."

This was a boldfaced lie, although Marea would, on her own, have guessed the new laird's intent eventually. As it was, Zander MacVin had told her of the Graham's plans, and together they'd had a good laugh over the man's foolishness in not preparing for the Douglas's inevitable ambush. She did not, of course, confess this to Chase, since it was doubtful, in his present foul mood that he'd either see or appreciate the humor in it.

Unfortunately, she had a feeling he knew she was lying. She could feel it in her bones, see it in the way he scowled down at her. Marea decided an abrupt change of subject would not be out of order. "So what be your plan now, *Sasunach?* Now that you've used up your legal right to a trod. Will you ride against him?"

Chase's scowl deepened when he heard the anticipatory note in her annoyingly shrill voice. And then his scowl eased. Like himself, she was a product of the Borders. She knew his options for recourse as well as he did. If one went solely by her age, she probably knew them better.

He shrugged. "A missive has been sent to Robert Carey, alerting him to the problem. As Warden of the Middle March, 'tis up to Carey to issue the Douglas a summons to the next day of truce, and to see the bill filed."

"And if the Douglas does not wish to show his ugly face? What be your plans then?"

Chase grinned. Rumor had it the witch had lived in Kinclearnon all her life—God knew how long that was. She knew what would happen if the Douglas did not appear at the next day of truce slotted for the end of the month. But the conversation flowing between them was a pleasant, relaxing distraction, and he humored her by way of an explanation. "If he does not appear, then his guilt will be proven. He'll have fouled the bill and will be forced to offer his pledge in the form of himself or one of his men. Of course I'll have to accept the pledge, or risk a bloodfeud by declining."

"Bah, I know all that. I be talking about the beasties he stole," Marea pointed out shrewdly. "He'll not offer himself as a pledge, but one of his men who he does not care to ever get back. The mon, in turn, will sit in your prison for years, eat your food, wear the clothes *you* provide him, and all with no ransom paid. *You,* on the other hand, will still be lacking a goodly portion of your herd." She shook her head in disgust. " 'Tis a fine law we live with, is it not?"

" 'Tis the way of the Borders, Agatha."

"A way my young king will see end."

"Aye, that too," he agreed. His arm slipped from the mantel and he moved to join her on the bench. "But I didn't come here to talk of King James, or the Douglas."

"Nay?" Marea asked suspiciously. He was sitting beside her, the leather and sweat smell of him teased her nostrils. His firm, warm thigh grazed her own. The contact didn't seem to bother him. It bothered her to the point of sending shards of breathless excitement shooting up her leg, melting in the warm pool of her stomach. The herb her fingers toyed with snapped in two. She tossed the pieces aside before snatching up another. "What did you come for then? Not to ask me advice on a retaliatory raid, I'll wager."

"Nay, Agatha, keep your advice. 'Tis torturing you I've come for. And shall have."

Marea's gaze snapped up, and locked with emerald eyes that shimmered with sincerity. Although he could not see it for the veil, her face drained to a deathly white, and her eyes rounded. Had he discovered it was in her company he'd passed the previous night? Aye, it would be torture of the worst order if he'd discovered

123

her secrets, and come only to torment her with his knowledge and vibrant presence.

"What's this, mistress? No reply? No glib retort?" He mocked her silence with a throaty chuckle, all the while watching her carefully. *Damn the veil that hid her features from view!* "Might I guess the reason behind your silence?"

"If it pleases you." She was careful to keep her tone neutral, not wanting to give away her inner trepidation—of which there was a sore good deal.

"Damn it, witch, I'll not stand for your toying with me a moment longer!" His fist slammed down hard enough on the craggy table top to send stalks of herbs flying. "I want the truth from you. I'll not leave here until I have it."

"What are ye talking about, mon?" Marea gasped as her long fingers flew to her throat. Her eyes widened when she realized what she had done.

Chase opened his mouth to respond, then snapped it shut again. His gaze was drawn to the long, slender fingers fluttering against the backdrop of her midnight black collar. Where his gaze traveled, his hand was quick to follow. "You've a slender hand, Agatha," he said, as his roughened thumb enjoyed the silk of her flesh.

"Aye, so you've said." Marea tried to tug her hand free. His grip held incredibly firm, and only by yanking would she free herself. She didn't attempt it: to do so would draw more unwanted attention to her hand. If he thought her reluctant to bear his touch, then he'd want the reason why. It was a reason she was determined he would never know.

Her tone turned derisive. "Is this your form of torture? 'Tis a wonder the Douglas dares reive your land. Mayhaps he'll not appear for your day of truce after all, for fear you'll hold his hand for retribution." She leaned forward and whispered lightly, " 'Tis not the way he usually compensates his wrongs."

" 'Tis not a humorous matter, that," Chase replied tightly. "And I'll thank you not to make it one." His voice hardened; his eyes narrowed. "Need I remind you, witch, that 'tis not the Douglas we speak of right now, but yourself?"

"Aye," Marea nodded solemnly, "and the untruth you think I've told you. I know." Or do I? she wondered. Lord, but it was difficult to feel the roughness of his skin scraping her palm while trying to form coherent words on her tongue! Her whole body felt abruptly warm and tingly, and the tumultuous sensation seemed to stem from the place their flesh entwined.

"Did tell me," he corrected. His grip tightened. Marea winced. Thankfully, the veil hid her features. "You *did* lie to me, Agatha. I know it. Now, I'll know why."

"Mayhaps you would like to tell me what I lied about," she suggested through clenched teeth. Her fingers felt as though they would snap like a dry twig in his grasp, but she doubted he was aware of the pain he caused her. "Och! mon, 'tis powerful hard to concentrate when you're breaking me fingers in two."

" 'Tis no worse than what I've suffered due to your lies, witch," he barked, and shoved her hand away.

"Mayhaps," she snapped as her hand hit the herbs scattered amidst the table top. She hugged the sore limb to her breast and glared at him angrily. "But 'tis a sore lot better than what I'll do to you should you ever

125

hurt me again." Her eyes narrowed, and for once Marea wished the veil gone so he could see the rage he'd stirred. "Or did you forget how great me powers be?"

"I forgot nothing."

"Aye?" she scoffed coldly. "I saved your life, mon, but I can just as easily take it. Do not think I'd hesitate, for I would not. Not for a second." That he appeared singularly unimpressed by the threat only fueled her mounting anger. This time it was Marea's fist that slammed the tabletop. "Listen to me, you simpleton! The villagers are not wrong. Their fear of me is very real, and very well earned."

Chase fixed her with a glare that bespoke of his own simmering rage. He leaned toward her until he was close enough for his hot breath to rustle through her veil. His words were low and menacing. *"Their* fear, mistress. Not mine." He paused, his gaze piercing her to the core. "Never mine."

"Nay? You harbor no fear of me? *None?*"

"Not an ounce," he growled.

"Then your be a bigger fool than I thought. 'Tis your father's death still to be accounted for, mon. Until you can be sure I did not murder him, you have every reason to fear me. Only a fool would not. A fool, or a very brave, very smart man. Your encounter with the Douglas speaks for itself. Of course, 'tis possible I'll not stop at murdering your father." The muscle in his jaw jerked as her hand swept over the dried plants atop the table. " 'Tis possible these be going into a potion to assure that you'll never see the light of morn again."

"And 'tis *just* as possible I'll snap your brittle neck in two to assure myself that you *do not.*"

126

Marea felt a thread of fear at that, not at the words themselves, but in the way he'd said them; firmly, with staunch conviction. "Aye," she whispered hoarsely. "That too. But then, if you break me neck, you'll never know the truth about me lies. Did you think of that?"

"Aye, I've thought on it. I've also given serious thought to simply throttling the truth out of you."

She swallowed hard. "Another option. But a poor one. I'll not tell you anything I do not want you to know. Torture or not, my tongue holds fast."

Chase's hand curled into a tight fist. His face reddened with rage. " 'Tis a tongue I'm tempted to wrench out right now. I warned you once, I'll but do it once again. Do not toy with me, Agatha. I've no patience for it."

"And I've no liking for being branded a liar."

" 'Tis a brand well earned."

"Is it?"

"Aye."

"You're sure of that?"

"Aye!"

His fist pounded the table, but this time Marea was prepared for it. The sound ricocheted off the tight walls of the shack, rivaling the crackling in the hearth as the flames snapped and danced. More herbs and roots fluttered to the floor. She ignored the mess, instead sending him a disdainful glance from behind the safety of her veil as she pushed to her feet. What she couldn't ignore was the sudden coolness of her thigh where it no longer pressed against his.

"Tell me about me lies," she said flatly, "and I'll see what can be done about correcting them. *If* I'm of a

127

mind to." Her feet crunched over the dirt and, now, herb-scattered floor as she crossed to the counter and poured herself a tankard of tepid cider. After a brief pause she poured a second. Her fingers trembled when she set the mug on the table in front of him, then quickly moved to the chair near the hearth. The old wood creaked beneath her as she settled into it, and fixed his broad back with an inquisitive gaze.

Chase lifted the tankard to his lips. The pottery felt cool against his flesh, slightly rough where the brim was chipped. The spicy scent teased his hungry stomach. He took a sip of the sweet-tasting liquid, and let it play over his tongue before swallowing. He wiped his mouth on the sleeve of his jack, then set the tankard aside and spun on the bench to face her. His legs were planted firmly on the floor and separated wide at the knees. Firm thighs were used as a cushion for his elbows; his hands were clasped.

"I remember a conversation with you, Agatha, shortly after I'd awakened to find myself mending in your shack." Though the words were spoken unemotionally, there was a tinge of desperation lacing his tone. "Do you remember it?"

"Aye," Marea answered cautiously. She raised the tankard to her lips, remembered the veil, then lowered it to her lap. "Though not every word precisely. 'Twas then I lied to you?"

"I asked you of the other nurse who tended me. You said 'twas no other nurse, only you who nursed me. You said the herbs you'd fed me for the fever gave me visions."

" 'Tis not uncommon. Some potions are powerful enough to do it. And since you be such a — er — rugged

128

mon, 'twas more I had to feed you than I'd have fed most."

"Mayhaps, but I don't think your potions were so strong as you'd like me to believe." He frowned when he saw how quickly her head snapped up at that remark. "I've since met again the woman you say does not exist. The woman you say lives only in my mind. In my dreams."

Marea swallowed hard and closed her eyes. Her feet set the rocker into agitated motion. Her voice was raw, although it still held its Agatha shrillness. "Have you now? And what potions have you been drinking to give you such sights, mon?"

"No potions. No herbs. No berries. I had a bit of wine, and though I may have been slightly drunk, I had enough wits remaining to know what I saw. "

She sighed, remembering the sore state he'd been in when he had found her hiding behind the bushes. He could barely walk for the liquor he'd consumed, and his speech had been slurred almost beyond recognition. A "bit of wine" wouldn't do that to a man. It would take a drink more powerful than fermented grapes, and a staggering quantity of it, to bring on such intoxication on a man his size. Unfortunately, she couldn't say that without incriminating herself.

"And what did you *think* you saw, *Sasunach?*"

He cleared his throat and his voice grew ragged. The sound of it, of his torment, rippled up her spine. The memory of a night spent wrapped in his brawny arms, set her blood on fire. "A vision," he said simply. *My* vision. And I've need to see her again."

"Then drink some more wine," she answered quickly. Too quickly if the narrowing of his emerald

129

eyes and the tightening of his fingers around each other was anything to go by. "I canna help ye, mon. Me powers do not go that far. The best I can do is make you a potion to bring on sleep. What you dream about, however, is beyond my control."

"I don't wish to sleep, witch. I've no need. My vision was *not* a dream!" He thrust himself from the bench and stalked toward her as though his body harbored an overabundance of energy that was in dire need of being spent. He stopped next to her chair, legs spread wide, balled fists riding lean hips. He towered over her, glaring down at the veil concealing her face. "My vision was *real*," he snapped, and thrust his hand, palm up, beneath her nose. "I touched her hair, Agatha. I tasted her skin, and smelled the sweet scent of her in my nostrils. I smell it still. *Feel* her still. She was real, I say! *Real!*"

Marea thrust his hand aside, and noticed her own fingers were trembling. Badly. She concealed one in the black muslin folds of her lap, lest he see—and suspect the cause. The other gripped the tankard so tightly she half-expected it to shatter in her grasp. " 'Tis not your word I doubt, 'tis your memory," she replied shakily. "The drink does strange things to the mind. In me own time I've drunk too much wine and had dreams that seemed real. But then I awoke and saw them for what they were: *dreams*." She paused, studying him carefully. "Wake up, mon, and see the truth. See the dream for what it be—a pleasant night journey that canna be returned to nor repeated, no matter how badly ye wish it. If you canna see that, this dream will eat at you."

"It already does. It eats at my mind, at my gut. I

carry the image of that lovely woman in my heart, yet it devours me and leaves me empty." He raked a hand through his tousled hair, and turned his back on her. "I need my vision, Agatha. My life is empty without her."

"I am sorry," she whispered softly, bowing her head, "but I canna help you. Some things are not meant to be, and me thinks this be one of them. 'Tis God's will." *And my own,* she added silently.

"Nay, I'll not believe it. The God I've always looked upon with reverence and respect is not that cruel."

"Then mayhaps 'tis out of his power too. Surely, 'tis out of mine."

"Is it?" he said thoughtfully. Slowly, he turned back to her. Before she could stop him, he'd lifted the tankard from her grasp and set it aside. The hands that dragged her to her feet were firmly insistent. His fingers bit through the padding that distorted her arms. "Is it?" he repeated darkly, his hot breath invading her veil, while the heat of the fire warmed her back. "I wonder. You see, Agatha, I wasn't mistaken when I said I knew my vision was no dream. She was as real as the sheet she left behind." His eyes narrowed and his tone grew harsh — as did his hands. "You stiffen, Agatha. Why? Have you finally realized I do not lie about this?"

"Nay!" she cried, shaking her head as the fringe of veil scrapped her shoulders. "Nay, I — I just do not believe you, 'tis all. You had a dream, mon," she pleaded desperately. "A *dream!* 'Tis all it was. Why can you not see that and let it go?"

"Because 'tis not the way I am, Agatha," he barked angrily, giving a vicious shake to her plump, soft shoulders. "I won't let it go because my vision *was no dream!* I have the stain of her maidenhead to prove it."

"Y-you what?" she gasped.

"You heard me. 'Tis too late to claim poor hearing now, Agatha."

Marea's head spun, her mind raced in endless, beginningless circles. Her breath came in slow, ragged gasps that ripped through her lungs like a sharply honed dirk. Her heart throbbed in her breasts; her knees felt too weak to support her weight. If not for the harshness of his grip, she might have crumpled into the chair that pressed hard against the back of her knees.

The sheet! her mind screamed as her fingers curled into his padded leather jack. *Sweet Lord, how could I have been so blessed foolish as to leave it? But how could I have snatched it out from under him unnoticed?* She didn't know if he slept deeply. Every movement she'd made had risked awakening him. And even if she had tried to take the sheet, she'd still have been doomed. She'd sensed it then; she knew it with a dreaded certainty now.

"Tell me who she is, Agatha," he coaxed. His eyes shimmered with emerald hope. His warm breath filtered through her veil to seduce her cheek. Marea shivered, her breath caught with confusion. "Tell me where I can find her. Please, Agatha."

"I canna tell you," she muttered hoarsely. "Do you not see? The wench must know who you be. If she wishes you to find her, you shall. If she does *not* wish it . . ." She shrugged, a difficult thing with his grip so tight. " 'Tis not my place to tell you, for 'tis not my secret to share. 'Tis hers."

132

The urge to throttle the words from the old bitch's throat was strong, not easily suppressed. Thankfully, Chase had enough control left to realize it would earn him nothing. He thrust her into the chair, unable to bear the feel of her a second longer. "I could have your shack watched," he threatened. "I know she visits you. 'Twould be only a matter of time before my men apprehend her."

"And I'll tell her of your search, and warn her to stay away from the bog."

His hands clenched and unclenched at his side. The muscle in his jaw jerked furiously. "I could take you back to the keep with me and put out word that you'll not be released until she comes to me."

Marea did not laugh at that; the situation was indeed humorless. Instead, she thrust her chin high with the MacKenzie pride that ran so thick through her veins and said, "I'll use me powers to turn your irons to dust. There be no walls thick enough, nor chains strong enough, to hold me in a place I do not wish to be."

He seemed taken aback by this. "I though you said your powers were not that strong."

"And you believe me? Why that and naught else I've said?"

"I've good reason, Agatha!"

"Mayhaps, but do you really wish to test me, *Sasunach?*" she challenged coldly. "I'll tell you now, once I've slipped from your keep—and I *will*—I'll not go back again. I'd be gone from Kinclearnon come dawn, and I'd take your vision with me. Scotland's not so small a place that you'd ever find us, so do not hope it. Remember, I've had over two thousand years to ferret out hiding spots."

Chase bent over the chair and thrust his face level with hers. Had the veil not been secured in place, their noses would have touched. "Run, witch," he taunted hotly, "if you think you can. And when I find you—*when*, not *if*—I'll kill you with my bare hands. Never doubt it."

"Aye, *Sasunach*, I hear ye," Marea sneered as she rose from the chair, forcing him back. She stood a hand's breadth away from his chest, her anger making her strong beyond her size. With the heels of her balled up palms, she shoved at his shoulders, moving him back still more. "Now *you* hear *me*. No matter what you think, the lass does not want you. If she did, you'd not be here, you'd be in her arms." Her eyes flashed when she wrenched her hands from the warm firmness of his chest. "And if by chance you someday find her, 'tis best you be warned that I will think nothing of driving a dagger through your heart before I'd let you harm her. Devil take the consequences."

"Is it so difficult to believe that the wench may desire me as much as I do her? Or haven't you thought about that? Mayhaps you should ask her the ways of her mind and heart before you *presume* to know what's best for her."

"Nay, 'tis not that way. I know the lass, which is more than you can say. I know her mind and her heart as surely as if it were me own. I've tried to be gentle with you, but you'll not listen. You force me to say it. She hates you, mon. Hates you beyond reason."

"She didn't hate me last night, Agatha."

"Mayhaps. And mayhaps the guilt and regret of that one night of passion cuts her to ribbons inside.

Mayhaps she's hating herself right now for having done it. And mayhaps she hates *you* all the more for not putting a stop to it."

" 'Twas not rape," he growled. "She came to me willingly. Little coercion was needed, and even less used. Ask her. She'll tell you I speak the truth."

Marea's heart fluttered. Aye, it was true. He'd had her willing. But the circumstances were not normal. Still, how could she defend such actions? "Rape or not, it does not make what happened right!"

If she'd thought his expression hard before, it was nothing compared to now. His jaw was harsh, his lips tightly compressed. His emerald eyes shot daggers that pierced her to the core. His voice was cold, precise, ringing with conviction as it bounced off of the shack's walls and drowned out the crackle of flames. "You're wrong, Agatha. Dead wrong. What happened last night was right. Nothing you can say will taint my memory of it, nor will I allow you to taint the wench's memory of it, either. I want her to remember the experience often, and to savor it with a sweetness to match my own." His voice lowered to a threatening snarl as he leaned toward her. "For 'twill happen again. 'Tis inevitable. You cannot stop us, witch, no matter how hard you try."

Chase spun on his heel and stalked to the door. He threw it wide, letting in a blanket of mist to curl over the threshold. The shape of a pregnant black cat disentangled itself from the wafty fog.

He didn't step out just yet, but turned to regard her fully. "Brew your potions, cast your best spells, witch. Do your worst, if you think 'twill prevent me from finding her. But know that I'll fight you every step of

135

the way. My methods aren't so cruel as my father's, but they're effective. This you'll soon learn . . . and 'twill be a fine lesson I'll teach you."

He disappeared into the mist. Marea's last sight was the powerful broadness of his back, and the scabbard of his deadly broadsword as it slapped against his thickly muscled thigh.

Corbie brushed against her skirt with an insistent yowl and purr, but Marea barely noticed as she stood in the doorway, shaking badly as she stared into the gloom, unseeing.

Chapter Nine

The day had come, the men were in place. All that was left was for Marea to sound the alarm that would commence the seige.

In the end she'd decided on a plan that mirrored one the Douglas had used on her father fifteen years ago. A brilliant strategy, one so effective it was only an odd twist of luck that saved the keep from falling back into Douglas hands.

Now, Marea prayed for the same stroke of luck, for if Chase Graham had heard the tale of the Douglas's seige, or had heard the ballad that had since been written about it, all would be lost. He wouldn't be looking for a strike to come from such an unexpected angle, so he'd be unprepared for a forceful defense.

She hoped.

"How much longer do we wait?" Randy asked moodily from her side. The whites of his eyes were tinged blue and streaked with red, bespeaking a night spent lifting a tankard—or a wench. His complexion was lighter than normal, making his beard seem

137

brighter. More than once she'd caught him stifling a yawn.

She nodded toward the castle, an ominously dark outline set against the first vibrant fingers of dawn. "We'll move once Zander gives the sign that all inside are ready."

Randy sent her a quick look from the corner of his eyes, then winced at the new throbbing it brought to his temples. "All? You mean you've more spies than Zander?"

Marea nodded, never lifting her gaze from the craggy stone battlement. "Aye. Do ye think your men have reached the end of the tunnel yet?"

"Let's hope so. 'Twould go easier on us if there was someone to unlock the door within, though."

" 'Tis already done. And the men who guard the portcullis should be taken care of by now as well."

Randy chuckled, the sound touched with admiration as he turned his full attention on his small cousin. It was the first time in years he'd seen her totally without her Agatha garb. He liked very much what he saw. Her cheeks were ruddy from the cool morning air, the length of red-gold hair snatched in a long, thick plait at her nape. Her amethyst eyes were narrowed and intent, never waving from the castle. The forest green of her plaid blended well with the trees concealing them, draping her body in proud highland fashion. He thought the color complimented the porcelain quality of her skin.

Randy considered telling her how beautiful she looked with the first light of dawn caressing her delicate features, dancing over the satin of her hair until each red highlight looked like a glistening streak of

138

flame. Then his mind hinged on words he'd shared with her many years ago, and he thought better of it. She did not want to be considered beautiful. The word *bonnie* made her pale, and made her limbs shake, her breathing shallow. Only Randy knew why.

Though he doubted Marea remembered their conversation, Randy remembered it well. That she'd confessed a great guilt over her family's death still troubled him deeply, as did her reasons; she truly believed it was the loveliness of her face that had brought on her father's particularly gruesome end and her mother's untimely one. Though he'd tried to convince her otherwise, her distorted reasoning held fast. Indeed, of late it seemed to have blossomed into an obsession. He'd no doubt it was the reason she'd taken to her Agatha garb so readily, the reason she so enjoyed padding and distorting her figure. Agatha's ugly trappings concealed what Marea had grown to regard as a vital flaw: her uncommon beauty.

Randy cleared his throat and looked away. His gaze settled on the castle. Though the solid walls were etched clearer now that the sun was rising on the horizon, it was the only change.

"Mayhaps we should go on to the tunnel, lass. If ye want to surprise the Graham, 'twould be best to do it soon, before the whole castle stirs."

Marea's gaze swept the area in indecision. She could see the men crouched behind bushes and pressed against trees, but only because she knew they were there. She heard the crackle of their feet shifting over cold, dry leaves. The men her uncle had guided around the firth, who now stood nearly invisible and still wet from the water they'd waded through, pressed against the castle walls as they awaited the order that would see them ascend. Her plan hinged on her reaching the Graham's chambers before the alarm was sounded.

Marea opened her mouth to respond when a movement atop the battlement caught her attention. Her eyes widened, first with familiarity, then with relief. She sent Randy a brilliant smile and said, "There, do ye see?"

He followed the tip of the finger with which she pointed. He scowled, his gaze fixing on the man who casually strolled the walkway. "Aye, I see your lack of concern, lass. Should you not be worried the mon up there will see your troops and shout a warning?"

"Zander's no traitor, Randy," Marea replied stiffly, which made her cousin's gaze, which had begun to stray, now sweep back and narrow on the man in question.

"Zander? Nay, he's no traitor, I'll grant ye that, but that's not—" He shielded his eyes with his hand. "I believe you're right, lass. Who else but a MacVin has *that* shade of hair? Orange as a carrot and twice as coarse." The scowl was back. "He's walking a mite slow, do ye not think?"

"Would you rather he ran and waved a big red banner, Randy? Nay, he's doing exactly what I asked him to do. When he reaches the other side, he'll descend to the storehouse floor and meet us at the end of the tunnel. 'Tis all been well planned." She jabbed him in the ribs and indicated it was time to leave their hiding place. "Come on. We've not a moment to waste."

Slipping stealthily through the trees without detection proved simple. Finding the boulder behind which

140

the entryway to the tunnel was located took a bit longer.

The tunnel was dark, but Marea didn't dare light a torch and risk attracting attention. The smell of the place was rank and moldy. Her feet splashed in the muddy water that seeped through her boots. The walls she slipped her hand along to guide her were moist and slimy. Her other hand loosely gripped Randy's, whose hand in turn held the one of the man behind him, and so on. There were six men in all, all armed to the teeth and ready to do battle. More than one scabbard scraped loudly against the ooze-coated walls.

"How much farther?" Randy grumbled, his feet slurping in mud and puddles. His voice bounced off the cold stone walls, echoing in all directions when he paused for breath. "I'm beginning to think you do not know where your going, and—"

"Shhh!" Marea hissed over her shoulder.

She knew exactly where she was going. Her keen memory was a guide finer than any map. Many an afternoon she'd spent in the dark, drafty tunnels as a child, and it was because of her youthful fascination for dank, musty places—and her need to hide from her father's quick Scottish temper—that she was now able to pick her way through what seemed like a labyrinth of passageways. In reality, there were but three, however the way the passages twisted and turned at odd angles, crossing over each other more than once, gave the impression of more.

Two steps before she would have collided into it, Marea knew she had reached the wooden door that would open as a cupboard into the storage chamber on the first floor of the keep. She stopped short, and

141

Randy's firm chest collided into her back.

"Be careful, mon," she hissed, the sound drowned out by the water dripping at their backs, and the tiny paws scurrying through the muck and water at their feet. "If you'd slammed me into the door while someone was passing . . . well, I do not want to know what would have happened."

"Where would they be passing, cousin?" Randy asked tersely. "What room have you brought us to? The great hall?"

"Nay, the storage chamber," she answered softly. Her voice was a loud, echoing hiss. "Do you not remember playing here, Randy? We did it often enough as bairns."

"Ye left me fumbling down here more times than not, if me memory's correct."

"Cease your whining, cousin. Did I not always come for you?"

"Aye, when it was demanded," he admitted with a soft chuckle. "And not a second before."

"Close enough." Marea pressed her ear against the cold, moist wooden door and listened carefully. " 'Tis quiet," she said, and turned toward Randy. Her gaze was met with unbroken blackness. Only the sound of his ragged breathing, and the feel of it brushing her cheek, said he was still there. "Zander is to meet us after he's let the other men through the higher tunnel to disperse the guards. Either he is not there yet, or he is quieter than a mouse."

" 'Tis not a MacVin's way to be quiet, lass."

"Then he is not there."

"Do we leave without him?"

Marea hesitated, torn between the urge to set her

plan into motion, and the need for Zander's assurance that the upper guards had been relieved of their posts. As it turned out, it was a decision she was spared from making.

The echo of Randy's voice had barely ceased before she heard the rattle of the padlock on the door against which she was leaning. Pushing forward, she turned and expectantly faced the velvet blackness that cloaked the door.

The sound of the padlock slipping from its thick metal loops was loud and grating. It was followed by three quick raps on the six-inch thick wood. Marea returned the knocks, paused, then repeated them. The door was then thrown open wide.

Though the day had matured only into the wee hours of dawn, the filter of morning sun blinded her. Marea squinted against the haze, a tight smile playing over her lips when her small friend's squat shape materialized. Zander's rounded features were etched with concern.

"What is it?" she asked, suddenly leery as she stepped into the storage chamber. It was a large room, cluttered with everything from kegs of ale to crates filled with various foodstuffs. "Has the call been given so soon?"

Zander rubbed the wisps of beard clinging to his jaw and let his gaze settle on the man at Marea's back. His eyes narrowed with distaste before he settled his attention on his mistress. "Nay, m'lady, but not five minutes ago I heard footsteps from behind the Graham's door. He rises early this morn, and if 'tis hoping you are to catch him, you'd best hurry. The rest of the keep will be awake soon."

"You've taken care of the guards?" Randy asked from over his cousin's shoulder. His dislike of the small man showed clearly in his eyes.

There were only so many MacKenzies Zander would take orders from. Raonull MacKenzie was not one of them. He answered the question as though Marea had asked, addressing the woman who had his loyalties. "Aye, m'lady. The bumps atop their heads say they'll sleep till midday if not longer. Your men have taken their places atop the battlement with none the wiser. Though, I'd be thinking you'd best hurry before any take a closer look."

Marea gave a brisk nod toward the door leading to the hall. Zander smiled, bowed his head, and moved in the indicated direction. His gait as he rounded the corner was slow, as though he was out for nothing more than an early stroll in the twisting hallways.

"Where be you sending him, lass?" Randy muttered in her ear.

"Do not sound so suspicious, mon, I know what I be doing," she whispered, slapping him lightly on his padded shoulder. She moved toward where Zander had just disappeared, indicating the rest should follow. "He's guiding us to the Graham. 'Twould not do for us to be caught walking the halls, armed as we be. Zander will make sure we encounter no—er—resistance on the way."

Twice Zander's low hum of warning made the band skulk amidst the shadows until her small friend waylaid the passersby. The third time, the intercepted man had almost taken to the hall in which they hid. Only Zander's quick thinking made him decide otherwise.

144

By the time they reached the door leading to the Graham's bedchamber, Marea's heart was throbbing, her fingers trembling. Zander continued to the end of the hall that branched off in a T and was cautiously inspecting both ends. The men behind her shifted restlessly as Marea put her ear to the door.

She heard footsteps. They didn't come muffled from the other side of the portal, as she had expected, but from behind. The men caught the sound as well and a prickle of tension charged the air as their attention abruptly shifted to the rear.

"You there," a surprised, youthful voice called out. The tone trickled familiarly down Marea's spine. "What are you doing by my lord's door?"

Randy spun on his heel. His demonic expression gave the young man pause. It was enough time for Randy to reach his adversary's side and rest the deadly point of his broadsword against the young man's throat.

The scrape of half a dozen swords being dragged from scabbards rang loud. The young man's eyes widened, for now he faced not one deadly blade, but seven.

"Wh-what is th-the meaning of this? What are you doing?"

Marea spun on her heel, and saw the young guard that Godfrey had left to guard her those many days ago. Guy Falken's face drained to ashy white. His brown eyes glistened with fear as the razor-sharp blade pressed into his windpipe. The arrogant gleam in her cousin's eyes said he would have no compunction about ending the young man's life then and there.

" 'Tis plain enough that we be paying your laird a

visit," Randy said, his gaze never wavering from his helpless captive. "Have you a problem with that, lad? If so, state it now," he paused sinisterly, *"before* I slit your cursed *Sasunach* throat."

Instructing one of the men to keep watch over the door lest Chase Graham appeared to surprise them all, Marea approached her cousin's back. "I said no bloodshed, Randy," she reminded him softly but sternly. "Not if it can be helped."

Randy snorted. The movement of his broad chest rippled down his arm, causing the blade to slice the upper layer of skin on Guy Falken's throat. The young man gasped when a warm ribbon of crimson twisted down his pale flesh, soaking into the collar of his ivory tunic.

"Sometimes it canna be helped, lass," Randy growled.

"This is not one of those times."

A scowl furrowed his bushy red brow as Randy's attention snapped to the side. He fixed Marea with an angry glare. "What do ye suggest, lass? We canna bring him with us, and if we let him go he'll awaken the rest of the keep. 'Twould make for an even bloodier end."

Proud MacKenzie gazes locked in open challenge. Guy Falken's gaze shifted between the two, and, seeing the silent power struggle, opted for immediate escape. His arm came up to knock the broadsword away. Years of practice made Randy's grip too fast to be easily broken. The sword did not fall, but it did waver enough for the young man to take a step back. Then another. He spared Marea an odd glance, as though for a split second he'd recognized her—or thought he did—before turning and rushing down the hall.

Randy lurched to follow, as did two of his men, but Marea quickly stopped them. Knowing it was her cousin they followed, it was him she aimed to halt.

"Nay, let him go, Randy," she ordered, her fingers wrapping around his thick forearm.

He glared down at her. "Are ye daft?" he demanded, his angry gaze shifting to the corner of the hallway Guy Falken had just disappeared around. The thump of retreating footsteps echoed around them. "The lad will sound the alarm and bring the entire keep down on our heads. 'Tis not the way to win a battle."

" 'Tis if we be quick, and get to the Graham before the rest of the keep gets to us." She refused to explain to her cousin exactly *why* she'd spared the life of the young man he seemed so eager to kill. Randy MacKenzie was Highlander born and bred. He would not understand. "They'll not dare overtake us if 'tis their laird's throat we threaten. 'Twas my plan from the start."

"Then let's be about it, lass," he grumbled, obviously not pleased. "The sooner the Graham tastes the bite of our sword the safer we'll all be. This hallway is quiet now, but 'twill not be so for long."

Guy Falken used his sleeve to dab at the half-caked trail of blood on his neck as he burst hellbent into the hall. His exerted breathing rang through the air.

"The keep has been infiltrated, m'lord!" he panted, leaning heavily against the arched stone doorway.

147

The spoon of porridge Chase was in the process of raising to his lips clattered to the table. His was not the only one. The four men who were to accompany him to collect rents tensed, their morning meals quickly forgotten.

In a second Chase was on his feet, his fingers flexing over the hilt of the broadsword strapped to his hip. "Scots?" he asked. Guy Falken nodded, and Chase groaned in response. "Was it Douglas? God's teeth, the man grows too bold!"

"If 'twas Douglas, he was not with them."

Chase nodded. "How many? What is their location?"

"Six men and a woman, m'lord, in the hall outside your bedchamber. They were the only ones I saw."

Chase stopped mid-stride. "A *woman?*" When the young man nodded, his expression darkened. "Nay, you must be mistaken. Raiding a castle is no woman's task."

Guy Falken stiffened. He was no liar, and the defensive tone of his words stressed that fact. "I know what I saw, m'lord. 'Twas a woman who led them, and a beautiful one at that. Were it not for her desire that no blood be shed, I'd be lying upon the upstairs floor with my throat slit ear to ear."

One of the men behind Chase stepped forward. He was a seasoned reiver, with the anticipation of a bloody battle etched in his craggy face. " 'Tis not the Douglas. The only woman in his keep is his sister, and even a blind man would not mistake her for beautiful. The rest are serving wenches, and his men are too well trained to take an order from them . . . unless 'twas put to them atop a mattress."

As Chase digested this, Guy Falken confessed, "It shames me to think 'twas the softly spoken words of a tiny, copper-haired girl that sees me breathing long enough to sound a fair warning."

Chase's head snapped up. His emerald gaze flared. Falken took a quick step back when he saw the intense anger etched in his laird's rugged features. The men grew silent, and a crackle of tension sparked the air.

Chase's hands clenched into tight fists as he fixed Falken with a glare that made the young man stumble back another step. His mind ran in circles, but he had no time for idle speculation. There was only one way to be certain. "Her eyes. What color were her eyes?"

Blinking stupidly, Falken answered, "A funny shade of . . . well, *heatherish*, I suppose. Why? Do you know her?"

"Aye!" The single word tore from Chase's lungs. For just a second he indulged himself in a stab of regret. It was not the way things should be between himself and the wench. Her boldness didn't conform to his plans. Then again, neither had intoxication and, ultimately, seduction been part of his plans, yet he had done both.

Regret, however, quickly melted to white-hot betrayal, then all-consuming rage. Chase pushed aside the former and focused on the latter, until not a scrap of compassion remained.

The treacherous bitch didn't deserve his sympathies! Not when her goal was to steal what belonged to him. That was something he would allow no man—or woman—to ever do. Nay, what she deserved was to taste the bite of his broadsword against her too smooth flesh. What she *needed* was to be taught a lesson, a les-

149

son he was not entirely sure she would walk away from with her life intact. That realization brought a stabbing pain to his heart, but, like the regret, her betrayal cut deeply enough to push the emotion aside before it had time to take root.

Chapter Ten

"How was I to know he'd not be here?" a woman's aggravated voice echoed down the deserted hall. "He was heard roaming these chambers not ten minutes ago. 'Tis doubtful he's gone far."

Chase paused on the stone landing. His hand twitched over the hilt of his broadsword as the lilting sound of her voice swept over him. Familiarity prickled the nape of his neck, alerting the wisps of golden hair there. A vision of red-gold tresses and wide amethyst eyes floated in his mind, tightening in his heart and his gut. The memory was brutally shoved aside. He needed no weaknesses hampering what he was about to do. Instead, his fingers gripped the sword's hilt as he focused his attention on the conversation drifting down the hall. The angry words fueled his already fierce anger.

"Ye should have been more thorough, lass," a burly voice scoffed. The gruff words were followed by the click of footsteps and the rush of skirts. " 'Twould not have happened had *you* checked your sources."

" 'Twould not have happened had I some *help*," she argued hotly. "Or is your memory so short you've forgotten 'twas agreed we go by my plan? 'Twould it not have been simpler had you or your father helped me concoct a more thorough one? Mayhaps we'd have the bastard now if you had."

"Do not blame this catastrophe on us. We agreed to *help*, not plan." A masculine sigh bounced off stone as Chase inched down the hall, clinging to the wall. Following behind him were twenty of his best men. " 'Tis not like you to blame your own shortsightedness on others, lass."

" 'Twas not shortsighted to expect the mon to be where he always is at this time of morn, cousin!"

" 'Tis not too clever either, for the mon's not here. Think of another plan, and think of it quick, lass. Time's running out. That boy you let go not ten minutes ago will sound the alarm any second. I'm surprised they're not clattering to battle already."

"Aye," she replied warily. "So am I. You do not think—?"

Chase gave her no time to finish the thought. The click of his heels atop solid stone announced his entrance. Her gasp of surprise was overridden by the hiss of swords being drawn.

He saw her pull free her own, shorter sword, then unconsciously step back. For a second, amethyst locked with emerald green. The former glistened with surprise, the latter with raw hatred.

"M'lady," Chase greeted coldly from the doorway, nodding his head in a stiff caricature of politeness. A sneer of disgust curled his lips when he brandished his sword before him.

152

He kept the six men trying to rush him at bay. The early morning sun filtered in through the long narrow windows and the golden rays glistened off blades as deadly as the gazes that clashed over them.

The big redhead made a fast jab with his sword. His aim was Chase's tunic clad shoulder. Steel crashed against steel. The sound of blades meeting was deafening as Chase parried easily, then counterattacked. The burly Scot had barely enough time to raise his own sword to deflect the sweeping blow.

"Surrender, pig," the burly Scot growled as he looked for another opening to bring Chase down. The sword he gripped in his meaty left hand was never still. "We've seven to your one. You'll never win."

"I won't lose. My men are just outside. I've only to summon them." His golden brow arched a challenge as a cold smile twisted his lips. His free hand lifted, and the fingers snapped crisply together.

In moments the room was filled with twenty bloodthirsty men. With drawn swords, the English quickly sized up their opponents. More than one smiled hungrily at the prospect of dousing the life from the now-outnumbered Scots.

His gaze wavered between the burly redhead and the woman, settling finally on the latter. He saw that her spine stiffened with pride, but it took effort for her to do it. He gestured to her with his sword. The deadly tip just grazed her neck. She didn't flinch and, damn, but he had to admire that. "My guard says you lead these men. I don't doubt it, but I've need to hear you say it."

"Aye," she answered, her voice low and gritty. She knocked his sword away with the blade of her own. The sound of steel scraping was harsh and loud.

153

"They be mine. All this and *more*."

Chase's gaze narrowed, his bushy brows furrowed in an assessing scowl. His weapon lowered, but stayed at the ready. "More?"

"Aye, mon, we are not complete idiots. The six men you see are not all of us. I've more in position atop your battlements. Still more surround the outer walls. Mayhaps they've already scaled it and subdued the rest of your clan." Her eyes and voice hardened with determination. "If 'tis a bloody battle you want, we've come equipped to give it."

His scowl deepened. "Then why sneak into my room with the assurance of only six armed men? Surely an open confrontation at full force would have benefited you more."

"She is not practiced in the art of raiding, *Sasunach,*" the big redhead barked, cutting short anything else she would have said. "She aimed to spare your slimy lives by demanding no blood be shed. 'Tis only because of that foolish order you're alive and standing here now. 'Tis grateful to her you should be." The point of his sword arched toward the open laces of Chase's tunic, and the wedge of sunbronzed flesh exposed there. The blow was not meant to draw blood, only to threaten. With a flick of his wrist, Chase deflected on the downward stroke. "We could have murdered you all in your sleep, *Sasunach,* with none the wiser."

Chase ignored this last, focusing instead on the words that set his mind to racing. "If she's not a skilled raider, then why the hell are your men obeying her orders? I'd think even a bunch of thick-skulled Scots like yourselves to have more sense."

The redhead snorted, and since he'd apparently

been repeatedly asking himself the same question, he declined comment.

"I'll speak with your mistress alone," Chase said, and slipped his sword into its scabbard. He glared at the burly Scot as though challenging him to defy the command.

Challenge was not what ran through Randy's mind, however. 'Twas more surprise that the Englishman would put down his weapon in a display of trust the Scots did not deserve. Concern for Marea circled in his brain as well, but knowledge of his cousin made the emotion shallow. She could take care of herself, she'd done as much on many occasions. And Randy doubted the Graham would send the captives farther than the corridor.

"Do we have a choice?" Randy asked finally, not wishing to give in too easily lest he look weak.

One golden brow arched as Chase's gaze clashed with the redhead's. "The twenty swords aimed at your heart say you do not." Dismissing the man, he turned. "Bring them to the hall, and for God's sake, don't harm them before I've finished here."

His gaze swept back to the big redhead, then shifted to the woman. A muscle twitched in his jaw when he saw her cheeks color, and her amethyst eyes grow wide. His next words were spoken for her benefit and hers alone, although they were loud enough for all to hear and understand. "Afterward, if all goes ill, dispose of them."

"Nay!" she cried, brandishing her sword with a skill not usually found in her gender. "They'll not pay for me own foolishness with their lives. 'Twould not be fair. Take your vengeance out on me, *Sasunach*, not them."

155

"I intend to, mistress," he answered slowly, meaningfully.

Chase supervised disarming the Scots and ushering them, with guards, into the hallway. From the corner of his eyes he saw her inch toward one of the long, slat windows and rest her shoulder against the cold stone wall. The heavy footsteps of her men clomping over stone echoed in the room, as did the English and Scottish voices murmuring their disapproval.

"Falken, feel free to divest our little dove of her talons," Chase said coldly from the doorway when only he and his young vassal remained. "I don't want to be skewered the second my back is turned."

Guy Falken's youthful gaze wavered between Chase and the woman who was suddenly rigid. Her head snapped up, her unusual eyes sparked with purpose as the sword in question was lifted even with her shoulders. The tip was pointed at Falken's heart. Though she'd spared his life before, for reasons he'd yet to contemplate, the young man knew such generosity would not come a second time.

Licking his lips, he glanced uncertainly at Chase, who leaned against the arched doorway and nodded for him to proceed. He swallowed hard, took a hesitant step toward the woman — and stopped dead when her lips pulled back in a feral snarl and the razor-sharp blade of her sword did a lightening quick arch. Guy Falken's sword sliced thin air as he belatedly strove to protect himself.

The muscles in Marea's arms screamed as she carried the blow through, then repositioned herself. Sucking in a ragged breath, she fixed her gaze on the torn left sleeve of Guy Falken's tunic, and the stain of crimson soaking through it. His face paled when he looked

156

down at the wound in shock. "Had I been of a mind, your arm would now be a part of the stone," she hissed. "Be warned, bairn, next time you come near me, 'tis what I intend to do."

"M-m'lord?" Guy began, sparing Chase a brief, plaintive glance as his fingers sought out his wound. They came away soaked in blood.

"Disarm her." The emerald eyes narrowed as they settled on her. He seemed as surprised as the boy by her deadly skill with the blade. "And remember, she's but a woman, and therefore no match for you."

"Aye," the boy agreed weakly, "a woman with the strength and dexterity of *two men*. I've never seen a girl who could wield a sword so well."

Marea's gaze shifted between them. Neither man gained her full attention, and so when Guy Falken charged, she was prepared for defense too late. He thrust. She parried. The two blades crashed together, meeting at the hilt. They held that position for a beat, then Falken shoved her against the stone. The smell of his blood stung her nostrils as he pinned her roughly. With a flick of his wrist, her blade went crashing to the stone.

She scrambled after it, but Falken pinned her to the wall and kicked it from reach. The sword twirled over the floor, spinning to rest at Chase Graham's feet.

He reached down and plucked it up, handing it to Guy Falken as the young man passed through the archway. At the same time, he wondered how such a veritable slip of a woman could manage the heavy blade with so much strength and dexterity.

"This door is to be locked, and a guard with the key posted outside," Chase ordered as he pushed away from the stone. His gaze swept the room and locked with hers.

Guy Falken's rigid affirmation that his orders would immediately be carried out was drowned by the slamming of the door. Within seconds, the sound of a padlock slipping into steel rungs grated through the air.

Marea moved not a muscle as she watched a satisfied smile cross his lips. His arms were crossed over his chest. The firmly sculpted muscles of his biceps and broad shoulders strained his ivory tunic. His hair gleamed in the newborn sunlight streaming in through the window at her back. His eyes were a single, iridescent spot of color against the dreariness of a stone backdrop; they burned with hot emerald fire.

"I'll not ask you if I am asleep this time, vision," he said from across the room, as he leaned his back against the door. He reached up and rubbed the smoothness of his jaw, surveying her coldly. "I know I'm not. What I do *not* know, but intend to find out, is what you hoped to gain by all this. What earthly purpose could such stupidity serve you?"

Marea swallowed hard, and pressed her back harder against the wall. His very presence unnerved her. Without a sword, she felt bare, as defenseless as a scrappy kitten. She was no match for him in strength, and she was beginning to think he ousted her in intelligence as well. All in all, it was a feeling of utter defeat she nursed now, and that glistened in the gaze she fixed on him. " 'Tis not stupid to fight for what is rightfully yours," she answered simply, glancing away. She didn't like the way the heat of his gaze made her tingle. Her reaction to it was too confusing—especially now.

"I've naught that's yours."

"You've everything that is mine, *Sasunach*. *That* is

158

what my foolishness hoped to gain. I did not come to harm you, as my cousin's attested, though such could have been easily done."

Chase pushed from the door. His bootheels clicked over the stone, marking his approach. He stopped a hand's breadth away. Of a sudden he was engulfed with her sweet, sweet scent. It touched a chord that he tried to suppress—tried, and failed. His voice sounded gruffer than he intended. "You attempted to steal what is mine, wench. 'Tis a different form of harm you sought to inflict, true, but a grievous one. An *intolerable* one." He paused, studying her. "Come, tell me what you hoped to gain for your troubles. Tell me what you *think* I possess that should, by rights, be yours."

The heat of his body melted through her plaid, and through the thin cotton rail. His warmth caressed her flesh in inviting waves that left her shaken and breathless. She gasped when his fingers cupped her chin and roughly forced her gaze up. He wouldn't let her look away.

" 'Tis Kinclearnon I was after," she admitted, hating the anger that had so rudely abandoned her. "The keep, the title, all of it. 'Twas my father's by birth. It should have passed to me upon his death."

His eyes narrowed lazily, but lest Marea think he had relinquished the fight, she noted the emerald depths remained sharp as he held her gaze. The fingers cupping her chin tightened. He said, "I know only legends of the man who held this land before my father. If the tales are true, the MacKenzie was a fine reiver. But the man's heroics can't dispute the fact that Kinclearnon was wrested from him a half score ago, and given in good faith to my father. 'Tis mine now, wench, and as you will soon learn, I don't part with my possessions. You'd do well to remember that."

Marea pulled her chin from his grasp. For some reason, he allowed it. "You, sir, would do equally well to know that a MacKenzie, lad or lass, does not give up. Kinclearnon is mine. I'll not give it up without a fight."

He stepped back. His strained expression said he was having a difficult time suppressing the urge to beat some sense into her. "I am sorry to hear that," he said, while raking angry fingers through his tousled hair, "for your words, so bravely spoken, have sealed your fate. 'Tis not a fate you'll enjoy."

" 'Tis not a fate I'll endure," she countered hotly. A surge of unease rippled through her; she was hard-pressed to push it away, and just as unsuccessful. "Short of killing me outright, there's naught you can do to stop me. I'll not rest until this keep is mine again. Even if it means battering your portcullis every fortnight until I taste victory."

"You'll taste only blood. Mayhaps your own, for I'll never give anything to you. What say you to that?"

"Time, *Sasunach*, will tell the victor. I'll not be defeated in this."

"Nor will I." He inclined his head, again crossing his arms over the firm wedge of his chest. "Which leaves us at an impasse. I'll not surrender the keep to you, and you'll not rest until I do. You leave me no choice but to assure myself that that never will happen — in any manner I am able to do it."

Marea steeled herself for the inevitable. Lifting her chin, she met his gaze and asked, " 'Tis death for me men? Can I not convince you to unleash your wrath on me instead of them? 'Tis where your hatred belongs, you know." Her chin jutted to the closed door. "What they did they did out of love and loyalty. They do not deserve to die for it."

One golden brow slanted, his gaze glistened with open speculation. "You wish to save their lives, do you?" Marea nodded cautiously, and saw him grin slyly. "How much are you willing to pay for their safety, wench? And how do you intend to pay when you've naught to bargain with?"

Why did she feel like a mouse who'd just stumbled into a steely trap from which there was no escape?

He watched the emotions glisten in her amethyst eyes, and wondered at their origin. Surely a woman who seemed so brave would not be averse to what he'd just suggested. Or was she? He didn't know. The woman was a mystery to him, one that grew more perplexing with each minute spent in her dangerously beautiful company.

"What do you suggest, *Sasunach*?" she asked, her voice a pitch huskier than normal. Her cheeks had taken on a healthy pink glow once she'd guessed his lurid intent. "A bargain canna be struck if there's naught with which to bargain."

His grin broadened, and despite herself, the sight pricked at her heart.

He reached out and snatched the ends of the burnished gold plait draping her shoulder, rubbing the silky tresses between his fingers before his gaze lifted to hers. His eyes were dark, liquid, searingly intense as they roved the delicate bones of her face. "Two things leap to mind, but I'd think you reluctant to part with either." His head tipped to one side, the ragged fringe of his hair scraped the broad shelf of his shoulders as he studied her. "One is your compliance in

161

matters of battle—which I'd never get, and never believe if you did give it. The other, the pleasure of your body to warm these brisk autumn nights. A more likely option, since you know the fate of your men lies in the balance of your decision."

Marea swallowed hard, her gaze fixed on the gaping collar of his tunic. It was a mistake. His sunbronzed, rippling flesh made her pulse soar. Slipping her hands behind her back, she leaned against the wall. The rough stone scraped her knuckles, but the twinge was a welcome distraction. "The lives of people I love are at stake. I am not so selfish that I'd place me own pride above something so precious—*if* I thought 'twould do me men good. Methinks you be right in not trusting my word. Then again, were I to give you myself, I promise 'twould be no pleasure for you."

The braid dropped from his suddenly slack fingers. The tip bounced against the plaid wrapped around her waist. Chase watched it settle, then turned on his heel and stalked across the room. The tip of his scabbard scraped the wall as he whirled back around. His composure was beginning to crack, and unguarded agitation was beginning to peek through.

"You'll not be allowed to leave the keep until I have your word another attack will not be launched," he told her coldly. The muscle worked in his jaw as he fixed her with a penetrating glare, as though daring her to argue his order.

"Is that *all?*" A ghost of a smile etched Marea's lips when she said, "You have it, then. Me word that I'll not raid your keep again." She took a step toward the door and felt the heat of his eyes boring into her. "Might I leave now?"

Like a taut piece of twine, Chase's patience

snapped. He punched a fist into the opposite palm. The sound of flesh slapping flesh stopped her.

Slowly, she turned toward him, poised halfway between the window and the door. "I'll be taking me men with me. That was our arrangement."

" 'Tis no game we play, mistress," Chase growled. He cleared the distance between them, and grabbed her hard by her upper arms. Giving into his anger, he shook her roughly. Her head snapped back on her neck as he was treated to the hot anger of narrowed amethyst eyes. That gaze burned into his soul. Small fists pummeled his chest, but it was her eyes that finally brought him to his senses.

Dear God, what was wrong with him?! Hurting women had been his father's practice, his brother's, but never his own. That he'd allowed this woman enough power to provoke that perversity in him disgusted Chase. With a snarl, he thrust her away. She stumbled back, chafing at the biting pain in her arms.

"Does manhandling a lass make ye feel better?" she taunted, and backed away.

"Watch your tongue, wench, or you'll leave this keep without it," he growled as he took a threatening step toward her. "*If* you leave, that is."

"I'll leave. 'Twas our agreement." Her heart hammered in her breast, the tempo increasing with each step that drew his rugged form nearer to her. "I've given my pledge I'll not attack you again. 'Tis time you honored your word and let me go."

A humorless smile twisted his lips as he stopped so close their toes touched. "Nay, wench. The offer's been rescinded. I no longer want your word, nor will I accept it. You've convinced me you cannot be trusted."

His hands came up, hooking over her slender shoulders. It was a heavy, pinning weight that made her squirm. Desperately, her gaze sought out the polished hilt of his sword where it brushed against the lean indentation of his waist. It would be an easy thing, she reasoned, to shift her weight, then carefully reach out and wrap her fingers around the hilt, pulling the blade from its—

"Your attack this morn proved your gift for strategy is lacking, wench. Don't make yourself a complete fool."

His harsh breath blasted over her cheek and brow as her gaze snapped up. Her hand, halfway to the sword hilt, dropped to her side. "You promised to release me, now you've reneged, proving 'tis not only I who canna be trusted." Her chin lifted, and her gaze grew stormy. "I'll not go to your smelly dungeon without a fight. In fact, I'll be thinking a slow death by torture to be better than rotting down there."

"You won't be put in the dungeons." One hand left her shoulder to sweep the sunlit room. His gaze didn't leave her as he added, "What think you of your prison, wench?"

His insinuation brought a splash of color to her cheeks. "I'll sink a blade in your back whilst you sleep at the first opportunity. Do not doubt it."

"I'm not concerned," he replied smoothly. "First, you'd need to find a blade to sink, and I'll not make that easy for you. Then, of course, you'd have to accomplish the bloody deed. I'm not so sure a woman who's already shown a strong aversion to bloodshed would be able to murder an unarmed man in his sleep."

"Mayhaps you should think again. Me aversions are not that strong. If it gains me freedom, I'd not think twice about spilling your blood on the stones."

Chase's jaw clamped hard. The fingers on her shoulders tightened. "Fine words, but they have a hollow ring. Deeds speak louder, and yours say you've too soft a heart for such actions."

"Again, mon, time will tell in the end," she said, and shrugged his hands away. They fell to his sides, and he made no move to stop her as she turned and walked to the window.

The sun was bright, set low on the early morning sky. From this position she had a clear view of the firth and the rolling hills surrounding it. Her gaze lowered to the craggy stone walls, and her heart stopped when she saw no sign of her uncle or his men. Where were they? Surely not all of them could hide themselves from view. Even the men atop the battlement were gone. The keep looked eerily deserted.

Marea spun on her heel. Her plaid billowed around her legs, then settled around her ankles as she leaned heavily against the wall. Until this second she'd been playing for time, waiting for her uncle to surge to her rescue. Now she had a sinking feeling that not only was Thomas not out there planning her escape, but he'd been taken prisoner along with the rest of the men. How? How had it happened? And so quietly? If there'd been a skirmish, surely she would have heard it!

" 'Twill not be easy for you if you plan to keep me here," she said suddenly, affecting an air of bravado she did not feel. Desperation curled like tangible fingers in her stomach when she eyed the door, her only route of escape. But it was locked, and guarded. "You've captured some of me men, but not all. There's many more who'll look to setting me free."

165

He'd spanned the distance between them without her realizing. Now he leaned an elbow against the stone beside her shoulder. The heat of his arm seeped into her. Her senses filled with the heady male scent of him—harsh lye soap and sweat. The aroma had the same powerful effect on her as the man from which it emanated.

"Sorry, but I don't consider your witch a threat."

"She's not a witch, she's a *healer*," Marea scoffed automatically, as she tried to melt her body into the stone wall biting into her back. "And you'd do your health well to nurture a fear for Agatha. She can take away good health as easily as she can restore it. Her powers be fierce, her temper short. She'll not be pleased to hear you're keeping me here against me will."

"There are ways of dealing with her sort. 'Twouldn't be hard to brand her the witch she so vehemently denies being. The punishment for witchcraft is, as I'm sure you know, most severe." His hand came up, a roughened fingertip outlining the soft, trembling line of her jaw. Her eyelids flickered shut, a second before Chase snatched his hand back. "Need I add that her fate also lies in your slender hands?"

Marea swallowed hard when she felt his raw strength seep through her. She was very much aware of just how precarious her situation was. Chase was physically strong, his orders powerful. Her handful of spies were useless, the men she'd brought with her captured, all of them. No help would be coming to her from any quarter.

And if, by some miracle of God, she was successful in perfecting her escape? Hot tears burned her eyes. This man would slay her men in retribution for such flagrant disobedience. He was ruler here, he was within his rights to do it. Very little punishment would come to him from the Warden of Middle March.

Marea could not live with herself if that were to happen, for she knew the men he held, knew the families that would grieve to lose them. She'd been on the receiving end of such grief herself, and the pain in her still ran deep. She couldn't knowingly inflict it on another.

"I'll do whatever you ask if you'll spare me men," she whispered huskily, her eyes still tightly closed as she pressed the back of her head hard against the cold stone. "I swear it. Just . . . please, do not ask me to share your bed. Is that fair enough?"

Chase sucked in a ragged breath and shook his head. Of its own accord, his palm reached up to cup the velvet softness of her cheek. He was surprised to feel moisture clinging to her skin, and just as shocked to hear his own breathless sigh echoed by her gently parted lips.

"Open your eyes, vision. I'll have you looking at me when I give you my answer."

Her lashes flickered up. Their gazes met like two swords crashing together. His thumb stroked her jaw, her cheek, the line of a dimple etching the corner of her mouth. His touch burned. So did the eyes that bored into her. If not for the wall at her back, Marea would have collapsed.

"Nay, 'tis not only unfair, 'tis not possible." His fingers slipped over her neck, then buried themselves in the tight tresses above the braid. "Even if I had the power to deny myself, the passion I've seen in your eyes would tear my resolve to shreds. I can't forget the pleasures our bodies bring to each other. Nor do I think you want me to."

"You bring me no pleasure." But her voice was too high, too shaky to be taken seriously.

"Liar," he growled, leveling his nose with hers, until the tips were touching. His hot breath washed over her chin and neck when he added huskily. "Shall I prove it to you?"

Chapter Eleven

He gave her no time to answer. His mouth slashed hungrily over hers. One arm circled her waist, crushing her to him, while the other held her twisting head firm. His heart throbbed against the fingers splayed across his chest. Like the howling wind of a hot summer storm, his breath rushed in her ears.

His kiss was hard, punishing; it demanded a response she fought hard not to give. But when his lips turned soft and coaxing, she was lost. Her body fired to his touch, to his kiss, to his raw masculinity, in ways she'd never dreamed possible.

She quivered, even as the blood in her veins heated. She tensed with passionate awareness wherever hard muscle pressed against her. Her legs turned to water when the moistness of his tongue invaded the honeyed recesses of her mouth. Hesitantly, her hands snuck around his neck. Her fingers twisted in the silky strands tickling her palms. Her tongue parried the moist thrust and retreats, making her surrender complete.

He'd meant only to test her strength. The moment he felt her compliance, Chase planned to end the embrace as well as the kiss. But now that the time had come, he couldn't do it. Her body inflamed him with its softness, the sweet scent of her fueled his passion beyond reason. Her wild response was more than he'd bargained for, and it made his heart swell. He couldn't let her go, he realized with a jolt, because he didn't want to. He needed to bury himself within her, to lose himself in her velvet softness. Damn the bloody consequences!

All the energy that crackled between them from the raid and its powerful aftermath rechanneled itself through their bodies in a different direction. A sensual direction that begged and demanded in turn. What had begun as a test, a challenge issued and grudgingly met, was now a mutual battle for release.

His breath quickened when his hands roved her, touching, stroking, setting her on fire. His lips devoured, the moist tip of his tongue left not an inch of her sweetness untasted.

She felt a heady surge of sexual promise tear through her like a knife. Her response was immediate. She couldn't control the need gathering within her, like a dam ready to burst. She clung to him desperately, her mouth answering his plea as her body begged him for release from the bittersweet torture.

Panting, Chase tore his mouth from hers and bent to slip his hand beneath her knees. His groan punctuated the air when the gentleness of her curves was drawn against his throbbing need. His knees trembled with the urgency humming through his blood as he carried her to the bed, and pillowed her atop the soft bedding.

As he climbed on top of the bed, his first instinct was to cover her with himself, and seek that which he wished most to possess. Yet something deep inside him prolonged his physical need, and honed it to a sharp edge. His breath caught as his hand touched her cheek. His fingers poised a mere fraction of an inch away, as though afraid he'd touch her and find her not real at all, but a vision, a figment of his imagination.

Then his palm dipped, his calloused flesh instantly seduced by her quivering skin. Chase sucked in a ragged gasp when she turned into his touch. She was more lovely than words, what with her soft hair shimmering in the morning sun, and her warm breath wafting over the throbbing pulse in his wrist. Her amethyst eyes, lidded heavy with desire, glanced up at him. The reality that she was truly there, lying atop his bed, left him humbled.

"I've dreamed of this," he rasped, his fingers slipping to her braid and quickly loosening it. He rubbed a fistful against his cheek before spreading the silky, red-gold tresses around her shoulder. Her hair glistened against the rich blue spread like a burnished cloud. "Aye, dreamed of having you in my bed, in my arms. Tell me you're real, vision. Tell me."

His hand slipped down to caress her neck, his fingers tickled her sensitive earlobe. She trembled. Her eyes flickered closed as she reveled in the rapturous sensations of his touch. Her hands slipped down his muscular biceps. She felt the sinew beneath the coarse sleeve ripple in response. Aye, if this was a dream, he wasn't the only one who didn't want to awaken.

" 'Tis real," she sighed. Her hand hesitated at his elbow, then slid down the firm forearm to meet his. Their fingers entwined. The curling hair on the back of his knuckles teased her palms, heightening an awareness that was already razor sharp.

With a groan he ripped the scabbard from his side and tossed it to the floor, where it clattered loudly against the stone, then eased himself down to her side. The dip of the mattress made her roll toward him. Chase captured her to him, reveling in the feel of small, soft curves pressing against his male hardness.

Burying his face in the flowery satin of her hair, he rolled her onto her back and covered her fully. Only a portion of his weight was supported by the mattress now, the rest pressed her back against the feather ticking. His mouth found hot skin. The tip of his tongue licked the salty flesh of her neck as his hands slipped up her arms, and stretched them high above her head. Her breasts thrust firmly into his chest. The tempting curves made Chase groan.

His breath whispered over her flesh, the feel of it tingled through her already fevered blood. Her body was on fire, the need that curled within her thighs and trembling stomach was white-hot and demanding. Her back arched. Though she could go nowhere, she increased the pressure between them.

"Ah, vision, I won't last if you keep moving like that," he growled against her throat.

She turned her head and found the curl of his ear. Her tongue teased the pliable flesh, while the ends of his golden mane tickled her cheek. The scent of soap was finely woven into each silky strand. She breathed in slowly, and thought she would burst when the soapy scent mixed with the spicy aroma of hard male flesh.

He lifted his head, and gazed deeply into her eyes. A low groan scratched the back of his throat as first his eyes, then his mouth, devoured the shell-pink perfection of her lips.

Her arms circled the thickness of his neck. She was vaguely aware when her fingers tangled in his hair, and very aware when his big hands began to frantically stroke her body.

His insistent fingers seared the flesh beneath the wool, stripping away the coarse cloth. He tasted patches of creamy flesh as it was exposed. Each brush of his lips made her weak, hot with desire. Soon, she was left with nothing but her rail for covering, and the intensity of his emerald eyes stripped even that away.

She didn't know when he'd stripped away his own clothes; she'd not seen or felt him do it. She only knew that when she glanced down, her gaze was met with sun-kissed flesh, covered thick with curling gold, and glistening with a sheen of perspiration.

He arched above her. His elbows flanked her shoulders, supporting his crushing weight. His position made tight cords of sinew ripple with his every ragged breath. His gaze searched her face. His warm breath washed over her cheeks.

" 'Twas victory I sought from you, and victory I've gained," he said huskily. His words made her heart hammer. Oddly enough, he wasn't gloating, though his voice was thick with emotion. "Now, vision, I've a need to taste surrender. Will you give it?" He shifted, drawing the tip of his calloused index finger down the tender curve of her jaw. His gaze darkened when he saw her tremble beneath even that simple touch.

His finger moved, covering her lips when they parted to answer. "Your body says aye, but that's not enough for me any more. I want all of you, Marea, body and soul."

It was the first time he'd ever spoken her name. Indeed, she'd begun to think he did not know it. The three syllables rolled over his tongue, as though he'd said it often. On his thickly accented voice, her name sounded oddly sweet. It touched a tender chord within her, a chord she'd thought long buried.

"There's not much left of me to give you. But what there is be yours." But only for today, she thought. The feelings singing inside of her now were too hot, too exquisite to last. But she'd not break the fragile strands binding them by telling him so, even if he demanded it.

Sensing his hesitation, she gripped his forearms tightly and moved beneath him. Her hips pressed to his. His lips thinned, his jaw hardened. He started to lower himself to her, but quickly checked the impulse.

The Graham was not the only one to taste victory this morning; the heady flavor shot through Marea's soul. Her gaze clashed with his as her hands trailed up his arms. Her fingers closed over his shoulders as she arched into him again, and stayed that way for one exquisitely long moment before collapsing back to the mattress, and pulling him down atop her.

Their lips meshed in a demanding kiss. Moist tongues parried and thrusted. Both gave and received, but neither received enough, and both searched deeper still. Hot breath mingled and washed over feverish skin.

A small palm swept over rippling, hard flesh. A large palm seared the outer curve of a creamy thigh. Two groans shattered the morning, entwining as one when his hands slipped beneath the hem of the rail and dragged it up over the tempting curve of her hips, over the gentle indentation of a stomach that quivered, over temptingly ripe breasts, over the slender porcelain shoulders, then, finally, over her head. The scrap of cloth was tossed aside. Before it had fluttered to the stone, the two bodies atop the bed were fervently entangled once more.

Chase's restraint had long since reached its end. When he nudged his knees between her smooth thighs, he found his wasn't the only patience that had snapped. Her legs opened to him like the dewy petals of a rose blossoming under a summer sun.

He lifted himself above her, until the hairs pelting his chest tickled the swollen buds of her breasts. He paused against her dewy softness, and drank in the sight of her lying atop his bed, beneath him, hot and willing and, oh, so very ready. The image flared in his mind, embedding itself there the same instant he plunged into the moist velvet sheath of her body.

Marea's hips arched. She gripped his rock-solid forearms and wrapped her legs tightly around his hips, drawing him deeper. He filled her completely, wonderfully. She luxuriated in the feel of him buried inside her before he moved, pulling out of her almost completely, then quickly filling her again.

The demand of his body sent a bolt of sensation throbbing first in her thighs, then quickly sweeping to the rest of her body. She arched, meeting each hard thrust, her eyes tightly closed as she strained into the mounting spiral of exquisitely alive senses. Her fingers curled, digging into muscled tendons.

Her head twisted against the pillow and her ragged breathing echoed in her ears as her body demanded more. A crescendo was building, like a rhapsody it sang through her blood, setting her nerve endings on fire.

The tempo increased to a breathtaking pitch. His

breaths came in short, labored gasps. Satisfaction was only a step away, but he'd no wish to climb that sensuous peak alone. The throaty moan that punctuated the air, and the ragged breath that rustled the golden hair swaying against his cheek, told him he would not.

Gritting his teeth, he shifted. Holding tight to the curve of her hips, keeping them joined tightly together, he rolled. He didn't release his hold on her until the back of his head was cradled against the pillow, and she was straddled atop him.

Gently, he grasped her hips and guided her into motion. When she'd struck a rhythm, he found a more sensuous use for his hands. He pushed her up until she was sitting atop him, impaled to the core, then slowly began to explore the curves of her body, the ones he'd previously ignored, but hadn't forgotten.

Marea conformed to this new position easily. His only encouragement was the hands that felt like liquid fire burning her flesh. His roughened palms cupped her breasts. He flicked the nipple until it peaked, then rolled the rosy nub between his index finger and thumb. She sucked in a sharp breath, shocked to discover that what he was doing to her breasts tugged and throbbed in another, more intimate part of her body.

The power this position evoked was heady. The tempo struck was her own. Fast or slow, teasing or hard, it was her decision. She liked that. She rocked against him, shyly at first, weighing each movement for the optimum impact. Her hesitation didn't last long. She found out quickly that even the simplest movements brought exquisite pleasure. In a matter of seconds, her body had taken control. This time it was *her* thrusts that were matched, and her need that spiraled out of control. She slowed the pace, wanting to prolong this torture of the senses forever. But Chase had other ideas. His palms slipped up to her shoulders, then swept down over her breasts, over her stomach, and settled on her hips. His hands were strongly insistent as they coaxed the fire within her until it raged.

The feeling came on her slowly, the tiny bursts of sensation grew in magnitude. Each spasm was increased tenfold by the fingers on her hips digging into her flesh, driving him deeper, deeper. Her thighs flamed, she moved in time to his urging, faster, faster.

Marea gasped as wave after wave of white-hot fulfillment burst through her. Her body tensed with spasms of pure, raw sensation. The man beneath her was hot, alive. He wouldn't let her rest and enjoy this wonderful feeling. Just when she thought she'd felt the ultimate release, he drove in deeper, and carried her higher and higher until she was soaring.

She heard his guttural moan, and knew he was climbing with her, meeting her at the top, his thrust driving them higher still. Her breath clogged in her lungs, her heart felt as though it was about to break through the restraining cage of her ribs. Over and over their bodies met, parted, then met again, until finally they were both panting, both spent.

When it was over, when the last wave had receded over her, Marea collapsed weakly atop the firm cushion of his chest and buried her face in the hollow of his neck. His pulse fluttered against her lips, and her tongue darted out to taste the flesh covering it before she snuggled against him. She felt him shudder as his strong arms came up to encircle her waist and back, the heavy weight hugging her close.

He slipped from her, shifted, then cradled her at his side. "Ah, vision," he panted against the tangled mass of red-gold hair blanketing them both. " 'Tis a powerful spell you've cast on me. One I've a sudden desire not to break free of."

"You've no choice," she whispered throatily, her words thick with regret. She ran her fingers down the side of his neck, over his shoulder, and felt his body tense. "What happened just now will not happen again. I'll not let it. 'Twas wonderful, but 'twas wrong."

He snatched her wrist and tossed her onto her back. His elbows flanked her sides, his face loomed a scant few inches above her. "Nay, Marea, 'twas right. *Right*. Open your eyes and you'll see there's naught wrong in what we just shared. Can you honestly think to stop it from happening again? *Can you?* Bloody hell, answer me, wench!"

She opened her eyes, surprised by the roar of his tone when he had, up until now, shown her only gentleness. What had she said to cause this much fury? She'd spoken the truth. His strained expression said it wasn't a truth he wished to confront.

"I *can* stop it," she said, her words thick conviction. "I *will*. I'll fight if you ever try to take me again. 'Twas wrong. More wrong because I allowed it to happen . . . again."

"You weren't the only one making allowances, Marea. I made my share." His lips tightened to a fine line. "When I first heard of your attack, and your methods of gaining my keep, I was furious. I vowed never to let your enchanting ways hold sway over me again. Obviously, the oath didn't last long."

His furious gaze raked her. Disgust shimmered in his eyes, but Marea wasn't sure if the emotion was directed at her ability to make him want her so badly, or at himself for not having the willpower to resist.

The muscle in his jaw jerked as his gaze captured hers. " 'Tis not the first time I've broken a vow to myself. I doubt 'twill be the last. Still, nothing has ever disillusioned me the way you have." His gaze darkened to stormy green as his hot breath kissed her pale cheek. "You make me forget myself, and *that* could be dangerous."

His words brought great joy, and great despair. "Mayhaps you should not protest when I ask for my freedom. If my presence twists your senses, you'd do best without me near."

His lips smiled. His eyes did not. "What? And risk you sneaking into my chambers at night so you can sink that blade you mentioned earlier into my back? I think not. I'd be better off to have you close, where I can keep my eye on you."

"Close where I can tempt you to madness, you mean?" she taunted, her tone tight. "You'll not survive living so closely with me, mon. Can you not see that?"

"What I see right now is my lack of choice." With a quick thrust, Chase pushed himself up to sit on the edge of the bed. He regarded her coolly from over his shoulder. "I've asked for your word, and realized I can't accept it. You leave me no choice."

" 'Tis my word I've given you!" she cried, thinking he meant to kill her men. "What more do you want from me?"

"Honesty. I want the truth!" Snatching his tunic from the floor, he shoved the wrinkled cloth over his head. He punched his arms into the sleeves, then went in search of his trews. "You've proved your loyalty extends no farther than your little finger, and is reserved

179

solely for yourself. I'm not so generous I'd risk testing it more than once." He tugged the trews up over his sinewy thighs and secured them at his waist, then fixed Marea with a meaningful glare. "You'll stay in this keep until I decide what to do with you. Don't entertain the notion of escape, for you'll be well guarded."

"But—" She sat up, gathering the bedspread around her to cloak her nakedness.

His hand slashed the air, cutting her short. "Don't argue with me! 'Tis the way things will be until I decide they will be different."

Marea watched him grab his sword and stalk to the door. A crisp order saw it unlocked and thrown wide. Her next words made him pause over the threshold.

"What about me men?" she demanded. "Have I not just done enough to at least buy their freedom?"

He turned to see her kneeling in the middle of the mattress, the spread clutched tightly to her breasts. The creamy flesh spilling over the rich material made his gut churn, as did the tousled cloud of burnished-gold hair. His voice clamped in his throat as he spun on his heel and stalked out of the room. The door was slammed loudly behind his rugged back. The sound of a key turning in the lock was harsh and grating.

Strong footsteps were retreating down the stone hallway by the time the first sob ripped through Marea's body. Weakly, she collapsed atop the bed and surrendered to her tears. It was a long, long time before they passed, and longer still before she could see past the thick fog of humiliation.

Chapter Twelve

Marea stood in the arched doorway of the great hall, tears clouding her vision. The curious stares of servants and a few men at arms wasn't what held her rooted to the spot; it was the hall itself.

Much had changed in the ten years since she'd last been in this room, and the changes were glaring. Where her father had preferred simplicity, the Graham opted for ornamentation. Once-bare stone walls were now graced with flowing tapestries. The fireplace wall was reserved solely for the hanging of various weapons—claymores, dirks, an assortment of richly carved broadswords, and hunting knives. Even the small, unreliable pistol known as a dag was represented. Every weapon known to the Borders was presented in one form or another, all artfully arranged to enhance the large coat of arms holding precedence above the exquisitely carved mantel.

A roaring fire crackled in the hearth, but the fingers of warmth could not stop Marea from shivering and burying herself deep within the woolen plaid's folds.

To her right was a screened passage separating the hall from the kitchen, pantry, and buttery. To the left, long tables—the most prominent of which was close to the fire and raised on a dais to distinguish it from the rest. It was the table reserved for family and honored guests, the table upon which Marea now fixed her attention.

Her vision grew misty when she pictured her father seated at the head of that table. She remembered the way he would tip his beloved red head, bending to listen in rapt attention to the blond beauty who shared his trencher. Her parents had made a fine couple; her father's volatile Scottish temper complemented to perfection by his wife's soft ways.

Marea thrust the bittersweet memory aside, and focused on the table itself. It was not empty now, as respect for the MacKenzie would have made it a half score ago, but cluttered with burly Englishmen. Their rumbling chatter had come to an abrupt halt at her entrance and had not resumed, except for a few speculative whispers. More than one appreciative English eye roved her head to toe.

Her chin rose higher when she spotted a comely girl rushing to her side from the screen that hid the kitchens from view.

"Och! m'lady, 'tis true, then," the woman squealed, coming to a skidding halt. She was tall, and her unusual height forced Marea to arch her neck to meet the shimmering green eyes.

Her own amethyst gaze flashed, silencing the girl and reminding her of the guard who'd grudgingly escorted Marea to the hall—and who was now positioned outside of the stone archway. "Hush, Sally, before they hear. You do not know who I be. To admit you do will see you thrown in the dungeon with the rest."

"Aye, m'lady." The dark brown head dipped respectfully and she made ready to sink a curtsy. She must have thought better of it, for she straightened instantly, and fixed her mistress with a questioning look.

Most of the men went back to their ale and chatter. But not all. There were a few who could not yet tear their gazes away from the small woman and her regal bearing. That they were openly ogling their laird's captive—and that he might very well take exception to their lusty scrutiny—didn't seem to matter.

Marea bristled under the unwanted attention. Her tone turned gruff. "The Graham sent me to work in your kitchens. Please, show me what I am to do."

"The kitchens?" The green eyes widened in alarm. "Nay, m'lady, I canna allow it. You should be gracing the table, not working like a servant. Can m'lord not see that?"

"I do not know what *m'lord* sees, wench. I only know what I was told to do." Her chin jutted to the screen covering the far right wall. "The kitchen, Sally."

"Aye," the girl muttered, a confused scowl furrowing her dark brow. Twisting her apron, she turned. "But I still do not think 'tis right."

"Nor I, for what it be worth," Marea muttered as she followed Sally's tall, unfemininely broad back. "But 'twill not go well on me men to disobey the Graham in this. 'Tis me men I think of now, not meself."

"The men be well cared for."

This, coming over the girl's shoulder, was spoken with an amazement that was echoed in Marea's heart. Although she wanted to believe Sally, it was difficult. She was too aware the information might be false, and had been offered only to appease Marea's sore conscience.

Sally scooted behind the screen, and Marea followed. The shielding was a welcome barrier to the Englishmen's hungry eyes.

Entering the kitchen brought its own form of pain. The sight of the scratched stone floor where her mother had died made Marea gasp. More unwelcome tears stung her eyes. Dashing the moisture away, she glanced around. A woman was bending over the fire, stirring the contents of the pot slung over the flames. As though she'd felt the gaze warming her back, the woman slowly straightened and turned.

She was as tall as she was wide, with the creases of age lining what had once been a bonnie face. Brittle salt-and-pepper hair was pulled back in a tight plait, which was woven over her head like a crown. No hair dared to escape the rigid coif. Unlike Sally, whose apron was stained with her morning chores, the large woman's apron was a splash of white which covered the crisp gray skirt beneath. Her eyes were dark and sharp as they fixed Marea with a hateful glare.

"Why do you bring her here?" the woman demanded of Sally, although her gaze never left Marea. "We've enough to do as it is. We've no time to coddle her as well."

" 'Twas m'lord's order," Sally replied with more pluck than Marea would have given her credit for having. "He'll not like it if you cast her out, or make things hard on her, Martha."

"Hmph!" Martha tossed the spoon onto the counter, then turned away. Cupboards were opened and closed loudly. Items were removed, then slammed atop the counter. "Don't dawdle, get to work. 'Tis

184

what you're here for." Martha's sagging chin shook like aspic when she jutted it in their direction, no longer looking at them when she spoke. "There's bread to be made for the midday meal. *She* can do that whilst you churn the butter, Sally. And take a care not to curdle it this time."

"Old coot," Sally grumbled, and stuck her tongue out at the woman's large back. Although Martha remained oblivious to the disrespectful gesture, Marea did not. Sally's childlike antics helped lighten her mood.

Since the kitchen had remained virtually unchanged, finding the ingredients to make bread was simple. More than once Marea caught Martha sending her a skeptical glance as she busily set about the chore.

An hour later, Marea's plaid was coated in flour. Her hands were wrist deep in springy bread dough. Her arms ached from kneading such a large mass, but the physical labor was a welcome distraction from disturbing thoughts.

She was in the process of shaping the dough into loaves when she felt a prick of awareness tickle her nape. Her spine stiffened, but she did not turn around to see who was gazing at her from the doorway. Nor did she have to. In a few short seconds, the man approached the table on which she worked and thrust one booted foot atop the bench beside where she worked.

Marea was not immune to Sally's reaction, nor Martha's lack of one. A slim, reddish gold brow arched when Marea glanced up. A grin of familiarity tugged at her lips when she saw a flush-cheeked Guy Falken.

"Good aft," she greeted, the easy smile still in place as she pressed the dough beneath the heel of her palms. "You appear . . ." her gaze raked him head to foot, "well recovered."

"Aye, mistress, I'm well enough." His eyes shimmered. His gaze pierced her to the core, making the meaning of his next question excruciatingly clear. "And yourself?"

This time it was Marea's turn to blush. Her attention strayed to the dough her trembling fingers were kneading. "Aye," she whispered throatily, unable to meet his gaze, "I be . . . well enough. Now, if 'tis all you've come to ask me—"

"Nay, mistress, I've another question." His candid reply made her glance up, as did the sound of his scabbard scraping against the table edge. The sound scraped across her suddenly raw nerves as well. "Your answer would be most appreciated, if you please."

Marea slapped her hands together, dislodging the dusty flour that clung to her fingers. She shrugged. "Mayhaps. 'Twould depend on what it is you be wanting to know."

He cleared his throat, and sent Sally a glance that had her scurrying to turn the lever on the butter-churn. His gaze darkened, fixing on the long, creamy legs beneath Sally's hoisted skirts, and the shapely knees flanking the wooden churn. But his attention was only briefly distracted. Lowering his voice, he inclined his head toward Marea and said, "I want to know why you stopped that red-headed beast of yours from slitting my throat this morn. He seemed ready enough, and Lord knows things would have gone better for you if you'd let him have me."

Marea shrugged. "I canna abide bloodshed." She

186

would not tell him that, by sparing his life once when she could so easily have ended it, she now felt responsible for him. To do so would brand her even more of a fool than she already felt, for he would surely never understand such reasoning, and she had no wish to explain it.

"What?!" he cried, gaining the attention of the others. "You detest bloodshed yet you lead a *raiding party?* 'Tis not logical. Mayhaps your men would have tasted a bit more success if they'd followed the orders of another."

"Mayhaps," she agreed through gritted teeth. Martha's throaty chuckle did nothing to heighten Marea's abruptly sour mood. Her fist pounded the dough with unnecessary force as she sent her companion a glowering stare. "I'm growing tired of having me faults this day thrown back in me face, sir. I'll thank you not to remind me of it again."

His expression melted to stark seriousness as he pillowed his elbows atop a firm thigh and leaned toward her. "Is that your only reason for having me spared, mistress?"

Again, she began shaping the dough into plump loaves. "I do not know you, so I've no other reason to spare you. I would have done the same were any other to have met us in the corridor."

Though his eyes narrowed, his young head briskly nodded. Her answer seemed to pacify his curiosity — for the moment. His foot came off the bench and echoed on the stone. Marea did not glance up as he disappeared into the passage that led to the screened hall.

"What be that about?" Sally asked as she slid onto the bench across from Marea. Her green eyes were

187

shimmering with curiosity and jealousy. " 'Tis rare for Falken to be wandering into the kitchens. Most of the men do not like this place." A thumb jerked over her broad shoulder indicated the reason why the Englishmen preferred the solitude of the hall. Martha was busy at the counter, and appeared to be ignoring them.

Appeared to be. Marea knew better. The shrewd ears caught every word that passed within her kitchen. Her amethyst gaze shifted from the meaty back to Sally, warning the girl to guard her tongue. "How goes the butter, Sally? You did not curdle it, I hope. Martha would not like it if you did."

"Nay," Sally muttered, scowling. " 'Tis not curdled. But I do not see what the butter has to do wi'—"

"Here, put yourself to use taking these to the bakehouse." Marea shoved the newly filled pans, heavy with dough, into the girl's surprised arms. Spinning Sally on her heel, she pushed the girl toward the door. "And do not hurry back," she hissed in Sally's ear.

"But—"

"Do it, lass," she said loudly. "Do not make trouble by dawdling." Marea gave the girl an insistent shove between the shoulder blades. "Martha's made it clear she cares not for a dawdler."

Reluctantly, Sally went. But she stopped at the door and sent Marea a confused stare before disappearing through it.

"I'm thinking there's more you'd want me to do now that the bread be finished," Marea said once Sally had gone. The comment brought a glance of open surprise from Martha, who was obviously unused to services being offered instead of avoided.

Wiping the sticky apple juice off her hands and

onto a towel, Martha turned. Her dark eyes, sunken in the folds of her face, glistened with mistrust. "Would you now? And why would you be so eager for work, wench? Most of my girls spend their days trying to think of ways to avoid it. Are you trying to make me believe you're so different?"

A ghost of a smile played about Marea's lips when she stepped over to a bucket of water in the far corner. She sank her flour-smeared hands in the icy depths and felt the shock of it ripple up her arms. "I be telling you only to make use of me services whilst you can, woman. From the looks of it, you be short of help. And me services won't be yours for long."

"Think you to find a better position in the household?" Martha scoffed, and laced her plump arms over an impossibly large chest. The ample curves of her breasts spilled over her loglike forearms. "Then think again, wench. Had m'lord favored you elsewhere, 'tis there you'd be now. *Not* in my kitchen."

Marea dried her hands on her plaid and shrugged. "Between you and me, Martha, 'tis in your kitchen I prefer to be. Now, what else would you have me do? I do not like being idle."

Martha's overfull mouth pursed as the dark eyes strayed to a large stack of carrots perched on the edge of the table. "I suppose you cannot be trusted to wield a knife without sinking it into my ribs?"

"Me word be good," she replied, eyeing the carrots. "Though I'd not blame you to not believe me in such a serious matter."

"The carrots need peeling. And the potatoes and celery. The meat must be chopped. And m'lord's favorite custard made, then set to gel."

"Och! You maun be busy to manage all this by yourself."

"Busy?" Martha stared haughtily down the large bump distorting the bridge of her nose. "Hmph! I'm that and more. And thoroughly unappreciated, as well. These men are of a mind to think leprechauns sneak out of the hills and into the kitchens at night to make their food and scrub their dishes, then sneak back into the hills—only to return come morning. They care not a whit from where the food comes, so long as 'tis tasty and 'tis quickly laid out for them when their stomachs grumble for it."

"Aye, Martha, they be chiels. And chiels—English or not—be unappreciative. Where would you be wanting me to start?"

The dark gaze strayed back to the stack of carrots. Her thick hands swiped down the apron, and for the first time Marea saw the crisp white linen marred by a stain. "I've but two hands, wench, and no time to do all that must be done. God's blood! and where did that Sally go off to now? The silly, good-for-nothing—she's too busy chasing after that jackanapes Falken to be in here where her help is needed."

In the end, Martha settled for Marea's word that she would not use the knife on anything but the carrots. The older woman's mistrust was evident in the way she placed herself on the opposite bench and watched her charge with a keen eye as she set about her own work.

If Sally had been shocked when she'd left the kitchen, she was doubly so upon returning to find her gruff warden smiling at something Marea had said. Framed in the doorway, her green eyes widened when she listened to the companionable, if not exactly

190

friendly, conversation. And her mistress plied a knife in her hand! Now, how on earth had she convinced shrewish Martha that she could be trusted with it?

Sally pushed away from the door. Her hushed footsteps and the rustle of her wrinkled skirt alerted the two at the table to her presence. They both glanced up, but only Marea's eyes glinted with warmth. The darker gaze was alive with reproach.

"Where have you been, Sally?" Martha barked, waving a meaty hand over the carrot and potato peelings scattered atop the craggy table. "Marea has done most of your work, with half of your complaints. I'll take an explanation, please."

Sally blushed when she noticed the amount of work her mistress had indeed done. "I—I was on me way back from the bakehouse when m' lord stopped me." She didn't miss the way her mistress tensed.

Martha turned with a "Hmph!" back to tearing the leaves off a stalk of celery. Her motions were harsh and jerky, causing the stalk to snap in two.

"More of your lies?" Martha snapped. "You're too bold to be spinning such tales. As if the Graham has nothing better to do than to pass his time with you."

" 'Tis true! I've no reason to lie."

"Don't you? Just like you had no reason to lie when you said you were going for fresh eggs earlier. Lord knows when you would have returned had I not found you behind the coop . . . in Falken's embrace. Have you no pride, girl?"

A pout pulled at Sally's full lips as she fixed her gaze on Marea. " 'Twas a slight indiscretion."

"Slight!" Martha bellowed. The roar of her voice set the pans on the table to rattling. "I'd hardly call your passionate kisses a *slight —* "

" 'Tis not important," Sally snapped, her gaze still on her mistress. The color in those flawless cheeks had heightened. "M'lord bid I tell m'la—Marea that she was to take the midday meal with him."

Only the barest hesitation of Marea's hand as she reached for another potato indicated she'd heard. The potato was plucked up, the sharp blade of the knife viciously scraped over its gritty surface. "Tell him I do not care to join him, Sally. Tell him me surroundings have stolen me appetite. Tell him . . . tell him whatever you please, but I'll not share his meal."

"Oh, m'lady, I could not do it. He'd slit me throat thinking I'd not obeyed his orders."

The knife came down hard enough to slice clear through the potato cradled in her palm. Only a quick flick of the wrist prevented Marea's tender flesh from being slashed. "He's cruel, but not *that* cruel. He'll take his anger out on me, lass, not you."

"Are you sure of that?" an intrusive third voice asked from behind. It was rich, that voice, and husky; it curled down Marea's spine in a warm, familiar rush. "Methinks 'tis wise I've come to see firsthand that my orders were properly given. I had a feeling you'd not obey them."

Sally's eyes widened, her gaze shifting to the door at Marea's back. Muttering something under her breath, she hurried to complete her chores about the kitchen. Snatching up a bowl of semigelled custard, Sally started whipping the mixture with a vengeance. Martha, for her own part, showed a sudden interest in the stalk of celery clutched in her meaty grasp.

"A kitchen be no place for a mon, *Sasunach*. Why be ye here?" Marea asked, the majority of her concentration focused on rhythmically working the knife. It

192

didn't work. She could still feel his eyes boring holes into her back. Each scrape of the blade as it peeled away gritty brown skin from the juicy white pulp grated on her already tattered nerves.

" 'Tis my kitchen, mistress. I visit it when I please." His steps across the stone were long and bold. In an instant he was towering beside her, glowering down at her. Although she could feel the heat of him, Marea refused to return his gaze. "Right now it pleases me greatly to see my orders carried through. You will take the midday meal by my side or I will see that—"

Chase's gaze fell on the knife. The long, thin fingers wielded it against the potato with the same expertise she used to brandish a heavy broadsword. Anger flared through him, clouding his senses as he reached down and wrenched it from her grasp. With a growl, he threw it atop the counter, where it clattered loudly before bouncing off the edge and falling to the stone floor.

Marea had anticipated his reaction. She wasn't surprised. What did surprise her was the swiftness with which he had done it. Certainly a man of his size and stature could not have moved so quickly! But he had. Clasping her hands together, she filed the observation away.

"If you've a brain lurking in that beautiful skull— and I do harbor doubts on that score—you'll be on your feet within seconds. 'Twould not be wise to push my patience further. Nor would it be safe."

"Mayhaps a wise woman would think it so," she replied contritely. "But, as you've already pointed out, my intelligence be lacking." Finally, her eyes lifted. Their gazes clashed with vicious intensity. "What be your worry, mon? Afraid that if the blade stayed in me hands it would have found a better home than on yonder counter?"

Martha's gasp snatched Chase's attention away for the space of a heartbeat. When it returned to Marea, the fiery emerald eyes were coupled with the strong bite of his fingers wrapping harshly around her upper arms.

Marea was powerless to stop him from dragging her off the bench. Its wooden legs scraped the stone as she stumbled to her feet. Swallowing a surge of rage, coupled with humiliation, she gave a toss of her head and met his glare head on. "Manhandling is not the way to woo a lass over to your way of thinking, mon."

The fingers on her arm loosened, but didn't drop away. "I no longer wish to convince you of anything, vixen. I do wish for a single order to be carried through. Not much to ask, methinks."

"Aye, 'tis *too* much. I'll not share food with you, *Sasunach*. Do not ask it of me again."

"Would you rather starve?"

" 'Twould be preferable."

"And if I told you that one of your men would be hanged for every minute you delay seating yourself at my table?" he asked softly, precisely. One finger shot out to trace the length of her jaw. The tip scratched her tender flesh, and made her shiver. "What would you do then?"

Her face drained of color. Did she dare chance him making good on the cold-blooded threat? Nay. Her pride was strong, but soothing it was not worth the risk, nor the lives it would cost.

Her spine stiffened. She fixed her gaze on the top of Martha's bent head, and said tightly, "Were you to threaten it, I would take the meal with you." Her gaze

194

slipped back to his. *"Are* you threatening it?"

"Nay, mistress. Even I am not so cruel." Chase had intended to lie. He took them both by surprise when it was the truth that slipped out.

Marea stared at him long and hard, knowing the words were not the ones he'd meant to say. Her hand lifted, her warm palm covering his even warmer knuckles as she tried to pull his hand away from her face. It would not budge. "I'll pass the meal with ye, were ye to rephrase the . . . request."

His hand twitched over the velvet of her cheek, then dropped limply to his side. His lids lowered, the emerald depths beneath shooting her daggers of warning. "Nay, mistress. I stand behind my orders and shall see them carried through. By force, should the situation require it."

"Very well," she snapped through gritted teeth. "I be willing to offer a compromise. I'll sit at your table, as you wish, but will not eat. How does that suit you?"

"It does not."

" 'Tis the best I can offer."

"I think not."

"Then think again."

"I have, mistress. I doubt you'd appreciate hearing the path my thoughts have taken." His gaze dipped to the pulsebeat throbbing in the creamy base of her throat.

Marea stiffened. "Aye, I doubt I would." With that, she spun and stalked from the room. Her destination was the hall, and the higher table warmed by the heat of a crackling fire.

From behind she could hear Chase's footsteps clapping over stone. The sound hesitated long enough for him to mutter a sharp rebuke to the two silent women left behind.

She was too far away to hear his exact words, but she knew that Martha was being taken to task for having supplied her with a knife. As she walked, chin held loftily high, Marea promised herself the subject would be broached and explained to Chase before the woman could be punished for it.

Chapter Thirteen

The soles of Marea's boots slapped at the stone as she paced the Graham's bedchamber. With every step, the anger simmering in her veins heated a degree closer to boiling. It didn't help that with each spin her furious gaze encountered the vast expanse of that horrible man's bed.

"Aye, Zander," she cried, spinning to face the small man sprawled in the chair nearest the window. " 'Tis humiliation he was aft, and 'tis what happened. I've never been so humbled in me life, and 'tis that *Sasunach* dog's fault."

" 'Tis not humbling to be seen taking a meal with him, lass," Zander replied, his hazel eyes assessing. "Me loyalties have always been MacKenzie, as you well know, yet 'tis shared a table with Graham I've done myself—many times."

"Nay, 'tis different. He started his foolish games the moment he seated himself aside me. 'Have a slab of mutton, vision,' he said. 'My men cannot eat until your sweet lips have tasted it,' he said." Her jaw hard-

197

ened. "Did he think I'd be looking to poison him? Nay! 'Twas by his orders I worked in the kitchen. Mayhaps he should have set me scrubbing the stones if he'd thought 'twas poison I had on me mind."

"And mayhaps 'twas more his way to test you. To see what did be on your mind." The gritty voice lowered at her furious glare. He shifted in the chair uncomfortably. "M'lady, I'd not pretend to know what the Graham be about. But you said yerself he's aware of your association with Agatha. And he's suspicious about whether or not she killed his da. Though it pains me to give any *Sasunach* a compliment, I think 'twas wise for him to test you that way. 'Twas the only way to know for sure if the witch be practicing any of her teaching skills on you."

Marea huffed, and stalked to one of the windows flanking the chair. The sun was sinking over the hills. A few last rays of light streamed from a cloudless sky, sparkling over the firth and setting the crystal surface on fire. The color reminded Marea of Chase Graham's hair.

With an angry growl she shoved from the window and commenced her frustrated pacing anew. "Were I of a mind to feed him poison, Chase Graham would have been dead long since, Zander. Plenty's the opportunity I've let slip through me grasp."

"Aye, m'lady. I know it. The Graham does not." With a restless sigh, he shoved himself from the chair and approached her rigid back. His large hand reached out to touch her shoulder, a scant inch above eye level for him. He hesitated, then scratched the wispy red whiskers sprouting from his chin instead. "To him you are Marea o' the MacKenzie, a woman who be trying fiercely to take his castle away.

He does not know you also be the witch."

"And he never will," she agreed tightly.

"And how would you be stopping him from knowing, m'lady? He'll suspect something amiss when he finds Agatha gone on the very same day you materialized in his keep. Only a fool would pass that off as coincidence. We both know the mon be no fool."

"Aye, Zander," she muttered. Turning, she leaned a shoulder against the sharp stone corner of the window. A cool breeze slipped in through the glass casing, making her shiver as she regarded her small friend from over one shoulder. "What would ye have me do? 'Twould be easy to slip from the keep. I know the tunnels, the fields, the forests. I could leave without him knowing the how or whens of it. But I canna. 'Twould be selfish and 'twould risk the lives of me uncle and cousin." Her voice cracked. She swallowed hard, hating the weakness but unable to suppress it. "I canna lose more family, Zander. I could not bear it."

"Aye, m'lady." This time he did place his hand on her arm. Her flesh trembled beneath the wool as she blanketed his knuckles with her warm palm. "But I'm thinking those beastly relations of yours would rather know you be safe. Even were that information to cost them their lives."

Marea shook her head, and dashed away the tear glimmering on her cheek. "Nay. 'Twould not be right."

Right?" His large hand squeezed her arm before dropping away. It was Zander's turn to pace in frustration, and his small body did it with flare. "Why must everything you do be right? Why can you not, just once, put yourself before others? If ever there was a time to do it, lass, 'tis now. Take the chance to escape whilst you can. Then, once free, plan a way to rescue your men."

"Do you not think I *want* to? 'Tis not a pleasure to be locked in this room, at the beck and call of that arrogant piece of English scum. But I've no choice! I'll not let rash deeds bring harm to me men. When I leave here—*and I will*—'twill be the same way I came. With me men guarding me back, down to the very last one of them."

For the first time in his life, Zander raised his voice to a MacKenzie. "Aye, 'tis a fine vision you have, m'lady, but not a realistic one! To wait for their freedom could be to wait for the rest of your life."

Crossing her arms tightly over her chest, Marea showed him her back. "Again, I've no choice."

He raked his fingers through his orange curls and heaved a sigh. "What about Thomas? If he were to *tell* you to leave, would you do it?"

"Me uncle is not here to tell me aught, Zander. 'Tis a rhetorical question. One I do not feel the need to answer."

"He not be *here,* aye, but 'twould be simple enough for his *words* to be."

Marea turned to him with a scowl. "What are you talking about, mon? I've no time for games, and 'tis a stomach full of them I've already had this day."

A sly grin turned the small man's lips. His hazel eyes glistened in the late afternoon sun streaming in through the windows. "Do you not wonder how I came to be in this room, m'lady? The door is guarded, with orders that none are let in but the Graham himself." His short, thick arms swept the sparsely decorated chamber. "Yet here I be."

" 'Tis further proof you be more clever than most give you credit for being."

He nodded, beaming proudly as he strutted before her. "But me point be this: the Graham's orders for the dungeons be much the same as the one's for your own soft prison. I'm of a mind the walls below can be breached as easily as the ones which surround us now."

" 'Twould be risky, Zander. Were you caught, 'twould mean death. The Graham has shown a measure of compassion — a wee, *wee* measure — but he'd not hesitate to slay a proven spy. As you said, he be no fool."

"I'd not be caught," he replied, his voice brimming with confidence. " 'Twould be a risk worth taking were the result to see you safely from this keep — and the clutches of the Graham."

"I'd not ask you to do it. Your death would weigh on me already heavy conscience."

"You ask nothing of me that's not freely given," he scoffed. " 'Tis in your best interest to be away from here. And soon. The rules of border warfare are painfully clear. In losing the raid, you be the Graham's prisoner. Must I tell you what the Graham be free to do with you if no ransom is paid?"

A shiver rippled over her shoulders when her gaze sought out the bed. A blush warmed her cheeks, and her breath caught when she quickly wrenched her gaze away. "Nay, Zander, 'tis well I know it. And since there be not a soul to pay him . . ."

As her words trailed hopelessly away, heavy footfalls echoed in the corridor. They both heard the guard shift into position.

Zander's eyes flicked nervously between the door and Marea. "Your decision, m'lady. Quickly."

"I—"

The footsteps stopped outside the chamber door

and the low rumble of voices slipped through the crack beneath. Marea's chest tightened when Zander rushed to the wall where the door would swing wide and conceal his presence.

His hazel eyes pleaded with her as someone left the door. Chase Graham had returned, and sent his guard away.

She gulped. "Aye, I'll be going. I have your promise to help me rescue me men once safety be reached?"

The key grated in the lock as the redhead gave a brisk nod. Zander pressed hard against the stone, as though trying to melt his miniature body into the cold rock. "Midnight, m'lady. The Douglas plans a raid for late this eve. 'Tis certain I am you'll be alone."

There was no time for more. The door swung open, and the only thing to stop the thick slab of wood from clattering against the wall was the softness of Zander's body.

Chase and Marea's gazes met. The sound of their ragged breaths entwined, and the world around them swirled then dimmed. For the space of one breathless heartbeat the world did not exist but for the man and woman who stared penetratingly into each others eyes.

Chase seemed not to notice the door's lack of noise. His emerald gaze seared into the woman standing dead still near the window. Nothing could have distracted him from drinking in the intoxicating sight of his lovely vision.

The light pouring in from behind silhouetted the flowing lines of her body. The glow of sun turned each strand of hair to fiery burnished gold and cast her features in enticingly vague shadows. His fingers flexed, and he remembered how soft her cheek felt beneath his fingertips. He had a need to feel that softness again. Now.

Releasing his breath, he took a hesitant step into the room. Then another. His body gravitated toward her soft feminine curves, like a freezing man would seek out the warmth of a fire. But this fire in his blood was sweeter and hotter than the crackling flames found in a warm stone hearth.

His heels clicked against stone. The sound made her delicate chin rise. She turned, and he caught a flash of bright amethyst fire in the dwindling light of day. The sight burned him, rooting him to the spot. He stiffened, raking his hand through his shaggy golden hair as he studied her carefully. With her face in shadows, her mood was indecipherable. The tension that snapped in the air told him more; it was so real it felt as though it were alive.

"Go away, *Sasunach*. 'Tis enough humiliation I've had this day at your hand. I've no desire for more."

The anger in her voice made him bristle. Instinctively, his own chin rose. "I've not come to humiliate you."

"Nay?" she snorted. "Then why have you come?"

He scowled, his lips thinned with impatience. " 'Tis my chamber."

'Tis my dream.

Marea backed hard against the wall. Her fingers dug into unyielding rock, and her face drained of color as though she'd just sustained a blow. She had. Not delivered to her cheek, but to her pride. It stung. "I—I'd be only too happy to leave. Just say the word."

He chuckled. The sound lacked humor. His gaze darkened. "The last time you left this room, you were found in the kitchen wielding a knife. I don't make the same mistake twice."

Chase turned and swung the door closed with a resounding slam. It was then Marea saw that her small friend had slipped away. She'd not seen him leave, but was thankful he had.

Slowly, she became aware of being alone with this man. And the consequences. If she could have taken another step back, she would have.

His eyes narrowed. Where she had been cloaked in shadows before, now a stream of sunlight filtered in through the window by her side. It covered her like a shimmering blanket of gold.

He fought the urge to grab her and pull her out to where his gaze could travel over her at will. Clenching his hands into fists, he turned away. He muttered a curse and stalked to the wardrobe, yanking open the top drawer. The force almost made it come free of its slot and topple to his feet. Layer upon layer of crisp, freshly laundered clothes greeted his eye. All were stacked in tidy rows. He eyed them dispassionately, venting his frustration by digging through the neat stacks until he at last found the tunic and trews he sought.

By the time he was done, clothes spilled over the top of the drawer. A few tunics lay in a wrinkled heap atop the stone floor. He seemed not to notice as he stepped through the pile and proceeded to the bed. There he threw the clothes he intended to wear atop the mattress and began working free the laces of his tunic.

"What are you doing now, *Sasunach*?" Marea asked coldly. Sheer willpower kept her voice from shaking. She was glad his back was to her, glad he could not see the way her cheeks flamed and her eyes greedily devoured the firm musculature of his back and waist before she could tear her hungry gaze away.

She watched his spine stiffen, and his head snap to the side. Her gaze was blurred by the sunlight that warmed her cheek and neck, but not so much that she could not see. If anything, the sunshine softened and enhanced her view, lending it a dreamlike quality.

"I am not preparing to ravish you—again—if that's your concern. What I am going to do is change for the evening meal."

Crossing her arms over her chest, she stepped past the wall of sun. Her gaze, when it settled on him, was dispassionate. "I'll not sup with you, so do not think it. As I've said, I've already suffered enough humiliation this day."

"Aye, so you have," he growled, thrusting the tunic over his head. His golden brows arched then drew down in a dark scowl when he heard her swift inhalation of breath. He tossed the tunic aside and snatched up the fresh one. "But what you've said, and what you think and feel, means naught. As laird here, you'll take your meal where *I* say you will take it."

Slowly, he turned toward her. The fresh tunic was held in a tight fist, the yellow material dragging on the floor. "I can make your life miserable, wench. Never doubt it, nor forget it."

His superior tone rankled. It was that, not the sight of his half-naked body, to which she responded. "I've not forgotten, *Sasunach*," she sneered. "Do your worst to me, if you dare. But it canna be worse than what you've already done."

"Done?" he shot in a sarcastically cajoling tone. His emerald eyes flashed a warning, saying his patience was nearing its end. "And what, pray tell, have I done

205

to you that you did not want me to do?"

"You've made me life a living hell, mon!"

"How? By keeping my castle and thwarting your ill-planned raid? Is that what I've done to make you suffer so miserably?"

" 'Tis a part of it."

"Mayhaps bending you to my will this aft did not sit well?"

"Another wee part."

"The taking of your men?"

"Another."

His pause was eloquent. "And the taking of you?" he asked, his voice a husky whisper as his gaze raked her.

" 'Tis the worst part, methinks," she rasped, her skin burning under the scrutiny. Her blood heated, her heart hammered. The breath that tore from her lungs was hard and labored. Try though she did to fight the liquid reaction, she'd no practice at it. In the end her body was the victor, the memory of his possession too sweet and too new to be cast aside. Against her will, she savored the feel of his gaze as though it was the warmth of his calloused fingers caressing her body, not merely his eyes.

"Nay, vision," he said on a ragged sigh, his gaze settling on her breasts. His palms tingled, and his body responded in other ways. " 'Tis not the worst, but the best."

It wasn't a safe topic. She knew it, and instinctively strove to change it. With a toss of her head, she glared at him. "I'll not sup with you. Your English fare is too bland. And I'll not comment on the filthy English company you'd have me endure."

"Endure? Mistress, I can have you endure 'muckle'

206

worse than sitting at my table, should I choose to," he growled, his lips pinched with anger. *"Endure?* Nay, mistress, 'tis my men who must endure. 'Tis they who must tolerate your sharp Scottish barbs. 'Tis they who must look upon you and be constantly reminded of who you are.

"As yet, they've tolerated you admirably. But their patience extends only so far. When it comes to an end, you'd best pray to whatever God you worship that you've not alienated me. For *I* am the only thing that stands between you and *certain* . . . humiliation."

Marea bristled when a prick of fear worked its way down her rigid spine. She clasped suddenly moist palms together and lifted her chin with false pride. "I do not like threats."

"No threat. 'Tis merely a statement of fact. Take it any way you please." He turned back to dressing before he could surrender to the urge to grab her and give her a rough shaking.

Marea did not intend to let this particular subject drop. "If I'm such a burden, then do not insist so strongly I share your meal. Many's the time I've done without. You'll be doing me no great service by nourishing me."

"I'll not starve you either," he replied coldly, yanking the tunic over his head and punching his arms in the sleeves. "However much you'd care to languish away from malnutrition, I'll not allow it. You won't escape me so easily. Not this time."

Something in the way he had said it — the abruptly husky pitch of his voice, his passionate pronunciation — made her gaze snap to his face. An emotion was being carefully concealed, avidly guarded, in the sharply molded lines there. A tremor coursed up her spine.

Chase reached for the trews, but his mind was not on the chore. From the corner of his eye, he saw her gaze widen. One golden brow arched when he saw her spin on her heel, and retreat to the window like a wounded pup. The fringe of her thick, burnished gold braid brushed the curve of her hip. He enjoyed the sight for a brief second before tearing his gaze away.

"Your uncle and cousin fare well," he said as he slipped the old trews down sinewy thighs and calves. Normally, he would have taken the time to sponge the day's dirt from his body. But he knew the boundaries of his own self-restraint, knew that to wash now would be too great a temptation. The mere thought of cool water and flesh, when this tempting woman was within arms length, was almost more than he could bear.

"I—I wondered but was afraid to ask." Her voice shook.

"They ask constantly of your welfare," he continued, reaching for the fresh trews. "I've done my best to re-assure them of your continuing good health, but I doubt they believe it."

"And what have you told them to make them doubt it?"

"That you've not been mistreated *yet*."

"Then you've lied, for—" Without thinking, she spun to face him. Her cheeks flamed when she was met with the seductive sight of his undress. A pang of something she did not want to feel ripped through her. She gasped, and spun back around. The plaid bil-lowed around her ankles, the hem kissing cold stone. Though she strove to focus on the scenery swimming outside the window, it was a fruitless effort. She was too engulfed with the memory of muscular, sun-kissed thighs, lean hips, and—

"I did not lie," he said. It was a light protest, for he'd caught her reaction and was suddenly engulfed in a hot, pleasant sensation himself. "You've not been mistreated. You're alive and reasonably intact. Were my father alive, and had he been the one to take you instead of myself, I doubt you'd be able to boast of as much."

She buried trembling fingers deep in the concealing folds of her skirt. "A-and the father d-does not resemble the son?"

"Nay, mistress, most assuredly not!"

The anger riding his voice made her curious. She wasn't stupid enough to turn around to see if his expression matched the harshness of his words. She knew that if she did, it would not be his face her eyes would seek; although her gaze might light there eventually—when it was far too late.

"I know only a wee bit about your da," she said, when clear thought had returned. "None of it be complimentary."

"Then what you've heard must be true." The trews were tugged up his legs. He stared thoughtfully at her stiff back while securing them at his waist. "Tell me, did you never meet the man? He was in and out of Kinclearnon for the better part of half a score, reiving your neighbors and causing quite a stir on the Borders. You must have come face-to-face with him."

"Never," she lied, her fingers curling into fists when she remembered her last sight of David Graham. He had been lying on the bed behind her, his forehead pasty and coated with sweat. For the first time, she

209

had seen a desperate plea in eyes that only now reminded her of his son's. They were the same green color, only the father's were narrower, and much, much colder. "In passing, mayhaps once or twa. But only from a distance."

Chase's gut tightened. The thought that she had never met his father was even more unreasonable when he looked on the woman's obvious beauty. David Graham would have been hard-pressed to resist her. No, David Graham would not have even tried to resist. Yet he knew she'd been untouched until that night in the forest. He scowled. Something here did not ring true.

She hadn't lied. *Marea* had never met David Graham. Agatha, on the other hand, had confronted the man on one score or another quite often; and dearly regretted each heated encounter.

"I'd think all in Kinclearnon to be familiar with the man after so many years. Do you not live around here that you'd miss having met him?" The question was asked, seemingly, in passing as Chase perched on the edge of the mattress and tugged the heavy boots over his hose-encased legs. Only the glint in his eyes spoke of his impatience to have her answer.

She was not so addle-witted that she couldn't glean what he was about. Ridicule thickly laced her tone. "Where I live is no concern of yours. I'll not be tricked into telling you something you've no need to know."

" 'Twas worth a try," he muttered. He reached for his scabbard, strapped it to his waist, then thrust off the bed like a man ready to do battle. His eyes glistened as his hand strayed over the hilt of his sword. "Ready to go below, mistress? My men are hungry, and I doubt they'd appreciate having their meal delayed due to a stubborn little Scot they already dislike."

Hearing his approach, Marea turned. She met his gaze with a confidence she did not feel, for the sight of his rugged body a mere inch away sapped her anger. "Your men can starve if 'tis my presence they be waiting for. Here is where I'll be staying."

"I think not." A grin turned his lips as he reached out and stroked the soft line of her cheek with his palm. The flesh beneath his hand trembled, and set his own skin on fire. He cupped her jaw, dragging her attention up. "There is only one alternative I'll offer to supping in the hall with my men. And I do not think it would be agreeable to you."

It was childish, she knew, but Marea had never wanted to scream so badly in her life. Why was this damn Englishman so set on constantly bending her to his will? Couldn't he see that where and how she took her meal wasn't really of such great importance?

So why do you continue to fight him if it's not important? She thrust *that* comment from her conscience quickly aside.

"Why," she said, her tone strained with impatience, "is it so important that I eat in your blasted hall? 'Tis a small enough thing for me to eat here."

"Because it is so important to you to eat elsewhere." His hand dropped, as though her satiny flesh burned. His gaze darkened. "Your position here is tenuous. You are a prisoner. You have *no* rights. You are mine to do with, or dispose of, as I please. I can see only two ways to make you understand that, as well as the magnitude of what it means. One way is to force you to carry through even the most menial orders, and in so doing hope that, eventually, you will get used to obeying my commands until your ransom is met."

"And the other?" she gulped, knowing that with her uncle languishing in his dungeon, there would be no ransom.

"You don't want to know. But you might benefit from knowing I've no compunctions about using that particular method if you continually disobey me. Aye, to me 'twould be preferable."

"When you phrase it that way, I can see I'll be joining you after all," she gritted. Her hands itched to slap his arrogant grin away. But she did not dare.

Cutting a mock bow, his hand swept to the closed door. He was scorched with the amethyst fire of her eyes before she lifted her chin high and marched angrily in that direction.

Chapter Fourteen

The men gave only a few restless glances at the proud Scot seated by their laird's side. Those who objected wisely kept their hostilities reserved to covert glances and an occasional murmur of disapproval.

For her own part, Marea dulled the sharpness of her tongue. Though she talked only when spoken to, she kept her tone as well as the subject matter neutral. As a consequence, she was spoken to more often than she had been at the midday meal.

Chase was unusually quiet.

More than once she'd caught his gaze ravishing her profile. Burning inquisition seemed to be forever shimmering in his eyes. It warmed her blood, and heated the color in her cheeks. Avoiding his gaze was futile. Though her determination ran strong, her curiosity ran stronger. Her gaze was drawn time and again to the harsh angles of his face, and more than once she had been snagged by the way his eyes glistened like polished jewels in the flickering orange light.

Another gaze that was avidly avoided was Sally's. The girl had served the food, and every time she had stopped by Marea's side to set down a platter, Marea died a bit. She could feel the green eyes boring into her downcast face. She knew if Sally kept staring at her with such avid attention, Chase would guess their alliance.

When he suggested, shortly after the meal, that they retire to his room, Marea jumped at the chance.

The corridor was deserted. A heavily carved chair had been dragged to one side of the closed door. The room, when she entered it, was cloaked in velvet black shadows that seemed to dance. The only spot of color was the dim slivers of moonlight coming in through the windows. But the moon was not high and full; the light was vague. Poor ventilation made the air cold and stuffy.

Marea shivered, snuggling within the folds of her plaid. She stopped a few steps past the door, and waited expectantly for a lamp to be lit. She knew the layout of the room well enough by now, but rational thought had been abandoned to the knowledge that she was now alone in a bedchamber with Chase Graham. She would not enter farther and risk humiliation by stumbling over a chair or, worse, the bed.

The silence stretched taut. The door swung closed and the breeze it created stirred the hem of her skirt. No key grated in the lock, and had she not already had plans for escape, they would now have been formed. Footsteps echoed over stone, their progress slow and oddly unsure.

"Where did you go, vision?" a husky voice asked from the darkness. It sliced through the deafening quiet like a knife, tingling up her spine and snatching

214

her breath. Of its own accord, her heart hammered in response.

Her only reply was to risk humiliation and slip farther into the darkness. She didn't go near the windows, for fear he'd see her shadow passing. Instead, she neared the wardrobe. Her eyes quickly grew accustomed to the darkness. The large piece of furniture she approached looked as hard and rugged as the man who stalked her through the darkness.

"Marea, 'tis no game we play here. Tell me where you are."

She slipped past the wardrobe and disappeared on the far side. Pressing her back hard against the stone wall, she waited, ears pricked.

Footsteps neared then receded. A muffled curse cut the air when he stumbled over a piece of furniture. She could feel his frustration, and knew she was fueling his anger. Still, she kept her tongue.

Aye, Chase was angry. But his anger was directed at himself. How could a man born and bred on the Borders, a man who had led many a midnight raid without falter, lose a slip of a girl inside a sealed bedchamber? Yet that was exactly what he had done. One minute her stiff back was illuminated by the light of the hall, the next she'd slipped into the darkness and become one with it.

A stab of panic gripped him when he wondered if she'd gone from his room for good. The feeling passed as quickly as it had come — where could she go? — but the wavy aftereffects left him tense.

Raking furious fingers through his hair, he spun toward the door. She hadn't left. He would have heard her. Therefore, she was still in the room. "Methinks you've kept company with the witch too long if you

215

can so easily turn yourself into cold air and stone." His voice was harshly grating.

The remark, made mostly to himself, elicited a response. Chase heard a throaty giggle before it could be suppressed. His attention snapped to the far corner, and the wardrobe. A smile laced his lips as he silently peeled off his boots. The stone floor felt hard and cold as, with the grace and stealth of a wildcat, he moved toward the wardrobe. Only the disturbance of the cold night air marked his progress.

As he grew accustomed to the lack of light, his body honed in on different areas. There was a soft, feminine scent in this corner of the room. If he listened closely he could hear an occasional rasp of breath. Coarse wool whispered in his ear.

Chase flattened himself against the front of the wardrobe. The carved handles bit into his back. He barely noticed. His body told him quite strongly that he'd neared his quarry. Blood fired through his veins, pounding in his temples. His palms itched to feel satiny flesh. His breathing came slow and long, and he savored each sweet whiff of her heathery scent.

She hadn't heard him approach. Therefore, the scream that ripped from her when she found him towering ominously in front of her was genuine. Her scream was quickly silenced by the mouth that crashed furiously down on her.

Rough fingers bit into her arms, drawing her up hard against the unyielding wall of his chest. He eased her chin up, and intensified the assault on her lips. His demanding kiss soon stole her surprise, and replaced it with smoldering passion.

Her hands had lifted to fight him off. Instead, her fingers curled into his arms, capturing fistfuls of his

216

soft tunic. The muscles rippling beneath felt warm and firm and wonderful.

Her scream melted into a husky moan—echoed by his own. He dropped his hands and encircled her waist. His fingers dug into her bottom. He brought her up hard, grinding their hips together. The coat of bristly stubble on his jaw scraped her tender flesh. In a country where most men sported beards, Marea found the feel of day-old whiskers shocking. And seductive.

Her arms wrapped around his neck and she pulled him closer. With a groan, Chase pushed her back against the stone. His tongue found the honeyed sweetness of her mouth. It was a greedy, all-consuming invasion. A welcome one.

What happened will not happen again. I'll not let it. 'Twas wonderful, but 'twas wrong.

Her own words came back to haunt her. They sliced through her heart like a knife, echoing in her ears and her mind. They had a hollow ring. What was happening did not feel wrong. Her blood was singing, her body tingling with sensual promise. The body pressing against her was as hard as the stone against her back, but his chest was warmer, more inviting. Never had she heard a sound to match his breath rushing hotly in her ears.

How could this be wrong?

Chase sensed her hesitation, and sought to abolish it. One hand cupped her cheek. His head lifted, but only far enough to speak. "The first time I thought you a dream." His mouth dipped for a gentle kiss. "I was right." His next kiss was longer. His teeth nibbled at her trembling lower lip. "The second time I was a fool. I sought to bend you to my will by force." He planted small, hot kisses on each eyelid in turn. Marea trembled. "I was wrong. 'Twas my own will that was smashed to pieces." His mouth met hers, hungrily stealing a kiss that left her breathless, clinging and aching for more.

"And now?" she breathed against his lips. Her fingers curled into his hair as she struggled to bring his mouth back to hers. His neck seemed suddenly cast of iron. It wouldn't bend. Her gaze lifted and locked with his. His lids were thick, his eyes shimmering with bright emerald promise.

"And now," he answered, his voice a husky seduction all its own, "I simply want you. The way a man wants, *craves*, a woman. Will you deny me, vision? Will you deny yourself?"

She wondered, fleetingly, if he would stop should she ask it. But stopping this bittersweet madness was not at all what she wanted. She sighed, "Nay, I canna."

"I didn't think you could." His voice was light, filled with the sweet jubilation pumping through him. His mouth dipped to taste her again, and yet again. He reveled in the feel of her small hands shyly exploring his shoulders, his back, his arms. Her fingers felt like delicate wings fluttering against his flesh. The delicacy of her touch, coupled with the willing curves molded against him, drove him to madness and beyond.

The kiss deepened to a frenzied pitch as he bent and scooped her into his arms. She went voluntarily. Her hands caressed, but did not think to fight. In his arms, with his heart drumming beneath her fingertips, she felt safe. So very much alive. She even, for just a second, felt beautiful. For the first time in years the beauty she'd fought hard to deny felt comfortable and right. She attributed that to the magic of his touch.

The mattress felt soft against her back. The pillow cradled her head, its downy softness nuzzling her cheeks.

He did not join her on the bed, as his body demanded, but perched on the edge and let his hands boldly roam the curves that had haunted his dreams for too long. His inspection was slow and breathtakingly thorough. It honed her senses until she smoldered and arched toward him. Her hands sought to bring him the same sweet pleasure, but he brushed them aside.

"Nay, vision," he rasped. Gripping her wrists, he tugged them above her head. There was something seductive about the contrast of steely fingers and soft pillow pressing against her flesh. "Tonight, we go slow." His mouth lowered toward her, so slowly Marea died with longing for each inch that seemed to take a lifetime to span. "Tonight, we achieve perfection. This I pledge to you with my heart . . . my life . . . my very soul."

His lips were almost upon hers. Marea's lashes flickered down when she felt the warmth of his mouth on hers. Her lips parted, accepting the first feel of his mouth teasingly grazing her lips. Her hands were still above her head, his hands covering hers. Their fingers entwined as his body at last covered her.

Their mouths fused together. The kiss was wild and demanding, the hunger for possession fanning out of control.

"Ah, vision, I—"

A sharp rap on the door brought his head up. Another knock was accompanied by a muffled voice of alarm seeping in through the slats of the door.

Amethyst and emerald eyes locked. The former shimmered with confusion and unquenched passion; the latter mirrored the passion, but was laced with frustrated anger.

Chase cursed harshly. Reluctantly, he thrust himself to a sitting position and barked a command to enter.

The door was flung wide. It crashed against the stone and Marea started, her passion only a sweetly fragmented memory.

The figure in the doorway was breathing heavily from exertion. The light pouring in from behind bathed the room in a soft orange glow, silhouetting the man who stood there. She didn't know who he was, but one thing was for certain: he was deeply upset.

"Come quick, m'lord . . ." the man panted. "The Douglas returns. And raids."

Chapter Fifteen

Marea smoldered, remembering the deep look of regret Chase had flashed her before disappearing down the hall in the wake of his man. In his haste, he'd left the door unlocked.

Their steps had barely receded down the hall when another set was heard approaching. Unlike the others, these footsteps were light, precise, cautious. When the door cracked open and Zander MacVin slipped inside, Marea wasn't surprised.

" 'Tis not midnight," she said by way of a greeting. Her words were harsher than she'd intended, but her emotions were roiling, and she seemed to have no restraint over them.

"Aye, m'lady," he nodded. His curly red hair was a bright splotch of color in the otherwise dark room. "But the Douglas, now, he does not take me into council about when he'll be riding against the Graham. Methinks even he be a wee bit surprised by the good time he made in coming."

Marea scrambled off the bed, her heart throbbing

as she approached him. "Do we wait, Zander, or do we leave now?"

The desperation in her tone caught his attention. Even the dim light couldn't hide the color splashing her cheeks, or her eyes, wide with apprehension. He wondered what had happened between her and the Graham to bring about her unease, but didn't ask. It wasn't his place. "We leave now."

"Good," she sighed, her mind never straying far from the soft mattress that stretched out like a battlefield behind her. "I be ready. A far muckle *past* ready."

The hallway was empty. Still, Zander insisted on leaving Marea behind to check it. He wouldn't risk anyone seeing them leave the room. Standing alone in the darkness, with only her ragged breathing and pounding heart for company, the minutes stretched on. The sound of raised male voices filtered in through the windows. There was no mistaking the angry tones.

Curiosity, finely interwoven with apprehension, coaxed her to the windows. Outside, the slight expanse of land that circled the castle was bathed bright orange from the torches held by the men who surrounded the barmkin. The soft light was a stark contrast to the purpose that had brought the men there.

Since the gate was on the opposite end of the castle, she could see nothing but foreboding shadows that looked like men arming catapults, readying crossbows, and lifting ladders in preparation for a full-scale attack.

"Hurry, m'lady. 'Tis doubtful the corridor will stay deserted for long."

Marea needed no prompting to fall into step behind her small friend. Although they took the long way

222

through twisting halls and an occasional room, the storage chamber was reached quickly and without incident. The men were too busy preparing for the seige to be bothered looking toward thwarting an escape by a captive they didn't want within the walls to begin with.

The storage chamber itself was another matter. The large, cluttered room was a flurry of commotion, with people rushing in and out of the doorway in no discernable order. They all entered empty-handed, and came out lugging crates and kegs that were awkward to maneuver up the twisting stone staircase. Everyone from the laird's closest guards down to the lowliest scullery wenches appeared at one time or another.

The storage chamber made up a large part of the bottom floor, and housed the bulk of foodstuffs. It had to be closely guarded, since it would most likely be the first attacked. The Douglas was a seasoned reiver. He knew that if the Graham could match his strength, the keep would need the supplies in the storage chamber to withstand a long and tiresome stalemate.

Marea and Zander made it to the bottom of the stairs without detection. Reaching the inside of the chamber, and the tunnels, proved more difficult. Every time a person would appear in the door and rush up the stairs ladened with his burden, another would take his place. Once they had come very close to being spotted. While Marea had frozen with indecision, Zander had tugged her down behind a large crate before they could be seen—and caught.

They huddled behind a wooden crate that smelled of salted venison. Marea's legs screamed at the cramped position. Zander shifted as two voices were raised a few feet away.

"You clumsy oaf!" a voice that sounded like Martha of the kitchen bellowed. "I was in this doorway before you. Now move and let me pass before I see to it your ugly face kisses this chunk of stone beneath my feet."

"Ugly, is it? 'Tis plain you've no looking glass or you'd reassess your opinion of the word," a man's voice answered. It was thick with anger. "I'll not go anywhere, you nagging old hag. Just because you fill up the doorway with your fatty bulk doesn't mean you were here first. Move aside and let me enter."

"I'd as soon drop this crate of dried pork on your toes."

"Sitting on me would like do more harm."

"Why you scrawny little—"

Crash

"You've broken it!"

"Not yet, but I—"

"Enough!" There was no need to be told who *that* voice belonged to; Marea's body reacted to it instinctively. "We're preparing for an attack, not a fist sprint. Put your differences aside and get those crates above." A tense pause was followed by, *"Now!"*

The two who fought hurried to make amends. In less than a minute the scene was over and the chamber vacant. A flurry of voices above could be heard. That, and Chase Graham barking orders from the hall. The chamber was oddly still.

" 'Tis now or not at all," Marea hissed. She reached for Zander's hand and jerked him to his feet. She caught a brief glimpse of the hazel eyes, studying her curiously, and knew he'd seen her reaction to the Graham's nearness. Be that as it may, this was no time for explanations—or delay.

Her skirt rustled around her legs, their feet clattered over the stone. From behind could be heard at least a dozen men rushing down the stairs. Chase's voice still rang loud, but not as loud as her heartbeat pounding in her ears.

Marea almost breathed a sigh of relief when they reached the cupboard concealing the tunnel's entrance. Almost. She checked the impulse, knowing that true relief would only be savored once the velvet mustiness beyond the door enveloped her.

The footsteps neared, as did Chase's voice. More voices quickly joined in. He was just around the corner of the storage chamber now. So close she could feel his nearness radiate from behind as surely as she felt the agitation of the small man at her side.

She began yanking sacks of oats off the shelves and tossing them aside. The second her fingers brushed the cold metal lock, Zander was there with the key. She was quivering badly; so badly she had trouble inserting the key.

If she'd been a split second quicker, what happened next might never have happened. But it did. There was no forgetting it, nor was there any stopping it.

Chase's cry of outrage cut the air. Her name being bellowed from behind froze her to the spot like a petrified tree. And stole her only chance for escape.

From close by came the Douglas's roar of victory as he gained the inside of the keep. The sound was loud enough to rattle stone and mortar, or at least appear to. Marea startled. Her grip slackened, and the key tumbled from her fingers and clattered to the floor. She stooped to retrieve it and almost banged into Zander, who was doing the same. Her toe kicked against the side of the key and sent it flying. It skipped across the stone, its path too quick to follow as it disappeared beneath the crates lining the far corner.

"There ye be, ye little cur!" a deep, weather-worn voice shouted. The rumbling tone was mixed with laughter. "Thought to keep me from taking ye, did ye? Think again, boy. The Douglas be here, and this time he comes to stay."

Chase, in the process of stalking Marea, spun on his heel. The sword hissed from its scabbard, brandished all in one lithe motion. The doorway was filled with Ian Douglas's burly form. Not a small man by any means, Chase's rugged body was painfully overshadowed by the size and virility of the man he faced.

"Are you requesting you be buried under Kinclearnon soil, you red-headed brute? 'Tis the only way you'll be staying," Chase countered. For all appearance he was undaunted by his adversary's intimidating stature. His fingers tightened on the sword hilt when the Douglas's men continued to file rowdily into his keep. Some filtered up the steps, and the sound of battle soon clashed through the air.

A grin of pure delight split the Douglas's thick, reddish brown beard and moustache. His sharp green eyes glistened out of the craggy lines of his face. "Do ye think it? Hmph! You're more like your da than I thought, if you're aiming to fight for something that does not even belong to you."

"Kinclearnon is mine. And so it shall stay."

"By default. And as for the staying part . . ." He took a step forward.

Chase did not retreat. Instead, his sword blade glistened in the light as it made a threatening arch toward the Douglas's huge chest. The blow was not meant to connect, only intimidate. It accomplished the former. The latter was debatable.

"Och! lass! 'Twould appear we've underestimated the lad. Methinks he does not wish to surrender the keep."

The Douglas's words dragged Marea into a conversation she had no wish to enter. She saw Chase tense when the Douglas's attention drifted to her. The Douglas spared a doubtful glance at Zander, who was inching toward the crates in the far corner, but Marea doubted the burly Scot actually saw him. His attention was rooted on Chase Graham, and there it would stay until the clash of battle had ended. That, or until a call for defeat was sounded, which the determination etched hard on Chase's face said not to expect.

"Methinks ye be right," Marea replied, her voice sounding oddly controlled. She could feel Chase's thoughts stray to her, then just as quickly shift back to his opponent.

Zander had reached the crates and disappeared on his hands and knees. No one but Marea seemed to notice, although she thought she caught a glimpse of speculation in the Douglas's eyes when he glanced in that direction.

A cry rang out from upstairs, then the shrill scream of a woman. Footsteps thudded on the floor above. The doorway behind the Douglas's broad back was filled with scraggly, eager faces. The pungent scent of sweaty bodies filled the air, and mingled with the sickening odor of fresh blood. None of the men rushed in to help their laird. For good reason. There was no need. The Douglas had the situation under control—as was his way.

Tossing his long sword from left hand to right, the Douglas sent Chase a speculative glare. "Well, pup? Be ye ready to meet your maker?"

"Nay," Chase replied. His sword raised, the tip slashed the air. The blade whistled as it whipped toward the Douglas's arm. The sleeve of the Douglas's jack tore under the blade he was too late in deflecting. A crimson stain quickly spread over the dark padded leather. "But you may tell him I was asking for him," his blade arched down and met loudly with steel, "when you see him. Which should be shortly."

"You think it?" the Douglas snorted. His nostrils, normally flared, flared more. His voice was edged with laughter. He seemed impervious to pain as he launched a counterattack that was quickly thwarted. "Your as arrogant as your da, 'twould seem."

That comment brought a surge of red to Chase's face, and an angry thrust of his sword. The two blades met at the hilt; the sound of steel rasping against steel was harsh. The two men met nose to nose, of a sort. Since the Douglas stood half a head taller, Chase was forced to glance upward in order to meet those laughing green eyes.

"My father would have sliced you to ribbons had this foolish attempt been made on his keep," Chase growled. He planted the ball of his hand on a meaty shoulder and gave a vicious shove. Surprisingly, the Douglas stumbled back a step. "I, however, am not so generous."

Steel crashed against steel time and again. By the time the men had come full circle, their cheeks were red with a mixture of determination and exertion.

Marea thought the Douglas looked to be having a fine time, as though he was merely playing with Chase, testing his skill until he grew bored with the game. Chase was big and boasted a strength she rarely found in the English, but he was still no match for the Douglas. And what will happen when the Douglas does grow bored? she wondered, a knot of fear coiling in her gut. She knew the answer without being told, and it disturbed her deeply, much more than it should have.

" 'Tis threats your weapon of choice, lad? If ye canna best me with steel, ye think to do it with words? 'Twill not work."

A grin that spoke nothing of the disadvantage he was under turned Chase's lips. The sight of it shocked Marea. Of their own accord, her feet moved toward the two men, stopping a few short feet from the close circle of the fight. It was not a smart thing to do, but right now intelligence, or lack thereof, was not a concern. Fear was.

"I've only just begun," Chase retorted glibly, as his blade ripped the Douglas's other sleeve. "Wait until I've warmed to my subject, then we'll see how ineffective my words are."

"M'lady," a soft voice hissed in Marea's ear.

She didn't hear Zander over the pounding of her heart, nor did she notice his approach. At the moment, her gaze was wide, riveted on the long, deadly blade that arched toward Chase's throat. A nervous scream tore from her lungs at the feel of a hand impatiently tugging her arm.

Chase's blade deflected the blow, but Marea's scream grabbed his attention. His head snapped to the side, and his gaze clashed with hers. He held her gaze for only a heartbeat, but it was enough.

Light shimmered off the Douglas's blade as it raised for the final strike. The sword drew Marea's gaze like a magnet. Chase did not see the deadly blade being swung at the back of his head. But Marea saw, and it struck in her terror unlike any she'd ever felt before.

With a strangled cry, she broke from Zander's grip and rammed her shoulder into Chase's sinewy chest. Her angle, coupled with his surprise, staggered him. The blade whistled overhead, so close she felt it slice through the strands of hair at her crown.

They crashed onto the cold, hard stone. She was cushioned by the solidness of Chase's body. Chase had no such padding. Hard stone slammed into his head, and shoved the breath from his lungs. She lifted her head, and for the length of a sigh their gazes met. His glistened with confusion over what she'd just done and . . . something else.

She had no time to assess what that something else was. Before she could draw in a shaky breath, a powerful hand wrapped around her upper arm and yanked her to her feet. Her back was brought up hard against a chest that felt like it was carved out of the same steel that abruptly pushed against her throat.

"Your sword will be clattering to the stone or her heroics will have been wasted." The chest behind her vibrated with each coldly uttered word. Marea was reminded of another time, another raid, and her terror fueled to a boiling degree.

Zander was standing near Chase's head. His face revealed his confusion and fear for her life. "She means naught to him," he sneered. "He'll not surrender so much as a pence for her, let alone his keep."

The Douglas's gaze shifted over Zander briefly. His opinion of the tiny MacVin was plain to see, for it was an opinion commonly shared. "The mon be winded, but he can speak for himself. I'll be thinking to hear this from his own lips." His gaze swung back to Chase, who was beginning to rise.

The grip on Marea's arm tightened. She winced. Both Zander and Chase paled, which caused the Douglas to chuckle dryly.

"Aye, the look on your face be answer enough, lad," the Douglas said. "Now, do not embarrass yourself by spouting a lie I'd not believe anyway. Just tell me if you'd have me kill her so ye can lose your land by honor of the sword instead of blackmail . . . which, I might add, be just as honorable."

Chase's jaw hardened to granite. A muscle jerked in that sun-bronzed hollow where jaw met cheek. His emerald eyes shimmered with indecision. His attention drifted between Marea and the Douglas. A hot glare was spared for the blade that threatened her quivering porcelain flesh.

Marea glanced away, focusing on the stone wall as though it held great interest. She cursed herself as a coward, but she'd no wish to see the look of raw hatred she knew would flash in Chase's eyes when he gave the Douglas permission to kill her. A tear burned her eyes, and moistened the burnished roots of her lashes. Resolutely, she refused to let it spill over her cheek.

Chase's fist tightened on the sword hilt—that was no longer in his hand. Surprise sparked in his eyes as he stared in disbelief at his empty fist. When he looked up, his gaze was met with the Douglas's gloating countenance.

Marea felt the broad shoulder behind her shrug. "So, 'tis not much of a choice I be giving," the Douglas remarked. His tone was that of a man who tasted imminent victory. "It still be right nice of me to offer it." He shifted impatiently. "Well? What be your choice, pup? I've a keep to settle if you surrender; and a battle to wage if you do not. Not to mention . . ." The sword moved in such a way as to make his meaning plain.

"I be telling ye, mon, he'll not—" Zander began, only to stop when the Douglas gave a fierce jerk of his furry chin.

The men behind him responded. Three large Scots rushed into the room, and dragged Zander away. He did not go easily.

Marea would have screamed a protest, but she didn't dare. The blade at her throat forbade swallowing, let alone talking. Though he had been dragged up the stairs, Marea could still hear Zander's shrieks of outrage over the gritty roar of battle.

"Will you force me to make the decision for you, lad?"

"And if I do?" Chase snapped, raking stiff fingers through the sweaty hair clinging to his brow.

A mirthless chuckle rumbled at her back. "You'll not like the choice, methinks. 'Tis only Border fair of me to ask: do you surrender or do I slit her lovely throat?"

The emerald gaze lowered to half-mast; Chase's gaze fixed on the sword. He couldn't ignore the pulse leaping in the hollow of her creamy neck, or his gut response to the sight of sharp steel pressing against it. His gaze lifted and he looked into her confused eyes. That, too, tightened his gut, and made his glaringly empty fists clench hard at his sides. Chase had never before felt such ragged emotions as the ones now gathering inside him. He felt powerless, as though he had been stripped not only of his weapon, but of an integral part of himself as well. The feeling was frightening in its intensity.

His gaze lifted, his eyes shimmering with hatred as

he focused on the Douglas. His voice, when it came, was as hard as the stone walls around them—just as cold, just as uninviting. His lips twisted into a sardonic smile, and his hand briskly swept the room. "Welcome to Kinclearnon, Douglas. 'Twould appear you'll be staying after all."

Chapter Sixteen

Marea's fingers were numb from the rope coiled tightly around her wrists. That was the least of her worries. Right now, every fiber of her body was aware of the hard surface molded against her back. A surface that was as flexible as it was firm. A surface that breathed, and that, with each steady rise and fall, made her even more conscious of it.

Physical contact with Chase Graham was not what should be gnawing her thoughts at that moment. She should be busy planning a way to escape the hall and the barrage of rowdy people filtering through it. Instead, she wasted precious time enjoying the spicy male scent of the man whose wrists were linked to hers, while at the same time trying hard not to think of another raid, the result of which had been vastly different.

Zander was nowhere to be seen. She felt a stab of fear when she wondered where he'd been taken. And whether or not he was still alive. It was common knowledge Ian Douglas cared naught for any who went by the name MacVin.

234

Chase felt her sudden, ragged breath. His head turned to the side. He could see only the soft curtain of red-gold hair, and the trembling shoulder that peeked from beneath it. The sight of her fear ripped through him, causing a silent, helpless burning that twisted deep in his gut.

He knew a momentary urge to whisper comfort, but the few words that tumbled through his mind sounded stiff and inadequate when he weighed them on his tongue. Too, the sight of her preparing to flee his keep was still strong; it quenched the traitorous words before they could be spoken aloud.

And so they sat, in a stony silence that seemed as endless as it was consuming. Until the Douglas took it upon himself to check the welfare of his most precious prisoners.

"Methinks I like seeing the twa of you thus," he said with a rumbling chuckle. His voice was light, filled with genuine good cheer. It bounced off the cold stone walls and outstripped the sound of the people milling in the hall.

Marea glanced up, her gaze settling on the large, bearded man of whom her father had taught her long ago to be wary. He towered over her. One hand was curled into a thick, dirty fist and rested atop his hip. His bushy red eyebrows rose high in his craggy forehead as he awaited her response.

From this vantage point, she thought he looked more menacing than when, in her youth, she'd caught a glimpse of him riding away from her father's keep after a successful raid. He appeared to sprout from the stone floor like a gigantic tree, his body easily as thick and solid as any trunk in the forest outside.

Chase grumbled. His words were uttered too soft and

low to be deciphered, but his tone made his meaning crystal clear. Just the feel of him against her back made Marea relax. A wee bit. It was because of the courage his nearness fostered that she was able to meet the Douglas's laughing gaze and say, " 'Twould appear you've finally succeeded in winning Kinclearnon. Och! it took ye long enough."

She felt Chase stiffen at her glib remark. The Douglas had quite a different reaction. His wide, furry chin tipped back and he let loose a laugh of pure delight. The sound captured the attention of more than one person in the hall, but not for long.

"Ah, lass, the years have not changed ye much, have they?" he asked, and wiping a tear of laughter from the weatherwrinkled corner of one eye. "Your tongue be as sharp as when you were a bairn. In fact, methinks the years have honed it."

Marea shrugged. "You'd have no way of knowing, mon. Me da made sure you did not know me when I was a bairn."

"I'd not have to. I knew the MacKenzie. That summer I held him and waited for your mother to pay the ransom, your da and I spent many a night talking over a tankard of ale. He told me of his wayward daughter, and her penchant for speaking her mind."

"And a week after he was settled back in Kinclearnon you were back stalking our beasties." She nodded, a soft smile playing over her lips. Her gaze fixed on the flames crackling in the hearth beside her. "Aye. I remember it." The smile melted and she glanced up sharply. "Me da held great respect for ye. He'd be sore disappointed to hear of the trouble you've wrought this day."

"You think it? Nay, lass. Your da and I knew each other, respected each other. 'Twas only a matter of time,

236

after all. Conner knew it." His bushy brows furrowed in a scowl, his mind apparently lingering on a memory that was buried deep, now suddenly resurrected. "He once told me that if you keep battering your head against a wall, eventually the bricks will weaken and tumble. Today, the bricks have tumbled."

"A sorrier day Kinclearnon has never seen." She paused, her gaze misted. "Well, mayhaps just once before."

Again, he shrugged. His green eyes sparkled with an exuberance that looked almost bairnlike. "Aye. But even you maun admit, lass, 'tis been a grand day for the Douglas."

Marea felt a flash of her anger return. White-hot and quick, it rushed through her. "Did you come over here to gloat, mon? If so, 'tis not appreciated."

"Gloat? Nay, lass, I came to offer you refreshments." His expression grew serious as he held out a tankard she hadn't noticed he carried. "You've been sitting here for hours, with not even a drop of water to wet your sharp tongue. Had I realized it, I'd have offered sooner. Let it not be said I mistreat me prisoners."

"And the Graham?" she asked without thinking. She felt the back behind her stiffen, and immediately wished she could bite back the words. Since it was too late, she continued primly, "Does your offer extend to him?"

"Aye. If that be your wish."

"It is."

He extended the tankard, and sent her an odd look when he was rewarded for his kindness with a softly derisive chuckle.

"Me hands are tied, mon."

"And so they'll stay," he said, his features hardening until he looked more like the fierce Border reiver she'd

237

always known and feared.

"Ye mean you'll not untie me?" she asked with feigned sweetness.

He quickly saw through it, and she just as quickly dropped her look of veiled innocence. "I'm not so big a fool as you think, lass. I'm aware of how well you know these twisting halls and chambers." His eyes glistened a bright green, and she knew his thoughts had also turned to that raid so many years ago. The one where he had almost succeeded in winning Kinclearnon two score before his rightful time. "Only a great fool would let ye slip away so easily, lass. And I am not such a fool."

"Pity," she said with a light shrug. In truth, she'd never expected him to untie her. Still, she'd had to try. "I'll take that sip of ale now. If you still be offering it."

The Douglas, his spirits lifted, knelt beside her and lifted the tankard to her mouth. The ale was warmer than the cool brim pressed against her lips. She took great gulps of the yeasty-smelling contents.

He let her drink, feeling a need to stop her when she drank too much too fast, but not a great need. Her eyes told him when she was done. He pushed the bulk of his body to his feet. Her gaze told him something else as well — that he hadn't completed his chore.

With a brisk nod, he stepped over to the Graham and offered the younger man the remaining ale. Chase was not polite about his refusal, telling the Douglas in succinct detail exactly what could be done with his ale, and the mug that contained it.

"And you thought my tongue sharp," Marea muttered, trying to contain an irrational urge to laugh. The stiff back behind her said her mirth would not be appreciated. As did the darkening of the Douglas's rounded cheeks.

"Aye, lass, that I did," the Douglas growled. " 'Twould appear 'tis not as sharp as some." He spun on his heel, took two steps, then stopped and swung back. His gaze, abruptly serious, locked with Marea's. She felt a prick of apprehension trickle down her spine. "The keep be in *my* hands now, lass. You know that, do you not?"

"Aye," she answered, echoing his seriousness, though her tone was laced with confusion.

"Do you also know I'll not tolerate any of your tricks?"

Marea's spine stiffened. She had a nagging feeling she knew what he was about, but fear kept her tongue still.

Silence, however, was not good enough for Ian Douglas. He wanted her word, and he had every intention of getting it. " 'Tis no game we play here, lass. 'Tis sore real."

"Aye," she whispered. Her fingers dug into the rope chaffing her wrists. She sucked in a sharp breath when she felt the heat of another's flesh sear her knuckles. "Well I know it. And neither am I such a fool."

He nodded thoughtfully, his thick fingers scratching the bearded underside of his chin. "Then I'd not have to be telling you how your tricks will be received in this keep. Or the punishments they'll gain you. I'll have your word you'll not be using your magic or potions on me men, lass."

Her lips tightened and she looked away.

"Yer word," he prompted.

"Aye, mon," she answered distractedly. Her mind was too busy focusing on the body behind her. A body that suddenly felt as though it had solidified into a chunk of steel. "You've my word. No magic. No potions. No tricks."

"I'll be seeing to it you stick by that, witch."

"I'm not a witch, I'm a *healer*." Marea grumbled the

239

rebuke that had long since become second nature to her. The words hung in the air, and she detected belatedly the note of Agatha shrillness her voice had automatically adapted. She bit her tongue, but it was too late. Far too late.

"Agatha?" The single word came, low and deadly, from the man joined to her at the wrists.

She stiffened, swallowing hard. Anger emanated from Chase; it rolled over her in hot waves.

"Agatha?!"

"Be whatever ye like, lass—in your bog, not in me keep," the Douglas reminded her lightly, ignoring Chase's outburst, and the string of angry curses being muttered under the young man's breath.

The Douglas muttered something else. She never heard what he said in that split second before he turned and rejoined the others. Her heart was pounding too loudly to hear anything else. No, on second thought something did override her hammering heart and ragged breaths. It was Chase Graham's furious voice. With an effort she concentrated on it.

"—hands are not free, witch, for at this moment I would like nothing better than to tear you limb from lovely limb."

Silence stretched taut in the air. Marea could feel the tension crackle between them; it was hotter than the heat pouring out of the hearth. She felt Chase's fury as though it were a tangible cloak settling heavily about her shoulders. Abruptly, she felt tired, and not at all pleased that it was in this offhand way he'd come to learn the truth about Agatha.

When she said nothing, he continued hotly, "I knew the witch for a traitorous bitch. A murderess and a liar. Never did I suspect the same of you. *Never.*"

His fingers flexed into steely fists. The movement pulled the rope more tightly around her burning wrists. She winced, and was unsure if the reflexive gesture was due to pain caused by the rope cutting into her flesh, or by the single word that cut into her very soul.

"Were you ever planning to tell me of the deception?" he demanded icily when, still, she refused to speak. "Answer me soon, wench, for my anger is great enough to break these ropes. I don't think you'd care to know what I plan to do to you should that happen. *Answer me, damn you!*"

"I —" she gulped. "I've naught to say."

He huffed. "There's not much *for* you to say, is there? Except that you played me for a fool. And that I allowed it." His voice hardened, the coldness in it frightened her. "Tell me, *Agatha,* did you have a good laugh over how easily you duped me?"

"Nay," she answered softly. "'Twas no reason."

" 'Twas no reason to lie to me about who you were either, yet you harbored no compunctions about doing that."

" 'Tis different. I could not tell ye the truth."

"Could not?" he countered icily. "Or *would* not? There's a difference, witch. One I do not think you know."

"I know what ye be thinking, mon, but —"

"Nay, witch, I doubt very much you do."

"If you'd let me explain!"

"Explain what? Treachery? Deceit? Betrayal? Nay. I've had a stomachful of it from you. I'll hear no more of it."

"But —"

"Enough!"

She fell silent, as did more than a few others in the room.

Chase inhaled deeply, as though the warm air from the fire could control the fury that was threatening to get the best of him. When the others turned back to their chores, he again glanced over his shoulder. His timing was poor, for Marea did the same.

Their gazes locked. She could see enough of his face, bathed in flickering shadows, to know that his anger was not going to be quick and fleeting. His skin was drawn taut over his cheeks and the hard line of his jaw. His complexion was ruddy with ill-suppressed rage. The eyes she had to struggle at this angle to see blazed with emerald fire, fueled by the bitter hurt of betrayal. A vein throbbed maddeningly in his temple. His voice, when it came, was as ragged as his breathing.

"I'll have your reason, witch."

"M-me reason for what?" she asked softly, turning away. The raw hatred she'd glimpsed in his face and eyes had drained what little fight she had left. She collapsed weakly against him, only to find the cushion of his back stiffen and pull away. That hurt her more than she would admit. Sighing, she straightened, but her shoulders remained slumped forward, her chin pillowed atop her collarbone.

"Your reason for saving my life when it would have gone better for you to leave me to die. Kinclearnon would have been yours had you acted quickly. But instead you nursed me. Why?"

She sighed heavily. "I'd no wish to regain me lands by adding to the killing. 'Twas the method used by the Graham to gain this keep. I'd not use such vile tactics to get it back."

"Why not? These are the Borders, witch. Killing is a

fact of life here, as natural as breathing. Besides, you showed no hesitation when it came to disposing of . . . My father! 'Twas not the witch who—God, 'twas *you!*" This revelation hit him hard. Marea felt him reel against her back, as though he'd been struck with a mighty blow.

Then, before she knew what he was about, he'd moved, shifted ever so slightly. She gasped when her fingers were clutched tightly in his strong hands. Hands that could easily crush her fragile bones, if that was his wish.

"Now you know why I did not tell you the truth," she said through gritted teeth. The pain in her fingers shot up her arm, past the insistent sting of the rope on her wrists. "You were so sure Agatha killed your da. So set on having your revenge against her. I could not tell you Agatha was really myself. If I had, you would . . ." her voice trailed away. It was a confession she did not want to make. Even to herself.

"What?" he rasped, his tone still kissed with an anger that refused to be shaken. "It would mean what?"

"That you'd fix your hatred on me. 'Tis not what I wanted."

"And now?" he prodded, his voice anything but gentle.

" 'Tis not what I want. I do not want you to hate me, mon. I do not know why." When he did not answer, but sat rigidly still behind her, she continued weakly, "I saved your life to repay you for saving mine so long ago." Her voice cracked, as it always did when she spoke of the night her family had been slaughtered by Chase's father. "That brute would have killed me, or w-worse, had you not come along when you did. You gave me the chance to escape. Good God, you even killed for me! 'Tis not

243

something I could forget."

She could feel his thoughts stray in that direction as well. It seemed an agonizing lifetime before he spoke. His words, amazingly enough, lacked their previous anger as he was consumed by memories that were mirrored in her own mind. "I killed no one, mistress, though I'll admit that was my intent at the time. Only wounded."

"Wounded?" she repeated shakily. Her shoulders trembled and she rested her head back weakly. The nape of her neck leaned on the hard shelf of his shoulder. Against her temple she could feel the beat of his heart throbbing beneath the sun-bronzed flesh of his neck. The torn tunic scraped her cheek.

Surprisingly, he did not pull away, but turned his cheek into the soft cloud of her hair. "Aye," he whispered, his lips brushing her scalp. "The dog still breathes."

Marea fought a wave of dizziness. She shivered uncontrollably. "I-I thought to see him once or twa, from a distance," she said weakly. "Always, I thought him an illusion. A nightmare. 'Twas so sure I was that you'd killed him."

"And 'twas wishing I was that I had. Many times."

Chase shifted, resting his head back against her shoulder, the way she had on his. She welcomed the weight as much as she welcomed the feel of his ragged hair tickling her cheek and neck. Hesitantly, she turned her head. Her gaze lifted. At this angle, they came face-to-face. The anger she'd expected to see in his eyes was there, but it was tightly leashed.

"He won't hurt you, vision," he said, his voice husky with conviction as his gaze roved over her face. "I won't let him."

She looked at him long and hard before reminding

him, "He'd have no chance, mon. Or did you forget . . . 'tis *you* who be threatening to tear me limb from limb."

His eyelids thickened. A veil of dispassion covered his expression. "And well I may, witch," he replied dryly. "But not before I've an answer to whether or not you killed my father."

She thought to lie. But then she remembered all the lies she had already told him, and knew she could not cast another. "Nay. Though I would have killed him had someone not stolen the pleasure from me." She shook her head and looked away, but her eyes were drawn back again. He was watching her carefully, gauging her sincerity. "Och! does it not always seem a fine muckle easier to blame the witch for everything, rather than look for the real culprit?"

She gave him a few minutes to think about that, and to assess her honesty. As it turned out, he assessed every inch of her face, his gaze finally settling on her lips.

She asked, "Do ye believe me?"

"Do I have a choice, vision?"

His breath was warm against her face, and oh, so sweet! She closed her eyes and willed rational thought to return. Their sudden silence was only vaguely uneasy.

He hadn't answered her, Marea realized suddenly. But she knew better than to push him. She thought there was still a part of him that wanted to believe Agatha had killed his father. A part that *needed* to believe it.

She gazed at the stone-and-timbered ceiling above. *Isn't it always easier to blame the witch?* Hadn't she long since grown accustomed to shouldering the blame for even the most menial infraction? Why was this one different? Why did she chafe now at being held accountable for a crime she hadn't committed? It had never bothered her before. She'd never thought a thing of being blamed for

245

someone's cow suddenly running dry, or their butter unnaturally curdling as she passed their door, yet she wasn't pleased to be accused of a murder she hadn't committed. Not when the life taken was one she had sorely wanted to take herself.

Guilt ate at Marea with gnawing fingers as she shifted restlessly against Chase's shoulder. She'd been close to taking David Graham's life that night. Very close to paying him back for the slaughter of her family. She hadn't. She had discovered that she could not take any man's life if it was not in self-defense. Even the pitiful excuse for a man who'd lain crumpled against bed linen as white as his sunken face. A man who deserved to die more than anyone she'd ever known.

How she'd wanted to kill him! Her fingers had trembled with the need to do it. The ability was at her disposal, as was the desire. She simply did not possess the courage to back them both up. She'd let motive and opportunity slip by. Someone else had not.

Even now she had chastised herself for the weakness that did not do her MacKenzie heritage proud. Border reivers took lives daily. It was a fact of life here; Chase had not exaggerated on that point. But she was, plain and simple, no Border reiver. And she was no murderer.

But would this, the Graham's son and heir, believe that?

Closing her eyes, she rationalized that his need for revenge would be matched only by how close he'd felt to his sire. If the relationship had been loving, his need for vengeance would be great. If not . . . ? Somehow, she couldn't imagine any relationship of which David Graham was a part as being loving. But she had to consider it.

Much would also depend on how alike Chase and

David Graham were. As yet, she'd seen little in Chase to compare with his father. As yet. But she couldn't ignore the possibility that the son was much better at concealing his cruelty than his father had been.

It was a distinct possibility. One she would be a fool not to consider. Or to forget.

Chapter Seventeen

"You're the witch, mistress. Melt the damn things. Or transform them into snakes. Whichever." As he said this, Chase's fingers continued to pick at the ropes that bound them together. Already a few coarse layers had fallen away. But it wasn't enough—yet.

A dry, Agatha cackle split the drizzly gray afternoon. The sound made the two burly Scots who drove the wagon quiver. The guard seated in the creaking wagonbed beside Marea and Chase had the same reaction. The rest of the men, crammed tightly into the four matching wagons jostling behind, ignored the sound as though it had been made in passing. Except for the Douglas's men, the rest were accustomed to the brittle laugh that sounded as though it could make glass shatter.

"Would that I could, *Sasunach*," Marea whispered shrilly to the man still joined at her wrists. "Would that I could. Had I such powers, you'd have been transformed into a newt weeks ago."

"Are you threatening me?" the husky voice demanded close to her ear now. Chase had turned his head and in so doing his lips grazed her cheek. Her hair, moist from the drizzle falling from the overcast sky, tickled his cheek. The dampness ignited each strand with the sweet scent of blossoming heather. He drank deeply of it. Their shivers were simultaneous.

"For, if you are I swear I will—"

"Och! Do not get your feathers ruffled. 'Tis only a statement of fact."

"You said you would turn me into a newt," he argued, but the argument was weak. Her closeness was wreaking havoc on his senses. Where his thoughts should be on escaping the Douglas, he instead found himself concentrating on the smell of her hair and the unusual color it turned when dark with water.

"And so I would have, had I the powers for it." She paused, as though testing his good humor before continuing slyly, "You maun admit, you've sore tempted me."

"I retained my keep. 'Tis the only wrong I've done you."

" 'Tis enough."

The guard at her side grunted heavily at that. Marea sent him her most charming smile. A red tinge kissed his thick cheeks as he crossed his arms over his chest and looked quickly away. Rain glistened like fresh dew on his rumpled beard and head, sparkling like crystal in the dingy sunlight. The air was rich with the scent of the moist hay beneath them.

Marea squirmed when she felt the calloused tips of Chase's fingertips against her wrists, fluttering like the silken edges of a moth's wings. A jolt of sensation shot up her arms.

For some time she'd been aware of him trying to

work free the ropes. She hadn't thought he'd be successful. She let her fingertips investigate, and her heart quickened with excitement. He was close. Very close.

Licking suddenly dry lips, her gaze strayed to the guard. The Douglas had spared only one for this wagon, besides the two who drove it. The fierce-looking man stared at the dreary, passing scenery with rigid intent. The hilt of his broadsword, strapped to his meaty waist, glistened in the flickering gray light. Her fingers flexed at the sight.

"Have you ever met a witch?" she asked the man as the wagon bounced over the rock-strewn path. Chase's back was jostled in time with her own. The guard didn't respond at first. Then, slowly, his gaze shifted. His gray-blue eyes were awash with amusement when their gazes met.

"Are you speaking to me, lass?" he asked, and there was a good measure of laughter interlaced in his words. One bushy brow rose in his wide, weathered forehead.

"Aye," she said, her expression the epitome of innocence. A few coy blinks of her lashes had his full attention. "I be asking if you'd ever met a witch."

His laughter was quick, and oddly pleasant. The sound washed away the harshness of his features. "Nay, lass. No witch, though me wife's mother could be passing for one."

"I mean a *real* witch, mon," she corrected lightly, the smile still in place. Her cheeks were beginning to ache with the stiffness of it. "A sorceress . . . in the flesh."

He shook his head, and eyed her strangely. "Nay, I canna say I ever have. Why do you ask?"

Her eyes widened, her moist lips pursed. "Why, because ye be talking to one now, mon. Did ye not know it?"

"Nay!"

"Aye!"

His eyes narrowed, piercing her as she felt Chase shift. Another layer of the rope peeled away, and she tried hard not to let her excitement show.

"I'll not believe it. Not a word."

Her chin rose proudly. The back of her head scraped the nape of Chase's neck. "Why not? 'Tis the truth."

The guard's bushy brown brows drew down in a confused scowl. "You're not a witch. You're too . . . too . . ."

"Bonnie?" she said, almost choking on the word. It was the first time in years she'd willingly associated the compliment with herself. It sent a shiver of unease icing down her spine.

"Aye!"

"Thank you. But a witch can be bonnie, don't you know?"

"Mayhaps. But you're still no witch."

"I am."

"Nay." Then, after a thoughtful pause, he added, "Prove it then, lass."

The second the words slipped out, she could tell he wanted to take them back. But since this demand was what she was after, Marea wouldn't allow it. She watched him shift nervously, his gaze flicking about, as though he was trying to look anywhere but at her. A slow grin tugged at her lips. "And how would you have me prove it? Me hands be tied."

"I'll not untie you. Don't even think it."

She shook her head, her smile turning secretive. "I

251

did not expect it. Tell me how I can prove myself. 'Tis a matter of pride now. I ask only that you keep in mind that me hands be tied, so I canna do grand miracles . . . just wee ones."

"Miracles?" the man asked, surprised.

One of the guards riding in front snapped gruffly over his shoulder, "The best miracle you could do, lass, would be to smooth out that ugly face of his and make it bearable to look upon. 'Tis a sore sight to see after a night spent deep in the ale."

His companion up front laughed heartily and slapped the horses flanks with the reins.

"I said *wee* miracles," Marea corrected with a throaty Agatha chuckle. With a toss of her head, she flipped back the wet curls clinging to her brow. "What you ask be too much even for a seasoned witch with her hands free."

She felt the ropes drop away in the same instant she was surrounded by the men's burly laughter. Free. Her hands were free! Free for an instant, that is. The second the binding had slipped onto the hay, Chase's fingers were there to encircle her wrist in steely manacles. He held them firmly in place as she struggled to suppress the urge to rub her chafed flesh.

"I have a miracle for you," she said, her voice abruptly serious. Their laughter quickly fled as her sharp Agatha cackle gained the guards' attention. Even Chase stiffened.

"Aye, lass?" the guard in back murmured. He seemed to be growing bored with her game now, although his gaze remained alert—just in case. Agatha, after all, had earned her reputation well. "And what be it?"

"A dragon, methinks," she answered, as though

252

muttering to herself. She didn't miss the look of shock on the guard's face or the grunt of surprise that came from the two up front.

Her voice dropped to a low, cajoling pitch, thick with the witch's shrillness. "Aye, a dragon," she continued as though casting a spell. "As big as he be wide, with fangs the size of Kinclearnon's portcullis. And a fierce hunger, of course, though it be reserved solely for a man of the Douglas." She nodded, satisfied. The eyes were narrowed, glistening with amethyst challenge as she fixed her taunting gaze on the abruptly squirming guard. " 'Tis a wee miracle. Will it do?"

The man blinked, his gaze shifting uneasily between the girl and the guards up front—who seemed to wait expectantly for his answer. Only the glint of apprehension in his eyes said he no longer found the game amusing. Slowly, he nodded.

"Ah, a dragon it be then," she whispered a moment before her thick lashes swept down to caress moist cheeks.

The words came to her lips easily, a mixture of familiar Gaelic and nonsense syllables, woven together in no necessary order. As she breathed the words, she felt Chase's fingers drop away from her wrists. The wagonbed creaked when he shifted his weight, and she knew he was preparing to spring on their guards. When she wrapped her fingers around the thick cord of his wrists, telling him the time was not ripe, she felt his confusion ripple up her spine.

Her eyes snapped open so quickly that the guard gasped. He pressed his back hard against the wagon's side when he found himself captured by dazed eyes.

" 'Tis done," she whispered, her voice so high and tight that the man blinked and stared through the drizzle, as though to assure himself it was she who had spoken. A cold smile turned her tightly compressed lips. Her eyes were as hard as polished jewels when she lifted her face to the misty air and laughed.

The witch's cackle rang through the air, easily overriding the clap of horse hooves squishing in the mud, the jostle of wagons, the low murmur of male voices. More than one broad back shivered, as men quickly sketched the sign of the cross over their suddenly pounding hearts.

They were nearing a crossroads. Forest densely covered the land, lending the damp air a sappy aroma. Trees obliterated all but the twisting road they were on, but even that well-trod path was cast in ominous shadows by the overcast sky.

The man atop the wagon pulled sharply on the reins. When the wagon rolled to a stop, he held up a hand, indicating the wagons behind should do the same. As the creaking wheels stopped, another sound became apparent. Not the normal sound of the forest. It was a low, pounding noise that throbbed over the ground and made the wagonbed beneath them tremble through the hay. The noise rumbled behind the barrier of trees and drew closer with every passing heartbeat. It was echoed in the hiss of swords being yanked from scabbards and the thump of men climbing over the wagon sides and landing heavily in the mud.

"He be coming. Just as I said," Marea whispered, her voice shrill and sharp, yet oddly lulling. "And my dragon be fiercely hungry, looking to feast on Douglas men. Mayhaps if you kill him fast, the death toll will not be so great."

The man's eyes fixed on her in horror as he pulled

his sword free and thrust himself to his feet. His eyes were large, filled with disbelief . . . and fear. Like any good Scot, his superstitions ran deeply. She had played upon them and the result was indecision. His reaction was mirrored in the rest of the men. They didn't outwardly believe she had conjured up a dragon—of course not—but they weren't positive she hadn't either.

Her guard made a decision. With a feral growl he joined the others who scattered to the ground. The two who had driven the wagon were already there, inching toward the trees and the noise that grew steadily behind them. Their swords were poised in the air, leveled too high for an encounter with mortal men.

Marea almost laughed at their gullibility. The sound withered in her throat when Chase clamped a hand over her mouth. Her attention snapped up, and locked on shimmering emerald eyes a mere hairsbreadth away.

"We will speak of this later, vision," he growled as his fingers wrapped tightly around her arm. His gaze darkened when he was met with laughing amethyst eyes. "For now, we move."

With a flick of his wrist, he yanked her to her feet. He just as quickly released her, disappearing over the endboard.

Marea stumbled after him, trying to keep time with his long strides as he ran to the wagon behind them. Her skirts tangled in her legs, but she hoisted them high and charged after him.

One guard had been left behind, but he was near the front of the wagon, his gaze trained on the first rider to clear the trees from the path beyond the forest. The man's eyes widened when he realized the attack being launched came not from a dragon, but from a family of reivers returning from an afternoon raid. His gaze widened still more when Chase's fist connected with his jaw.

The guard toppled to the ground, landing in the mud with a squishy thud. He was unconscious by the time his sword had been wrested from his slackened grasp.

The scene was repeated at the next wagon, and the one after that. The second sword was thrust on Marea. The one after that pressed into Guy Falken's hands.

Marea scrambled into the second wagon and sawed through the bindings that held the prisoners tied to one another. When each was free, she shoved them over the wagon's side before turning to the next. One by one they ran to the shelter of the forest.

The last prisoner was free. Marea straightened as she watched him disappear over the side of the wagon. Her arm ached from the unaccustomed sawing motions. She shifted the heavy blade to the other hand and hurried to the end of the line. A quick glance saw Guy Falken working like a demon to cut the prisoners free in the last wagon. Chase was nowhere to be seen.

Since the sword was too unwieldy to maneuver as she climbed down, she tossed it onto the mud below. Lifting her skirt, she jumped awkwardly to the ground. She landed heavily, the wet dirt swallowing her ankles and making her skid to a sit. Her hand reached out to claim the sword at the same time she tried to thrust herself free. Her fingers met with sticky mud, and nothing else. The sword was gone.

She was instantly in a crouch. Her head snapped to the side, her gaze frantically scanning the ground.

The sword was truly gone, vanished, as though it had been sucked down into the mud without a trace. She wasted no time searching for it. Pushing herself to a stand, she hoisted her torn, dirty skirts and prepared to bolt for the trees, and safety.

She never made it so much as a step, for the instant her foot came up, her arm was grabbed from the side and the deadly tip of a sword was pressed firmly into her waist.

Her captor's laughter was as cold and sharp as the steel biting into her side. "A dragon?" the familiar voice taunted as he yanked her hard against a chest that smelled of sweat and mud. Lifting her gaze, Marea stared into the glowering countenance of the guard she'd duped.

"Did I say he would be large?" she asked, breathless. Fear coursed through her, but she shoved it aside. Holding up her free hand, she put her index finger and thumb, almost touching, beneath his flared nostrils. "I meant a *wee* dragon. Surely 'tis not my fault you misunder—"

"Enough!" The raw anger in his eyes made her wince. So did the fingers tightening around her tender arm. She waited for her fragile bones to snap in two under the pressure. "Your witch's tricks have played me for a fool. I'll not tolerate that."

"And what do you intend to do about it?" Common sense bade her to appear meek and pleading. Mac-Kenzie pride refused to allow it. Her chin thrust high as she met his gaze unflinchingly. She tried to wrench her arm free, but his grip held strong. "Will ye kill me? Me death will not salvage your pride, sir. 'Tis something ye threw to the dogs—or dragons, as the case may be—with little coercion needed from me."

He growled, his angry face lowering until they were nose to nose. "You'll pay for embarrassing me, witch. And pay dearly."

The point of his sword jabbed her side. The tip sliced through her clothes, and sank into her waist. He didn't slice deeply, only sinking the blade far enough for her face to pale and her eyes to widen. The cries of battle receded in her ears.

A chuckle of satisfaction rumbled through him. "Where be your spells now, witch? Where be your dragon when you need him?"

"Right behind you, you clumsy oaf!"

Marea caught the shimmer of a blade being lifted high. The hilt was brought down hard on the back of the guard's head. A look of surprise registered on his face, a second before his features melted to blankness. His fingers uncurled from her arm. The sword fell away as his eyes rolled back. The ground shook with his weight when he collapsed, unconscious, atop it.

Marea stepped back quickly to avoid being taken down with him. A sharp pain shot through her side. She pressed her palm to it and felt the hot stickiness of blood seeping through the layers of clothes. Stifling a gasp, her gaze lifted.

"M'lady," Guy Falken said, while cutting her a mock bow. He lifted the hilt of the sword to his forehead, then gestured with it to the forest. "After you."

Marea glanced in the direction he indicated, but the line of trees was already beginning to spin before her eyes. Her head felt strangely light, while the wound in her side felt as though it was on fire.

Guy Falken's brow furrowed with concern. Marea opened her mouth to assure him she was all right. She took a stumbling step toward him, and it was then she noticed how badly her knees were shaking. The sound of the battle was mere buzzing now, blotted out by what sounded like rushing waves in her ears.

Again, she opened her mouth. The words of reassurance never came. Her knees buckling beneath her, she was unconscious long before the mud rose up to meet her.

Chapter Eighteen

"If ye touch me again, I'll kill ye. I swear it."

This was spoken through gritted teeth. A thick fringe of burnished gold lashes snapped up. Dark amethyst eyes sparkled sharply beneath finely winged brows.

Marea's gaze locked and held glistening emerald eyes as she struggled to push herself up from the soft, moist cushion of the forest floor. Her hair had worked free of its plait; the red-gold strands now tumbled around her shoulders and face in a damp, tangled mass. "Stop your fussing, mon, I be fine," she snapped, and swatted his hands away from her waist.

Chase, who was hunkered down by her side, rocked back on his heels. "You aren't fine; you have a nasty gash in your side. I want only to staunch the flow of—"

" 'Tis but a flesh wound." Swiping the damp curls from her brow, she glared at him, silently challenging him to deny it.

Chase did so readily. His fingers flexed, then dropped to his lap. One golden brow cocked as he raked her face. Her skin was beaded with crystalline drops of rain and sweat. "A flesh wound?" he growled. "Nay, mistress, people do not swoon from flesh wounds, they gasp and look mortally offended."

" 'Twas not why I fainted." Her nose wrinkled with disgust. For herself, him, or the wound she was trying to brush off? Neither of them knew. Shivering delicately, she gathered the plaid close. The fabric was torn and tattered, and damp with rain and blood. The smell of the latter was pungent. It made her stomach roll. " 'Twas . . . 'twas the *blood,* mon. I canna stomach the sight or smell. Never could."

"Correct me if I'm wrong, mistress, but you didn't seem to mind the sight or smell of mine."

She shrugged. " 'Twas different. 'Twas yours."

"And because 'twas mine, you enjoyed watching it flow. Is that what you are telling me?"

His voice had turned softly coaxing. The tone immediately set her on guard. "Nay. I be telling you 'tis me own blood with which I have trouble. Me own blood that makes me stomach turn and me senses reel. If it belongs to another . . ." Again, she shrugged. This time, the gesture was stiff and brought a twinge to her stinging side. She winced.

Chase reached out to cup a cheek that went beyond white. His hand poised midair, then dropped back to his lap with a muffled *plop*. His gaze shifted to the men who mulled in hushed whispers at his back.

Behind the line of trees concealing them, Marea could hear the clash of steel. The cries of battle continued, but did not ring out as loudly. " 'Twas not wise to stop, *Sasunach.* Good ground could have been covered in the time you've wasted."

Slowly, his gaze swept back around. The hard glint in his eyes said he'd never considered continuing their escape. "You were wounded; no one knew how badly," he replied, his brows furrowed in confusion.

"So? You could have left me behind. I'd not want to think 'twas me and me weak stomach that foiled your escape."

"I'd not want to think of you bleeding in the dirt. 'Twas my decision. There's still time to make good an escape, now that you've woken and admitted the wound means naught. Can you ride?"

The spark of emotion she'd glimpsed so fleetingly in his eyes disturbed her beyond reason. It was gone now, but it had been there. She was sure of it.

"I can ride, *Sasunach*," she said finally. The pain in her side sharpened, but she voiced no complaint. For some reason, she didn't want this man to think she felt pain. She didn't want him to know she had any weaknesses at all. She didn't know why. A half smile pulled at the corner of her lips. "Mayhaps I can even ride better than yourself—*if* you've a beastie for me."

He returned her grin, though his eyes remained guarded. "I've a beastie, vision. Compliments of the Douglas. Right now, my concern is whether or not you'll fall off."

" 'Tis never happened before."

"Before." He inclined his head, his eyes sparkling. "I've no wish for today to be the sight of your first tumbling."

"Have a care, mon," she scoffed with an indignant toss of her head. "I'm stronger than I look. And a fine muckle more stubborn."

This time his hand did make contact with her face. He ran the tip of his calloused index finger down her outthrust jaw. " 'Tis not possible. You already look quite stubborn, witch."

"Be that a compliment?"

"Take it however you like." He grinned at her, and his hand opened to cup her cheek. The coolness of her skin against the warmth of his palm surprised and concerned him. As did the quivering he felt beneath the flesh. "We've miles to cover if we want to put good distance between ourselves and the Douglases. Are you sure you feel up to it?"

"Never better." Pride made her snap those words at him.

Two hours later, it was a pride she sorely regretted having. Her posterior knew every angle and bump of the jostling saddle beneath her. Her side had been throbbing when she'd mounted the beastie she'd grown with each mile to hate. Her plaid had been sliced by the sword point, the gap of cloth exposing her wounded flesh to the elements. At times, the cool autumn breeze made her skin icy. At others, like now, the wounded flesh felt as though it had been singed with the scalding hot tip of a poker. The pain was enhanced with each clomp of the mighty hooves trodding beneath her.

Her side was damp with blood that refused to clot. She could smell the ripe scent of it in the air, and it made her stomach roll. She refused to inspect her wound. She knew her shortcomings, knew that the sight of her own blood would make her swoon again, and topple into the mud that was beginning to cake under a beating, late afternoon sun. Such humiliation a MacKenzie must never suffer!

Instead, she suffered in a different way; silently. Her back ached from keeping it so rigidly stiff. Her eyes burned from the dirt the horses in front of her kicked up. Her mouth was dry, with remnants of that same dirt gritting between her teeth, scratching her throat. Her temples throbbed from grinding her teeth together. And her tongue was sore from where she had bitten it more than once to keep from crying out when her mount had quickened its pace.

An hour earlier, Chase had dropped back, his mount falling into step beside hers. As it had then, her gaze now sought out his rugged form. Her attention kept drifting to his swaying back. Twice she'd glimpsed his chiseled profile, and both times her heart had involuntarily leapt. Then, as now, she regretted the impulse to watch him. But her gaze refused to budge.

His seat on the horse was magnificent. He moved in time with it as though he and the beast were cast from the same iron mold. The legs gripping the horse's sinewy ribs were encased in dark blue trews. The tightness of cloth displayed each curve of steely muscle and tendon to perfection. Unlike the plaid she'd swathed her body in, he had only the thin yellow tunic to protect his broad shoulders and chest from the bite of the elements. Yet he seemed not the least bit cold.

His back was straight. The fingers encasing the reins were thick and tight and powerful. His cheeks were a healthy pink from the brisk air snapping at his skin. His hair was pleasantly ruffled and fluffed to a soft cloud of gold, threaded with strands of honey brown. Marea's grip on the reins tightened when she remembered the soft texture of each strand slipping between her fingers.

An hour before, he'd come, he said, to check on how she fared. But her horse, sidestepping a broken tree trunk in the path, had sent a pain shooting through her side and temples that had forced clipped answers through gritted teeth. Her amethyst eyes had shot him daggers, mirroring the ones that sliced through her side. Her foul mood had seen to it that he didn't tarry.

Sighing, Marea lifted her chin and tore her gaze away from Chase. The confusion the sight of him brought to her already floundering senses was a peril she couldn't afford. Right now she needed every ounce of willpower merely to keep herself in the saddle.

A movement at the front caught her eye. She squinted and focused, welcoming any distraction from the pain scorching her side and throbbing in her head.

The late afternoon sunlight glinted off the broadsword hanging at Guy Falken's side as he leaned toward Chase. The two exchanged a few brisk words she couldn't hear before the young man disengaged himself from the six men up front.

Guy Falken picked his way through the confusion of ragged men and stolen horses, his gaze seeking out Marea. Her heart tightened when she realized his destination was her side. She plastered a strained smile on her face to suit the man who'd saved her life, and called out a weak greeting.

"I've come to see how you feel," he said, reining his horse in step next to hers. Trained for the press of battle, the two mounts had no complaints about sharing such close quarters.

" 'Twould seem 'tis a popular pastime," she said with a hint of a smile. "The Graham inquired the same not an hour ago. I do not think he was pleased with me answer."

"And what was your answer, mistress?"

Despite the pain in her side, her grin blossomed. She sent him a mischievous glance and shrugged. "I told him to leave me in peace, and if he did not, I'd turn him to a pile of dry cinders so he could not ask it again."

Guy tipped his head back and laughed heartily. "Ah, so that explains his foul mood. I did wonder."

She'd made Chase cross? Now, why did the thought

please her ever so much? For just a second, the grinding pain in her side ebbed. "He does not share your good humor, sir, for he found nothing funny about my response."

"I'll wager he didn't." His laughter died to a strained chuckle. "Did you really say it to him? Most would not dare."

"I did." Then, with an obvious lack of concern she added, "Perhaps 'twas foolish of me, but—"

"Oh, nay, mistress." He waved aside her concern, such as it was, with a thickly gloved hand. "I've not known him long, but I'd say 'tis a refreshing thing to see that *someone* can get under his skin. Until now, we'd begun to think the young Graham not human. His lack of emotion is a rare thing in a man."

"Rarer still when it be genuine," she replied, thinking back on all the times she'd been in Chase Graham's company. Lack of emotion were not the words she would have chosen to describe a man like the Graham. In fact, she would have said he was *ruled* by his emotions. "Are ye sure we be talking of the same mon? 'Tis Chase Graham you be speaking of, not his da?"

A shiver of disgust rippled over the young man's shoulders. Though his distaste was quickly concealed, Marea knew she had seen it. "Aye, mistress, 'tis Chase. Only a blind man or a fool would confuse him with his sire, or compare them. 'Tis difficult to believe he sprang from the old laird's loins, so different are they. Beyond the physical resemblance, and that is fleeting, they are like dawn and dusk—one bright and promising, the other murky and dark."

Marea scowled as she contemplated this, but Guy Falken continued to speak as though he had not noticed her thoughtful lapse. "Now his brother Henry, from

266

what I hear, is the devil's own spawn. I've met him twice, and each time I came away from the meeting less than impressed." He leaned closer and confided over the clomp of hooves and rustle of leaves. "A meaner child I've never set eyes upon. Nor would I care to."

Henry Graham. Slowly, the image came to her. His hair was light and looked softer than spun silk. His young body promised a growth comparable to his brother's. At a glance, it was plain he would one day be strikingly handsome. But his good looks were deceptive. Even as a boy, there was something sinister about his eyes. It was that feature Marea remembered most about Henry Graham, his dark devil eyes, glistening like evil crystals beneath gold brows that slanted down in a sardonic V.

She'd never met him, but once, years ago, their paths had crossed. Quite literally. He'd bolted past her on a narrow dirt road, riding hellbent toward Kinclearnon. Marea was never sure what made him notice her, yet she'd known the second his malevolent eyes had settled on her. Those eyes had sparkled with evil intent when he yanked brutally on the reins. The horse, brought up unexpectedly, reared at the pressure to his mouth. The hooves that seconds ago had kicked up a suffocating cloud of dust danced treacherously close to Marea's veiled head. For one very long second, she had tasted imminent death. It had a bitter sting.

A shiver coursed up her spine when she recalled the boy sitting atop his flailing mount, his cruel laughter ringing in her ears before he jerked the horse around and charged off.

She'd been eighteen summers at the time, and the sight had fueled more than one gruesome nightmare. As a woman of twenty-five, Marea still found it hard not to sketch a quick cross over her breasts whenever his name was mentioned.

Her fists tightened on the reins. "Aye," she murmured, her gaze drawn like a magnet to Chase Graham's back. " 'Tis well I know the lad to be a cruel one. And 'tis thankful I am 'twas not he who inherited the title, but his brother."

" 'Tis thankful we all be," Guy agreed with enthusiasm. "One rough laird per century is all the men and I can stomach. I'd not be here today had things happened differently."

It was the closest Guy Falken would come to admitting the old laird's shortcomings. Marea nodded, deciding a swift change of topic was in order. "You'd not be here at all if 'twere your normal practice to sip witch's brews either, mon. Or did you forget about that?"

The young man's eyes widened, and his cheeks took on a pink tinge. The color could have been caused by a sharp breeze. But Marea knew better.

" 'Twas different," he said with a weak shrug, his gaze trained on the prickly pine they passed. "I—I didn't know who you were then. And . . . well . . ."

"Aye?"

"Truth to tell, you frightened me," he admitted bluntly. "Few can boast of surviving an encounter with the legendary Agatha. And even you must admit to having been less than . . . welcoming that day."

One of the horse's hooves caught in an animal's hole. Her mount lurched to the side, and Marea gasped when the pain in her side fired. To cover her wince, she sent the young man a look of feigned indignation. Her voice was slightly breathless. "I welcomed you. Few can brag about an encounter with Agatha, but even fewer can boast about sharing a table with her. You should be proud of the fact that you did—and lived to tell of it."

"Barely," he groaned good-naturedly. If he harbored any anger over what she'd done to him, he hid it well. "I was sick for days afterward. And had the most horrid nightmares. What was in that potion anyway? Eye of the newt? A few bat's toes? Frog's spleen? 'Tis how it tasted."

Even the pain that ripped through Marea's side couldn't stop her from chuckling. "Nothing so elaborate, I assure ye. 'Twas but herbs you were fed. Not tasty, mayhaps, but effective. I did not want to do it, mind you—you seemed fair nice—but your captain left me no choice." She grinned when she met and held his gaze. "Did it work?"

"I slept like a babe for hours, if that is what you're asking," he answered evasively.

" 'Twas not me question, as you well know. I know the herbs for sleep worked—'tis the others, in that combination, that tickle me curiosity. Tell me. Did it work?"

His brown eyes widened, sparkling like amber in the sun filtering down through the leaves. "Don't you know?"

"Nay. 'Twas my first love potion."

"First?" His face drained white, then flooded crimson. "Do you mean to tell me you'd never made the brew before? That you tested it for the first time on," he gulped, "me?"

"Aye. But answer me question. Did it work?"

If possible, the splash of color in his cheeks darkened. His answer seemed to surprise even himself. "Aye, it did."

"Sally?"

"How did you know?"

Her gaze shimmered with mischief. "I be a witch. 'Tis not much I do *not* know."

269

"I thought you said you were a healer?"

"To most, 'tis one in the same."

He nodded, and they lapsed into companionable silence. A satisfied smile played over Marea's lips. Her first love potion had worked! At least, it appeared to have. As with every new concoction she brewed that was successful, she was as surprised as she was pleased.

Her gaze fixed on Chase Graham's back. The beginnings of a plan hatched in the back of her mind and her smile broadened. The idea was immediately dismissed, of course. The Graham would never be as foolish and gullible as this man had been. Still, the thought made for interesting speculation. And it took her mind off the pain.

"I return to the front," Guy Falken confided in a hushed tone that made her strain to hear him. "If the dark looks being cast my way have anything to say about it, my company back here is not appreciated."

Marea's wandering attention now snapped to the young man. A bolt of foreboding, mixed with an anticipation she tried hard not to feel, shot through her. "Oh? By whom?"

"Who else?" He grinned, jerking his chin in the direction of Chase's swaying back.

Her eyes narrowed and she shook her head. "I do not see any dark looks. Methinks you're imagining them."

"Nay, mistress. 'Twould appear my lingering at your side has increased my laird's displeasure. I've seen that look in his eyes before, and it bodes no good. There'll be hell to pay when we break for camp. Of that you may be sure."

She scowled. "But why? You came back to check on me. 'Tis no more than he did an hour ago. He canna find fault there."

"He can. And he will." The brown eyes sharpened with an intelligence that did not belong on his youthful face. "You sent the Graham away when he dropped back to speak with you. *I* am still here. 'Tis reason enough for him to want my blood."

"Nay, you maun be mistaken," she argued, shaking her head and glancing away. "I see no reason to merit his wrath."

"Can you not? Truly?"

Her eyes shimmered with confusion. "Truly."

His chuckle of pure delight rang through the air. The sound bristled up her spine as it mingled with the soft chirp of birds.

"Stop that snorting. I do not see the humor." She jerked hard on the reins as they rounded a corner. "I tell you he does not care who I be talking to, nor for how long."

"Aye. If you say so, mistress."

She glanced at him sharply. "Are ye saying differently?"

His smile melted as his lips pursed thoughtfully. "I'm not saying anything at all—either way. 'Tis none of my affair."

With a flick of his wrist, he guided his horse away from hers. Marea knew a moment of despair, for his company had helped pass the time and take her mind off the agony in her side. She was reluctant to see him go.

"I'll drop back to check on you later, if you don't mind," he said from over a shoulder as his horse stepped around hers.

"I would enjoy it."

His gaze narrowed assessively, until he spotted the sincerity that sparkled in her eyes. A friendly smile turned his lips, and he seemed pleased to find the gesture instantly returned.

"You saved me life," she said. "And I've spared yours twice. It should make us friends, would you not agree?"

"Aye. Methinks 'twould go better for me to have the infamous Witch o' the Mist as an ally, not foe. If you're offering friendship, 'tis willing I am to take it — and offer up my own."

" 'Tis willing I am. And glad of it."

He started picking his way through the scattered horses and men. "I'll return," he said by way of farewell.

Marea's gaze softened as she watched him go. Although she'd never expected to strike up a friendship with the man, she found herself pleased that she had.

Sighing, she pulled her attention away. It automatically settled on Chase. Their gazes met.

Her breath caught, and her heart skipped. The fingers that had been about to cover her wounded side poised in midair. She tried to wrench her gaze away but it refused to budge.

The skin over his cheeks was drawn tight, his gaze shifting between herself and Falken. The muscle in his jaw ticked. Anger radiated from him like the heat of a roaring fire; it covered her like a smothering blanket.

She swallowed hard and noticed his free hand was poised on the hilt of his stolen sword. There wasn't a scrap of warmth in the gaze that was torn from her own and fixed steadily on the young man who fell silently into step beside him.

Chase faced abruptly forward. Without a word, he jerked hard on the reins and dug his heels deep in the sinewy black's flanks. As one, horse and rider bolted down the twisting path, and soon lost themselves to the murky shadows playing in the distance. Only a gritty cloud of dirt spoke of their passing.

The look on Guy Falken's face, in that split second before he turned away, said clearly, "I tried to tell you, mistress, but you chose not to listen."

Chapter Nineteen

It had been a long day, and Chase felt every commanding hour of it in the soreness of his aching muscles. His body protested when he lowered himself to sit in the shaggy carpet of grass.

Though he feigned interest in the conversations around him, his mind drifted. He mouthed clipped answers, but none that demanded him to think. Those who tried to include him in conversation soon gave up when they noticed his emerald gaze was trained fast on the place where the hazy firelight melted into a flickering circle of velvet darkness.

Men muttered, a few laughed, all drew closer to the fire in search of warmth. The smart ones gave Chase a wide berth. Most had seen that look in his eyes enough times to know when their company would not be appreciated.

The horses were tethered to trees. They snorted their own form of disdain as their hooves restlessly clapped the ground. The air was sharp with the scent of scorched wood and the close press of bodies who'd ridden the day hard. Even the aroma of burnt rabbit was overridden by the smell of leather and sweat. The cold night air could do nothing to dispel it.

His eyes still trained on the night outside the circle of fire, Chase lowered himself to his side. His weight forced the ground to conform to the rigid contours of his body. With elbow bent, the knuckles of his fist supported his eagle-sharp cheek. The fringe of his hair caressed his sun-bronzed forearm and wrist.

His eyelids were lowered to half-mast, his emerald gaze apparently indifferent beneath sharply drawn brows. As it had for the better part of the afternoon, the muscle in his cheek ticked. The fingers of his free hand combed through the grass. The stalks felt like icicles against the warmth of his flesh. Three steady breaths were drawn deeply into his lungs, then released. The brisk, cleansing air had no effect on him.

Where the devil was she?!

An hour before, Chase had watched Marea sneak away from the men and delve into the shadows of the night. Chase thought he was the only one who had noticed her absence. His first instinct had been to follow at a safe distance—only for her protection, of course. The sight of Guy Falken also slipping away scarcely a minute later, a scowl of concern furrowing the young brow, had stopped him cold.

Rage had sliced through Chase, burning him to the core, shocking him with its intensity. One of the hardest things he had ever done was to suppress it. But suppress it he had. For the last hour his anger had simmered, twisting in his gut. But he was only human and, since his fury refused to be banished, he could only deny it for so long. It was only a hairsbreadth away from the boiling point. Rigid self-control had held it in check until now. But it was a control that wouldn't last, for he could already feel it chipping away, leaving him raw and furious.

His fingers closed around a handful of grass. The delicate green stalks were ripped from the ground and tossed away. He shifted his gaze to the stars glittering like fiery diamonds over the silhouetted treetops. Every throbbing beat of his heart rang clear and pronounced in his ears; the sound taunted his mounting rage when his gaze once again dipped . . . and focused on the darkness out of reach of the flickering firelight.

The decision, if there truly was one, was made in the space of a single heartbeat. Scarcely another had passed before Chase was on his feet. The man who had been asking him a question was now rudely shown Chase's back as he stalked toward the covering of trees and night.

Brisk autumn air soon undid the warmth drawn from the fire. To compensate, anger raced through his veins, igniting his skin to a fevered pitch. It heated him far better than mere flames. The crackle of burning wood dwindled behind him, as did the sound of men and horses. Soon, all noise was overridden by the crunch of leaves beneath his boots, and the rush of his breath hissing through gritted teeth. His hands were tight fists that rhythmically clenched and released at his sides.

He had no idea where he was going. Marea and Falken could be anywhere in this forest. For all he knew, they could be on their way back to Kinclearnon. He wouldn't be surprised. He was no longer shocked by anything Marea did.

Marea. Her name wrapped possessively around his heart, as though it belonged there. He couldn't shake the feeling free. In fact, it was so strong he was almost staggered by it. What was it about her that attracted him? And how often had he asked himself that question without ever finding an answer to it?

Oh, he knew their first meeting—when his father had raided the keep—had played on his pity and compassion. How could it not? But the scene was a repeat of many played out before it. In the time he'd been with his father, Chase had seen many women thrust into the same circumstances as those in which he'd found Marea.

But those women were vague, shapeless memories. Marea was not. Marea he had never forgotten, as he'd thought he would, *should*. Something about her obsessed him.

Time had softened his memory, enhanced it until no woman could favorably compare. Even that dreadful night in her kitchen, there was something about her—much more than just her beauty—that fascinated him. Even then, when she was at her most defenseless, he'd sensed her pride, her determination, her presence of being. And he'd been strongly attracted to it. For some reason, it was an attraction the years had honed, when they should by all rights have faded and diminished it.

As Chase plunged headlong into the forest, his thoughts took an abrupt turn. Though he had always held the girl of his memories as an ideal, his dreams had gifted the lovely creature with quite a different personality. He'd pictured her as a woman who sat by the hearth pricking needlework and awaiting her man's return from a Border raid unharmed. Such was what he expected from his own wife, when he found one to suit him. Yet he could not imagine Marea meekly waiting for anything or anyone. More likely, she'd be found *leading* the raid. Oddly enough, though it infuriated Chase to think of her risking her life, it also filled him with a certain sense of pride.

Her need to be in the thick of action was but one of her traits that angered him beyond reason. Ironically, it was that same trait he found admirable. She tested his patience by trying to take something that, by right, was his. Kinclearnon. She infuriated him by duping him into believing her a two-thousand-year-old crone. But what really rankled was that she defied him at every turn, refusing to bend to his wishes. That taunted him . . . and enticed him beyond reason.

As for the passion he'd tasted twice—oh so briefly—well, that haunted him most of all. No matter how strongly Chase told himself he *could not* be attracted to her, the memory of her softness twisting beneath him ate into his nights, igniting a fire in him that only her sweet surrender was able to quench.

He wanted her. Again. Even now. The heat of his anger couldn't abolish white-hot desire. It was untenable to think that Guy Falken might now be quenching her passion. For a split second, bloodlust coursed hot through his veins. This time, he made no attempt to suppress it.

His footsteps quickened, guided by animal instinct alone. Water gurgled in the distance. Slowly, another sound disengaged itself from the night—the tickle of soft, fleeting, feminine laughter. The sound rippled up his spine, pricking the hairs at his nape. The laughter was gone as quickly as it had come, but not so soon that Chase could not decipher its direction.

His reaction was fast and fierce. Clamping his teeth together, he bounded through the underbrush like a charging lion. His broadsword slapped at his thigh, unnoticed. No attempt was made to hush his approach. He found the two sitting atop a boulder, their heads bent together as a confidence was exchanged. Their voices whispered in the air, but the words were swallowed by the angry throb of his heart.

A stream gurgled, twisting near their feet. The water's churning matched the emotions roiling through Chase.

He stood at the border of trees, his shoulder leaning against rough bark, his arms crossed tightly over his chest. Waiting, watching, angering. He could have been a vital part of the tree against which he rested, so still was he. Neither acknowledged his glowering presence, and their blatant disregard did nothing to ease his fury.

"Nay," she said, her tone rising above the softly churning stream and rustling leaves. Chase's gaze narrowed on the indignant toss of her red-gold head, on hair that had taken the pale quality of satin-spun moonlight. Her skin looked soft and white, a glowing contrast to the black velvet night. " 'Twas me da's before, and 'twill be mine next. 'Tis me fate. Not a soul can wrest it away, though many may try."

"And succeed from the looks," Guy Falken responded, his tone dead serious. " 'Twould seem more than one soul has already tried, mistress. And succeeded. The Graham. The Douglas. Methinks the latter will not surrender without a fight, while the former has already proven as much."

"Then 'tis a fight they shall have. Kinclearnon belongs to the MacKenzie. 'Tis there it will pass next, and stay." She paused for the space of a heartbeat. Her next words sliced through Chase like a finely honed dagger. "For too long me people have lived under the tyranny of a rough laird. They be good, kind folk. Undeserving of Graham or Douglas harshness. I'll see peace restored, or I'll die in the attempt."

Guy Falken responded. Chase never heard the young man's softly spoken words. Blind fury pumped in his ears, echoed in the throbbing of his heart. For so long he had striven not to be like his father, yet all his effort seemed for naught. This woman believed him to be a mirror image of the man he detested. Nothing he had done had changed her opinion. The knowledge infuriated him, luring him into a decision he would not have ordinarily made. If she believed him to be like David Graham, who was he not to live up to her expectations?

Chase pushed away from the tree. The crunch of his boots over dry leaves and twigs announced his presence. "The keep was given to a Graham in good faith by *your* young king," he announced, his voice a deadly pitch above the rustle of night sounds and the splashing of his feet as he carelessly walked through the stream. "And *there* is where it shall stay."

The two heads snapped up simultaneously. Guy Falken had the good sense to look chagrined as he automatically slipped from the rock and stood on shaky feet. His hand drifted to his sword hilt, then dropped away as recognition dawned.

Chase spared Falken a passing glance, then ignored him. His gaze fixed on Marea, bathed in flickering silver moonlight, and nothing on heaven or earth could have budged it.

Her chin jutted up. Their gazes locked. "Good faith? And what would a Graham be knowing of that?"

"Apparently, more than a MacKenzie."

"Ye think it? You, son of the man who slaughtered me family?"

If she'd been hoping to antagonize an answer out of him, she succeeded admirably. Only his response was not verbal.

The second his fingers closed around her slender arms, Chase knew he'd made a mistake. Touching her was never wise, but he would rather die than admit to it. With a flick of his wrist, he dragged her from the rock and drew her up hard against him.

Another, bigger mistake. Now he had the sweetness of her breath against his whiskered jaw with which to contend. Her body was pliant, wiggling against him, struggling for a balance. The anger churning in his gut channeled into another, baser emotion—one that jolted through him like a sizzling bolt of lightning.

Guy Falken shifted from one foot to the other. Only a blind, deaf man wouldn't know there was something more than a disagreement going on there. The sparks flying between the laird he'd pledged his life to protect and his new found friend crackled in the air. For a second he toyed with the idea of slipping away, knowing neither would notice. But his sense of honor ran too strong; it left no room for such a cowardly retreat.

"She meant no harm, Chase. Truly," Falken interceded, and was rewarded with a sharp glare that made him squirm.

"You're needed back at camp. Don't delay in finding your way there, or in telling the others to stay clear of this forest until I return."

Chase held tight to her slender arms and velvet gaze as he listened to Falken's hesitant retreat. He saw a flash of alarm in Marea's eyes. It was quickly doused, but not before he felt a ripple of tension in the soft arm crushed by his fingertips. He thought he saw a moment of fear twist her expression. Real or imagined, it ate at him.

Common sense told Chase to push her away before her soft curves could do more damage to his melting composure. Instinct kept his fingers curled around her arms. His iron grip reminded him of where his anger should be. He let that anger flow through him as he barked, "Say it. I dare you to say it."

Obstinately, she held her tongue. He gave her a brisk shake. "Say it." Her jaw hardened. *"Say it,* damn you!"

The eyes sparked with an anger to match his own. She could hold the words back no longer. "Say what? That I hate you? Aye, I'll say it over and over if 'twill make you believe it." Her fingers, splaying his chest, curled inward, fisting his tunic. "For everything you stand for, for everything you and your family have done to me and mine . . . aye, *I hate you!"*

"Liar."

The word cut through her at the same time his

282

mouth crashed down on hers. If any distance separated them, it was spanned by his hand, dragging her roughly against his length.

Chapter Twenty

Agatha had once said that a moth could feel the heat of a fire on its wings even as it drew closer to a deadly flame, but that instinct compelled it onward. Marea felt that way now. Her anger peeled away, and she couldn't stop from drawing closer to his heat.

Chase Graham was her deadly fire; his hot kiss was slow and sweet, hard and punishing in turn.

"You don't hate me," he growled against her lips. His breath wafted over sensitive lips and cheeks. "You can try—with your dying breath you can try—but you can't hate me any more than I can hate you."

"But I do." It was a weak argument. The moist flicker of his tongue on her lips elicited a groan she would have given her life to suppress.

"I'll not believe you. I *cannot* believe you."

"You must."

"I'll not." His hands slid down her arms. When she made no move to pull away, but instead leaned weakly against him, he circled her waist and pulled her up hard. There was but an ache in her side; the salve she had applied not an hour before was working. That, and his warm palms riding the curve of her hips, rubbing her against him until she thought she would die from the pleasure of it, kept the pain at bay. Her body pulsed in response to the feel of his hips grinding against hers, and the feel of her breasts straining against the firmness of his chest.

"Your da—"

"Is dead." His lips trailed feverish kisses along her jaw.

"But—"

"I'm not like him, dammit!" His head lifted. His hands slipped from her waist, cupping her chin and wrenching her gaze back when she tried to look away. His voice rang with steely conviction, as though he was trying to convince himself as well as her of the truth in his words. "I'm not like my father."

"You're his son." She tried to twist away, but his grip was now as hard as the boulder grinding into her back.

"I cannot deny it, much as I would like to," he snarled. The scowl drawing his blond brows together told Marea how much that admission cost him. "The man was my sire, but he was never a father to me. 'Tis a fact with which I've long lived. It has taken my entire life to realize I do not have to be like him. That I am not like him. Many's the year I've wasted thinking I was."

"You've not proven it to me, *Sasunach.*"

His gaze, if possible, sharpened. His fingers loosened, and slipped down to gently curl around her throat. There was no pressure, but it was insinuated there could be soon. "Haven't I? I could have killed you easily, many times. That first night. In your shack. The morning you raided my keep." His tone

285

lowered to a deadly pitch. "Now. Even the Middle March Wardens would agree I am well within my rights to do so."

Marea swallowed hard. It was impossible to ignore the calloused thumb stroking her neck, impossible not to realize that it would take only the slightest bit of pressure to steal her precious supply of air. "T-then do it."

He shook his head, and she caught a momentary flicker of horror in his gaze. It was quickly concealed, but the memory of it rippled down her spine. "I've no desire to hurt you, but that is not the point!" he shouted, as though in raising his voice the words might have a better chance of penetrating her skull. "What do you think David Graham would have done had he been the one to catch you raiding his keep? What do you think he would do to you now? Providing, of course, he'd have let you live this long—which I sincerely doubt."

She shivered, but did not answer. His hands slipped over the curve of her neck, until his warm palms were shelved atop her shoulders. His anger made the weight feel like lead.

"I think we both know the answer, do we not?"

"Aye," she snapped. Shrugging his hand off, she stepped away. A twig snapped beneath her boot, and she wondered why he'd let her go.

"But you still compare me to him?"

"Aye!" She crossed her arms over her chest and leaned against the rock. At that moment, only the rigid firmness of the boulder kept her upright. "Guy said you never liked your da. I've seen as much myself, but I canna trust it. I'll not be duped by a Graham again."

Her back was to him. Marea did not see the way his jaw hardened with fury, and his eyes darkened to tiger green. Battle-roughened fingers curled into tight fists at his sides. " 'Guy,' is it now? 'Twould appear you and he have come far since this morn," he growled through gritted teeth. "At dawn you could hardly stomach the sight of each other, yet now you address him familiarly. Is there a reason for this sudden intimacy, mistress?"

"I do not like your tone, mon."

"Pity. I've no intention of changing it."

"How dare you — !"

Marea spun on her heel. Her stained plaid whipped around her ankles. She hadn't heard his stealthy approach, and she almost collided into him. Her hands lifted to steady herself, until she realized she was about to touch his firmly worked chest. The heat of his body seeped into her palms and shot up her arms with alarming swiftness. Inhaling quickly, she dropped her trembling hands to her sides, as though she'd just grazed a very hot, very lethal flame.

"I dare much where you are concerned, wench," he snapped, his fingers clamping around her jaw. His skin was warm, his breath hot as it singed her cheek and neck. Neither could compare to the fire in his eyes. " 'Tis but little compared to what I will dare if you don't spit out the truth. Now!"

Her gaze widened. In her lifetime, she'd seen many a man angered. But none had she feared as much as this man, this minute. She arched, trying to put distance between them.

He bowed forward, until his face loomed threateningly above her. The moonlight sculpted his features hard. His eyes glinted like cold stones in the flickering silver rays.

The rock ground into the back of her head and her fingers curled into its gritty surface. There was no give, much like the firm maleness pinning her to the boulder.

"Should I take your silence as guilt?" he asked. A sliver of ice laced his tone and settled around Marea like a blanket dipped in a cold mountain spring. "Will you make no halfhearted defense of yourself or your lover? Or is it that you cannot bring yourself to deny the truth?"

Whether by accident or design, his hips ground against her. Lightning sparked through her veins. She fought her body's response, fought it with all her might, but she was no match for it. Her hands came away from the rock and encircled his back. Her fingers dug into the rippling flesh beneath the tunic. She told herself she did it for balance. But she knew better than to believe such a blatant lie. And so did he.

A groan tore from Chase's throat. His mouth lowered for a bruising kiss, one that was returned measure for hungry measure.

"Tell me, vision," he growled against her lips. His hands roved her body, quick and urgent, leaving a trail of tingling fire in their wake. "Tell me you've not lain with Falken, for if you have, you seal his fate. By all that's holy, I'll tear the pup limb from traitorous limb."

Her lashes flickered closed as her tongue darted out to flick over his moist lips. He tasted of roasted rabbit and sparkling sweet water. He smelled of leather and sweat. These things sensuously combined with the heat of his flesh beneath her fingertips. Her wall of resistance crumbled, if indeed there was one left.

" 'Tis not a lad I be wanting, *Sasunach*." Her voice was a throaty moan, unrecognizable as it mingled with the night sounds echoing around them. Her eyes opened and she was captured by a sea of emerald green.

"Then what do you want, vision?" He pulled back. Holding her shoulders firmly, he looked into her eyes, into her soul. His hips ground against hers, leaving no doubt as to his own lusty wants. "Tell me. Say it now, while you can. 'Tis the last chance you'll have to stop this madness."

"Nay, do not stop! I-I mean, I . . . I want a mon, not a bairn," she confessed almost shyly. Almost. "I want . . ." Her gaze dropped to his lips, moist and full from their kisses. The taste of him still warmed her tongue, and left her craving more. Her eyes darkened to purple fire when she added breathlessly, "You, Chase Graham. God help me, 'tis you I want."

It was the first time he could remember her saying his name. It rolled over her tongue, touched by her lilting brogue until her lips transformed it into what seemed to his ears like a prayer. His heart tightened, as did his grip on her shoulders. He was excruciatingly aware that his body possessively sandwiched her softness between hard stone and equally hard maleness.

"Marea. Sweet, sweet Marea." He buried his face in the satiny cloud of her hair. "You've no idea what you've done. No idea of the demons you've just unleashed in me."

"I know," she rasped. "And they be matched by me own."

She lifted her chin. Hungrily, his lips sought her

sensitive throat. His tongue flicked over her jaw. His teeth nipped the delicate hollow beneath. Her skin tasted as creamy as it appeared in the shadowy moonlight. Chase knew, for he devoured every inch.

With his hands pinning her to the boulder, Marea could not feel him the way she wanted to. Her palms burned to stroke his back, to feel the rigidity of his muscle bunching under her fingertips. A moan of frustration rumbled in her throat, and was mirrored by his husky chuckle.

"Nay, witch, you'll not hurry me. Not this time," he growled against the pulse beating desperately in her throat. "Twice I've let you drive me too far too fast. Past the point where I can enjoy you fully. 'Twas no way for you to learn of loving. But tonight . . . aaah, tonight 'tis *my* pace we follow. And my pace is set torturously slow."

This was a command he gave to his own traitorous body, for even as he said it, he had doubts about upholding such a promise. His need for her was hot and fierce, humming through him like a battle cry demanding swift, sure action.

"Witch," he hissed as he peeled away the plaid. In seconds, he'd exposed her from the waist up. His hungry gaze roved the body he had pinned to the rock. The pulse beating wildly in her throat fluttered against his knuckles and set his blood on fire as his passion-darkened gaze drank in vivid perfection.

"I'm not a witch," she said, then whimpered when he leaned into her, and suckled a rosy bud into his hot, moist mouth. "I'm a healer."

Marea's fingers dug into the tunic and flesh of his steely forearms. Her chin rose in pleasure, not pride. Her lashes flickered down.

290

"I stand . . . corrected. You're worse than a witch, you're . . . a bloody sorceress," he replied huskily, between lapping at one swollen nipple—his teeth teased until she thought she would die—while his calloused index finger flicked at the other. "Not that you'll find me complaining."

Her back arched away from the boulder as he drew her into his mouth time and again. The other breast was experiencing similar delights as the firm contours were molded and remolded to the shape of his palm. A prickle of whiskers scraped her flesh. Marea found an uncanny pleasure in the masculine feel of it.

She clutched at him. The only thing that held her upright was the solid wedge of rock, and the equally solid man, for her own knees were too weak to support her.

Chase's promise of slow and easy evaporated as he felt her fingers slipping between their bodies. They brushed his taut stomach, poised in the act of straying lower. He relaxed, allowing her room. Her touch was slow, hesitant, almost coy. It stopped almost as soon as it had begun. He groaned.

Had he not closed his eyes to savor the aching pleasure of her touch, he would have seen Marea's hesitant grin of victory; would have seen her amethyst eyes darken with unknown sensual power. As it was, he was having a devil of a time not taking her here. Now. Fast and hard, with her back pressed against the stone. Lord knew, his body cried out for it, begged for it, *demanded* it.

"Did you like that?"

Her voice was so soft it might have been the breeze that caressed his cheek when his head snapped up. Their gazes met as, in a moment of extreme boldness, she caressed the bulge beneath his trews. He was long and hard and hot.

"Aye, vision." His voice had the gusty quality of a hurricane about to be unleashed. "Very much."

"And this?" she asked, not quite as shyly. Her fingers found what little give there was to the cloth. She gripped the long, smooth sides of him and slid her fingers down to the base in one satiny stroke. "Do you like this as well?"

His hips arched forward and her inquisitive hand was abruptly crushed between them. His firmness on one side, her softness on the other. Marea thought she could die from the pleasure firing through her.

His reply was a long, husky gasp and a distinct darkening of his eyes. Her heartbeat quickened, and she thought she would gladly drown in those bright emerald pools, pools that glistened with desire as her fingers began a leisurely ascent. The softness of the cloth as it slid against her fingertips was a stark contrast to the hot firmness beneath, a firmness that grew in her palm.

She opened her mouth. Chase, knowing his control was now only a solid shaft of power held in long, soft, playful fingers, sealed her words with a scorching kiss. His body covered her — hungrily, possessively, and oh, so firmly — as he pressed her against the boulder. Her breasts strained into his chest, branding his flesh.

The kiss deepened. Tongues met and thrusted. Parried and retreated. Mated. He nibbled her lips. She tasted his, running her tongue along the rigid line of his teeth. He sucked the honey-pink tip into his mouth. She ran her tongue along the length of his before coaxing it back into her own mouth.

Her hands were never still as they explored the rigid

firmness of his body. Her palms burned with each inch of male flesh they touched.

His battle-roughened fingers closed over her breasts, rubbing the aching tips against his tunic. He pushed the plaid lower. It fluttered to her small feet in green folds that were quickly stepped out of and kicked aside. Her boots came off and were thrown aside. Her travel-wilted underclothes were swiftly stripped away.

Chase groaned, a sound of animal lust, as his gaze devoured what the cloth had hidden, and hidden well: High, thrusting breasts, the nipples rosy in the moonlight; a small waist that could be spanned by two hands with room to spare — he knew because he did it; hips that were slim, but not boyish; creamy thighs and calves that were perfection.

His hands trembled as his palms worshipped the hidden valley of her stomach. Silky smooth, it quivered under the skilled caress. He took special care not to disturb her tender side. His tongue paid homage to the pulse beating wildly in the hollow of her throat — such a long, glorious expanse of flesh, and so tasty. He died a little at the feel of her fingers fluttering over his body. She dragged the tunic over his head, then worked clumsily at the fasteners securing his trews and hose.

She never got to the boots. With a growl of impatience, Chase moved away from her only long enough to strip the trappings away. Where they landed after being tossed briskly aside, he didn't know. Didn't care. Three throbbing heartbeats later, his body was again pressing against warm feminine softness. There was only time for a single shiver of cold to shake her shoulders.

And then there was no cold—only white heat. Heat that emanated from the rock-solid maleness grinding seductively, demandingly, against her. Heat from her own inflamed senses and the urgency that matched his.

Ah . . . tonight, Marea thought as she was lowered onto a bed of moonlit clover. Tonight she was going to be loved as never before—and probably die from the pleasure of it. Slowly. Torturously.

The grassy blanket tickled her back as she wrapped her arms around the thick cord of Chase's neck and pulled him down on top of her. He pinned her to the ground, his arms scooping her close as though trying to melt into her. His heart hammered against her breasts. The fevered tempo excited her own heart to racing.

He sucked in a thick breath when she wiggled insistently beneath him. The air was released in a ragged groan. Her hair smelled of fresh forest sap and sunshine, a heady combination to tease his already fevered senses.

His restraint was gone. He existed on willpower alone and even that was tenuous. His need for her was so great it was palpable. It was a need surpassed only by the desire to give as good as he got.

Her body was alive, coiled with anticipation, hot wherever he touched her. The smell of him, leather and sweat, pine and wind, was more intoxicating than the spiciest of colognes. She inhaled deeply, reveling in the sharp, tingling sensations the smell of him inspired. She released her breath slowly, heavily, letting it ruffle the soft golden hairs against his cheek.

The torment of anticipation was beginning to eat at her. How much longer must she wait? She was no longer the giggling maiden, no longer innocent in physical pleasures. She knew what was possible, knew what she wanted, and she wanted it *now*. Her legs came up to grip steely hips and wrap around them. Her own hips arched in blatant invitation, coaxing him to break his restraint.

His elbows flanked her sides. The fingers of one hand toyed with a rosy, achingly erect nipple. Her whimper fired down his spine. Chase lifted his mouth from the delicate earlobe on which he'd just been dining. His hair scraped her neck, and he heard her pull in a quick little breath. Her fingers tightened, her nails biting into his back. If there was pain, he was beyond noticing it. She strained urgently into his chest, trapping his hand between heaven and hell, sweetness and light.

"I'm thinking I won't be as slow as I would have liked, vision," he rasped. His gaze searched out every contour of her face, committing it to memory. His breath wafted over her skin as his eyes devoured.

"I do not want slow," she replied thickly, huskily. Her fingers scraped down his back, and she saw his eyes darken. Her undulating hips told him exactly what she did want.

He entered her slowly, by his own design, fighting the insistent legs wrapped around him that would have him move faster. When she arched up, her body demanding more, he held back. He captured her confused amethyst gaze. He forced his words through tight lips—lips that wanted to do anything but talk. "What, exactly do you want, vision?" His voice was as deep and as gritty as the floor of the stream gurgling at their feet. His hips applied more pressure, and he sank in a little deeper. But not enough. Not nearly enough. "Tell me. Say it."

"This," she hissed, her lips drawn back in pleasured torment. "Now." Her hips teased him, her hands slipped down to cup his buttocks, trying to draw him deeper, failing. "Chase, *please!* Do not tease me. I could not bear it."

The sound of his name on her lips was his undoing. He closed his eyes and tried to summon back some of the control that had so rudely abandoned him. But it was too late. Control was gone. Patience was forgotten. Restraint was a foreign term. Right now, he needed to feel himself completely surrounded by the warm honeyed softness that was even sweeter than he remembered. Much, much sweeter. And warmer. And wetter. And tighter.

He was poised at her very threshold. The moist sheath beckoned him, lured him, invited him inside with a silken promise that threatened to devour him whole. Arching his back, he gave one quick thrust and buried himself inside her. A groan shattered the night, and it was only in afterthought that he recognized it as his own.

"Ah . . . tonight," Marea sighed huskily in his ear. It was all she said, all she was capable of saying. He made sure of it.

His mouth covered hers. His kiss was bruising in its intensity, his tongue matching the fevered strokes of his body, a body that told him his desire to last through this sweet torture for anything longer than a minute was nothing more than a wild, unrealistic dream.

His pace quickened. His heart hammered. His chest and palms were moist with perspiration, almost as moist as the softness enshrouding him. If his body had its way, he would have already reached the precipice towering before him. That snowcapped mountain of satisfaction. But he had no intention of scaling those cliffs alone. He would bring the delicate beauty who clutched at him and whimpered plaintively with him, or he wouldn't go at all.

She was ready. More than ready. For a lifetime, Marea had waited for this moment and now that it was here she wanted to savor it for another lifetime. But she couldn't. What had started out as a gentle lapping of sensations in the crossroads of her thighs and stomach soon had built into a tidal wave of rhythmic excitement. She was drowning in a sea of desire, but she was a willing victim. An eager one. She wanted to die, enfolded in the pleasure that was tugging at her body, building, churning within her like a tumultuous ocean storm.

And then it washed over her. So sudden in its impact that her entire body reeled with the force of it. The spasms crashed over each other, heightening with each hard thrust and retreat. She reveled in the tingling feel, not wanting to let go of such exquisite sensations for so much as a heartbeat.

The muscles beneath her fingertips bunched and turned to steel. His breathing came harsh and ragged, caressing her hot skin. His flesh was slick, and, oh, so smooth as it glided beneath her suddenly sensitive palms, slipping against other parts of her body. She felt him quiver, felt him drive his last thrust, hard and deep. And then she felt the liquid warmth of him burst like a flame inside her.

They lay entwined for seconds, minutes, hours. The brisk night cooled their fevered bodies. The rustle of leaves, the gurgle of the stream, the scamper of small paws on the forest floor, were the only sounds that whispered over their labored breathing.

The intensity of what they'd shared was too new, too shocking for words. Instead, they let the gentle night sounds speak for them. That, and the beat of their hearts pressed intimately together, pounding in unison, spoke volumes.

Chase grudgingly withdrew from her and rolled heavily onto his back. Before Marea could utter a protest, she was scooped close to his side by a strong arm. Nuzzling into him was a natural thing that took little thought.

Although Chase was excruciatingly aware of her wrapped tightly in his embrace—he knew every time she drew breath, felt against his chest every time her lips turned up in a fledgling smile—he didn't speak until much later. By then he was able to keep his voice controlled and his emotions in check.

"What sort of spell have you cast on me, vision, that the feel of you excites me so?" he asked huskily. His fingers combed through her hair, pressing her head back onto the hard pillow of his shoulder when she would have glanced up. If his feelings were written as plainly in his eyes as they were in his heart, he did not want her to see them.

" 'Tis no spell," she whispered. Her breath stirred a male nipple to erection, and Marea smiled when she saw it bead beneath the wiry gold curls. Her smile blossomed when her tongue darted out to tease it, and she heard him groan. "There be some things that do not take magic. This be one of them."

"This?" His hand cupped her cheek. "And what, I wonder, is 'this'?"

"I do not know, but it has the same effect on me."

She nipped at him and the arm encircling her shoulders tightened.

His fingertip traced her lips, which were sealed, momentarily, around the rigid male peak. When she glanced up, it was to find his eyes dark with rekindled passion. She reached up and traced his jaw. The whiskered flesh softened beneath her touch and his cheek unconsciously turned into the warmth of her hand. The memory of him doing the same thing in her cabin, when he was wounded and unconscious, twisted through her.

She dragged her hand down and rested it on his chest. Cushioning her chin atop her knuckles, she glanced at him. A hint of a blush kissed her cheeks, but pride would not let the weakness creep into her words. "Every time you touch me I feel . . . hot. Tingly. Alive. I do not know why, but 'tis so. Is it"—she smiled weakly, her glance shy in the silver glow of moonlight—"always this way between a man and a woman?"

The golden brows arched. He regarded her skeptically. "Do you not have dozens of lovesick swains who've brought you release in . . . less intimate ways? Surely you must have known your share of them before our night in the forest beside your shack."

She shook her head, her voice haunted. "Nay, not a one."

"Impossible."

"True."

His voice hardened a bit. "I may be English, and therefore a gullible fool in your proud Scottish mind, but I'm no idiot. A woman as lovely as you is too rare to be missed by a rutting stag's eye. 'Tis hard to imagine a man, any man, setting eyes on you and *not* wanting to claim such beauty for his own."

She'd thrust herself stiffly to a sit before giving her mind permission to do so. After two deep breaths, she sent him a cold glance from over her shoulder. His face, bathed in moonlight, framed by a crop of shaggy gold hair, was hard, confused. "Are you calling me a liar, *Sasunach?*"

He sat beside her, his knees curled up to his chest, making a shelf for his elbows. "I am merely asking what kept you from experiencing the same pleasures as other young women."

"Did I not just do that?" Her shoulders were rigid, her spine extremely straight, her chin high. With trembling fingers she reached out and snatched up her rail, dragging the wrinkled scrap of white linen roughly over her head.

He didn't stop her, but regarded her quizzically. "Aye, but why not *before?*" His hand tightened into a fist as he imagined the cloth that now covered her from view clutched in his hands. He wanted to rip off the barrier she had just thrown up between them. "I know your age, and I know you were a maiden the night I thought I'd dreamt you. Now, I want to know why." His hand smacked the ground between them when she refused to answer. "Dammit! 'Tis not natural. Beauty such as yours is—"

"Stop it. Stop saying that!" she screamed, her voice strong but shaky as she clamped her hands over her ears, and rocked stiffly back and forth. It was a reaction usually reserved for bairns who'd just heard a night monster, but Marea didn't care. Her horrified mind had pushed her beyond reason. Shoving to her feet, she searched the clearing frantically for the rest of her clothes.

Chase scowled. That her reaction was unusual for a woman just paid a compliment—a high one by Chase Graham's standards—was an understatement. "Marea, there's naught wrong with being—" he began, only to be glared into silence.

"I'm not beautiful. *I'm—not—beautiful!* Do not say it again, for I canna, *will not*, stand to hear it. Please."

This last, a soft, horrified whimper, curled around Chase's heart like a death grip. Tears glistened in her wide, wild eyes, and an uncontrollable trembling shook her shoulders when she bent to hastily retrieve her clothes. For the life of him, he couldn't understand what he'd said to instill such terror. And it was terror that gripped her. He could feel it like a tangible, ugly thing. "Marea . . . ?"

He stood, extending a hand to her. She stepped out of reach and inched toward the trees. He started to follow, but the sight of her clutching the torn plaid and boots protectively to her heaving breasts, the sight of her frightened, glistening amethyst eyes, rooted him to the spot.

"Marea!" he called when she turned and ran like a frightened doe into the forest. Then, softly, "Vision, come back."

Stunned, he watched her flee. Her movements were graceful even when caught in the grips of terror. A piece of him died when she disappeared from view, and he collapsed heavily onto the clover. The fragile stalks were well crushed, and still warm from their bodies. He lowered his face to the grassy blanket, and still smelled her sweet, sweet fragrance.

"Bloody hell!" he growled, his fist slamming into the ground beside his cheek.

Chapter Twenty-one

It was only because Marea knew the land surrounding Kinclearnon so well that she had not become lost hours ago. It was the horse beneath her that needed guidance.

Stealing the beautiful chestnut mare from under Chase's nose had proven to be easier than she'd hoped. A few well-placed words to the grumpy man left as the horses' guard—coupled with a few well-placed threats—had seen the horse saddled before Chase had returned to camp.

Stealing the broadsword that now slapped at her thigh had been more difficult. She wondered at the headache the guard she'd left crumpled on the ground would have upon wakening, but not for long. It felt too wonderful to have the wind whipping her hair out behind her, stinging her cheeks, making her eyes water.

Her body complained at more hours spent in a saddle, but the ache in her limbs was a small price to pay for freedom. Her side no longer stung. The salve

302

of herbs and roots she'd found in the forest, with Guy Falken's help, had worked magic; as she'd known it would. Infection, though, was not a consideration. Freeing her men from the Douglas was.

Marea lifted her face up to the moonswept sky. The stars above guided her whenever uncertainty reined—which was rarely. According to her calculations, Kinclearnon lay at the end of the wagon path she was now clomping down. The northernmost tip of the firth should come into view at any moment.

A few minutes later, she was there. The boulder beside which her old friend was buried lay to her right. A sketchy outline of Kinclearnon could be glimpsed through the swaying tree branches to her left. Noise from the keep echoed in the chilly air, blending with the hush of late-night sounds.

Throwing the reins over the horse's head, she slipped to the ground and guided it to the moonlit water. The mare snorted before dipping its neck and drinking. Kneeling on the sandy bank, Marea cupped her hands and enjoyed the crisp liquid herself. Ice-cold mountain water trickled down her chin and arms as she drank. She sighed with contentment and wiped the moisture away on her sleeve.

She was never sure exactly what alerted her. The snap of a twig, the scampering of wee paws in the underbrush? The sudden tightening of the horse by her side? Whatever it was, suddenly she was very much aware she was no longer alone in the clearing. Danger pricked up her spine, and her hand automatically drifted to the sword hilt, enclosing it in tight fingers.

The blade hissed from the scabbard. Dry leaves

crunched when she raised the sword high and spun around and up in one fluid motion. Her mouth opened, but the cry of alarm wilted.

She was alone. From there to the line of trees, and as far beyond them as the pale moonlight would allow her to see, there was no one. This, her searching gaze told her. The apprehension that continued to prick at her nape told her quite a different story. Her lips pulled back in a snarl when she felt a concealed gaze studying her.

"Tulach Ard!" She raised the sword higher, her chin higher still, and yelled the MacKenzie war cry that had been instilled in her since birth, then added the Douglas' for good measure. *"Buadh no bas!"*

"Victory or death?" a voice inquired from the shadows. The ceiling of leaves rustled as more than one frightened bird took to flight. The man's accent, she was alarmed to hear, was most definitely English. "Are you, a mere woman, threatening *me?*"

"Aye, *drabach doup,* and I'll be saying a fine muckle worse if you do not get out here where I can see you." She brandished the sword, though she was unsure at what since she still could not see him. His voice came at her from the right and it was to that quarter she focused her attention.

"Say it then," he encouraged. His feet stirred leaves and twigs, and she knew he'd moved closer in the darkness. "We've all night. Just remember, wench, I'll hold you accountable for every insult. Whether I can understand them or not."

So he did know he'd been insulted. She'd wondered. "I'd not realized 'twas an insult to speak the truth," she sneered. Her arms were beginning to ache

304

from holding the sword; she'd not lowered it. A MacKenzie never lowered his guard in the face of an overconfident English dog. "You'll have to forgive me if you took me words in the wrong light. 'Twas no insult, 'twas a statement of fact. There be a difference, don't you know?"

"Aye. The difference being that the former is worth a flogging, while the latter is worth your life."

"Now who be threatening whom?" The challenge was issued with a calmness not reflected in her trembling fingers and quickening heartbeat.

" 'Tis not a threat, wench. 'Tis a promise."

As the man spoke, he stepped forward. The swaying branches above kept him cloaked in shadows, but not enough so that Marea could not make out his basic shape. She gulped. He was tall, broad, and fair. His bearing, as he leaned a broad shoulder against a birch trunk, was arrogant and surly. She couldn't see his eyes, what with the distance and dim light, but she could feel his gaze. Her skin crawled with it.

"I'll not slaughter you if you leave now," she warned. The words far surpassed the courage needed to back them up. This was evident in his chuckle, a sound that sent shivers up her spine.

"How very kind," he mocked. He took a step closer, but stayed beneath the shadow of trees. "However, I feel I must decline your generous offer."

Marea's patience snapped. She had work to do. A half-baked plan for freeing her men had nested in her mind, waiting to be hatched. She had no time for games! "What do you want? I've nothing to give you but the clothes on me back and the provisions in me sack." Her gaze raked his attire. Even in this light, the expensive cut and cloth did not go undetected. "You do not look to be needing either."

She saw a flash of pearly teeth. "I've no need for the provisions," he agreed, like a wolf who'd just offered a fox the protection of its cave. "However, if you are willing to *give* me your clothes, who am I to refuse you?"

"Be serious, mon."

"I am. Dead serious." His words were clear, precise, and menacing. Each was punctuated with an ominous step forward as Marea took a counterstep back.

She petered on the sandy river bank. She could retreat no farther without tumbling into the brisk water. Her arms ached with the effort it took to hold the sword up. The rest of her ached from her arduous journey.

The man stepped closer and he appeared even more ominous. With the moon at his back, he was a dark, foreboding silhouette. Taller than he'd seemed at a distance. Broader. More powerful. Infinitely more menacing. The bay snorted and stepped to the side, as though sensing the danger that emanated from the man like tangible fingers.

"Put down the sword, wench," he ordered when he was only a few short feet away.

"Nay!"

"Would you rather I wrestled it from you?" His laughter was cold, merciless, delighted. "Not that I'd mind. In fact, such sport sounds amusing. I prefer my women to show spirit—up to a point. You'd do well not to push me, though."

"I am not your woman, dog." Just the thought of it

306

made her skin crawl and heated her words. "Nor will I be. And as for pushing, the only thing I'm like to push is this blade through your black heart if you dare another st—"

He dared another step. And more.

Before Marea could finish the sentence, he'd knocked the sword from her hand with his fist. Her wrist throbbed from the blow as the sword tumbled into the high grass. Cradling her aching hand at her waist, she lurched for the horse, belatedly knowing it should have been her first move once she'd realized she was no longer alone in the clearing.

The silky mane slipped through her fingertips when a strong arm coiled around her waist, yanking her back. She was pulled up hard against firm hips and a taut stomach. The breath left her in a whoosh, aided by the arm that held her tight.

His free hand came up, clamping her jaw. He jerked her chin to the side and forced their gazes to clash. "Now, about those insults," he growled, his breath hot and ragged on her cheek.

"Which insults, pig? I spoke many and they all be true." She recognized him now, although time had redefined his features and frame. Time, however, could not eradicate the cruelty in Henry Graham's eyes, cruelty enhanced by flickering moonlight.

"We'll speak of all of them, wench," he growled. "One at a time," his fingers bit into her shoulders as he roughly spun her around, "so I can punish you appropriately for each in turn."

Though only eighteen, he was a good head taller than her. Marea had to crane her neck to look up at him. His face was well carved and menacing. Except for his nose and hair, he bore no resemblance to Chase. This one's features were too harsh, too cruel, his eyes too hard and punishing. Seeing him reminded her of how very much she wished she'd never left the campsite, and Chase, behind.

"I wouldn't try it, bitch," he sneered when her gaze shifted to the sword, lying buried in the calf-high grass. Just as quickly, his sneer melted to what could almost be mistaken for a smile. Almost. The tightening of his fingers on her shoulders belied it. "Come now, wench. 'Tis not as though I'm asking you to share anything you don't offer freely. Ouch!"

The feel of his toe grinding under her heel brought a surge of satisfaction singing through Marea. It was short-lived. The second his fingers loosened, she moved. Her knee came up hard, grinding into his manhood at the same time she shoved him away.

He landed in the grass with a thud, his body doubled.

She heard him moan, but didn't spare him a glance as she bolted for the horse. The bay was eager to leave the danger of Henry Graham behind. At the feel of Marea's weight atop its back, the bay bolted. She didn't chance a backward glance until she had reached the line of trees, and even then it was a brief look she spared.

Henry Graham was on his feet, his shoulders only slightly hunched as he watched her flee, making no move to stop her. She couldn't see his eyes, but she could feel the hatred in them. It seared her. As did the words that echoed around her as she leaned low in the saddle and galloped headlong into the forest.

"Run, bitch!" he taunted, his voice bouncing off

the tree trunks. He punctuated each word with a fist punching the air. "Run while you can. But never think I won't find you. I will. And when I do, I'll make you sorry you refused me."

Chapter Twenty-two

Marea was shivering by the time she reached the covering of woods that pricked the top of the hill. Below her spread the dark, jagged form of the keep. Guards from that distance looked the size of enlarged ants as they strolled the parapet. The moon glinted gray off centuries-old stone. The pale light played over Solway Firth, turning the dark water a shimmering quicksilver. The bridge leading to the keep looked like a black satin ribbon as it twisted through the night.

A soft breeze swept up the hill and Marea gathered the plaid tightly around her shoulders, snuggling into its meager warmth. But it wasn't the cool breeze that made her quiver. It was the aftereffects of her encounter with Henry Graham.

Her teeth clamped together hard when she remembered his breath scorching her cheek. The feel of him pressed against her back. Where Chase's masculine firmness caused waves of excitement in her, his evil brother caused only disgust. It was not a sensation she cared ever to feel again.

310

For a split second, she entertained the notion of casting her madcap plan aside and devising another. The only thing stopping her was the surety that, if the guards the Douglas had sent to see his prisoners safely to his castle hadn't returned yet, they would soon. The Douglas would have a fit when he found out how easily they'd escaped. Who knew what he would do with his MacKenzie prisoners once the news reached him.

She couldn't take that chance. What family she had was in the dungeon of that keep. It was her duty to free them — even if she couldn't retain the keep in the process. She owed Thomas and Randy that much. She owed Zander a fine muckle more.

Although her body ached and she needed nothing so much as a good night's rest, she dismounted. Guiding the bay in a half circle, she administered a brisk slap to its flanks and watched it charge into the forest. Leaves and twigs crunched as it dodged shadowy trunks and brush. When the thunder of hoofbeats receded, Marea entered the forest, heading in the opposite direction, picking her way toward the bog.

Although the man had been a faithful servant to David Graham, Chase stared at Cam McPhearson as though he were mad. His heart throbbed as he dragged anxious fingers through his hair. "Gone? What do you mean she's *gone?* Where the devil could she go in the middle of the night? And with no horse?"

Cam shifted uncomfortably. All the horrible things this man's father had ever done ran through his mind as he studied his boot toe. The gurgle of the stream almost drowned out his reply. "She — er — the wench *had* a horse, m'lord."

311

"She *what?!*"

"I said the wench—"

"I heard what you said." Chase's fists clamped tight as he restrained the urge to yank the words out of the man. The fact that it was exactly what his father would have done stopped him cold. "Now I'll ask you to explain it. How the bloody hell did she get a horse? And where the bloody hell was Hector?"

"Guarding the horses, m' lord," Cam replied uneasily. His hand strayed to the hilt of his stolen sword. If his young lord grew violent, he harbored no qualms about defending himself.

"Are you telling me the wench walked up to him calm as you please and snatched one from under his nose?" Chase raged. In an attempt to vent his frustration, he began to pace. It didn't help. "Did he not think to stop her? Perhaps ask her what she was about?"

"He couldn't, m'lord. He was unconscious."

"You just said—"

"He was guarding them," Cam quickly corrected, "until the wench came up and engaged him in conversation. She hit him in the head. *Then* he was unconscious. 'Twas when she stole the horse and his sword."

Chase spun around. His feet crackled ominously over the leaves, crushing clover as he stopped a scant inch in front of the anxious man. He towered over Cam McPhearson's dark head by almost a foot. "She knocked *Hector* unconscious? A mere slip of a wench knocked that giant senseless?"

"Aye. And Hector's not proud of it, either."

"Well, he should not be!"

"What are you planning to do, m'lord?" Cam asked nervously. In the short time he had known Chase Gra-

312

ham, this was the first time he'd seen the man angry. The sight was more than a little unnerving—especially when coupled with the cruel and well-earned reputation of his father. " 'Tis too dark to follow her."

"Bloody hell!" Chase spun again and stalked angrily to the boulder and back. The scabbard slapped his thigh with each angry step. In the short time since Cam had found Chase, the men had begun to cautiously sift through the forest. More than a dozen of them peered curiously from the safety of the trees. Only a few dared approach and that fact rankled a furious Chase.

God's teeth, they're afraid of me. Seasoned Borderers, the lot of them, yet they are *afraid—of me!*

Had David been *that* cruel? The question was rhetorical. Of course he had. It was his father's nature. Didn't these men have every right to fear the Graham's son because of it?

Chase made the trip between boulder and Cam three times. By then his anger had cooled enough to speak in a somewhat rational tone. Considering his fury, he thought his voice sounded admirably controlled. *"We ride!"*

Marea emerged from the shack. The hem of her black dress fluttered in the breeze around her ankles. Her shoes were swallowed up by the misty vapors that twisted almost to her knees. The veil felt oddly oppressive as it was tossed around her face, brushing padded shoulders. A leather sporran containing the articles that would, with a shred of luck, make her plan work was strapped to her waist. The three small tassels on the front flap jostled with each sure step.

313

Finding the boulder that hid the mouth of the tunnel was easy, even in the flickering moonlight filtering down through the leaves. It seemed to take forever to skulk her way to the end of the tunnel, but in reality it was only ten minutes. By the time she stepped into the deserted storage chamber and locked the door behind her, she felt as though the damp mustiness of the tunnels had seeped beneath her clothes and padding, and embedded itself into her skin.

There was only one place the Douglas could be. At this hour of the night, he would be abed. Everything her father had ever told her of Ian the Douglas said there was only one chamber in the entire keep that would suit him. Unfortunately, to get there she would have to climb the wide stone steps from the great hall to the floor above. In so doing, she would risk being spotted and having her plan divulged to the entire castle.

It was a risk she was willing to take if it meant the result was freeing her family and friends.

Marea was halfway up the steps—too far to go up, too far to go back—when she heard the click of boots on the floor below. Her breath caught as she pressed her back against the cold stone wall. Her dark clothes and veil made melting into the shadows an easy feat to accomplish. But for how long would her presence go undetected? And what if the intruder ascended the stairs? She would be spotted. All would be lost.

Closing her eyes, she held her breath and waited. She heard the footsteps near, then pause at the foot of the stairs. Her heart stopped, then skipped to life. She'd been spotted. She knew it, could feel it. She pried her eyes open and, not turning her head, glanced down the stairs.

She could barely make him out. His dark clothes blended with the murky shadows until she couldn't tell where broad shoulders ended and the shadows began. Only his light blond hair gave evidence to his presence, and each strand glistened like a fiery beacon. His head was bent over a piece of parchment. The paper rustled loudly as his right foot rested on the first stair.

"You asked to see me, m'lord?"

Chase's scowl deepened at the sound of Guy Falken's voice. His mind conjured a picture of the boy and Marea sitting close atop a boulder, laughing, and his blood boiled. His fingers curled tightly around the reins. When he looked up, it was to regard Falken with a hot emerald glare. "How much longer before we reach Kinclearnon?"

"A half-hour at the most."

"And at the least?"

"A quarter if the rain didn't wash away the roads."

They lapsed into uncomfortable silence, the clomping of hooves keeping time with their ragged breaths. Each sway of the horse beneath him jolted Chase's already sore muscles. It was a welcome distraction to his racing thoughts. His jaw tightened and the muscle beneath the bronze flesh jerked. "Did she tell you what she plans to do once she reaches the keep?"

"Tell me? Why would she tell me anyth—?"

"Did she tell you?!"

"Nay."

"Why not?" Chase knew he should stop—not say another word—but he couldn't. A tiny demon was gnawing at his gut, spurring his words on. "Do you two not share lovers' secrets?"

The young face hardened. Moonlight flickered over his angry features and gave him an air of maturity he normally lacked. When he spoke, his voice was softly controlled, but indignant. "I don't like what you're implying, m'lord."

"What I imply is the truth. Do you dare to deny it?"

"Aye! I dare that and more."

"Fool." The emerald gaze sharpened on Falken. A lesser man would have let his horse fall out of step. Or a smarter one. Or a guilty one. Guy Falken kept the pace. "I am not blind. I know what I saw."

Falken stared at him in astonishment. His fingers trembled on the reins, for he too had been the victim of David Graham's wrath on more than one occasion. His quivering fingers were his only outward show of weakness. His voice was strong and only a bit sarcastic—if one listened closely. "And what did you see, m'lord? The wench and I conversing? Laughing as we gathered the herbs and berries to treat her wound? Aye, 'tis incriminating stuff, that. Definitely worth lopping my head off."

"It can be, if your friendship did not stop there," Chase growled, but his tone lacked its bite. He was beginning to doubt his accusations. The thought did not sit well, for more than his hatred for his father, Chase hated to doubt himself or his instincts.

"Were the wench willing, I'd have taken my good nature to the extreme. Damn the consequences," Falken said, and seemed as surprised to say the words as Chase was to hear them. "But the wench was not willing. And I've yet to take a woman who was not. Especially one who has eyes for another."

Chase's gaze snapped to rigid awareness, scanning

his men. His eyes were sharp with accusation. "An-other?"

"You truly don't know of whom I speak, do you, m'lord?" Falken asked, visibly relaxing when his gaze raked Chase's angry features. His laird's fingers un-curling from the sword hilt meant the moment of dan-ger had passed, although the tension was still as thick. "Nay, you do not. You are no more aware of the wench's feelings for you, than you are of your own for her." His laughter was crisp and direct, and riddled with youth.

The sound scratched Chase's raw nerves. "I've no feelings for her," he answered suddenly, aware of how insincere the words sounded, even to his own ears. "And she hates me."

"Aye, if you say so." A patient smile curved Falken's lips. "If there's naught else . . . ?"

Chase grumbled something unintelligible, watching as Falken flicked the reins and dropped behind. His mind didn't travel far from the young man's words.

Marea stood statue still, afraid to move. Twelve more steps and she would reach the landing. But even if she were lucky enough to get there before being overpowered, it would do her little good. Her only route of escape, the tunnels, lay below. Charging up the stairs and finding a hiding place would only post-pone them finding her. Postpone, but not prevent.

It was worth the risk, she decided upon hearing his heel hit the second step. The third. She was pre-paring to bolt when a burly voice below stopped her cold.

"Henry! What are you doing about at this wee

hour?" The Douglas disengaged himself from the shadows of the corridor and stepped into the moonlight slicing through the window. His red head shimmered copper in the pale glow.

"Looking for you," was the immediate, albeit surprised reply. Parchment rattled. The slip of paper was crumpled into a large hand and quickly concealed behind Henry Graham's back. His heel scraped the stone when he turned to face Ian Douglas.

"Well, here I be, lad. What can I do for you?"

"Reubin informs me that Chase and his men have slipped through your fingers." The light fall of steps descending the stairs was a stark contrast to the weight of Henry's words. "Of course, I told him he was mistaken. My brother's freedom was not part of our bargain. Was it, Douglas?"

"I — er — 'twas not part of the deal, nay. But —"

"But?" The single word was snarled coldly as a step across the hard stone was gained. For the first time in her life, Marea felt a shred of sympathy for the man her father had fought so fiercely. A wee shred. "Well? Do you still have my brother or don't you? For your sake, I hope you do. I don't take kindly to being betrayed."

"I've not betrayed you," the Douglas argued weakly. "And 'twas not me men's fault. The lass played on their fears. Used their superstitions against them. We Scots hold our superstitions close to our hearts, don't ye know?"

"No, I *don't* know. Nor do I want to."

Marea used the cover of scuffled footsteps below to inch up the stairs. She'd gained six when the noise ceased. She stopped. Pressing against the stone, she glanced down. Henry Graham had a fistful of the

318

Douglas's tunic and was shoving him hard against the wall. Although the Douglas was bigger and broader, there was something dark and sinister about Henry Graham that gave him an edge over the Scot.

"Where is he?"

"I-I do not know. The lass duped me men into turning their backs. When they looked again, the lot of them were gone."

A hiss was followed by a razor-sharp blade being pressed with deadly intent against the Douglas's throat. The darkness did not conceal Henry Graham's dagger. "Where?"

"I do not know!"

Marea gained another three steps.

"Do you plan to find out?"

"Aye, if I can."

"Not good enough."

" 'Tis the best I can do, lad."

She reached the landing and skirted the corner. Instead of running down the deserted hall, as she probably should have, she waited. And listened.

"Nay, you bastard. The best you could do would be to finish the job for which I hired you."

"I could not kill him in front of so many witnesses. Not without a reason. The Wardens would have me head."

"You'll have no head left to take when I am done with you!" It was not an idle threat, as the Douglas's strained gasp attested. Henry's voice lowered to a lethal pitch. "You have until dawn to find my brother and kill him. If you cannot present me with proof the deed is done by the time dawn streaks across the sky, I will kill you. Slowly and painfully."

"Dawn? But that's scarce six hours away, mon. I canna—"

"Dawn! Not a second later."

Angry footsteps ascended the stairs, while shakier ones echoed down the corridor below.

Hoisting her skirt, Marea slipped down the hall. When she reached the second door on her right, she lifted the latch and slipped into the chamber. She leaned hard against the thick wooden portal. Her breasts were heaving with the nearness of her escape as the footsteps neared, passed, then receded.

A door down the corridor crashed open. Henry Graham's voice drifted through the slats in the door she pressed against. "Reubin, I didn't think you'd still be here. We need to talk."

The door slammed closed, cutting off the rest of his words. His voice still rumbled, muffled, down the corridor—as did that of another.

Marea wasted no time. She slipped from the chamber and retraced her path. She dared not waste a second for fear the Douglas was gathering his men to search for Chase, and would find her instead. She reached the tunnel, but barely. Already the scuffle of feet could be heard in the hall above. Slowly, she inched her way through the musty darkness.

"You're joking," Cam exclaimed, scowling. " 'Tis outrageous."

"Those are my orders. They will be followed."

They were on the border of trees sketching the top of the hill. The moon peeked from behind a layer of inky clouds, casting the keep below in a pale, eerie glow. The forest's shadows kept their hiding place secret—for now. But the secret could not be kept for long. There was little time to argue.

"But what if he's waiting for you? What if you're walking into a trap? Wouldn't it be better to attack and take the Douglas prisoner? Then we'd be sure of what he's up to. He'd not take us by surprise if we took him before he had the chance."

Chase studied the man carefully. There was wisdom in what Cam said—if he had the manpower to back such a plan up. He did not. His own plan, at the moment, also had reason to it. "At full power we were unable to retain the keep. What makes you think we could storm it now at only half strength?"

"The element of surprise," Cam argued. "Surely that must count for something."

"Aye. Were we not all so tired it would count for a lot. As it is, it counts for a disadvantage." Chase's gaze strayed to the craggy battlements and he wondered if Marea was now inside those thick stone walls. His gaze swept back to Cam. "We don't know the Douglas has her. We do know he holds half of our own men, and all of the MacKenzie. We'll have but one chance to free them. I do not intend to see that chance wasted on a plan too quick in the making."

"But—"

"Nay! My orders have been given, McPhearson. I leave it to you to see they are carried out."

"Very well, m'lord," Cam nodded grudgingly. "I don't like it, but I'll do it. I'll take the men and ride to Brackenhill for reinforcements, as instructed." The brown eyes regarded Chase cautiously, and for an instant concern shimmered in their depths. "And if you should need us?"

Chase dismounted and handed the reins to Cam,

pushing them into the older man's fingers when Cam seemed reluctant to take them. "I won't."

Turning, he left the men and entered the forest. It seemed forever before he passed the shadowy glen and emerged near Agatha's shack. The place was deserted. Though a part of him was surprised—and a bit worried that Marea had gone elsewhere—another part of him was not.

A fat black cat greeted him with a loud purr and affectionate rubs as he closed the thin door behind him. Picking up the swollen, furry body, he let the cat nuzzle his neck as he crossed to the rocking chair flanking the cold, dark hearth.

As he settled the cat in his lap, only a small part of him noticed the kittens quickening in her belly. The sharp claws kneaded his muscular thigh as Chase waited.

Chapter Twenty-three

The mist was not thick that night, but floated close to the earth. Jutting branches and bits of brush peeked from the wispy vapor. The air smelled salty and still acidic with the day's rain. No curls of smoke poured from the chimney of her shack. No delicious food smells spiced the air. No family waited. Still, the decrepit old place brought her a sense of contentment.

Marea had missed the bog. Missed the mist and the gnarled tree trunks silhouetted by inky sky and pale moonlight. It was here she'd first come to heal from the Graham's attack so many years before. Here where she'd grown into a woman and learned everything Agatha had to teach. This shack held a special place in her heart—tinged with sorrow—because of it.

She felt achy and tired as, stifling a yawn, she entered the shack. Corbie, who'd been lounging about atop the table strewn with herbs, jumped clumsily down to greet her.

"Aye, you brazen wench," Marea greeted the cat wearily. The muscles in her legs ached when she crouched and ran a hand down the cat's swollen middle. The kittens moved against her palm. She smiled when a loud purr filled the cluttered room. " 'Twon't be long now, lass. Your wee ones feel a might eager to be out. Almost as eager as you be, I'd wager."

Corbie meowed and twisted around her mistress's ankles. "You're probably hungry," she murmured as she scooped the cat up carefully and placed her on the table. The full black tail batted the air as Corbie perfected a stretch. Her large, round eyes watched her mistress search the darkness for a lamp.

" 'Tis here somewhere." With her fingers, she sifted through the shadowy clutter on the small table beneath the window. "Of course, if I were to put things back in one place, 'twould make it easier to find. Aye, Corbie?"

It was not Corbie who answered, but a deep, rich voice that sent a shiver up Marea's spine. "Looking for this, mistress?"

On the other side of the room, the lamp was lit. Large fingers turned the wick high, bathing the room in soft orange light. The glow was not nearly as bright as the determination sparkling in her intruder's eyes.

"H-how did you get here?"

Chase was sprawled in her rocker, the lamp on the floor near his feet. His broadsword lay next to the lamp, close enough to grab quickly. His long legs were crossed at the ankles, his strong hands laced atop his stomach, his head pillowed against the chair's headrest. Bathed in flickering lamplight, he looked every bit as tired as she felt. And a fine muckle angrier.

A reckless grin touched his lips when his shoulders rose and fell in a lazy shrug. "The same way you did, *Agatha*. By horse."

" 'Tis not what I meant."

His gaze pierced her. "Then what did you mean? Explain, please, for I'm too tired to play games with you this night."

Her own exhaustion was quickly being replaced by a spark of anger. "I left you behind, *Sasunach*. 'Tis not fair for you to catch up with me so easily."

His grin broadened and his eyes flashed a challenge. Marea pressed back against the table, her fingers curling around the molded edge. "Well, fair or not, I'm here. 'Twould seem my horse runs faster than yours. Hardly my fault."

" 'Tis your fault when you use that speed to follow me," she snapped. She pushed away from the table, her sore muscles cramping from standing in one position, and restlessly prowled the room. "I canna see why you'd bother to do that at all."

"Can't you?" The question was asked simply, as though there was no hidden meaning to it. They both knew better.

"Nay."

"Then mayhaps I should explain." His rugged body uncoiled from the chair. Standing, he seemed to fill the room, dwarfing it with his size and strength. In two strides he was in front of her. She felt the warmth of him seep through her tattered clothes. Despite the liquid heat, she shivered. "Did you think I'd let you leave me?" he asked, his voice soft and controlled as he lifted the oppressive veil from her face. His palm stroked her cheek. Her satiny flesh quivered beneath the touch. "Did you think I'd not hunt you down? Not demand an explanation?"

" 'Tis what I'd hoped." She tried to draw back from

his touch, but his other hand coiled around her neck and held her steady. Her chin raised and she met his gaze. "Apparently, 'twas more than I should have expected."

"Apparently." His head tilted to the side and he sent her a mocking smile. "Now would be a good time to tell me why you left so abruptly."

When she didn't answer, Chase's hands moved down to clamp over her shoulders. Even through the padding he thought she felt small beneath his palms. Delicate and defenseless. It was a ridiculous notion; of all the women he'd ever met, this one was the most sturdy. Yet the implication of fragility was there, and feeling it made his mood soften. It was a weakness not mirrored in his tone when he said, "I demand an answer, mistress. If need be, I'll wait all night, but I'll not leave without one."

"Stay if it pleases you. Demand if it pleases you. I'll still not give you answers." A grin pulled her lips when she saw a spark of anger light his eyes. It was gone quickly, but that it had been there, and that she had put it there, delighted her. "Do not be thinking I'll surrender me cot to you again, either. You're healed now. You sleep on me floor."

"Nay, mistress," he replied sharply, "I'll not be sleeping anywhere until we've talked. Too much needs to be said between us. You can start by telling me why you left so abruptly."

"I'd need of a ride to clear me head," she lied, stepping away from him when his hands dropped from her shoulders. Her feet crunched over the hard-packed floor when she approached the hearth. As though a fire crackled there, she extended her hands to it, then dropped them limply to her sides when she was met with only cold. "I'd also the need to free me men from the Douglas. Your campfire was warm, but sitting in front of it was not freeing me men."

"Liar."

Ignoring the aches in her body, she spun around. Black wool settled in thick folds around her ankles as she planted fists on her hips and glared at him. "A MacKenzie does not lie."

"This MacKenzie does."

"Were I a mon, I'd kill you for that."

He turned slowly. The lamplight made his eyes glisten with hot emerald fire. She warmed under the intimacy of his eyes and hated herself for it. "But you are not a man, mistress. If you were, I'd have met you over a sword long ago."

"And you'd be lying next to your da." Only Marea noticed that her fists had begun to tremble.

He acknowledged her threat with one of his own. "Or you next to yours." He took a menacing step toward her.

She took a step back and came up hard against the cold stone of the hearth. "Get out!"

He advanced another step. "I think not."

"I said get out! You're not wanted here."

He stopped in front of her, so close the tips of her breasts grazed his chest. He didn't press closer, though the desire to was there in his eyes. "Wanted or not, I'll stay." The tip of his thumb traced the tight line of her jaw. "For now."

"And if I threaten to kill you whilst you sleep?"

"You've threatened it before." His mouth twisted in a lazy grin as he threw her own words of so long ago

327

back in her face. "You can try. But you'll no have an easy time o' it, lass."

His mimicry gave her pause. The tiredness of her body and mind was beginning to ebb. She leaned wearily against the stone. Diverting her attention out the window, she asked, "What do you want from me, *Sasunach?* I be too tired to argue."

"An answer to my question. That's all I want," he replied. He inhaled deeply and his chest felt the strain of her breasts against it. There was no padding on her there and none was needed. The jaw beneath his fingertip tightened, proof that she was every bit as aware of the desire kindling between them as he. "After that, I'd like Kinclearnon back."

" 'Tis not yours to take," she answered, deftly avoiding the first request in favor of the last. This, she saw, did not go unnoticed. "Kinclearnon belongs to the MacKenzie."

"At the moment Kinclearnon belongs to the Douglas." His hand turned inward, cupping her cheek. Ah, so soft! His voice turned ragged. "And there's not a damned thing either of us can do about it, as things stand now."

"They'll not stand this way forever. Time has a way of changing things for the better, don't you know?"

"No, I don't." His gaze sharpened and he assessed her shrewdly. Her eyes were too wide, her soft, sweet mouth too innocently set. Suspicion tightened his gut. "You have a plan?"

"Aye."

"A plan you'll not share with me?"

"Aye."

His hand dropped and he stifled the urge to shake

the words out of her. No, there were more subtle, more enjoyable ways to wheedle information from a woman like her. Ways Chase wouldn't hesitate to pursue if it meant insuring their safety. Imperceptibly, his body moved toward her. It would, eventually, have done the same thing under its own power. That was inevitable. "A plan that would free your men and see the keep again under MacKenzie rule?"

"Aye." She scowled, her gaze trained on the thick cord of his throat. A pulse throbbed beneath the tanned flesh, its tempo as frantic and wild as her own. His warmth seeped through wool and padding. His heat caressed her flesh, his breath stroked her cheek. The effect was devastating.

His chest moved closer, until he could feel each rise and fall of her breasts. "A plan that does not include me?"

"*Aye!*" Devil take it, she'd no idea how he'd managed to pin her against the hearth without her noticing. His hips moved, pinning her against something harder still. Her fingers curled around his shoulders for balance. Her eyes widened in confusion when she was captured by the intensity of his gaze.

"A plan you'll put into motion tonight?" The eyes darkened as he raked her Agatha attire.

"Aye," she said. It sounded more like a ragged sigh, for his hips had arched, as though seeking her out through the material separating flesh from hot, hungry flesh.

A groan rumbled in the back of Chase's throat when his gaze fixed on her lips. Her warm breath kissed his cheek, snuck beneath the laces of his tunic, grazed his neck and upper chest. For an instant, he forgot his

329

need for information, forgot his need for delicacy of tactics, forgot everything except the insatiable need to taste and feel and possess her once more.

"You're a fine muckle curious about things that do not concern you," she whispered breathlessly.

The words yanked him from his thoughts. He blinked and stared at her stupidly. She repeated the statement.

"Everything you do concerns me, witch." His hands slipped down her arms, squeezing the padding that hid her from his touch. He resisted the urge to tear the false thickness away.

"It should not."

"But it does."

Marea groaned. Her blood simmered in her veins, her heart pounded wildly. Breathing was a torturous event, for it molded their chests together. Her arms itched to curl around his neck, her body begged to melt into his. Only knowing he was her enemy kept her strong. But it was a weak, faulty, insincere kind of strong, for her body, as always, betrayed her.

His palms scorched her wrists, which were easily ensnared by his fingers. His rough skin chafed her tender flesh. It was not an unpleasant feeling.

"Where have you been, vision?" he asked, as warm lips grazing her earlobe. He grinned when she shivered. "I've been waiting for you."

"I-I went for a walk to—er—to wash the dirt away."

His tongue lapped a fiery path down her neck. "I think not." His lips grazed the pulse racing in the hollow of her throat. He felt her heartbeat quicken. "I smell the forest in your hair, Marea. The scent of leather and horse on your skin is still strong." He lifted

330

his head and, cradling her cheeks in his palms, rested his forehead against hers. His breath came hard and ragged. "Where did you go? Tell me."

"To the keep," she whispered, and closed her eyes. The passion in his gaze was too much to look upon, for it mirrored that coursing through her soul. "I—I thought to scare the Douglas away. To play on *his* superstitions the way I did his men. It did not work."

"He can't be scared?"

Her eyes snapped open. "I did not try."

"Why not? 'Twas what you went there for."

"I had no chance." She didn't elaborate, even though his gaze begged her to. What could she tell him? That the thought of him being killed come daybreak had frightened her senseless? That, upon hearing the threat, she'd fled the keep thinking only of finding Chase to warn him of his brother's duplicity? That on her way back to the bog she'd faltered with indecision? That, though she knew she'd be better off without him, the thought of him dying tore her to shreds. She couldn't tell him those things. Wouldn't. A confession such as that would make her weak . . . and a Mac-Kenzie never showed weaknesses.

The hands cupping her cheeks tensed. His voice thickened. "Something happened, didn't it? What? What made you change your mind about scaring the Douglas away, Marea? What?"

"Nothing." She tried to wrench away, but his fingers held strong. Shoving against his broad shoulders was useless. The only thing wiggling her body accomplished was to darken his eyes and find herself pinned thigh to shoulder against the stone.

"I'm tired of your lies, MacKenzie," he growled, his

331

patience sorely strained. His mind wanted her, his body craved her, but his soul, ah, his soul wanted more. He needed *all* of her—including her honesty. "If you don't tell me what happened in the keep, Marea, I'll go there myself and find out."

"Nay!" Her fingers curled into his tunic, as though the grip alone could keep him there, away from the Douglas who sought to kill him. Away from his devious brother. She didn't ask herself why the thought of Chase's death brought so much pain. It just did.

"So something *did* happen. Are you going to tell me what it was, witch? Or will I have to discover it for myself."

"I told you, 'twas nothing."

"This 'nothing' seems to be very upsetting to you."

"Aye. Mayhaps it should not be, but 'tis."

"And does this 'nothing' involve me?"

She hesitated. "Aye. I canna tell you of it. I can only ask you to stay here, in me shack, where it be safe."

He frowned. "Safe? You care that I am safe?"

She sucked in a breath and closed her eyes. Against her will she leaned into him, pillowing her head against his shoulder until his heartbeat throbbed in her ear. The rhythmic sound brought comfort, as did the arms holding her close. It was a tender moment, one she savored if only because it might be the last. Clenching her teeth, she nodded.

Her answer was not satisfying. His hands strayed to her upper arms and he reluctantly eased her away. Her lashes swept up and he was met with her tortured gaze. "What do you seek to shelter me from, vision?" he asked, his voice a raspy whisper. She didn't answer, but nibbled uncertainly on her lower lip. "Tell me. I can't protect myself, or you, if I don't know where the danger is coming from."

"Everywhere, mon. It comes from everywhere." She rushed on before she could change her mind, for suddenly telling him the truth to save his life was very important to her. No matter that it shouldn't be, it was. "Th-there are those seeking to kill ye before dawn. Those you'd not thought your enemy."

"And that is why you would have me stay here?"

"Aye. To keep you safe. They'd not think to search for you in Agatha's shack."

"And it is important to you they not find me?" he murmured, incredulous. "You *do* care whether I live or die." The words were hushed, torn from his throat as though he was afraid of what her response would be.

Marea lifted a hand to his face. Her fingers shook when she stroked his cheek, and felt the bristle of stubble against her palm. Her vision blurred, her voice cracked with emotion. "Aye, I care. Too much, I care."

His arms slipped around her waist, hauling her close. She went willingly, nuzzling into the firm cushion of his body, molding her curves to his hard planes.

Chase turned his head, inhaling deeply of the fresh scent of her hair. Each red-gold strand felt like silk against his cheek. "I've waited a lifetime to hear you say that. In my wildest dreams, I never thought you would."

"Enjoy hearing it whilst ye can," she rasped, and her lips brushed his throat. "I'll never say it again."

"But you will, Marea," he promised huskily, his head lifting. His gaze seared her before his mouth dipped to claim a scorching kiss. "You will," he murmured against her lips, his breath heating her flesh before he deepened the kiss.

Her arms circled his neck, pulling him closer as she arched hungrily against him. It had been but hours since he'd held her, kissed her, loved her. It felt like days.

The short distance to the cot felt like a mile away. He scooped her into his arms and crossed the distance quickly, urgently, as though this might be the last time he would ever taste her sweetness and he intended to savor it. The straw crunched as he laid her on the mattress, then covered her with his body. She felt small beneath him. She felt like heaven.

Clothes were torn away and discarded. Impatient hands roamed naked flesh. A body arched, another responded.

Their lovemaking was hot and fierce, fast and scorching. Thrusts were met and received. Their ecstasy built to an excruciating pitch, then crashed over them in waves of mutual pleasure. Swift, simultaneous explosions ripped through their bodies, and their hearts. They clung to each other, breathless, spent.

They lay entwined for what felt like hours, but it wasn't near long enough. When Chase made to pull away, Marea's legs tightened around his hips and refused to let him go. With his weight on his elbows, he brushed the sweat-dampened hair from her brow and gazed down at her, confused.

"Do not leave me," she said, her voice high and strained, her breaths shallow and uneven. "Ever."

Chase knew exactly how much those words cost her, and how very vulnerable they left her. He lowered his mouth for a tender kiss. "I won't leave you, vision. Ever," he whispered hoarsely against her lips. "You're mine, now and always, as you were meant to be. I'll not let you go, even should you demand it."

A sigh of contentment rushed from her. She ran her palms down his back. His flesh was warm, solid. It rippled nicely against her fingertips.

This time they loved slowly, slowly.

This time, her body spoke the words her lips could not.

Chapter Twenty-four

The first fingers of dawn streaked in through the window. Golden slivers of sunlight warmed contented, naked flesh.

Corbie had found a home cushioned against Chase's thighs. Except for the sharp claws that occasionally found their way into his leg, he didn't complain. Loud purrs mixed with the crackle of a freshly kindled fire and mingled with the soft trill of a bird in a tree outside.

After their second encounter with perfection—long and torturously slow—Marea had told Chase of the conversation she'd overheard between Henry and the Douglas. After their third—hot and fierce and fast—she'd confessed her plan to free her men. That had been a scant few minutes ago.

"A half-baked scheme if ever I've heard one," he muttered, while nibbling the tips of her fingers. He dragged his tongue over her nails and tasted the sting of blood—from when she'd clawed his back during a particularly pleasurable moment.

"Half-baked scheme?" she repeated distractedly. At another time she would have taken exception to the insult. Right now, she felt too contented and good to take exception to anything.

She lay upon her cot facing him. With a sigh, she nuzzled into him and inhaled. He smelled of leather and sweat. It was a heady aroma. Twisting to the side, she glanced at him and grumbled, "Half-baked? 'Twas the best I could think up so quickly. 'Twould have worked, methinks — had I the time."

"Mayhaps." He reached down and, hooking his fingers beneath her knee, dragged her leg up over his hip. He watched her eyes darken when the long, firm proof that he still wanted her nudged her moist place. It was too soon to take her again — Chase *knew* it was too soon — yet his body was telling him differently. God, how he wanted her! And since she wasn't pushing him away . . .

He arched forward, plunging into her. She stretched around him, her body hugging him tightly. He continued to speak as though his body wasn't in the process of thrusting slowing in and out of hers. "Are you Scots really so superstitious? I can't imagine an Englishman — ah, God! — falling for such a trick."

"Aye," she said, her voice ragged as she stroked the line of his whiskered jaw. He shivered, and his fingers curled into her bottom, holding her close as his thrusts deepened. "And as for what you *Sasunach* believe — Och! that feels nice — I recall a time when you thought I be poisoning you through the flesh." Her fingertip traced a path down his throat, then circled the pink scar Randy had left on his shoulder. "Do you remember it?"

"Hmmm? Oh, aye, but I never believed a word." He guided her hips, moving her with him. When her finger returned to his face, he captured it with his lips, sucking it into his mouth.

The moist heat of his tongue flicked over her knuckle. She trembled, and her body fired, as though she had not already been carried to glorious peaks thrice that night—and was being carried there yet again. "You *did* believe me. Well, mayhaps only for a few short seconds—Oooh!" She groaned when he buried himself deeply, withdrew, then buried himself again. And again. And again. "I—I saw the look you gave me bowl—Oh, Chase!—and your d-doubt when you—yes, yes, faster—felt the bite of me salve. You canna deny that."

"I don't." Their bodies strained together, apart, together. Their breaths meshed, ragged and strained. "Say it again, vision," he whispered hoarsely.

"S-say what?"

"My name. Say my name. It sounds so sweet on your tongue."

"Chase," she sighed, her brogue rolling the single word into a silken caress. Her eyelids thickened when her gaze settled on his lips. His strokes were fast, deep, and, oh, so distracting. "I like the way it sounds."

"Not half as much as I," he growled. Shifting his weight, he tossed her onto her back. Her arms encircled his neck and her chin lifted greedily for his kisses.

His mouth was hot and searing as his body pumped into hers. His strokes were long and deep and filling. In a surprisingly short time he had her shuddering and crying out his name. In a surprisingly short time, he was doing the same. He collapsed atop her, his arms slipping beneath to hold her closer than he'd ever held a woman before. Or ever would again. "I shouldn't have done that," he said once his breathing had begun to regulate. "We've much to do this day."

The words hit her like ice water. Marea fought the urge to get up from the cot and put some needed distance between them. Of course, she couldn't when his possessive weight was sprawled atop her. The subject, she decided, needed to be changed and changed quickly. She voiced the first words that came to mind. "I watched you last night whilst you slept. You look good swaddled in plaid. If you were not to open your mouth, I'd almost mistake you for a Scot."

The second the words left her, Marea realized they were true. She remembered how the plaid he'd tossed over them in the night had looked against him. The forest green wool complemented his eyes, darkening them a shade. The yellow threads shot through the fabric matched the ones streaked through his sleep-tousled hair. The red enhanced his healthy complexion.

Oh, there was no mistaking Chase Graham's nationality. His nose was English, his cheekbones too regal for a Scot, his lips thin. And his lack of a beard spoke for itself. Was that clean-shaven jaw, now bristled and darkened with whiskers, his personal stab at rebellion? she wondered as, when he pulled back, her attention lifted and her gaze raked his face.

His eyes were guarded. Yet, it was in those eyes, and the low-slung brows slashed over them, that Marea found a hint of the Lowland features with which she was familiar. She watched closely for his reaction, and was surprised to see he had none.

Chase was as used to acquiring compliments as Marea was to handing them out. His lack of expertise in that area was evident in his wary response. " 'Tis the murky light," he replied stiffly. "You'd not see a trace of your proud Scottish ancestors in me in the clear light of day."

She scowled when a preposterous thought nipped at her. It was ridiculous, of course. Even if she were to ask him, she knew what his answer would be. She asked anyway. Just to see. "Wouldn't I? I'm not so sure. Until last night, I'd not looked for it. But now that I've looked . . . ."

Chase had been in the process of slipping over her to get off the bed. He was halfway across when her meaning struck him. He froze. His elbows were cushioned on either side of her head. Her hips were soft beneath his. His body pinned hers to the mattress as he cautiously glanced down at her. "What are you talking about?"

"Your heritage. Or, rather, the half you're hiding. Why have you not told me of your Scottish ancestors?"

"Why should I?" His voice was strained, hoarse, a mere whisper. "Is it any of your business?"

"Nay. But 'twould have been nice to know."

One golden brow rose accusingly high. "And it would have made a difference, wouldn't it, Marea? Wouldn't your views of me have been a little less harsh, a little less cynical, had you known there was a bit of the Scot in me?"

"Aye," she admitted, confused.

"You should learn to hide your feelings better," he snapped. Bracing his weight on his elbows, his palms captured her cheeks. "Your eyes mirror your soul, Marea. I can see in them that what you've just learned makes quite a difference with you. 'Tis why I've never told you. Why I never intended to tell you."

"Scottish or not Scottish, don't be thinking I'd ever forgive the Grahams for slaughtering me kin." The pain the words brought sliced deep. The need to make this man feel the same pain was as strong as it was irrational. With his body holding her to the cot, she lashed out in the only way she could: with words.

"'Twas a slaughter you took full part in, *Sasunach,*" she hissed.

"Aye, and I thank you ever so much for reminding me," he growled sarcastically. The hands cupping her cheeks clamped tight. He seemed not to notice the pressure he applied or the way she squirmed beneath him in response to it. He glared at her, his features hard. " 'Tis an act of which I'm so very proud. I boast of it to any who'll listen, you know."

Though his tone had been thick with self-disgust, Marea didn't dare believe that was truly how he felt. "I saw no one forcing you. What you did 'twas done willingly."

He chuckled dryly—at her, or himself?—and pushed from the bed. He was naked, yet seemed as immune to his state of undress as he was to the chilly morning air. Golden streams of sunlight filtered in through the window, melting over his flesh until it was ignited an appealing shade of bronze. Muscles coiled and rippled beneath his skin as he crossed the room and leaned an elbow atop the timbered mantel. His fingers plowed his hair.

"What is your definition of *willingly,* Marea?" He

341

didn't look up, but continued studying the chips of ash and cinder in the hearth. "If you mean did I ride with my father of my own free will, then, aye, I was willing. If you mean did I do things of which I'm not proud, things that compromised every principle I hold dear, then, nay, I was a most *un*willing victor."

She pushed herself up on the cot and leaned back against the headboard. Pulling her knees to her chest, she covered herself with the plaid. Her gaze never left Chase's harshly sculpted profile. He looked angry, tortured, but she could not muster up so much as a scrap of comfort to offer. Her own pain ran too deep. "A mon does not do things he believes wrong. He does not compromise his principles if he holds them dear."

"This man did." His expression flashed with an emotion that was as brief as it was unreadable. The muscle in his jaw jerked. The admission had cost him, that much was clear. Why it should was not so obvious. He turned his head and appraised her. "Do you think there is a single moment when I don't regret the things I've done?" he demanded harshly. "Do you think your cries do not haunt my sleep—or those of dozens of other women just like you?" His fist slammed onto the mantel. The force of the blow rained dry herbs and leaves to the hardpacked floor. "Think again, for they do! I hear the screams, I see the people dying around me. I remember it when I'm asleep, when I'm awake—when I'm *making love to you!* I remember the senseless bloodshed, and I remember *my* part in it." He shuddered, his voice thickened. "And I hate myself for what I did."

"Then why did ye do it?" she asked, and huddled deeper beneath the plaid. She averted her gaze, not daring to look at him for fear his tortured expression would make her soft. "You could have stopped. If you feel the way you say you do, you should not have ridden with your father at all."

"You'd not understand."

"Aye, not if ye won't be telling me."

There was a moment of tense silence before he asked softly, "You knew your mother, didn't you?" She nodded slowly, scowling, keeping her gaze trained straight ahead. "And your father. Tell me, mistress, what was the MacKenzie like? Strong? Loving? Trustworthy? Free with his praise for you? His thoughts only for family and clan, and how he could best serve them both?"

"Aye," she said, her voice edged with pride and sorrow. Her fingers plucked nervously at the frayed edges of the plaid. "He was a fine mon, Connor MacKenzie. Kind-hearted and strong." Her gaze narrowed. "What be your point?"

"David Graham was not so fine."

"But he was your father."

"Aye. Though 'tis not something to brag about."

"Y-ye did not love him, did ye?" Having been raised by loving parents, it was hard for her to imagine.

"Nay, Marea, I hated him with every fiber of my being. I still do."

"But he was your father," she repeated, shocked to hear the words ring in her ears. Was she defending David Graham? Surely not. She was merely trying to understand the son.

"I know *who* he was. I also know *what* he was: a cruel bastard whose heart was as cold as an ice-covered loch. If it makes you feel better, his hatred for me ran just as deep."

Her insides rebelled at that. "Surely he must have felt something else for you."

"Aye. Disgust. He said so. That, and disappointment."

Marea thought of the babe her mother had lost along with her life. If the child had been a son, he would have been raised with love and pride, respect and courage. He would have grown into manhood fine and strong, like his father. A MacKenzie would never turn his back on a child the way David Graham had turned his back on Chase. The very idea sickened her. "What about pride? Was he never proud of you?"

His laughter was cold and hard. "He could see nothing of which to be proud. If I raided a rival clan and returned with fifty beasts, the biting end of his whip told me fifty more should have been taken. If I organized a trod to go after our own stolen goods, and was lucky enough to return to Brackenhill with them, I was told I should have taken the robbers prisoner as well. And when I did that, my father's well-aimed fists reminded me of my right to kill thieves on the spot."

Marea flinched at the abusive picture he painted. She licked parched lips and chanced a quick glance at him. His back was to her. She didn't have to see the bitterness in his eyes to know it was there. "If what you say be true, then you've a right to your hatred," she muttered, not knowing what else to say. "No one can deny that."

"I can," he growled. "And I do. I should have seen what was happening when Henry was born. I should have seen that what I fought so hard to gain — my father's love, his respect—was not something I could ever have. You don't know what it was like for me to watch him dote on Henry, lavishing his love and attention on a child I'd learned to hate months before his birth."

Gathering the plaid about her, Marea rose from the bed. Her bare feet padded across the cold dirt floor. Her free hand lifted, pausing a scant inch from his arm. Hot, coiled tension rolled off of him and singed her hand. After a few seconds, her hand dropped limply to her side. "Do not be so hard on yourself, Chase. 'Tis only natural to feel jealous when that which you've worked so hard to gain is denied you and given to another."

He raked his fingers through his hair. Her words brought him no comfort. " 'Tis not something of which to be proud of, either, Marea. Only a monster would harbor ill feelings toward an innocent babe. A monster . . . or David Graham."

"I've met your brother. Any ill feelings you have for him be well earned."

He laughed coldly. "Dear little Henry's lived up to the Graham code of ethics, hasn't he? Surpassed them, in fact. 'Twas something I could never do."

"And 'tis glad I be to hear it. You're twice the mon your brother is. Let no one tell you differently. Even yourself."

His gaze snapped to the side at the feel of her hand on his arm. Her fingers felt warm and right against his flesh. The touch brought comfort, even if her words brought confusion. "If I didn't know better, Marea, I'd think you were trying to console the enemy. Is this softness because you know I'm half Scot?"

"Your brother be half Scot too, but I'd die before offering him the same words."

His hand covered her own. "Henry is English to the bone. 'Twas *my* mother who was the Scot. And me who paid the price for her nationality when she had the indecency to die giving me life. Henry's mother, on the other hand, was a proper English serving wench who lived to the ripe old age of twenty-two— before David Graham's beatings took their toll."

"You're a bastard?" she gasped.

"Nay. Margaret, my mother, he married. 'Twas Helen who stayed unwed. More than once my father was overheard swearing he'd learned his lesson on his first trip to the altar with the Scottish bitch. He said he'd no desire to repeat the mistake. 'Tis why I inherited Kinclearnon, although he would have given his life to see it pass further down the family line." His lips curled in a vengeful smile. " 'Tis a sick sense of pleasure I get knowing how much he would have hated to see me take what he spilled so much innocent blood to attain."

" 'Tis why you want the keep so badly?" she asked softly. "To avenge yourself on him?"

" 'Tis one reason, but by no means the only one."

"There be others?" The muscle beneath her palm bunched. Her fingers quivered and she tried to withdraw her hand. His grip tightened, refusing to allow it. The heat of his body melted through the plaid, warming her.

"Aye, mistress, there are others," he sighed, yet his voice was far from relaxed.

Marea waited, hoping he would confide these reasons to her. She didn't want to guess. Second-guessing a man like Chase had always been futile. When he didn't answer, she glanced up. The early morning sun filtered in through the window, igniting the fire in his eyes. They seemed unusually green: radiant, intense, probing. "You'll not tell me the rest?"

His answer was clear in the way he gave her hand a gentle squeeze, then stepped away. He scooped his clothes from the floor, then moved to the bed and perched on its edge. Only when the hose were halfway up his sinewy calves did he stop and look at her. "Get dressed, mistress." He stood, tugging the stocking into place. "I repeat, there is much we need do today."

Marea had turned away by the time the waist of his hose had reached his hips. Her cheeks colored when her imagination took up where her vision left off. Was there not a single inch of him that was not firmly sculpted and bronzed? If so, she'd yet to see it.

"Marea?"

"What?" The word was almost a scream, so fast and hard did it pour from her lips. She heard his approach from behind, but didn't turn toward him. She didn't dare. Who knew what traitorous emotions swam in her eyes, emotions she did not want him to see.

She felt him stop behind her. Felt the heat of his partially clad body melt through the plaid and caress the bare skin beneath. His breath was warm, sweetly scorching as it grazed her neck, and rustled red-gold wisps curling there. She sucked in an uneven breath and smelled his spicy scent mingling with her softer, flowery one.

She startled when his hand settled on her bare shoulder. Spinning on her heel, she almost lost the plaid in the process. She clutched it tightly before it

347

could fall away, holding the frayed ends in a protective bunch beneath her chin. Lifting her gaze, she found him watching her closely. His eyes were just as bright as before, only now they sparkled with amusement.

"I said you should get dressed. There is—"

"Much to do today. Aye, I heard you." She tried to side-step him, but he caught her arm. Even through the wool, his grip was intimidating.

"What the devil is wrong with you now?" he growled, his good humor abruptly gone. When she didn't answer, his grip tightened. "I asked you a question, Marea. I damn well expect an answer."

"Nothing is wrong." Her words were terse, uttered between clenched teeth. The fact that she refused to return his gaze seemed to irritate him. She could only guess why.

"That is no answer." With a flick of his wrist, he brought her up against his side. She struggled to keep the plaid around her, but his foot was on one corner, causing the cloth to dip threateningly low on her breasts.

"I said 'twas nothing," she insisted, tugging on the plaid. It wouldn't budge. "I'll be fine once you're—"

"Dressed?"

Marea froze. How had he known? She didn't have to look up to know he was staring at her. His breath on her face told her that. He shifted subtly, until she was treated to his chest grazing hers. The feeling did torturous things to her composure. She closed her eyes, not knowing where to look, only that she didn't want to look at him.

"Does the sight of me disturb you that much?"

She rolled her lips inward, refusing to answer.

"I asked you a question, mistress." His grip tightened.

"Nay," she lied. "It does not bother me at all."

"Sweet, beautiful little MacKenzie, you are a liar to the bitter end, are you not?"

She willed her voice not to betray the almost overwhelming surge of panic she felt. "I'm not a liar. And I'm *not* beautiful. Do not say it again. Do not even think it."

"Would you have me lie as well?" His voice was soft and cajoling, but Marea wasn't fooled. She closed her eyes tighter and ground her teeth hard. Angry words hovered on the tip of her tongue, begging to be said. "If my nakedness doesn't bother you, then open your eyes and look at me." The hand on her arm left, only to return at the small of her back. He applied no pressure, merely let his palm ride her hip. It was enough. "I dare you."

At that, her lashes snapped up. After all, she had her ancestors of which to think. A MacKenzie never refused an outright dare. But, though her eyes were open, she did not look at him.

The hand at her back slipped over her shoulder, then down the plaid concealing her arm. He reached her hand and enfolded her fingers in his. She kept her gaze on the wall behind his shoulder, even as he tugged her hand up. He held her at arm's length, and she could feel the coldness enfolding her now that his body heat had been removed.

"Look at me, Marea." He gave her hand a tug, but did not win her gaze. "Is the wall *that* interesting?"

"Nay."

"Then look at me."

349

She brought his face into focus. He was taunting her, she knew. Just as she knew she was letting him do it. Why?

"Look at *all* of me."

She did. Except for the pelt of curling gold, his chest was bare. She became interested despite herself. Her gaze traveled lower slowly. His stomach was taut, his navel a tempting dip in his suntanned flesh. Coarse gold hair swirled from there in a sweeping, downward stroke that disappeared beneath his hose.

Her gaze stopped abruptly and returned to his face. She inhaled quickly and fumed at what she saw. The bastard was gloating! His eyes were narrow, glowing, daring her to look more intimately. Her cheeks heated and her hands bunched into fists that yearned let fly at his jaw—hard. Her chin thrust up with MacKenzie pride as she returned his stare unflinchingly.

"Did you like what you saw?"

" 'Tis passably fair," she muttered noncommittally, and wasn't pleased to hear her voice crack.

"Passably fair?!"

His fingers tightened around hers and Marea felt a measure of satisfaction to see she'd bruised his ego. "Aye, passably fair," she repeated, her voice firmer. "What's the matter, *Sasunach,* are those not the words you wanted to hear? Mayhaps you should not ask a question if the answer does not suit you."

His expression grew stormy. "The answer suits me fine, witch. 'Tis the lie behind it that grates."

"I'm no a witch, I'm a healer. And a MacKenzie does not—"

"Don't say it!"

She looked at him, confused and stunned by the

force of his words. He took a step toward her, a step that brought them toe to toe. He didn't drop her hand, but his fingers were now caressing. His thumb trailed small circles in the center of her palm, while the rest of his fingers nestled securely in hers.

That unsettled her. Marea wished his grip had remained harsh. Harshness she could deal with. But this tenderness left her at a loss.

His other hand came up. The crook of his index finger settled under her chin, drawing her gaze up. What she saw in his eyes was yearning and desire, but not of the lustful nature.

"Why does your beauty upset you?" he asked. His roughened finger stroked her jaw. She shivered. "Twice now I've seen you run from words that come very naturally to me. Why?"

" 'Tis none of your affair." She started to look away, but his hand brought her back.

"Mayhaps. But I want to know." He studied her closely, watching the emotions that played over her delicately molded face. Then, when she did not speak he muttered, " 'Twould seem I'm not the only one in Kinclearnon with inner demons to fight. Methinks you've a share as well, Marea."

She slapped his hand away, surprising even herself with the force of the blow. "Leave me be," she snapped, her voice low and hard. "If I've demons inside, they be mine to fight. Alone. I need no god-forsaken *Sasunach* to show me how."

Chase's hand was poised midair. Her words made it drop to his side. Spinning on his heel, he returned to the bed and gathered his clothing—but not before she caught a glimpse of the pain and anger in his eyes.

The sight stung, but it was too late to take her words back now. Not that her pride would ever have allowed it.

Huddling within the plaid, she watched him move to the door. His hand gripping the door latch, he paused and glanced at her from over his shoulder. The plaid was a poor barrier to stave off the coldness in his eyes and tone. "Fight your demons. I'll not intrude again, unless you ask it." He turned his attention out the door, but made no move to leave. "Meanwhile, we've a keep to win back. Again, I suggest you get dressed. You will, of course, do whatever you bloody well please."

The door swished shut behind him. Marea would have given anything if only she could have let him go right then. But she couldn't. There was one other matter they'd not settled yet.

She hurried to the door and threw it wide. "Chase!"

He stopped two strides away from the border of trees. He did not look back at her. "What?"

"Do you—do you fight for the castle alone or do I fight with you?"

"I'd say that's up to you, Marea. But I'll tell you now, if a Graham reclaims the keep, it is in his hands 'twill stay."

"Aye, but for how long? You may fight and win Kinclearnon back, but so long as there's a breath in me body, your holdings will never be safe from the MacKenzie."

He turned to look at her. His gaze was narrow, hard, and probing. Possessive. "Fair enough. Because as long as there is breath in mine, *you* will never be safe from the Graham."

She leaned hard against the door. "Are you threatening me?"

He shook his head. "I state a fact. There is nowhere you can run to that I will not find you, Marea. Nowhere you go that I will not hunt you down and drag you back. You are mine. I knew it the moment I set eyes on you half a score ago. Our being together was inevitable. Why can you not see that?"

"What I can see is that right now the keep maun be wrested from Douglas hands," she said, thinking that this topic was by far safer than the one he'd broached. "We can either fight together or fight separately, but we still maun fight."

He'd walked toward Marea as she spoke. He now stood just in front of her. The top of her head, he noted, barely grazed his shoulders. He was again struck by her size and the way his own dwarfed her. A surge of protectiveness he did not try to stifle swelled in his chest. Reaching out, he took her hand and pressed her palm against his chest, holding her there when she would have pulled away. "You don't have to fight at all, Marea. You could stay here and let me do the fighting. Then, when 'tis over, you can join me in the keep and take your place by my side. No one would question it."

"I would."

His grin disarmed her. "Pride will not keep your bed warm at night, Marea."

"Mayhaps. But 'twill keep my heart in its place."

His thumb stroked her long, slender fingers. He felt her quiver and resisted the urge to pull her into his arms. It would do no good, only prolong the inevitable. He glanced down at her, his gaze carefully impas-

353

sive. "If we fight separately and I win the keep . . . what then, Marea?"

" 'Twill mean I failed." Her gaze fixed on the sky, pinking with sun, behind his back. "But I'll try again. And again. Eventually, I'll have what belongs to me."

"And if I told you *I* belong to you?"

His ragged tone made a shiver race down her spine. Slipping her hand from his, she moved back into the shack. She heard Chase hesitate, then follow.

Corbie had found a home amidst the dry herbs on the table. Marea ran a palm down the sleek, furry back. The room was filled with a loud purr. A nice distraction. She glanced over her shoulder but did not look at him. "You'd not say such a thing. 'Twould be foolish. There can be nothing between us, *Sasunach*. Not now. Not ever."

A cold laugh rumbled through the room as Chase stepped to her side. He hooked a finger under her chin and forced her gaze to the rumpled cot. "Nothing, mistress? Nothing at all?"

She flushed and looked at the timbered wall. Sucking in a deep breath, she thought she could still smell the earthy scent of their lovemaking in the air. It was unavoidable; it was everywhere. "Mayhaps *one* thing," she granted weakly. "But 'tis a physical thing. 'Twill pass, if we let it."

"I don't intend to let it. Nor will I allow you to. Lust is not all there is between us. There's more. Much more. You know it, though you refuse to admit it."

"I do not."

"Don't you?" He dragged her gaze back to his. His eyes smoldered. "Don't you?" he repeated, his thumb scraping her jaw. The touch was tender. So were his words. "I know you watched me last night when you thought I slept. And I watched you. I saw the look in your eyes, Marea, when your gaze raked my body. Say what you will, but there was more than lust in your gaze. There was affection. Warmth. Aye, and caring."

"I—"

He slashed a finger over her mouth, stilling her words. The roughened tip of his finger quivered against her lips; her lips quivered in response. "Fight *with* me to win the keep back. Together, I think we can beat Henry, beat the Douglas. I shudder to think what will happen if we strike alone."

"A-and if we do win? What happens then?"

"We fight the lairdship out between us." Her jaw rose as though to argue, but he didn't give her the chance. "Not clan against clan." His finger traced the delicate bow of her lips. "One MacKenzie. One Graham. The way God intended it to be. We settle the dispute between ourselves and honor the outcome."

She hesitated. "And if I win this battle between us?"

"I'll admit defeat," his eyes sparkled a warning, "but only if you agree to the same should I win." Chase noticed the way his body cooled when she pulled away and moved to the perch on the edge of the cot. He gave her the time and distance she needed, refusing to rush her even though the hour was late. It cost his pride to wait. Surprisingly, he found that pride was only one of the many sacrifices he would make for her.

At the crunch of straw, he turned toward her. Her eyes were dark with indecision. "Well?" he prompted.

Sighing, she shook her head and said, "I accept your deal."

"All of it?"

"Aye. All of it."

"And if I win, you'll become my wife?"

Her eyes widened. "*That* was not part of our deal."

"Aye, 'twas. I must not have explained myself too well."

She thought on that a second then, reluctantly, nodded. "Aye, I'll marry ye if ye win. But if *I* win, you must agree to leave Scotland and never return."

"Agreed." Inwardly, he promised himself that any attempt at victory on her part would be discovered and squashed before it had a chance to root. Whatever happened, whatever it took, this woman would lose their last, their most important battle. He swore it.

Chapter Twenty-five

With only the two of them to accomplish it, their plan was shaky at best. Unfortunately, not only was it all they had, but they'd very little time to see the scheme through. The Douglas and Henry wouldn't be long in figuring out where Chase had hidden. They had to move before that discovery was made.

Chase spent the morning scouting the castle. It appeared the Douglas had left before dawn to hunt Chase down. Not knowing Chase had already returned to Kinclearnon, the Scot set out on the path leading to his own castle. It was a fortuitous mistake, one that played directly into Chase and Marea's hands.

Marea used the time Chase was gone to collect herbs and roots, then cook a potion. By the time he returned, the small shack was filled with a pungent, spicy odor. Not foul, not pleasant, the scent hung in the air like steam. Only the tension that crackled between Marea and Chase was thicker.

Once the potion had cooled, she poured the concoction into a leather pouchan. The pouch, in turn, was secured to her waist with a scrap of rope.

They left for the tunnels at dusk. The tension between them had eased a bit. Scarcely an hour before they'd settled into a conspiratorial, if not friendly, mood. Both knew that if they were to succeed, their plan hinged on their ability to work well together. Though neither acknowledged it verbally, desperation was spoken with passing glances and an occasional touch.

The night was cloudy. The forest, treacherous in daylight, was even more so with no light to guide them. The trees were large and ominous, not easily seen. Animal holes were nothing more than abnormally dark shadows. More than once Chase lost his footing and Marea had to wait for him. Three times they had to hide when guards passed close by.

It was as they neared the mouth of the tunnel that Marea's steps faltered and she stopped and turned toward him. Chase, not prepared for the sudden stop, came up hard into her back. His hand shot out to steady her. The second her footing was sure, he let her go. "What's the matter?" he hissed into the swirling shadows. "Can you not find the opening?"

"I can," she whispered back. A breeze tossed the hem of her Agatha skirt. It rustled around her ankles and his. She backed up a few steps. "But I've a doubt I should be showing ye where it be, though."

"Oh, bloody hell!" Then, a bit more calmly, he continued, " 'Tis not the time for second thoughts, Marea. Need I remind you that our plan is based on gaining the keep? If you'll not use the tunnel, then we enter by the bridge. Forgive me if I'm wrong, but I

358

doubt the guards would see fit to open the gate once they see who is seeking entrance."

"Aye, but how do I know you'll not use the tunnels against me in the future?"

"You don't."

Marea felt a nudge against her shoulder and stumbled back a step. She braced her feet and refused to budge any further.

"You're being childish," he hissed.

The words shot at her from the darkness and she had only a sketchy silhouette to tell her from where they'd come. She fixed her glare there, standing her ground when he nudged her again.

He sighed impatiently. "If you don't move soon, Marea, I swear I'll throw you over my shoulder and carry you."

"Ye canna," she said imperiously. Crossing her arms over her chest, she glared at where she supposed he stood. "You do not know where you be going. Only I know where the entrance is."

"True enough. But I *do* know the way back to your shack," he growled. "And once there, I promise I'll take you over my knee and administer the spanking you so deserve."

"You'd not dare!"

His silence spoke volumes.

Marea's lips pursed in indecision. The sound of his booted feet crunching over the dry leaves that spanned the distance between them made up her mind quite quickly. Spinning on her heel, she delved farther into the woods. She heard him fall into step behind. Worse, she heard his soft, delighted chuckle.

As always, the tunnel was dark and murky. The

359

wetness lining the floor and walls seeped through the soles of her shoes, wetting her back as she slid against the wall. The familiar musty odor and constant dampness was tolerable. It was having to take Chase's hand in hers to guide him that was not.

His hand was warm and rough. His fingers wrapped around hers tightly, but not painfully. More than once she felt his thumb scrape her knuckles, stroking, caressing. Their sides bumped together and two hisses sliced through the darkness. She stiffened, but did not pull from his grasp. She couldn't. And he knew it.

"How much farther?" His whisper bounced off walls and ceiling. Their surroundings made his hushed voice seem loud.

"Not far," she said, and almost screamed when she felt his thumb nuzzle the sensitive center of her palm. A drop of water fell on the veil she'd pushed over her head. She could feel it pelt against the fabric.

Somehow, their shoulders brushed. This time, she had a feeling the contact was not accidental. Clamping her jaw hard, she hurried forward. With a vicious tug, she pulled Chase behind her, smiling when she heard him stumble. His curse bounced off the walls and her smile broadened then melted from her lips at the feel of his hand clamping down hard on her shoulder.

"If you'll not work with me say so now. I've no wish to reach the keep and learn of your insincerity then."

"Have I not already said I would?" she answered tightly. The echo of his voice had not receded before hers overlapped it.

"You have. Yet you continue to trip and yank at

me, hoping to make me fall. What else have you in store for me, witch?"

Marea tipped back her head and released a soft but shrill Agatha cackle. She couldn't resist — and when she felt his hand flex, she was glad she hadn't tried to. "You're no bairn," she told him sweetly. "Methinks you're strong enough, and smart enough, to dodge whatever I throw your way."

"I thought we were working together in this," he hissed.

She felt the tension that rippled through the body, oh, so close to hers, but she ignored it. She knew the tunnels well. He did not. Losing him in the twisting, turning passages would be easy. Though she wouldn't do it — their plan depended on them both reaching the hall — there was no reason for him to know that. For once she had the upper hand and she was going to enjoy it.

"You'll have me full cooperation once we reach the keep," she informed him lightly. "I'll give you no trouble then, but will carry out your instructions without question. However, until then I'd be fibbing if I said 'twould not do me heart good to hear the almighty Graham falter now and again."

"Why you—!"

She was ready for him. As soon as she felt his fingers tighten, she slipped from his grasp. Her timing was perfect. They had reached a cross road in the tunnel. Marea scooted silently to the mouth of the second passageway and molded herself against the wall. Waiting, listening.

His curses did not disappoint her. He quieted only long enough to draw breath and listen for signs of her, but Marea refused to give him even that much. Eventually, he continued on toward the hall, as she knew he would. His footsteps were hesitant, searching.

She moved into step behind him, timing her steps to fall in rhythm with his own. His spicy scent warred with the stale, musty odor of the tunnel. She was not close enough to touch him, but she could feel the heat of his body warming the moist stones beneath her palm. It was a nice feeling. And distracting enough so that when he stopped, she did not at first notice. Not until she had crashed into his side.

" 'Tis no time to play games, wench," he growled, his voice very close to her ear. "We've a job to do—the result of which should be your sole concern right now. Or did you forget about that? Does Kinclearnon mean less to you than I thought it did?"

Invisible fingers curled around her upper arms, pinning her to damp stone. A solid wall of thighs brushed her hips, pressing ever so slightly into her before arching away. The feel snatched her breath and made her heart race. "Nay," she whispered, feeling properly chastised. "I sought only to lighten the mood. 'Twas"—she choked on the humiliating words—"foolish and silly. A prank a bairn would play. I'll not do it again."

Even in the velvet darkness, she could feel his surprise. The fingers clamped around her arms tightened, then fell away. He surprised her yet again by slipping back to place at her side as though nothing had happened.

Their only contact now was linked hands. It was enough. Her palm felt hot wherever it touched battle-roughened skin. As if that wasn't bad enough, as she

362

moved slowly down the tunnel Marea noticed that her thumb had unconsciously begun to stroke and tease. Her mind ordered an immediate stop to it, but her thumb had other ideas.

She grazed his bluntly cut nails. The feel of them scraping her tender skin sent a shiver down her spine. The callouses on his fingers were more pronounced in the darkness, since her senses were sharpened to an acute pitch. His knuckles felt thick and weathered, the hairs on the back of his hand like threads of silk as they tickled her fingertips. His pulse raced against the inside of his wrist. Her thumb grazed it. She felt its frantic tempo and knew it matched her own.

By the time they reached the door hidden behind a tapestry hanging in the hall, her nerves had unraveled like a ball of yarn being played with by a kitten. Every noise reached her ears: the drip of water on stone; the scamper of small paws; the scuffle of footsteps; the rustling of her skirt; his scabbard scraping stone; uneven, masculine breaths; the hiss of two heavily muscled thighs rubbing. . . .

Marea stopped short. Squeezing Chase's hand, she indicated he should do the same. She then yanked her trembling fingers from his grasp. Resting a shoulder against the door, she glanced back at him, then wondered why she'd bothered. There was nothing to be seen but musty blackness, both ahead and behind. Yet, oddly enough, there was a peculiar sense of comfort to be had in knowing that Chase Graham was a part of that darkness.

"What is it?" From the sound of his voice, his mood had not improved. "Why have we stopped? What game are you playing now, Marea? Or would you rather I guessed?"

"Hush up. We be at the door and I be trying to listen," she admonished, while pressing her ear to the door. The panel was thick — three inches of solid oak — and sturdy. Only muffled sounds filtered through. "There be men out there." She scowled, listening closer. "A fine lot of them. Methinks 'tis the evening meal." Her breath caught. "Methinks we be too late."

"Bloody hell!" The expletive was released on a frustrated sigh. She heard his leather jack crunch in the darkness and imagined him plowing his fingers through his hair. "Oh, this is wonderful." Was he grinding his teeth, she wondered? Was the muscle in his jaw twitching as it always did when he was angry? "If you'd not played your silly trick back there we might have — "

"I wasted five minutes of your precious time. From the sounds of it, they've been eating for awhile. The time I wasted made no difference."

"Mayhaps. Not that it matters now. We'll have to think up a new plan."

"*You* will. As my foiled raid attests, I'm no strategist." She paused and, when he did not respond, added, "You're the born and bred Border reiver. Think of something."

"Aye," he whispered. Then, more fiercely, "Aye."

She felt him move past her. Automatically, her hand shot out. Sheer luck had her fingers find their mark. His jack felt cold beneath her palm, the leather cracked and weathered, the muscle beneath hard and alive. She bunched the sleeve in her fist and stopped him. "Where are ye going?"

"You said the door would be unlocked."

"I did. But we've no plan to work with yet."

"You need no other plan than to find your way back to the bog, Marea." The shadows in front of her shifted and she inhaled when she felt his palm cup her cheek. It smelled of must from the wall and of the leather wrapped tightly around the hilt of his sword. "I go alone from here."

"Are you mad?!" It was all she could do not to scream. "If you go out there now, the guards would have you skewered in seconds. Think reason, Chase! It'll not work."

His thumb stroked her cheek, her jaw. The touch was lightly caressing, as though the calloused pad sought to memorize each delicate line. " 'Tis time for action now, not thought. After all, 'twas you who reminded me which of us is the Border reiver." His sigh kissed her brow. "About time I started acting like one, wouldn't you say?"

"They'll kill you." And, oh, how she hated the way her voice cracked!

"Mayhaps 'twill be I who kills them first."

"There be too many. Ye can't kill them all."

She heard the leather shift and knew he'd shrugged. "Then they'll kill me. However things go, I want you safely back at the bog. I'll not have you witnessing more death and destruction in this keep, Marea. Not if I can help it."

"I'm no bairn who needs sheltering and protection. Nor will I be ordered about by you. I'll do what I please, and what I please is to see us win back this keep *together!*" She was trembling, her voice thick with an emotion she didn't dare analyze. Whatever it was, it had her heart in a mighty grip. Her palms were sweaty with fear—white-hot, coiled fear. It had been years since she'd felt terror this strong and all-consuming.

"Your concern is appreciated, but misplaced." His palm ascended. The curl of her ear was captured between his thumb and index finger. His rich voice caressed, the tone husky, almost pleading. "My mind is made up, mistress. Please, go back before it's too late. Leave me to do what I must."

"Nay!" She shook her head, the movement hampered by his hand. Her fingers fisted in his sleeve. The tightness in her chest was unbearable. Her soul felt like it was being brutally ripped in two. She knew why, but refused to acknowledge it. "What ye maun do now is make up a new plan . . . with me."

His tone hardened. "If you are worried about our deal, I swear to you it will stand as agreed upon if I live to—"

"Chase, *please*. What you suggest . . . 'tis suicide. I canna let you go out there. I *w-will not!*" Tears, as alarming as they were warm, weighted her lashes. She tried to swallow them back, but couldn't. One slipped down her cheek, melting in a warm, salty puddle atop his knuckles. His thumb absorbed the salty drop. Another was quick to fall. And another.

"Why are you crying?" he asked softly.

"Because I"—her voice caught on a sob—"I be a fool." Her head dipped, but his hand quickly brought it up again. "I must be, because th-the thought of you dying—" She swallowed hard, trying to gain some control over herself. It wasn't possible. "It should not bother me, yet it does. It . . . brings me pain." The last was said in a soft, breathless rush.

His hand slipped behind her neck and he drew her toward his chest, not content until he felt all of her leaning into him. His arms cradled her close, as though she was a priceless piece of art that needed to be protected and cherished at all costs. In his arms, she felt as though she was.

"I thought you *wanted* me dead," he rasped against the satin-soft hair beneath his cheek and the coarse veil covering it. "Many's the time you've said so."

"Aye. 'Tis what I thought I wanted," she admitted with a sniffle. Her throat stung and her head ached from holding the real torrent of tears at bay. "I hated you so much for what your family did to mine. I'd have cut you to pieces meself not so long ago. But now, to see it actually happen . . ."

"Say it, Marea." After a brief hesitation, he said, "Tell me what you feel for me now."

"I do not know. I—" Sobs tore her words away. The tears were pouring down her cheeks in salty rivers now, unchecked. He wrapped his arms around her and held her tight. She didn't pull away. Instead her hands strayed up his back and she clung to him as though she might never get another chance. Turning her head, she buried her face against the cold leather covering his shoulder and wept fiercely.

There was a great deal of comfort to be had in his arms. Marea fed on that comfort, on his warmth and strength. She felt safe, protected, as though she'd come home.

It took a while before her sobs eased. Chase still held her just as tightly. She wiped the wetness from her cheeks off on the coarse wool of her sleeve, but

367

didn't pull away. She never wanted to pull away from this man again.

"I love you, my proud, fierce MacKenzie. Never doubt it." His voice wrapped around her, hugging her as tightly as his arms. The words, so solemnly uttered, made her heart stutter, and brought her soul an equal amount of warmth and comfort.

She knew he was looking down at her in the darkness, waiting for her to speak, waiting for her to answer him in kind. She opened her mouth to do so, but her emotions were too tumultuous, her mind too fogged from her hard cry to form the words he needed to hear.

A lifetime passed before he cupped her cheeks in his palms. His mouth crashed down on hers. His kiss was hard and demanding, branding and possessive. He dragged the warm, moist tip of his tongue along the line of her teeth before plunging inside. He played with her, warred with her, made love to her mouth the way his body had done all through the night.

She pressed urgently against him, trying to melt into the firmness of his chest. Her hips arched and a whimper rumbled in the back of her throat when she felt the hard proof of his desire against her stomach. Her heart raced with promise as her hands restlessly searched the familiar terrain of his back. Even through the padded leather she could feel the sinewy cords ripple. They burned through her palms, tingled up her arms, and warmed a fiery pool in her stomach. Lower.

The darkness, the guards, the Douglas and Henry Graham, even the castle vanished from her mind. None of it mattered. Right now the only thing that mattered—the only thing that *existed*—was Chase and the fierce hunger he'd stoked within her.

"Take me," she whispered against his mouth. "Make love to me. Here. Now. Please. I've need to feel you moving inside of me, Chase Graham. Hard and strong and alive. I've a need for—"

"Better accommodations," he finished for her. He lightened but by no means ended the kiss, only shifted it elsewhere. His lips moved over her jaw. His tongue licked and teased, his teeth nibbled and seduced. "Or did you forget where we are? And why."

She drew a harsh breath and arched into him when he captured her earlobe in his mouth and made love to it with his tongue. "I did not forget."

His hands plowed through her hair, freeing the veil. It tumbled down her back, splashing in the muck on the floor. He cradled the back of her head, tilting it to the side to give him better access as he moved his lusty attentions to her neck. Ah, a longer, more glorious expanse of flesh God never created. "How do I make you feel, Marea?"

"Hot. I'm burning up for want of you."

The words scorched and elicited a stifled groan of desire from Chase. With a shift of his body, he pinned her to the wall and bent forward. He never lost the taste of her neck. The pulse in the base flicked against his tongue. He stroked it until it pounded. His hands moved to the buttons at her nape. He slipped loose the first. The second. The third. Cool, damp air rushed through the gaping fabric, caressing flesh that his hands and mouth had kindled to a degree just shy of boiling.

He never reached the fourth button. A sound

echoed close on the other side of the door, stopping them both cold.

They stiffened in the darkness, both instantly alert. After a few seconds of listening, a voice became distinguishable.

"I've agreed to spare your young mistress, Zander MacVin, and in return you've agreed to point out the tunnel and guide us through it. Need I remind you what will happen if you don't?"

Marea clutched desperately at Chase's shoulders as the voice of her worst nightmares echoed in her ears.

The voice belonged to Carl Reubin.

Chapter Twenty-six

Chase thrust Marea behind him at the same time the door crashed open. The mouth of the tunnel was bathed in flickering orange light. To eyes that had adjusted to shadowy blackness, the light was blinding.

Marea squinted, looking past Chase. Blinking hard, she made out the shapes of three silhouettes framed in the doorway. The first was poised in mid-step, while the second stood just behind the first, peering curiously into the shadows. The third, and smallest, looked ready to bolt.

The hiss of steel slithered off damp stone walls as Chase slipped his sword free. The murky light glinted off the blade when it made a deadly arch up. He held the weapon brandished and ready for battle.

"Marea," Zander gasped, taking an instinctive step forward. His rounded face was flushed, but now that her eyes had adjusted to the light, Marea could see bruises distorting his features. Some were old, but not all. A trickle of blood dripped down his chin from the fresh cut on his painfully swollen lip.

The second man, now recognizable as Henry Graham, reached out a restraining arm. Like an iron bar, it refused to allow Zander past. "Chase, how good to see you again," Henry greeted coldly. His eyes, however, were on Marea. Even in the shadows she saw recognition—and fury—glisten ominously in his eyes. His lips curled up in a sinister grin when he spotted her uncontrolled shiver of disgust.

"Pity I can't say the same for you," Chase replied, his attention split between Reubin and Henry. His muscles were coiled tight, prepared to spring into action should either of them try to rush him. Neither did, but the threat was there and Chase was ready for it.

"What are you doing skulking in the tunnels, brat?" Reubin sneered, his voice a nasally, bored whine. His gaze was also fixed on Marea, but more than mere recognition shimmered in the devilish depths of his eyes; realization glistened there as well. "And what, pray tell, are you doing consorting with Kinclearnon's lovely witch? I'd think you wise enough to keep better company. Or did you forget this woman killed your father?"

"Did she?" Chase heard Marea's frightened whimper, acknowledged it, but his sword didn't waver. He could only guess what seeing Reubin again was doing to her. "And how can you be so sure, Reubin? Have you taken to believing your own lies now?"

Reubin laughed. Leaning against the doorway, his gaze raked Chase. Disgust shimmered in his eyes. "And who else besides our dear 'Agatha' here would want David dead so badly? Now that I know who your witch is, I can see her motives clearly. I'm surprised you can't. 'Tis not like you to be so blind, brat."

"Nor you so stupid," Chase countered with the barest nod. His attention shifted to Henry, and the younger man's cheeks colored under the intensity of his brother's gaze. "I can think of at least one person who would have liked David Graham gone for good. Henry, can you think of another? Now might be a good time to cast suspicion in another direction."

Henry's cheeks darkened, but it was not from embarrassment. His hands clamped into fists, but still he did not reach for the sword hanging at his waist. "Nay," he snarled, jabbing a finger at Marea, " 'twas *her*. No other had the reason she did."

"And what reason would that be . . . *brother?*"

Henry faltered. His mouth sagged open, but no words poured forth. They couldn't. Truthfully, he hadn't a clue as to why the woman would want their father dead. Until that night in the clearing, he hadn't even known she existed! But Reubin had said she had motives, so she must.

" 'Tis an answer I am also curious to hear, Henry," Reubin muttered. His stance was casual, giving the appearance of calm relaxation. No one was fooled.

Henry's arm dropped from in front of Zander. He made no attempt to stop the small Scot from hurrying to Marea's side.

"Be ye unharmed, m'lady?" Zander whispered, enfolding Marea in his arms. The top of his scraggly head barely cleared her shoulders, but the comfort his arms offered was appreciated.

"I-I be fine," she answered shakily, and drew a palm down his battered face. She removed it quickly when he winced. "But you do not look so grand."

Zander opened his mouth to reply, but Reubin's voice snatched the words away.

"Well, have you no answer, Henry?" He pushed away from the wall and took a threatening step forward. Though Henry's eyes widened, he did not back up. "Methinks you've been given plenty of time to concoct a lie. Let's hear it."

"I've no reason to lie." Henry tilted his chin high and returned Reubin's gaze unflinchingly. "If you'll recall, I was at Brackenhill the night Father was murdered. The distance between keeps makes it impossible for me to know for certain who killed my father or for what reason."

"Yet you are positive our little witch committed the crime," Reubin pressed, now standing toe to toe with Henry. His anger was a tangible thing. "Why? No, Henry, don't lie to me again, or I swear I'll slice off one of your fingers for every untruth." The hiss of his sword being drawn sealed the promise.

Henry stammered a response, but Marea never heard it. Chase had turned just then and hissed to Zander, "Get her out of here." He jerked a thumb in the direction of the tunnel. "Take her back to the bog and keep her there. Sit on her if you must, but don't let her out of your sight."

"Aye, m'lord," was Zander's immediate response.

Marea opened her mouth to refute the order, but Chase's glare melted the words on her tongue. "I'll have his life if he doesn't do as I've instructed, Marea. And 'twill be on your head that the guilt for his death shall rest." He didn't wait for a response, but turned back to the two men who continued to argue.

"Come, m'lady. Please."

Zander tugged on her arm and Marea stumbled ahead a few paces. A few more and they were concealed in the blanket of shadows. Only their footsteps

374

and the angry words behind them could be heard.

"I do not want to leave him," she pleaded, trying to pull her arm free of his grasp. For a small man, Zander was strong. He wouldn't let her go, but continued pulling her behind him. "Th-that awful man will kill him, Zander, as he tried to kill me half a score ago. And I-I canna let the Graham die."

"I'll not ask ye why that should matter, m'lady," Zander hissed from the darkness. "But I'll tell ye. If ye stay by his side, ye force him to protect ye. A mon canna fight for his own life properly whilst he be busy protecting his woman's."

"I can protect meself. I'll do whatever I must, but I can't leave him to Reubin. I'd not be able to live with meself if . . ." Marea wrenched her arm free. She turned to run back to Chase, but had taken no more than two steps before Zander's small body slammed into her. The impact was sudden and fierce, forcing the breath from her lungs at the same time she was propelled hard against the stone. His grunt of pain as his battered body rammed into hers was loud in her ears.

"Do not make me knock you senseless, lass," he panted, pinning her to the wall and stifling her struggles, "But I'll do it if ye force me."

She pushed against his shoulders, but weakly. She couldn't hurt him more than he already was. "Zander, you remember your way through the tunnels. Leave. Go to Kintail and seek out me Highland kin. Tell them who you be. They'll take you in. Just, please, get off of me and let me do what I maun."

"Nay, m'lady. There be other MacKenzies in Kinclearnon who need your help right now. I'll not disappoint them."

At that, her struggles stopped. "What do ye mean?"

"Your Uncle Thomas and Randy, lass. Reubin gave orders to kill them in the morn." He heard her gasp, felt her melt limply against the wall. "I be thinking 'tis time they found their way out of the dungeons and did that which they came here for."

"Aye, Zander. They maun be freed. But how?"

" 'Twas a fine muckle of nothing I could do to help them whilst I languished in the next cell, lass. But, now that I be free . . ." He gave a fine rendition of an "Agatha" cackle.

She felt the release of his weight and heard him move in the darkness. Instinctively, she fell into step behind him, hurrying to catch up. "Think you we'll free them in time to help Chase?"

" 'Chase' is it now?" he muttered, hurrying down the passage. Even without light to guide him, he knew the twisting paths well. Marea had taught him all she knew and he was a quick learner. "Aye, lass. If you'd not be stopping me again, nor fighting me, methinks that's a possibility."

Marea drew a quick breath and for the first time indulged in a small measure of hope. "Then let's hurry, mon!"

"She's gone," Henry cried, jabbing a finger over Reubin's shoulder and ignoring the tip of the blade that threateningly jabbed at his abdomen. He turned furious eyes on his brother. "What have you done with her? I demand to know."

Until now, Chase had been content to watch the fight between Henry and Reubin from the sidelines, curious to see who would emerge victorious. Now that he was being dragged into the conversation, he couldn't say he minded. He had his own reasons for wanting to know why Henry had accused Marea of their father's death. "Are you trying to change the subject, Henry? Not too clever. We'll just change it back again."

"I'm doing nothing of the sort," Henry spat. He would have advanced on Chase, but for the point of Reubin's broadsword. "I simply want to know where the wench is."

" 'Tis not your concern." Nothing in Chase's expression or stance suggested the relief he felt to know Marea was safely away. The glint in his brother's eyes bespoke trouble for her. Henry would stop at nothing to cast suspicion off himself—and if, in the process, it fell back to Marea, so much the better. The boy would have no regrets.

"Answer the accusations and get on with it, Henry," Reubin sneered. "Hate though I do to agree with your brother, he's right. Where the wench went is of no importance. I've more interest in hearing the proof you have against her."

"If she is Agatha, then she killed my father," Henry said tightly. The gaze he cast on Reubin was brutal. "She was seen administering a potion to him the night he died. Apparently, the culprit is obvious to all but you two." His gaze narrowed on Reubin. Hatred shimmered in Henry's eyes. "You've the gall to let the wench go, then dare to turn your accusations on me. I'm starting to think my father's trust in you was ill-founded, Reubin."

It was not a wise remark to make to someone of Carl Reubin's reputable bad temper—as the reddening of the man's gaunt cheeks attested. His black eyes shimmered with fury as he growled and, with the heel of his palm, gave a shove to Henry's shoulder.

Henry reeled back, his feet catching in a tapestry that had been torn from the wall and tossed carelessly into a wrinkled heap. He stumbled, and with a grunt of pain toppled hard onto the hard stone floor.

A small crowd had gathered around the door of the tunnel. The group was growing larger. All were eager to hear every juicy word being uttered inside the dank-smelling recess. The sight of Henry Graham careening out, however, made them take a collective step back. A few mumbles rippled through the men, but most remained unnaturally silent as they watched Reubin step into the hall. The man's eyes were blacker than coal and trained on Henry Graham. More than one man thanked the Lord that it was the young Graham who would be victim to that one's fury, and not himself.

Reubin stalked to Henry's side, planting the sole of his boot atop his stomach. He kicked Henry back to the floor when the boy tried to rise. Henry didn't try twice. "Did I give you permission to stand?" Reubin sneered. Sheathing his sword, he crossed his arms over his chest and glared down at Henry, who was finally beginning to show his first true signs of fear.

Chase emerged from the tunnel only far enough to lean a broad shoulder against the stone doorjamb. His presence created a new stir amongst the men. Unlike Reubin, Chase's sword had not found its scabbard, though it was no longer brandished. It hung limply from his right hand. Only the tense bunch of muscles in his arm said he was ready to pounce on a second's notice.

"I'll have more than rumor from you, Henry,"

378

Reubin said, the heel of his boot grinding into Henry's gut. "I'll have the reason you're so sure the witch killed your father. And I'll have it now. No more delays"—he leaned forward, his gaze dark and threatening—"or lies."

"I've no idea *why* she did it," Henry whined. His hands rose, as though to push the breath-stealing weight off of him. His fingers grazed Reubin's boots before he realized what he was about to do and his hands dropped back to the stone.

"But you *know* she did," Reubin replied. "I wonder how you can be so sure?"

" 'Tis what I've heard."

"Rumor does not make it true." Reubin's eyes narrowed as he pulled free the dagger from his belt. The jewels embedded in the hilt winked in the sconce light as he turned the blade this way and that. "Tell me, Henry," he said with apparent distraction, "why do you think the wench wanted David dead?"

Henry gulped and looked away. His gaze fixed plaintively on the men who gathered around, listening intently. None looked willing to spring to his aid. "I suppose 'twas because she hated him," he muttered finally.

Chase pushed away from the wall and approached Reubin's back. The closer he drew, the more tension he felt radiating from the lank man's body. The feel of it surprised him, for he'd thought Reubin had parted ways with his emotions years ago. Apparently not.

"Speculation," Reubin snarled. "She had many chances to kill David before then. Why didn't she? Why *that* night?"

"Isn't it obvious?" Henry cried. "The facts speak for themselves. She had the motive, the opportunity. Who else could have done it?"

379

"Any number of people," Chase replied from over Reubin's shoulder. The older man was small by comparison and Chase had no trouble seeing his brother squirming atop the stone floor. He rather liked the sight. "Father died quite a few hours after the witch left the keep, Henry. Yet he drank her potion immediately—in the presence of a servant. Methinks if the drink was poisoned, the effects would have been quicker."

"Sh-she could have snuck back through her blasted tunnels and fed him the poison during the night," Henry argued, but the statement was weak, made even weaker by the way his voice cracked. "There's none to say she didn't."

"Aye." Chase nodded. "And none to say she did."

Henry gulped, his gaze scanning, trying to find a ready exit. The men gathered were mostly Reubin's. The group of them was thick, making easy escape an improbability. Henry's attention returned to Chase and his eyes burned with hatred. "Who else would want him dead?" he asked, his voice stronger now as his gaze began to glisten with renewed purpose. He started to rise again, but Reubin's foot still held him pinned. He didn't dare move it. Not yet. "Besides *you*, dear brother."

"Or *you*," Chase countered, one golden brow slashed high.

A dank center passage, poorly lit, twisted between the four large cells. When Connor MacKenzie used the dungeons, he'd had three guards patrolling the area—two at the door, behind which led the stairs, and another strolling the curved passageway.

Tonight there was only one — from the looks he was a Scot whose loyalties had switched from Douglas to Reubin. But only one? Either Reubin was astonishingly self-assured or the commotion from the floor above had drawn the extra guards away.

The two who hunkered outside the door cared not which it was, only that they had but one man to overtake. Peeking through the keyhole, Marea monitored the remaining guard's actions. The guard had drifted down the center passage, around the curve. His disappearance from sight was all that was needed. Quietly, she and Zander slipped through the door and hid in a medium-sized storage cubicle, sandwiched between the first cell and the wall.

The fit was tight and they were forced to squeeze together in the darkness. Zander barely had time to throw a threadbare blanket over their heads before they heard the guard approach.

The material was thick and coarse, blotting out what little light there was. The fabric scratched Marea's cheek as she turned her head away, holding her breath and wrinkling her nose at the foul smell clinging to the cloth. The smell of Zander's blood and sweat was just as pungently trapped beneath the cloth, but at least that odor was welcome. It meant he was alive.

When the footsteps retreated, she hissed into Zander's ear, "I saw a tankard set atop a keg near the door."

She felt him shift, and knew he was looking at her in the darkness. "I saw it too. What of it?"

"I could put it to use."

"How?"

"Shhh."

381

The guard was back. This time his steps were not sure and even. He paused at the halfway mark and a wicked chuckle cut the air in response to a mumbled remark made from one of the men in the cells. "Think you I care how you feel, MacKenzie? Ha! You could be losing the entire contents of your stomach and I'd still not be concerned."

The mumble, while indistinguishable, grew angry. Lifting a corner of the smelly cloth, Marea leaned forward and dared a glance down the shadowy passage. The guard was dark haired and bearded, large and well formed, intimidating to look upon. No wonder only one had been left behind—with this one's size and obvious strength, only one of him was needed.

She was just pulling the blanket back over her head when she saw an arm shoot out from the vertical space between the iron bars. The hand was grimy, the fingers thick and tight as the prisoner lunged for the guard's throat. The guard took a quick step back. His swift inhalation hissed through the air, as did the sound of his sword being drawn. The blade glinted in the flickering sconce light.

"I said get back. Me orders are not to skewer you, though I be thinking there's not a soul in this keep who'll be upset if I did. Now, get back!"

The prisoner grumbled something that sounded suspiciously like a healthy Gaelic curse, and the hand disappeared. The guard resheathed his sword.

Marea pulled the blanket back over her head. Her fingers strayed to the pouch strapped to her waist.

The footsteps approached, and stopped beside the door. She heard liquid splash into the tankard, swallowing, then a belch. After a few moments, he moved back down the passage again.

Marea unstrapped the pouch from her waist. Clutching it tightly, she waited for the guard to turn the curve in the passage. Then, after mumbling softly for Zander to wait, she slipped from beneath the blanket. With only the faint rustle of her skirt to mark her passing, she padded across the floor, ever watchful for the guard.

Scarcely a minute later, she was leaning against the stone outside the door. The corridor leading toward the stairs was pitch black and damply cold. Shivering, she clutched the half-empty pouch to her breasts, all the while willing her frantic heart rate and breathing back to normal.

A crash echoed from above. Marea's heart stopped. Her mind screamed out for Chase. Was he still alive? Would he continue to live if she waited much longer to act? Swallowing hard, she tucked the pouch in her pocket and pressed her ear to a crack in the door. Inside, she heard the guard approach. He paced the corridor four times before she decided not to wait any longer.

Henry's eyes widened in surprise, but the expression was quickly masked. "I'd no reason to want Father—"

"No?" Chase cut him short as he stepped to Reubin's side. He felt the older man's thoughtful gaze rake over him, but ignored it, concentrating instead on his brother. "Not a one?"

"Nay!"

"Not even your inheritance?" Chase countered with cold precision.

"I'd no inheritance to gain," Henry growled.

The colors that flamed in Henry's cheeks, combined with the anger hardening his gaze said Chase had hit a sore spot. Good. Unless he missed his guess, he was about to hit another. "You had no way of knowing that. In fact, Father said he was going to try and bypass me, leaving everything to you. Didn't he, Henry?"

" 'Twas what he wanted," Henry snarled. "He hated you. Despised you. You and your 'feelings' sickened him. He didn't want you gaining an inch of his lands. Not a shilling of his fortune. He would have done anything to prevent it."

"But he couldn't," Chase said coldly. "*I* was his son." Henry flinched. "As was I."

"Not legally," Reubin interrupted. "Legally, you were a bastard—and bastards inherit nothing." His expression was hard, merciless, his eyes glinted with dark realization as he glared down at Henry. "On your feet, brat!" Reaching down, he grabbed a handful of Henry's tunic and yanked, giving the startled boy no choice but to obey.

Henry's shortened stance put him on eye level with Reubin. His fingers curled around the older man's forearm as he struggled to free himself, but Reubin wasn't letting go.

"David never married your mother," Reubin snarled. "And for good reason. I don't believe he liked her." The black gaze raked Henry head to toe. Disgust shimmered there. "You, he liked. Mayhaps he even loved you, in his way. You were his only weakness, Henry; he would have given his life to spare yours." With a flick of his wrist, he yanked Henry close. Nose to nose, Reubin glowered into Henry's face and demanded, "Did he? Did David die because of you—

384

at *your* hand?"

"I was in Brackenhill!" The cry tore from Henry's throat, punctuated with the fist he threw at Reubin's head. His eyes widened when he hit his mark. Reubin grunted in surprise. Henry had no chance to savor the victory, for Reubin's retaliation was lightning quick. In one sure blow, Henry crashed to the floor at Chase's feet, the fresh cut in his lip bleeding freely.

A feminine scream cut the air when Reubin's dagger rose, poised atop a deadly arch. Henry shook his head to clear his addled senses. He barely heard the scream, but heard the woman's words quite well.

" 'Twas not his fault!" Martha sobbed as, skirts hoisted about her thick legs, she broke through the semicircle of men. They parted to let her past, giving her a wide berth, as though afraid that touching her would somehow draw them into the deadly encounter playing out near the tunnel's entrance.

The woman rushed to Henry's side, but was brought up short by the tip of Chase's sword when she made to bend over him. The blade pressed threateningly into her heaving, matronly breasts.

"She doesn't know what she's saying," Henry shouted, rising shakily to his knees. "Get her out of here."

"Nay." Chase studied the woman who had once nursed Henry tenderly through a bad bout of the fever. "I want to hear her out." His emerald gaze pinned Martha to the stone and he saw her flush. "What do you know of my father's death, Martha?"

"I . . ." Her meaty fingers twisted her limp white apron.

Her eyes were wide and nervous. Her attention flickered to Henry, who had been dragged to his feet, and whose back was now pinned against Reubin's lanky chest. With the jeweled dagger pressed to his throat, he could give no indication of what he wanted her to say.

Marea removed the padding from her clothes, ran a nervous hand down her skirt, and moistened her lips with the tip of her tongue. She worked her braid free, finger combing the red-gold waves and fluffing them around her face and shoulders. Then she pinched her cheeks hard, forcing back the rosy color she knew tension had robbed from her.

Satisfied, she opened the door and stepped inside. Just as quietly, she closed it. The guard was rounding the corner. She heard a sword being drawn, heard the pounding of footsteps spanning the rest of the passage, heard the mumble of prisoners as they became alert and moved curiously toward the bars. A few sharp intakes of breath hissed through air, and she knew a few of the men had recognized her.

The tip of a sharp metal blade was pressed to her throat.

Appearing meek and coy was something at which Marea had little practice, but desperation spurred her on. She slumped her shoulders forward—as far as she dared with a sword being pressed against her throat—and kept her eyes downcast. Her hand twisted in the folds of her skirt. The glossy curtain of hair fell forward over her shoulders, concealing her face from view.

"What are ye doing here, wench?" the guard demanded. Those prisoners who had slept until now were awakened by the guard's booming voice. His breath, as it wafted over her, reeked of stale whiskey.

"I — I'm lost," she whispered, her voice quivering. She'd softened her brogue, contorting her tongue around an awkward English accent. All in all, she didn't think it a bad imitation. "I've journeyed all the way from Brackenhill to see Henry Graham, but he was busy. He told me I was free to roam the keep." She smiled shyly, though the waves of her hair hid most of her mouth from view. "He declined to mention how easily I could become lost. Could you guide me to the hall? Henry must be sick with worry. I've been gone quite some time."

"I've prisoners to guard, lass," the man replied gruffly, indignant that such a lowly request would be made of him. "I've no time for playing escort to a silly wench. Find your own way."

"Prisoners?" she gasped. "Do you mean this is . . . the *dungeon?*" Marea inhaled quickly and backed hard against the door, as though just the thought made her head light. "Oh, my, I'd no idea." Her fingers fluttered at the creamy base of her throat as she lifted her chin. Blinking quickly, she turned the full effect of her wide amethyst eyes on him. Her reward was an open-mouthed stare and a lowering of his sword.

"Aye, mistress, 'tis the dungeon," he informed her, his broad chest puffing when he caught her look of open admiration. His sword tip swept the cells behind him before he slipped the blade back in its scabbard. "Ye did not know?"

"Nay." She shivered delicately. "I'd no idea." Her gaze strayed over his shoulder. Familiar faces pressed against the bars. She tore her gaze away and turned awe-filled eyes on the guard. Her words were hushed with feigned respect. "Are your prisoners *dangerous?*

And are you here *alone* to guard them?"

His smile was cocky and swift. Thoroughly male. "Aye, mistress, to both your questions," he boasted as he leaned a broad shoulder against the door, much too closely to hers.

One of his dirty fingers caressed a red-gold curl. Marea allowed it, pretended she hadn't noticed, and suppressed a shiver of repulsion. "You must be very strong and brave to be trusted with such a fine muck—er—a *large* responsibility."

"Aye, very," he replied with a severe lack of modesty. His attention was riveted to the delicate curl clinging to his large, calloused finger. "Would ye care to see the prisoners up close before ye leave, lass?" When her eyes widened in fear, and her sweet breath washed across his cheek, he rushed on, "No need to worry. *I'll* protect you."

"Nay, sir," she whispered throatily. Cocking her head, she met his gaze. The hunger shimmering in his dark brown eyes was unmistakable. She pretended not to see it. "I've no fear you could protect me—you're so big and strong—but I've also no wish to view men so . . . so . . . fearsome. Why just the thought frightens me into a swoon"—she batted her lashes coyly—"and I've a doubt you'd wish to catch me should I faint."

"Think again, lass. Catching a soft wee thing like you sounds splendid." His gaze darkened a shade as it fixed on her dewy lips. He moved closer to her side.

"You are so gallant. I am thinking that perhaps I've no wish to return to Henry right now after all." Her gaze drifted to his lips—too full and moist—and, placing a hand on his grimy tunic, purred, "Have you a drop of water to spare on a poor, lost waif like myself? 'Twould be sorely appreciated."

His face loomed closer. "I've a dram of good Scottish whiskey. If you've a thirst to quench, nothing will do the job as well."

"Oh, I," she blinked and dropped her gaze, "I shouldn't. Strong spirits make me giddy. Why, just the smallest sip and I become most unladylike. It Finally he muttered. mightn't be wise."

"I'll not let ye drink too much," he promised. The sparkle in his eyes bespoke the lie. "Just enough to quench your thirst." His bushy, dark brows drew down in a hesitant scowl. "Do ye not trust me, lass?"

"Aye, sir, I do," she soothed. She splayed her fingers on his chest. The muscle moving beneath the tunic felt firm and hot. "All right then, perhaps just a sip."

Capturing the hand, he placed a moist kiss on her knuckles, then turned away. He returned a second later with the tankard, which he pressed into her grip. Marea took a small sip, though she made it look as if she took three. The cough that tore from her throat was genuine as she passed the tankard back.

" 'Tis strong for such a wee wench," he said, lifting the tankard to his lips and taking a deep drought. His dark eyes regarded her over the bottom of the mug.

"Might I have another sip?" This time, she did not drink, only pretended to. The small amount of the potion she'd consumed so far would do her little harm. If she drank more, however, she would be unconscious in minutes. Passing the tankard back, she watched him drain the rest. His eyes never left her as he discarded the cup on the floor, then leaned hard against her.

"Ah, wench, ye be a might easy on the eye," he murmured. His calloused hand cupped her cheek as his head clumsily lowered. Already his lids were growing thick. Soon, his vision would blur. "Be a good lass and give us a kiss."

His lips brushed hers. The contact was brief and ended when he collapsed to the floor. The stone shuddered with the burden of his weight.

Zander popped up from beneath the blanket. His expression was a mixture of concern, awe, and reprimand. "What be ye thinking, m'lady?" he grumbled, then flashed her a smile that made him wince when it curved his swollen lips. "Never mind. Methinks I already know—and his name be Graham. Come on, let's free the men and see what can be done about helping the other."

Zander knelt beside the guard and relieved him of the key to the cells, as well as his sword and the dagger concealed in his belt. Quickly, he set about freeing the prisoners, not all of whom were Marea or Thomas's men. Those who weren't quickly agreed to help win the fight above in return for their freedom.

Her reunion with Thomas and Randy was brief and fierce, with no time for more than hushed assurances of health and tight bear hugs. Their ordeal not withstanding, her uncle and cousin were in sound health. Between them, Thomas and Randy quickly brought order to the group of haggard-looking men. In less than five minutes they were organized and heading for the hall—knocking out guards and collecting much needed weapons on the way.

Chase had always been an excellent judge of character. He knew Henry for the cruel bastard he was, just as he knew Martha for her gruff kindness. That Henry could have convinced the woman to commit murder on his behalf shocked Chase. But there was no

390

denying the evidence—it swam in Martha's frightened gaze.

Wisps of gray-black hair had pulled from the bun at her nape. She swiped the brittle strands back, her voice softly pleading when she said, "I didn't want to do it. But when Henry told me his father was going to kill him—"

"David?" Reubin cried in disbelief. "Kill *Henry?* His own son? David would never do such a thing."

Martha's head came up. Her eyes were wet with unshed tears. Whether they were caused from fright, grief, or the sword pressed to her bosom, Chase never knew. "I know that now, Lord Reubin. But Master Henry was most convincing."

"What reason did my brother give you?" Chase asked, his voice edged with impatience as his gaze flickered between Martha and Henry. "Why did he say our father wanted him dead?"

Martha's eyes rounded with fear. She looked at the sword pressed to her breasts, then let her gaze travel up the length of the blade, up the arm that held it steady, until she met Chase's gaze. "Henry killed Hannah when m'lord was visiting Brackenhill, beat her with his fists until she was dead. Lord Graham saw him do it. M'lord was in a fury. He said Hannah was his favorite, and that he'd see Henry pay for wasting a good serving wench."

A whimper left Henry as Reubin's dagger sliced into a thin layer of his skin. A trickle of blood twisted down his neck, soaking a crimson splash into the collar of his tunic.

"David wouldn't have killed him for that," Reubin growled, the arm around Henry's midsection increasing its pressure. "Beat him, mayhaps. Or whipped

391

him. But he wouldn't have killed him."

"Henry said differently," Martha cried. Her fingers trembled with nervous anticipation as they worked at the limp white apron. "I—I believed him. The poor boy was f-frightened to death."

"And so he solicited your help?" Chase pressed. He'd pulled the sword back slightly—afraid the woman would move and accidentally skewer herself on it—but not so far as to remove the threat. " 'Twas you who administered the poison, at my brother's urging, wasn't it, Martha?"

"Aye, 'twas I."

Until now, Chase hadn't consciously admitted he'd harbored doubts—even after Marea had confessed she was innocent of his father's murder. Now he felt the shock of her innocence cut into his soul. It staggered him. The feeling was made more intense by the realization that, deep down, he'd never really believed her, but had only wished to.

"She's lying!" Henry screamed, writhing in Reubin's grip, trying to break the unbreakable hold without slicing open his throat in the process. His face was set with desperation, his devilish gaze flickering between Martha and Chase. Both were bestowed with equal amounts of hatred and fury. "Hannah lives. She's at Brackenhill serving ale to the men there as we speak."

"Hannah's dead, boy," one of the men said. It was a deep, gruff voice that snatched the attention of all in the room. "I saw her body myself . . . and a sore sight 'twas."

The man stepped forward, recognizable as a Graham, far down on the clan ladder. Chase knew the man by name, knew at a glance the dark, forbidding-looking guard could be trusted. What he didn't know was how the devil the man had escaped the dungeon. Scanning the crowd, he noticed a few more familiar faces, all men who had been taken captive by the Douglas. All men who should, by rights, be languishing in the cells below but were not.

A frown etching his brow, Chase sent a quick glance to Reubin. The man was too busy keeping his hold on Henry without killing him to pay the speaker, or the others, much attention besides a curious glance. Chase turned his attention back to Henry. "What say you now, brother?" he asked, his sword arm tensing. "We've a witness who says Hannah is dead. Will you call him a liar?"

"Aye!" The single word was a strangled yelp, for Reubin had again gained control of Henry, and now held him excruciatingly tight. "The wench lives," he croaked.

"I've not seen her body, but I've heard rumor of her death," another voice called out. This man did not step forward, but his accent was distinguishably English amongst the murmuring Scots. "The wife was sore grieved to hear of it, too. 'Twas Hannah who helped deliver our last babe fine and sound. She was a good wench, was Hannah."

One golden brow cocked high as Chase coldly regarded his brother. Henry's cheeks had drained white. He hung limply in Reubin's arms, like a rag doll with no fight left in him. Chase wasn't fooled. He knew his brother, recognized the glint of desperation in Henry's eyes for what it was. He was biding his time, waiting for the perfect opportunity to escape. And when he did, all hell would break loose.

Chase's gaze shifted to Martha, who was quietly sobbing. Her rounded cheeks were paler than the

393

apron she twisted around her fingers. "You can go, Martha," he said and jerked his chin in the direction of the men who'd gathered closely behind her.

With a muffled sob, Martha lifted her skirt and scurried away, as quickly as a woman of her bulk could scurry. In seconds she had disappeared behind the semicircle of men.

"You're letting her go, too?!" Henry demanded, his face reddening as he glared at Chase. "Another who may have killed our father and *you are letting her go?!*" This last came out in a rush of breath as Reubin tightened his arm around Henry's waist. For a second, Henry's eyes bulged before the pressure was eased, but not released.

"She was a pawn," Reubin hissed in his ear, loud enough for everyone to hear. "We seek the one who conceived the game, not the one who was tricked into playing it out."

"Then look elsewhere," Henry cried, squirming. " 'Twas not I. I'd no reason to want my father dead. Not a one."

"Your brother and Martha say differently," Reubin snapped, his patience wearing thin. "For the first time in my life, I've a mind to believe him. You'd not be the first man to shed blood for a hefty inheritance."

"But—"

"Don't say it," Reubin growled. The dagger nudged Henry's flesh, drying the young man's words in his throat. "You'd no way of knowing David left you nothing. He never told you. This I know. The same way I know the greed that festers inside of you. And the hatred." He paused, his lips curling back in a disgusted sneer. "I took pride in you, Henry, but there's no pride to be had in a boy who kills his own father. Especially

394

when that man was my dearest friend." His grip tightened and Henry gasped. "I see you for what you are now, and what I see sickens me."

Henry's face contorted with rage. Although he made no attempt to break Reubin's hold, it was only a matter of time. Chase braced himself, ready for the moment his brother was free, morbidly anticipating it. His hand tightened on the leather-wrapped sword hilt.

Henry's chin jerked at Chase. " 'Twas that one who always sickened you, Reubin. Chase and his girlish ways. His softness. His weaknesses. How many times when I was young did I hear you and Father say what rotten luck it was to have such a sniveling excuse for a son sprout from David Graham's loins? And 'twas true! He's not half the Graham *I* am."

"Aye, ye feckless bastard, 'tis twice your sniveling hide he be worth—and I for one be proud of it," a hard, feminine voice spat from behind the tight gathering of men. The soft tap of heels on stone punctuated each furious word as the voice that rippled up Chase's spine drew closer. The men shifted, parting to let her pass, but he knew who she was long before she stepped past the men. The sudden throbbing of his heart, his abruptly shallow breath, the tingling in his blood, told him it was Marea.

She stood hands on hips, sandwiched between two burly Scots. Her diminutive height was dwarfed by their size, but the anger radiating from her, glistening in her fiery amethyst eyes, made the men flanking her seem no larger than woodland fairies.

Chase tore his gaze away. The tension in the room had subtly changed—charged, electrified—and he'd only to look at Reubin and Henry to discern the reason for it. Marea. They both looked upon her, and while the younger man's eyes were filled with vengeance and lust, the older man's gaze was wary.

Chase's gut tightened. Clenching his teeth, he crossed to Marea's side. He should be angry she'd flagrantly disobeyed him by coming back to the hall, but he wasn't.

Right now, the only emotion he was capable of feeling was the need to shelter and protect. His body was coiled tight, poised at her side, feeding on the warmth and smell of her. It stunned him to realize he was ready for anything, ready, even, to lay down his life and those of his men for this woman if need be.

Chapter Twenty-seven

"You fickle Scottish bitch," Henry sneered at Marea. "You defend my brother now when, just a few eves past, you played the slut for me. Don't tell me you've forgotten so soon the hours we spent beneath the stars when you lay hot and willing in my arms, begging me to take you."

Her fingers convulsed around the hilt of the dagger concealed in her skirts. "Liar! I'd sooner skewer meself with me own blade than lie in your arms, pig. And never, *never*, would you have me willing." She met Henry's gaze unflinchingly. His eyes sparkled a raw challenge as he raked her head to toe. Marea felt as though every scrap of cloth had just been ripped from her body. Her skin crawled at the thought of this man gazing at her naked flesh, even if it was only in his warped imagination. The urge to melt into the towering, comforting strength standing poised at her side was strong and not easily denied.

"There's no need for pretense, wench," Henry said. His precarious position at the end of Reubin's blade was belied by the leisurely quality of his voice. Although his attention was on Marea, the evil smile on his lips said he was very aware of Chase's reaction. "Nor reason to lie about what happened between us." His hand swept the room, stopping palm up in his brother's glowering direction. "Chase is used to sharing his wenches—of necessity. Many's the woman I've been called upon to satisfy where my brother could not."

"Like you satisfied Hannah?" the man whose wife the dead woman had saved called out. That question brought a murmur of unpleasant speculation drifting through the men. "No doubt she was begging you, too . . . to stop your flying fists."

If Henry had hoped to gain the men's respect, he failed. He swiftly tried another tack. Turning his attention to the men, he addressed the one who'd just spoken. "Aye, she begged loud and hard, Hannah did," he boasted with a sneer, "for more."

"Then ye admit killing the wench?" another, this one Scottish by brogue, challenged. Only Marea recognized Randy's voice and knew what he was doing. The tension in the air increased, and the men she had brought with her to the hall sought to add to it. They were doing a fine job.

"I said only that she begged me," Henry corrected stiffly. "Not what she begged for."

"Ye did not have to," another Scot called out. It was Thomas, artfully concealed at the back of the crowd. "Guilt is in your eyes, lad. Ye killed her all right and had a fine time doing it. 'Tis a pity ye were caught, but now that we know the truth of it—and since poor, dead Hannah is not here to do it herself—we'll have to seek vengeance on the lassie's behalf."

"By what right?" Reubin demanded, moved to speech by the eagerness on the faces around him. His grip on Henry loosened as he prepared to battle the men who closed in.

"By March Law," one of Reubin's guards growled angrily. "We be in the Middle March, on the Scottish side of the Border. Here, we do things the Scottish way."

"Aye," another voice, barely recognizable as Zander's, agreed eagerly, "and any Scot worth his salt avenges a wrongful death. It does not matter on which side of the Border the victim was born. Is that not right men?!"

A roar of approval rippled through the crowd. The sound of dozens of blades being freed from their scabbards hissed through the air. Bloodlust and vengeance shimmered in the eyes of English and Scottish alike as the crowd pressed forward, carrying Chase and Marea with them.

Marea tried to turn, reaching for Chase's hand as she planted her feet firm and fought not to be swept away. She felt the warm roughness of Chase's fingers graze her wrist and she lurched towards it, grasping desperately. But the men behind surged ahead, and his hand was gone before she could catch it. She was forced forward on a sea of hard, sweaty male bodies toward the one place she did not want to be — toward Henry Graham and Carl Reubin, the only two men on the face of the earth who had the power to frighten her senseless.

Impending death was all the incentive Henry needed to break free of Reubin's hold. A well-placed jab to the man's gut caused Reubin to double over, breathless. He hadn't time to straighten his stance before Henry had drawn Reubin's sword and dodged the first brutal attack.

Steel crashed against steel as Henry's blade was thrust high. Hilt met hilt and, with a feral snarl, Henry pushed away the man who was trying feverishly to separate his head from his shoulders. Henry lost his sword in the bargain, but quickly found the dagger tucked in the cuff of his boot.

Marea saw it all from a distance of barely two feet. Her own dagger was still hidden in the folds of her skirt, but she'd no need to protect herself from the men who formed an impenetrable wall at her back. They were working to draw someone else's blood, not her own. Still, she felt better with the metal hilt biting firmly into her palm.

Two seconds later, she was glad for it, because a brutal grip wrenched her upper arm and she felt her back brought up hard against Henry Graham's heaving chest. His arm slipped around her waist like a tight coil of rope, squeezing the breath from her lungs and threatening to snap her ribs. With his other hand, he held the tip of his dagger against her breasts.

"Come a step closer and you'll have another death to avenge!" Henry's voice boomed over Marea's head, piercing her ears in the sudden, quelling silence. Even the shuffle of uncertain feet atop the stone seemed deafening.

She scanned the sea of faces, searching for one. Chase stood on the border of men, his face set hard, his eyes sparkling furious emerald fire. His gaze wavered on the blade pointed at her heart. And for the first time since she'd nursed him in her shack, Chase Graham looked helpless.

Her gaze shifted. Thomas and Zander were toward

the left of the men, conferring, but they weren't close enough to offer the immediate help Marea needed.

"The wench and I will be leaving now," Henry announced, his gaze fixed imperiously on Chase. The victory that rang in his voice was a tangible thing; it curled up Marea's spine. "Unless you want this woman dead, no one follows us."

Henry backed up a step, dragging Marea with him. She had no choice but to comply. Collectively, the men around them moved closer with Chase at their lead.

"Tell them to do as I say, wench," Henry hissed in her ear.

Marea stiffened, stumbling back another step as she slipped her own dagger into the pocket of her skirt. "And if I do not?"

"Then you die."

She tried not to think of the last time her life had been threatened in this keep. Tried not to, but did. Her gaze lit on Reubin and a violent shiver worked over her shoulders. "Do as he says," she ordered, her voice shaking as badly as the rest of her. Her gaze met briefly with Chase's. In one look, a world of understanding passed between them. Words her lips would never utter, her eyes said, and his acknowledged. All too soon, the contact was broken.

Henry reached the mouth of the tunnel and his grip on Marea grew tighter. Breathing was nearly impossible, for every gulp of air she sucked in, there was a stab of pain in her ribs. Her head felt alarmingly light.

A cautious step was made through the doorway. Henry's empty scabbard scraped against the wooden door as the shadows of the tunnel fell over them like a dark, musty blanket.

Marea's heart throbbed as she looked back at the men. While a part of her pleaded with them to charge forward and rescue her from this insane man's clutches, another part, equally as strong, was terrified of what would happen should they dare.

"Close the door," Henry barked when they were fully engulfed by the shadows. Only a few brave rays of sconce light dared invade the darkness here.

The arm around her waist uncoiled, a split second before the heel of his palm planted a rough shove between her shoulder blades. Marea staggered, then hunched slightly forward, preparing to run out of the tunnel. The dagger that abruptly took the place of his palm on her back convinced her that running right now would not be wise. With trembling fingers, she closed the door, casting them into inky blackness that felt alive from its very impenetrability.

"The bolt," Henry growled. He was close enough for his warm breath to rush over her hair and cheek. His voice was hard and grating, impatient. "Throw the bolt, you stupid chit."

She did. Her compliance was in no small way prompted by his dagger, the tip of which bit into her back, nudging her to obey. Her hands were quivering, which made sliding the slab of iron that had not been used in centuries difficult. The bolt groaned as it slipped into place. Outside the door she could hear the shuffle of footsteps and eager voices plotting her rescue.

A sinking feeling churned in the pit of her stomach. It was too late. The door was bolted. The men could not get through.

A hand she couldn't see—and didn't want to—wrapped brutally around her upper arm, dragging her

402

hard against the wall. Henry's broad chest pinned her to the damp stone. Marea tried to assess where he'd put the dagger. Unconsciously, her hand strayed to the side of her skirt and the comforting bulge of metal there.

"Don't do anything foolish. That's the only warning I'll give you, wench," a gruff voice said from the darkness. "Be thankful for it, for 'tis one more than I usually give."

His free hand shot out of the darkness to drag down the length of her jaw. It was all Marea could do not to jump away as she bit back the scream bubbling up in her throat. *Where had he put the dagger?!*

"See us safely out of here and I'll take you with me . . . unharmed," he continued. The hand on her arm tightened until her fingers grew icy and numb. His voice lowered to a deadly pitch. "Try once to escape me and I'll kill you. Slowly."

"Kill me and you'll never find your way out," she snapped, surprised at how calm her voice sounded; it was a marked contrast to her hammering heart and rapid, shallow breaths. "The tunnels were made to confuse an intelligent mon. You'd not stand a chance."

His hand dropped from her jaw. A second later she felt it again — his warm, steady fingers closed around her throat. His grip was not so tight as to cut off the gasp that whispered through her lips, but tight enough to be alarming in its threat.

"Lead the way, wench," he growled, thrusting her away from him and toward the cloistering darkness. Since he hadn't let go of her arm, she didn't have far to stumble. "I'll see you pay for that remark when we're well away from here. *Now walk!*"

Marea walked — very slowly. Knowing he couldn't

see her in the darkness, she made a pretense of making it seem as though her knowledge of the tunnels was sketchy. She flinched dramatically at the scamper of small paws around them. She banged into walls, grunting when she crashed into the sweating stone. She tripped uncertainly through the muck that puddled on the floor. When they came to their first crossroad she pretended to be unbalanced by the sudden disappearance of stone, then stopped completely, as though debating which passage to take.

"Tonight's the first time I've been here in years," she muttered under her breath, just loud enough for him to hear. His sigh of impatience combined with the pressure of his grip, both told her not to toy with him overlong. "Methinks we should go this — nay, *this* way."

Henry muttered an imaginative oath as his hand slipped from her upper arm to her wrist. Then lower. His palm cupped her bottom, squeezing unmercifully tight, before he shifted. His fingers entwined with hers.

Since the darkness acted as a blinding shield, Marea allowed herself a quick smile. Before, with her side against his, she couldn't have reached her dagger without alerting him to what she was doing. Now, she could. Tugging him behind her, she careened into a wall, and slipped her right hand into her left pocket. In seconds she had the hilt of the dagger in her hand. She slipped it free, and pushed away from the wall.

"I am not so big a fool that I cannot see what you're doing, wench," Henry barked from close to her shoulder.

Marea tensed, her fingers curling around the hilt, ready to thrust, even though she wasn't sure of her mark. "And what be that, *Sasunach*?" she asked cautiously, skirting the edges of a puddle that was ankle-deep.

"You're hoping to waste enough time down here to give my brother a chance to meet us at the tunnel's opening. I'll not allow it." His fingers tightened in a bone-crushing grip. Against her will, Marea winced. "Don't think I can't find the way out myself, for I assure you, desperation can make a man do anything. Your purpose was served in seeing me safely away from the hall, so either you quicken the pace or I will relieve myself of the burden of bringing you with me."

"I do not wish to go with you," she argued, still creeping down the tunnel. They were nearing another crossroad. If she could only keep him distracted another minute . . .

"Then mayhaps I should kill you now, bitch."

She was almost there. Almost. A few more precious feet. "N-nay," she muttered, trying to sound cowered. It was difficult since the heat of nervous adrenaline was pumping furiously in her veins. "I-I'll show ye the way."

"I thought you would." His confident chuckle bounced over the close press of walls.

The damp stone beneath the heel of Marea's hand disappeared. The crossroad had been reached. Finally. her fingers tightened around the dagger, trembling in dreaded anticipation as she tried to assess his position behind her. He shifted, but she wasn't sure to where. She thought she felt the heat of him melting into her back. Thought, but was unsure. "I-I be not sure of the way from here," she lied.

Stopping, she waited until he had done the same, then turned to face him in the darkness. Even with her eyes accustomed to the lack of light, the tunnel was too dark to make out more than vague shadows. She needed to hear his voice to know where he stood. Exactly. If her aim went wild, escape would be lost. She knew there would be time for only one sure thrust before his dagger cut its own deadly path.

"I think we be lost, *Sasunach*," she whispered into the darkness, and heard his boots shuffle directly behind her.

"You'd best hope we're not."

It was all Marea needed. She knew where he was now. In her mind she could see him leaning against the cold stone wall. Her imagination conjured up a glimpse of his arrogant grin.

Her dagger lifted and, swallowing a steadying breath, she arched it downward with the brunt of her strength.

The dagger sliced air. For a moment Marea thought she'd misjudged. Then she felt the blade sink into flesh. A scream ripped the air, ricocheting off the walls as the tip of the blade grazed bone. Marea felt a surge of warm, sticky blood ooze over her hand as she pulled the dagger free and, in the same instant, hoisted her skirts and ran.

Her heart pounded in her ears, rivaled by the sound of a man's whimper as Henry collapsed onto the soggy floor. She didn't know how badly she'd hurt him, nor did she waste precious time finding out. She had aimed for his arm and there was a chance it was his arm her blade had found. There was also a good chance she'd killed him.

Shutting out the image of Henry Graham's dead body crumpled and bloody on the tunnel floor behind her, Marea ran. Her breath tore from her lungs, her legs screamed a protest. She was only half conscious of where she was and of how much longer it would take her to reach the woods at the end of the tunnel.

Behind her, she heard pursuit. She gasped, unable to believe it at first. But the cold, hard laughter that echoed down the tunnel said it was not her imagination, but that Henry Graham was following. His boots splashed over the puddled stone, the strides surer and stronger than they should have been.

"Run, bitch," he called, his voice growing closer by the second. "Run fast. But you won't escape. I'll find you, and when I do you'll beg me to make your death as easy as Hannah's was."

Marea gulped, her mind whirling. Another cross-road was coming up soon. It would be the last. The distance to the tunnel's opening and the safety of the woods was half the distance of the opposite tunnel, which spilled into the storage chamber. Taking the second passage could prove a fatal mistake, for there was no guarantee the door leading into the storage chamber would be unlocked. If she switched passages, she'd be trapped if the door was barred from the outside. Then again, at the rate Henry was gaining on her, there was a better chance he would overtake her before she reached the woods, at the end of the shorter passage. She didn't dare think about what he would do to her if he caught her.

The last crossroad was reached. The clomp of footsteps echoed from behind. Marea stopped, trying not to pant too loudly as she made up her mind. A muffled groan as Henry crashed into a wall a few hundred yards behind prompted her to move. Lifting her skirts in trembling fingers, she made her way cautiously into the mouth of the next passage. Just as there was no guarantee the door at the end of the tunnel would be open, there was also no guarantee help would be waiting for her in the woods at the end of the one she'd just abandoned.

Molding herself to the wall, she used her hands to guide her. The cold, damp stone slipped beneath her palm as she picked her way through the darkness. She was careful to keep her progress quiet so Henry would not know she'd switched tunnels, which meant she must go slow. Only the rustling of her skirts marked her passage, but to Marea's alert ears, even that slight sound seemed deafening.

The throb of Henry Graham's footsteps stopped abruptly when he reached the crossroad. He'd made the distance quicker than she'd expected and Marea breathed a sigh of relief to think she'd made the right choice after all. Had she continued straight, he would have caught her in minutes.

He stopped. She did the same, afraid the scratch of her heels would tell him where she had gone. She'd come scarcely a hundred feet. Closing her eyes, she leaned against the stone, her knees quivering as she waited for him to come to his own decision. Mentally, she willed him to go straight, even as she heard him shuffle with indecision.

"I'm coming for you, wench," he called out. "And in case you think I don't know where you've gone, you should know I can smell you. Hmmm, your scent is heathery and light. And strong. I'm close now. So close I've only to reach out to touch your shoulder. Can you feel me touching you?"

His voice was deep and taunting, bouncing off the wall. To Marea it sounded as though it came from mere inches behind. Instinctively, she started; half expecting to feel his fingers clamping brutally down on her shoulder.

Her dagger brushed against the stone. The sound was not loud. But it was loud enough. With a wicked laugh, Henry plunged down the tunnel after her.

A scream lodged in Marea's throat as she hoisted her skirt and bolted into the shroud of darkness. There was no need for quiet now and she made no attempt at it.

His footsteps drew closer, louder, more threatening. Breathlessly, she ran. Blindly. Frantically. With every step, the door and its uncertainties loomed closer. But he was gaining on her and she was no longer sure the storage chamber, if indeed she could reach it in time, offered any safety. She rounded a corner, tripping as her feet splashed in a mucky puddle. Almost immediately, he rounded the corner as well.

The door was at the end of that straight bit of passage, but Marea knew she would not make it that far. Her ragged breath burned as it tore from her lungs. Her legs were aching, her head spinning. With each step, her feet felt as though they'd been encased in a fresh layer of lead. The stitch that pierced her side almost landed her on her knees.

An arm reached out of the darkness and coiled about her waist. Another clamped over her mouth, muffling her scream until it sounded like a soft, plaintive whimper. Marea twisted, struggling like a demon, lashing out with her feet and flailing her arms as she tried to find a home for her dagger. Twice it scraped stone, but not once did it meet flesh. She tried to open her mouth, to sink her teeth into the calloused palm, but the bruising grip was too tight.

The arm around her waist tightened, forcing the rest of her breath to pour from her lungs. It was in that instant that she noticed the footsteps behind her had slowed, but not stopped. That they had, indeed, somehow lost distance on her.

"Chase." The word was unintelligible, thanks to the hand over her mouth. But that hand was no longer unwelcome. The hard chest pressed against her back seared her with its familiarity. The hand over her mouth loosened and a finger slashed over her lips, telling her to be quiet before slipping away. She nodded and felt the brush of Chase's lips against her temple before the arm around her waist uncoiled and she was allowed to drink in healing gulps of air.

Henry's footsteps had stopped by the time Marea caught her breath. She felt herself being reluctantly handed over to a man by Chase's side. She knew from his size and the coarse texture of his hair that it was Zander to whom she clung.

She heard Chase move away in the darkness and felt her heart lurch when she could no longer feel him close by. She heard a shuffling deeper down in the tunnel and another closer to her.

"Now!" Chase barked and almost immediately there was a loud scraping sound as half a score of sconces were lit.

Marea winced, closing her eyes against the sudden brightness as her hold on Zander tightened. Her lashes hadn't had a chance to flicker shut before she saw Henry Graham's look of shock — an instant before he turned to flee.

Zander held her close, murmuring words of comfort — words that did nothing to ease her terror as the tunnel was filled with the sound of pounding footsteps. The men who'd gathered inside the door of the tunnel rushed forward, hot on Henry's heels.

She lost sight of Chase almost immediately. She turned to Zander, her eyes wide and pleading in the flickering shadows of the single sconce left behind. "I have to go to him," she whispered raggedly, and Zander's arms tightened around her. "Henry is insane. He'll kill Chase without a thought to their kinship. I canna let that happen, Zander."

"Nay, lass." He shook his curly red head, meeting her gaze. His large, rough palm caressed her much too pale cheek. "He'll come to ye when he be done here. For now, you'll let him do what he maun, without hampering him by clinging to his side."

"But—"

"I said nay, m'lady." Zander guided her toward the door, his tight grip giving her no choice in the matter. "I know 'tis not me place to order you about, but this once I maun. This fight between the brothers has been a long time in the making. 'Tis time they ended it, and they canna do that with you there."

The door creaked open and Zander led a reluctant Marea into the cluttered storage chamber.

"And if he dies, Zander?" Marea asked, her voice thick with dread. She didn't realize her eyes had filled with tears until she felt one slip down her cheek. She watched Zander close the door, then turned back toward her. "What shall I do if he dies?"

"Ye be MacKenzie," he replied, as though the answer was that simple. It wasn't. The vicious rending of her heart in her breasts told Marea nothing was simple if it concerned Chase Graham. "If the lad dies—and I'm not saying he will, but if he does—you'll go on with your life the way you always have. The way any good MacKenzie would."

"I don't think I'd want to, Zander," she whispered.

Chase's death. Just thinking those words turned her blood to icewater. What Zander said was true, she'd only be a distraction if she went down into the tunnels after Chase now. But if she *didn't* . . . "I have to go to him," she whispered in a rush, trying to wrench from his grasp. "I should never have let you convince me to leave. If he dies . . ."

Zander's hold proved too strong to break. Clenching her teeth hard, Marea met and held the small man's unwavering gaze.

"If ye love him, m'lady, you'll wait until he comes back up and see him then." Abruptly, Zander dropped her arm and gestured toward the tunnel. His hazel eyes glinted with challenge. "If ye do not love him, then by all means go . . . and see that he dies for his need to protect ye."

Marea stood, teetering on the edge of indecision. Her conscience warred with her desire. It was a battle she couldn't hope to win. Finally, with shoulders held regally straight, she turned and left the storage chamber.

Chapter Twenty-eight

Dawn sliced pink and blue slashes across the sky. The rise of hill and mountain prevented the sun from peeking over the snow-crested tops just yet, but the golden brilliance of day was evident in the colorful lightening of the cloudless sky.

Marea stood poised atop the battlement, looking out over the splashing waters of Solway Firth. She'd given up her restless pacing a mere hour before. She was simply too tired to place one foot in front of the other. Now she leaned against the stone wall and gazed lovingly at her surroundings. Her heart ached, for she knew she was seeing her beloved home for the last time.

A brisk wind blew from the north, tossing the plaid about her legs and pulling free wisps of hair from the tight plait at her nape. Shivering, she snuggled deeper within the extra plaid she'd thrown around her shoulders. She was glad now that she'd thought to bring it.

When she'd received word Chase was alive and well, she'd retreated to her shack. No one had stopped her, nor had anyone but Randy tried to accompany her. She had a chore to do, a chore that grieved her sorely, and Randy had seemed to sense the emotional play involved. Regretfully, he'd left her be to search out Thomas, who'd accompanied the Graham into the tunnels.

Shortly before dawn she'd emerged from the shack with one small crate filled with clothes, and another housing Corbie and her newborn litter of kittens. No mist had wafted the ground when she'd made her two trips to the keep with her belongings. Somehow, the lack of curling vapors seemed curiously appropriate.

Zander had found her atop the battlement scarcely half an hour before. After sparing a brief comment on what he thought of the squirming little creatures in the crate—carefully set away from the wind near the stone battlement—he'd approached her. He stayed long enough to tell her the Douglas had been spotted near his own castle and that it was unlikely the burly Scot would return any time soon. Reubin had left the keep after being sequestered in a room with Chase for the better part of two hours. Zander didn't know what had convinced the *Sasunach* to leave, nor did he seem curious about it. Reubin was gone, that was good enough for Zander. Marea felt only relief.

After assuring himself Marea knew of Chase's safety, and after receiving only clipped, distracted responses for his effort, Zander had left. She'd been alone ever since, barring the few guards roaming the parapet walk, all of whom regarded her oddly. But she was too lost in her own whirlwind of thoughts to pay them much mind.

"Marea?"

She started, her heart racing as, for a split second, she thought the voice belonged to Chase. She spun on her heel, the wind catching the hem of her plaid and tossing it around her ankles. Her breath lodged in her throat, then released in a soft hiss as she focused on her uncle. She cast her gaze down, afraid he would see the disappointment mirrored in her eyes.

"Randy said ye were here," Thomas said, leaning a shoulder against the stone at her side. The musty smell of the tunnels still clung to his tunic and plaid, almost masking the stench of the dungeons. "We'll be leaving soon." After a brief, tense pause he added, "Are ye sure ye wish to do this, lass? 'Tis not too late to change your mind."

"Nay," she muttered softly, "I want to do it. There be nothing left for me here. Mayhaps I'll find a place for meself in Kintail."

"You're always welcome with us," he replied softly, his voice full. "I told you as much after Connor . . ."

His words trailed away and Marea felt the familiar stab of pain at the mention of her father. When she spoke, her voice was as thick with emotion as her uncle's. "Aye, ye did. And I knew it." Her gaze strayed over the Firth. " 'Tis half a score late, but I finally be coming to the Highlands."

"As ye should have done after—"

"Aye. I'm thinking you're right. 'Tis a journey I

should have made years ago." That statement made the pain in her heart slice a little deeper. She would have missed so much had she gone directly to her uncle instead of Agatha after the death of her parents. Not the least of which was the knowing of a certain arrogant Border reiver—the knowing of intimate caresses and softly spoken words. The knowing of—

"Have ye anything else you'd be wanting to bring?" Thomas asked. He reached out and tenderly cupped her shoulder. He felt her tremble under his hand, but no more so than the hand itself.

"Aye." She spared a quick glance at the box of kittens. Thomas followed her gaze and his grin was quick and wide. "But I'll be bringing that one with me when I come down." Her gaze strayed back to the water, but she couldn't see the foamy crests for the tears that blurred her eyes. "There's nothing else of this place I'd care to take with me."

Ah, but there be one thing, she thought, as her mind cruelly flashed her an image of piercing emerald eyes beneath a thick slash of golden brows. She pushed the image away, but those burning emerald eyes refused to be banished.

Thomas nodded and his hand dropped from her shoulder. He started to turn away saying, "I'll send Zander up to fetch ye when it be time."

"Zander?"

Her uncle's grin widened. "To me men's distress, your friend's decided to travel with us," he grumbled with a disgust that was too forced to be genuine. "I told him 'twas not wise for a MacVin to be seen with the MacKenzie, but he'd not listen to me now anymore than he ever did. The wee scamp said he'd only be following us if we left him behind. He'd a thought you'd be needing him."

"He be right," Marea said, casting her uncle a warm smile—her first and probably last of the day. "I'd not leave Zander behind if he's of a mind to come. Nor would I ask him to leave if he did not offer it. 'Tis glad I am to hear he made the decision for me."

"That he did," Thomas nodded. There was a trace of respect glistening in his eyes. A very small trace—one that would be vehemently denied should she ever ask about it. "And he was quite vocal about it, too. Got me men's dander up and had them fighting amongst themselves before the first crate was hoisted." He grinned to soften his next words. " 'Tis going to be a long, long trek to Kintail with that one in tow."

"And I'm sure Marea will be eager to hear all about it, Thomas . . . when next you visit Kinclearnon. Pity she won't be able to accompany you to the Highlands, though."

Marea's heart skipped and her breath clogged in her throat as her attention snapped over her uncle's shoulder. The intruder clung to the morning shadows cast by the high stone walls, but she knew who he was. If his arrogant stance, superior height, and broad shoulders didn't give his identity away, his voice did. His crisp accent combined with the rich huskiness of his voice to make it distinctive. The way it washed over her was sinful.

Marea's skin tingled with recognition even as she bristled at his remark. She felt her uncle's curious gaze shift from herself to Chase, then back again, but, try though she did, she couldn't tear her eyes off of the imposing silhouette that was a mixture of light, shadow, and raw masculinity. Nor could she stop her heart from throbbing with relief. She'd heard he was unharmed, but to see the evidence of it was a sweetness unto itself. A sweetness that threatened to engulf her.

Bathed in shadows as he was, she could not see Chase's eyes. But she could feel them. Hot emerald fire roved her face and grazed the tousled hair escaping her tight plait. Nothing was missed by his hungry gaze, not even the splash of color in her cheeks. His eyes stripped away the plaid, the too-large tunic, her shoes, and coarsely woven belt. Without touching her, he caressed her. Marea felt the burning heat of desire that went hand in hand with Chase Graham's nearness. The feeling alarmed her with its swiftness and intensity, but the warm fingers of yearning that licked at her gut, and lower, were nonetheless sweet and familiar.

Shivering, she drew the plaid closely around her shoulders. Her reaction was instinctive; it had little to do with the brisk wind that tossed her skirt and hair, and that whispered softly in her ears. It had everything to do with Chase Graham.

When she regained her bearings enough to look around, she was surprised to see that her uncle had slipped away. Surprised and alarmed. The last thing she wanted was to be alone with Chase.

Bloody hell!

She had not spoken the words aloud. At least, she didn't *think* she had. But when Chase stepped out of the shadows and she caught a glimpse of the laughter in his eyes, she knew she had. She also knew she was doomed, for with every step that brought him closer, her body became a little more aware of him.

He stopped scarcely three feet away. By that time, Marea's senses were honed to a fine edge. She could hear his breath over the whisper of wind and her skin burned when she remembered how each soft rush would feel on her upturned cheek. The musty, spicy scent of him was strong, the aroma countered by fresh air and her own flowery scent. Though he didn't stand close, her body was aware of the heat he cast off; the heat penetrated wool and linen and seeped into her suddenly too warm flesh.

"Ah, vision," he whispered huskily. His gaze caressed her face as though striving to immortalize it. "You aren't going anywhere, you know. Not today, not tomorrow, not ever. I can't allow it."

Their gazes locked. Brilliant emerald clashed with fiery amethyst. The two colors softened, melted together, blended. The result rivaled the breathtaking sunrise that neither of them were aware existed any longer.

"Ye canna keep me here," she said, and the trembling in her tone matched the one in her body.

"Can't I?" His gaze strayed to her lips, his eyes devoured. "Have you forgotten our deal, Marea?" His eyes darkened when he saw her shell pink tongue dart out to moisten her lips. Imperceptibly, he

419

tensed. "Should I refresh your memory?" His head dipped and he started to lean toward her, leaving no doubt in her mind as to his tactics.

She placed her fists on his chest — *so wonderfully warm and firm!* — and arched back at the waist. She gasped and stopped abruptly when her shoulders came into contact with hard, cold stone. She'd retreated as far as she could. And that wicked emerald gaze said Chase couldn't be more pleased to know it.

"Ah, I see you've remembered our deal after all," he said, pulling back to glance down at her. His grin was unnerving. "And here I was looking forward to jogging your memory." He shrugged. "No matter. There'll be time for that later, I imagine. For now, we've important matters to settle."

"Nay, mon, right now I must be leaving," Marea said. His suddenly light mood played on her already frazzled nerves. Only the spark of determination in his eyes and the hard set of his jaw said his mood was not as light as he'd have her believe.

She gave his chest a shove. He moved back a step, but she thought that was only because he was about to retreat. Lifting her chin and her skirt, she made to step around him saying, "I've a wagon to catch."

She heard a clatter of steel before he caught her arm. She'd taken less than three steps. "We have a deal to settle," he growled close to her ear before dropping her arm.

She traced the clank of metal to the broadsword he'd tossed atop the stone in front of her feet. She hadn't noticed him carrying it. She cocked an eyebrow and regarded him quizzically and saw yet another sword, the hilt of which was gripped tightly in his capable right fist.

His chin jerked in the direction of the weapon at her feet, but his gaze never left her. "The keep is Graham now, which means 'tis time we settled the matter of its vastly disputed lairdship."

When she still did not pick up the second sword, Chase bent forward. With a flick of his wrist, he slipped the tip of his blade through the hilt and offered the dangling sword to Marea. "Prepare to defend yourself, vision"—his lips curled into a devilish grin as he cut her a mock bow—"for you are about to come under seige."

The words, said with a lewd intonation, curled right up Marea's spine. Her flesh, traitor to the end, warmed to the insinuation. Her gaze dipped and she regarded the blade that dangled at the end of his sword tip with a disdain to match that in her voice. "I be leaving," she repeated as though she hadn't heard. They both knew he had. "There's no need for this now."

"Ah, but there is. We had a deal. A deal I intend to see honored"—his eyes flashed—"no matter what it takes."

Her gaze narrowed when he inclined his head. The morning light made his hair glisten a rich shade of gold. The strands were fluffed around his face by the breeze. His tunic flickered on the dancing currents of air, billowing the soft yellow fabric before pressing it against his chest, shoulders, and arms, outlining and defining each intricately carved band of muscle.

Marea tore her gaze away. Pushing away the red-gold curls tossing over her brow, she shifted her attention past the battlement. Although the churning currents of Solway Firth were not nearly as easy to look upon as Chase Graham bathed in morning sun, she forced her gaze to stay fixed there. "Our deal be cancelled now. With me gone, Kinclearnon and all its holdings be Graham. None will dispute it." Her spine stiffened. " 'Tis what you've wanted for so long, *Sasunach*, is it not?"

"What I want is not the point." His voice was soft, almost regretful. "The settling of our deal *is*."

"Our deal *be* settled," she insisted through gritted teeth. "I'm leaving Kinclearnon to you, even though it pains me to do it." Her gaze narrowed, shifting to Chase only to find him close by her side. Too close. "What be the matter, mon? Does this keep no longer hold the same fascination for you now that the ownership of it be undisputed?"

"Is that what you think?" His tone was casual. The hand that slowly wrapped the thick coil of her plait around his fist was not. "Do you think I'm a child, mistress? Wanting only what I cannot have, then not wanting it once I've attained it?"

With a corner glance, she raked his body. Her gaze was narrow and assessive when it traveled over muscular thighs, lean hips, a solid torso, broad shoulders. This was no bairn, but a man full grown. She met his gaze only briefly. Her cheeks were hot with color. "Nay," she muttered miserably.

His hand had wound its way up to her nape. His rough knuckles scraped her flesh and she could feel the wisps of hairs pulling at her scalp, but not painfully so. When he forced her to return his gaze, she did so reluctantly.

"Good, for I'm no child, Marea," he whispered hoarsely, intensely. His emerald gaze bore into her. "My desires are a man's desires. My dreams, a man's dreams."

"I-I know," she stammered. Was it his words that affected her to the point of near insanity, she wondered? Or the very nearness of him?

"Do you? If so, you'll take the sword, Marea."

"Nay! I do not want to fight you, Chase," she murmured shakily, her gaze fixed on the blade that glistened in the dawn breaking around them. Her fingers were trembling too badly to reach for it, not that she would have. "Take what I offer and let me leave in peace. 'Twould be best for us both."

"Never."

Her gaze snapped up. The desperate emotion that rang clear in that single word was mirrored in his eyes and the hard set of his cheeks and jaw.

Chase leisurely unwrapped her hair from his fist and took a step back. With their gazes still locked, he gave a flick of his wrist and tossed the offered sword up. The hilt slapped into his left palm as he snatched it from midair. The tip pointed at the chilled stone as his fingers curled in a white-knuckled grip around the hilt.

"Take it," he repeated coolly, pressing the hilt against the hollow between her breasts. The heat of his hand cut through the wool. The touch was searing, but no less searing than the intensity of his gaze as he stared down at her. " 'Twill be your last chance to defend yourself, mistress. I've no wish to strike down an unarmed woman"—one golden brow cocked high as the tip of his thumb grazed the inner curve of her breast—"but a deal *is* a deal. I'll not let you welch on your end of this one."

Marea jumped back from his touch. Her gaze sharpened as her previous confusion and, yes, weaknesses, slowly gave way to annoyance. "A MacKenzie does not welch," she snapped with a toss of her head.

"Aye," he agreed, his tone every bit as provoking as his grin, "nor does one lie—or so I've been told. I've yet to see the proof of it, though. To date, every MacKenzie of my acquaintance has displayed a penchant for fibbing. Indeed, they seem to have a gift for it. And as for the welching part—"

"Do not say it!" Marea clenched her fists tightly in the folds of her skirt before she could snatch the sword away from him. She did not want to fight him, she reminded herself. It would do no good. It would change nothing. But her logic was fading quickly, being replaced with proud indignation laced with cold, hard fury. There was no logic in fury.

"Why not?" he countered. His voice was light. His gaze was not. "I speak the truth, Marea. Admit it. If not to me, then to yourself. You've lied to me at every turn and now you'll not uphold your end of our deal. 'Tis not my fault the bulk of your ancestors came from a dishonest lot."

"Ye be insulting me ancestors now?!" she raged, her hand raising. It stopped before touching the sword hilt, but did not drop to her side as she directed it to. Her gaze narrowed as she added

424

shrewdly, "Ye be insulting yours as well, mon. Or did you forget there also be some Scottish blood running through *your* veins.

His expression went from openly scrutinizing to closed and guarded. She'd struck a nerve and she hadn't needed a broadsword to do it. Her spirits lightened a bit, but her anger did not fade.

"I forget nothing," he growled. "But then, I don't claim my ancestors as the proud, truthful, virtuous MacKenzies. The Grahams are known for their uncanny gift for blackmail and their penchant for intermarriage with other clans — Scottish and English alike, mayhaps the reason there are so many of us. We are not known for our honesty, integrity, or good will."

"And your mother's clan?" she asked, openly skeptical.

"Armstrong, which, I am sure in your eyes makes me no better than a full-blooded Graham . . . of the worst order."

"Aye," she murmured, her hand dropping to her side, "they be a bloodthirsty lot of reivers, the Armstrongs. We've been plagued by them off and on in years past."

A slow, almost proud grin slashed across Chase's lips. His eyebrows raised and lowered devilishly. "As has everyone from Border to Highland. The Armstrongs are not choosy about from where they steal their beasts." His expression clouded as, again, the sword hilt was pressed against her breasts. Marea thought he enjoyed that part. For herself, she found the touch singularly disturbing. "Shall we?"

She shook her head and took a quick step back, nearly tripping over her box of kittens. They mewled in protest, but the sound was snatched away by the wind. "I'll not fight you. Have I not said it already?"

His grin broadened. "You have. Of course, being a MacKenzie, I've no way of knowing whether or not you lie."

"A MacKenzie does not—!"

His challenging glare lodged the words in her throat. "Take the sword, Marea. Let's get this unpleasantness over with so we can get on with the rest of our lives."

Against her better judgement, Marea's fingers wove around the leather-wrapped hilt. As soon as she had it, his supporting grip dropped away. The sword was heavy in her hand. The muscles in her forearm and shoulder ached, telling her how long it had been since she'd rested. Still, she raised it up.

Taking a few steps back, she put enough room between them to take a test swipe. She used two hands, the way her father had taught her to do when using a larger sword to compensate for her sex and size. With that swipe and the next she evaluated the weight of the sword and the dexterity with which she could wield it.

Chase raised his own weapon, preparing to parry what he thought was her first attack. The tips of their swords missed each other by a fraction of an inch.

Marea smiled. Satisfied that she had a feel for the sword, she lifted it, tip pointing heavenward, and positioned the slice of blade so that when she looked through it, it ran cleanly down the center of her opponent's face, separating one handsome side from the other. "Do we fight to the death?" she asked with the cold calculation of one about to do serious battle.

" 'Twould make things more interesting, wouldn't it?" he said just as smoothly as he tossed his sword restlessly from one capable fist to the other. He glanced up only long enough to see her momentary alarm. "Then again, considering the prize for which we fight, mayhaps 'twould not be wise. I cannot marry a dead woman . . . and you cannot see a dead man out of Scotland."

"Och! but I can." Her gaze narrowed as she watched each expert pass of his sword. "Flat on his back and cold as stone."

"Let me put it another way. You *won't*." The hilt made its final slap into his right palm, then, with lightning quickness, he launched the first offensive.

Metal crashed against metal as Marea swiftly deflected the blow. The blades scraped together, meeting at the hilt and forcing them close together. Their ragged breaths mingled as they glared at each other.

"The winner is he who draws first blood," Chase informed her, his sweet breath washing over her face. From behind the crossed blades, his emerald eyes sparkled. "Notice, mistress, I said 'he.' "

"Aye." She shoved with all her might, pushing him away. Her blade lifted. The second offensive was hers. "But what I also be noticing is that you be wrong." Their blades crashed together, rhythmically, repeatedly. " 'Twill be *she* who draws first blood here. Make no mistake."

427

"Where you are concerned . . ." He jabbed. She parried. "I never make mistakes."

"Then 'tis past time you started."

His laughter echoed in her ears as he forced her backward. For every two steps back, Marea gained one forward. It was one more than he would have liked, judging from the surprised gleam in his eyes.

Still, it was not enough. Her original objective had been to force him into a corner, thereby limiting his defensive options. That, she realized quickly, was not going to happen. First, he was not on the defensive, she was. Second, he was going only where he cared to go, giving her only the victories he cared to give her. He was toying with her, tiring her, making it glaringly apparent who was the more skillful with a blade.

The clang of swords slapping against each other rang loudly in Marea's ears as she tried to devise another plan. Distracting him came to mind and, since no other idea was presenting itself, she went with it. "Zander said your brother be wounded," she panted. "Will he live?"

"He's not expected to." Chase's voice was hatefully firm, showing no signs of breathless strain.

"Oh." This, Zander had not told her. " 'Tis sorry I am to hear it," she offered breathlessly.

"Don't waste your pity where it's not appreciated."

His sword met hers in a blow that ricocheted up her arms, momentarily numbing her. She recovered just in time to slant her sword in front of her, point down, stopping his blade a scant inch before it bit into her thigh. Her reflexes were dulling and she knew it was only a matter of time before she felt the sting of his blade cutting her flesh.

"I can look in on him before I leave." Somehow she forced him back two steps. "Though, if he be bad off, there's not much I can do."

"Look at him if you like," Chase replied evasively, and gained a step. Their swords crashed together. He was vaguely aware of the guards who'd gathered to watch the match.

"I'll not try healing him if you do not want me to." She took a step back, and though her sword stayed up, she made no move to attack him with it. Already her muscles were cramping. This sudden relaxation was a welcome respite.

Chase stopped cold, his gaze openly assessive, his eyes sparkling in the morning sun. Like Marea, he made no move to attack. Her ragged breathing hissed in his ears. "Does what I want matter to you?"

"Nay," she lied. "Not at all."

"That's what I thought." His blade lifted, countering her thrust. "Do whatever you like. I'll not stop you."

"Would you rather he died?"

" 'Tis my wound that festers in his gut," Chase replied, winded. A quick sidestep and his leg missed the blade that whipped treacherously close to his thigh. Muttering a livid curse, he took up the offensive, determined not to let her words distract him again.

"That does not answer me question," she insisted. She was pressed backward two steps, but quickly gained one back. "I be a healer. There's a chance I could save him. Would ye have me do it or would ye let him die?"

Their blades met. Metal snicked loudly against metal. The hilts clanked together, forcing them close.

"He deserves death," Chase growled, his hot breath searing her upturned face. Their gazes met, locked, and warred. "For Henry, it's long overdue."

"Aye, I'll not argue," she panted. "Be that your answer?"

His jaw hardened, his gaze clouded over as his lashes flickered shut for an instant of indecision. His breathing was hard and ragged, but Marea thought the quality of it stemmed not from exertion of the body, but exertion of the mind.

"Get him now, lass, while his guard is down!"

The faceless voice echoed over Marea's shoulder, tightened around her heart. Her gaze narrowed. A glance told her Chase was so caught up in his own thoughts, he'd not heard the man's advice. She also saw that the man who had spoken was right.

A silent, lightning quick war was waged between her heart and her mind. She could push Chase away, and before he knew what had happened, her blade could slice open his arm. The fight would be over. The castle would be hers. Chase would be forced to leave Scotland and never return.

Her fingers trembled with indecision. The muscles in her body were coiled tight, ready to attack the second her mind gave the command. But her heart intervened. She couldn't do it. She could not slice open the body of a man she felt so strongly about. Her heart ached at just the thought. At the same time,

430

her pride told her she could not admit defeat any more than she could admit love. Aye, love. For only an emotion that strong could stop her from taking what she had fought years to attain.

"Defend yourself, *Sasunach*." she growled, shoving him away before she could change her mind.

Gold-tipped lashes flickered up as Chase stumbled backward, but the surprise Marea expected to see reflected in his eyes was glaringly absent. Instead, his gaze sifted over her—hungrily, possessively, victoriously—and she knew with shocking certainty that he *had* been alert. While his eyes had been closed, his expression turned thoughtfully inward, in truth he'd been aware of everything, including the silent war she'd waged within herself. His gaze said he was also privy to the outcome of that skirmish—and was extremely pleased by the results.

"You couldn't do it, could you, vision?" he asked softly. His sword came up with no time to spare as he deflected her angry swipe at his arm.

Marea flung a string of Gaelic curses at his head that would have made the devil turn blue. She brandished her sword like a demon. Chase's superior strength and skill saw that he stayed unharmed, while his gaze flashed in admiration, surprised by the strength and dexterity of her thrusts.

"What happened to Reubin?" she asked, panting and ignoring his previous question. "I hear he be gone as well."

Using what little strength she had left, she forced him back two steps and felt giddy from even that small a victory. It was short-lived, for she was just as

431

soon put on the defensive again. It was a weak defensive at best. She was tiring fast. They both knew it. Still, she fought. A MacKenzie always fought. "How did ye manage his leaving?"

"In a way I'll never tell you about." He grinned crookedly and glanced at her reddening cheeks. Her thrusts were getting clumsy. He had only to wait a bit longer before casting the final blow. The question was, did he have the grit to slice into her wonderfully soft flesh? Flesh that, even now, recalled memories of hot softness. Could he brand it? "Would you like to admit defeat now and save yourself the humiliation of feeling my blade cut into you, Marea?"

"Buaidh no bas! Victory or death." It was the Douglas' war cry, though she had no intention of airing this fact. The MacKenzie cry simply did not fit the purpose.

Again, their swords met at the hilt. This time when they came up close, Chase let his chest graze the tips of her breasts. Through the tunic and wool, he could feel the frantic pounding of her heart. Up close, he could see the perspiration dotting her upper lip and brow as her ragged breaths washed over him. His eyes softened, but not his voice. "Victory or death. Another virtuous MacKenzie statement. Is there any weight to this one?"

The sword, which had begun to feel alarmingly heavy in her hand, felt suddenly lighter. Her reflexes, which were dulling rapidly, honed and sharpened. With a loud oath, Marea shoved him away. Immediately, her blade descended, ready to swipe up and make the final strike.

Although Chase expected the movement, it was the strength of her push that took him off guard. He started to lift his sword as he stumbled back and would have recovered nicely had his heel not caught on the edge of the crate housing the kittens.

The wooden box clattered against the wall, the kittens mewling plaintively from inside. With a protective hiss, Corbie shot out of the hole in front, robbing Chase of what little balance he had when the cat protectively hooked her claws into his calf. Her back legs flailed madly, her sharp nails sliced bloody ribbons into his leg as she growled low in her throat.

Chase landed on his back with a resounding thud. The sword flew from his hands and clattered atop the stones as his wrist slapped the ground. His head was quick to follow and the impact was punctuated by a grunt of pain.

Marea did not laugh at this comical display, but she thought about it. With a glance, it was clear to see Chase wasn't badly hurt. But neither was he ready to take up the fight again.

Eyeing him carefully, she approached. His eyes were closed and he looked tired and winded. Still, in case it was a trick, she kept her sword up and ready to defend.

"Methinks victory should go to the cat, m'lord," she teased, the irony of the situation hitting her full force now. She felt good, really good, for the first time in a long time when she glanced down and saw the shredded hose encasing his calves. There were bloody slashes where the cat had branded him before hastily retreating to the safety of her wooden box and the small kittens she sought so hard to protect.

Slowly, the thick fringe of his golden lashes flickered up. Chase regarded her coldly, squinting to bring her into focus. There wasn't a trace of humiliation to be had in his gaze. If anything, he looked dazed — and not a little furious.

"Corbie *did* draw first blood," she clarified, pointing to his wounded calf with the tip of her blade. "And since those be your rules, should she not be declared the —" Her eyes widened when her gaze retraced its path. She stared in shock at the tip of her sword. The tip of the steely blade was wet with blood. The brisk air that swirled around her head was tinged with the scent of it and the smell made her stomach roll. Was it hers, or . . . ?

Chase regarded her evenly, watching as her face drained white. Even the brisk wind didn't put the rosy hue back into her abruptly ashen cheeks. Her sword fell from slackened fingers. He doubted she knew she'd dropped it. "If the pain in my hip is anything to judge by," he said, wincing as he rolled on his spine to a sit, "I'd say victory belongs in a different corner."

"I w-wounded you," she stammered, even as her disbelieving gaze picked out the evidence of it. A neat separation could be seen in his trews — much too close to more vital parts of his anatomy than the hip the blade had sliced through. Beneath the rending of fabric, she could see his flesh. That, too, was sticky with fresh blood. Her jaw tightened. "Bloody hell!"

Chapter Twenty-nine

Chase was in the process of inspecting his wound. The sound of his own expletive, enhanced by Marea's brogue, made his gaze stray up. Despite the pain in his hip, which shot down through his thigh, he smiled. "Problems, vision?"

"I-I did not mean to do that," she whispered huskily and dropped to her knees by his side. She closed her eyes, but the sight of his blood—blood she'd unwittingly drawn—refused to be banished. " 'Twas an accident," she rushed on. "You should demand a rematch."

The wind tossed Chase's hair about his face as he returned her gaze with level intensity. Though his thumb itched to smooth away the worried frown etching her brow, he checked the urge. "I think not. 'Twas as fair a fight as any. And a Graham, though not to be measured by the high MacKenzie standards, isn't so proud he can't admit defeat when he sees it."

Marea swallowed hard. Her heart hammered in her chest when she tried to assess his wound without actually touching him. How badly was he hurt? And did she truly want to know? "I cheated!" she exclaimed desperately.

He laughed. "I tripped."

" 'Tis *my* cat," she countered weakly. Red-gold curls danced around her cheeks as the cold wind lifted them. The breeze was not nearly as cold as her heart at that moment.

"Aye, I'll concede that point to you. It changes nothing, however. Corbie or no Corbie, you still drew first blood."

"We'll fight again." She started to turn away, her hand reaching for the sword she only now realized she'd dropped, but his fingers coiled around her wrist, stopping her. He dragged her palm back to him, pressing it firmly against the moist stickiness of his wounded hip. Instantly, she snatched her hand away, but it was too late.

Chase winced, but he did not release her. "I lost, vision," he said, his tone gritty. Reaching up, he ran the tip of his index finger down the slender line of her jaw. A thin red trail of his own blood was left to mar her beautiful flesh. The sight made his breath catch and his blood surge cold in his veins. "I can accept the loss. 'Twould seem 'tis you who cannot. Should I ask why? Or wouldn't you tell me?"

"I can accept it," she lied quickly, breathlessly, and very, very weakly. " 'Tis just that I . . . I did not expect to win. I be surprised is all. Nothing more."

"You little liar."

His tender tone snatched her attention. She glanced up and was captured by his piercing emerald eyes. She shivered when his hand turned inward, cupping her chin in his palm and holding her steady when she

436

would have looked away. His roughened thumb stroked her cheek. Her quivering increased tenfold.

"You did not want to win, did you, vision?" His gaze turned darkly probing.

Hot color splashed over Marea's cheeks. Since he would not let her chin go, she dropped her gaze. It was a mistake, that—for she was greeted with the sight of his slashed flesh and blood. It was a sight that affected her as much as if it had been her own blood. Her head spun and her stomach lurched, even as her heart throbbed with vibrant life. "I fought ye well, did I not?" she countered finally, breathlessly. She closed her eyes against the sight of his ripped trews and what they concealed. "Would I have fought so hard if I'd no mind to win?"

"You were a most worthy opponent," he conceded softly. "But you still haven't answered my question. Tell me, Marea, was it me you fought so fiercely," his hand slipped to the nape of her neck, drawing her closer, his lips hovering a scant inch from her own, "or yourself?"

"I do not know what you mean," she gasped, pulling away from the confusion of his touch. He let her go and she thought that was for the best. She couldn't think when he touched like that. Indeed, she could not think when he touched her at all!

"Don't you?"

"Nay!"

"Then mayhaps I should say it for you, since you seem reluctant to admit it even to yourself."

"Aye. Mayhaps you should," she replied stiffly, rising awkwardly to her feet. She towered over him, hands on her hips.

Chase made no move to rise. For the moment, he conceded the physical upper hand to her, while settling for the verbal one himself. "You'd no desire to win, vision. I know it. Mayhaps, deep inside, you know it too. 'Twas the reason you couldn't draw my blood when I gave you the perfect chance. Now, would you like me to tell you why?"

"Aye," she croaked, unable to stop herself. Though her mind screamed to take the word back, her heart yearned to hear him say what her tongue refused to. Words her heart cried out to hear.

He bent his knees and, wincing, used them as a pillow for his elbows. Squinting against the sun rising at her back, he gazed up at her. The golden rays of morning shimmered around her; her slender shape a perfect silhouette against the bright light. "You love me, vision. *Really* love me. You have for some time. 'Tis as simple as that. Only your fierce MacKenzie pride has stopped you from admitting it—to me, or to yourself."

Their gazes clashed for what felt like an eternity. Each searching, each hotly probing. Marea was the first to look away. Her feet shifted nervously atop the stone when she felt his eyes bore into her. They were pleading, those hauntingly green eyes. And filled with emotion. She didn't have to see them to know it.

"Even if 'twere true, it does not matter," she said finally, evasively. "It changes naught." She heard him shift, knew he had risen and now stood towering by her side. Her arm burned from his nearness and her cheek tingled at the feel of his warm breath caressing it. Her nostrils stung with the smell of blood and sweat. It wasn't the unpleasant aroma it might have been.

"Ah, there is where you're wrong. It changes *everything*," His words caressed her, enveloping her in a bittersweet embrace. "I meant it when I said I couldn't let you leave. What I neglected to mention was that, no matter what the outcome of our battle this morn, I never intended to leave Kinclearnon either. Not so long as you are here."

Joy, hot and sharp, shot through her like a lightning bolt. Even the indignation she tried to summon up was not strong enough to counter it. "You lied to me then?" she whispered throatily.

"Of necessity." He nodded gravely, the golden fringe of his hair scraping the collar of his soiled tunic. "I'd hoped by the end of our battle you'd have changed your mind and ask me not to go. What I didn't take into account, and should have, was that damn MacKenzie pride of yours. I should have known it would blot out what your heart truly desires . . . again."

Anger took a long time in coming, and when it did come it was in a weak trickle, easily quenched. Wrapping her arms about her waist, she kept her gaze riveted to the wooden crate, hidden in the shadows beside the stone. "And how would ye be knowing me heart desires, *Sasunach?* Have I not proved I want ye out of Kinclearnon? Out of me life forever?"

"If you had, would I be standing here arguing with you now, witch? Would I not be busy readying my men for the journey back to Brackenhill?" His fingers coiled around her upper arm. While the touch was not rough, it wasn't tender either. It was merely insistent, determined. It was wonderful.

439

When he drew her close, she went willingly, melting her side into his solid feel. A sigh of contentment whispered past her lips before she could stop it. The wind was a poor mask for the sound, as the tightening of his body attested.

Marea could deny it no longer—to Chase or herself. She'd harbored a physical ache to feel his firmness against her. Now that she felt it, languished in it, the feeling inflamed her. Fascinated her. Filled a very real void deep in the pit of her. But that was not all. While his touch kindled desire, his presence kindled something deeper, something stronger, something that touched her heart, her soul, her very life. She could find no words adequate to describe the feeling of total bliss, the feeling of utter contentment, so she remained thoughtfully silent, basking in the warm golden glow of . . . yes, of love.

"Do you deny it, witch?" he asked huskily in her ear. "Do you deny that, had you truly wanted me gone, you'd not have saved my life that night in the mist." His other hand wrapped around her waist, the palm splayed over her stomach as he pulled her back against him. "Admit it, Marea, you don't want me to leave. You never did. Indeed, you never had any intention of winning our battle today or any other day."

"But I fought—"

"Shhh." His breath was like a warm breeze rustling the wisps of hair clinging to her cheek and brow, searing the sensitive flesh beneath. "The wound in my hip tells me how hard you fought. Pardon the pun, but that is not the point."

With a torn sigh, she rested her head against the firm cushion of his chest. It was a warm, comforting pillow. She had only to turn her head to feel the material of his billowing tunic against her cheek, to hear the throbbing of his heart in her ear. Was his heartbeat be as frantic and wild as the one throbbing within her own breasts? Somehow, she knew it was—and that knowledge brought a sweet smile to her lips.

"What be your point?" she asked finally, wearily.

"That you did not wield the sword with the dexterity with which I've seen you wield one before. That your attack was halfhearted and insincere." His head turned and he grazed his cheek against the silky, fragrant curtain of her hair. She smelled of soap and heather, a scent that had long ago become a very real part of him. Inhaling deeply, he placed a light kiss atop her head and felt her quiver in response. His hold tightened protectively. "Would it not have sat better with your fierce MacKenzie pride to see me win? To see me wed you by force? Would it not have saved you the trouble of having to confront your feelings for me?"

"Aye," she whispered raggedly, "things would have been a fine muckle easier had you not tripped over me cat." She took a deep breath and plunged on. "A-and you be right. I did not want to fight you because I did not want to win. Not truly."

His hand slid upward. Gripping both her arms, Chase turned her around to face him. Her skirt twirled around their legs, grazing his torn hose and trews. "What *do* you want, Marea?" he asked, his voice low and husky. His gaze searched her face. The hair blew back from his brow, his pleading expression unconcealed. The sight of it touched her, and touched her deeply. "Tell me, vision."

441

"I . . ." her voice caught and she glanced away. Like a magnet, her attention was drawn back to him. Her gaze caressed his face, even though her vision blurred with the tears that stung her eyes and threatened to course down her cheeks. The fingers she'd splayed over his chest for balance tightened as she balled his tunic in her fists.

"Say it, Marea." His fingers bit into her arms as he suppressed the urge to shake the truth from her. "Please."

This last was a low, desperate groan. It was Marea's undoing. To see this fierce Border reiver pleading was too much for her. The sight sliced her to core and tightened like a knot in her stomach until her own heart forced her to respond to him. "I be wanting what I canna have," she confessed, her voice high and shaky. Swallowing hard, she met his gaze as the first traitorous tear slipped down her cheek. "I want you, Chase."

His lashes flickered shut as he lifted his face to the wind and savored her words. Her declaration washed through him, fueling his hunger for her. It brought with it a joy unlike any he'd ever felt before. The pain in his hip felt like a minor inconvenience when compared to this blinding wave of elation.

The easing of his harsh features fascinated Marea and she watched, mesmerized. His ragged sigh kissed her cheeks as she felt the tension in him ebb. The muscles beneath her hands unbunched, softened about as much as they ever would, as did the ones that pressed against her hips and thighs. Beneath her fingertips she felt the beat of his heart — wild and erratic, but calmingly firm. Unbroken.

"Do you love me?" His eyes were still closed, as

442

though he couldn't bear to look at her when she answered.

"Would I have nursed you that night I found you bleeding in the mist if I did not?" she countered, brushing the tears from her cheeks with her fists.

His eyes snapped open and she saw a flash of confusion in their emerald depths. "I don't know. Would you?"

She chuckled. "Aye, I would," she answered. " 'Tis the way I am. Beside, how could I not? Ye did looked so pitiful. Pale and bloody, but proud as a strutting peacock. 'Twould have taken a stronger will than mine to leave ye there."

"And that was your reason?" he asked, his tone etched in caution as his fingers tightened perceptively around her arms.

She shook her head even as her hands strayed over his chest. He felt warm and firm. Strong and mighty. Wonderful. "Nay. I had a debt in sore need of repaying. And a MacKenzie always repays his debts." His golden brows furrowed and Marea quickly answered the question shimmering in his eyes. "You're forgetting the night you saved me life." Her smile froze, her expression clouded. "I never did. 'Twas much I owed you. Had you not come along, Reubin would have—"

"But he didn't."

"Thanks to you." A dark chill settled in her bones. The arms wrapped protectively around her, hugging her close, quickly dispelling it. "But he might have. Many's the night I've dreamt of what could have happened. And each time I woke, 'tis with a heartful of thanks to you that I was spared."

"You owe me nothing," he whispered sharply into

443

her hair. "Not now. Not ever. Life on these Borders is fierce—I'll be the first to admit it—but not so fierce that innocent women and children need be abused. My sense of justice, warped as many think it is, rebels at that. What I did for you I'd done before, for other wenches found in similar circumstances."

"But you rode with your father, Chase. Even knowing what he did to those he was victorious over." Marea felt him stiffen against her and she wished she'd bitten the hateful words back.

"We've talked of this already. You know I can't deny it. But think of this, Marea. Had I not spent my youth trying to win my father's approval, who would have been there to rescue you? Or the others? Make no mistake, I don't claim to have saved a great many lives from David Graham's wrath, but I do claim a few. Of that, at least, I can be proud."

Marea lifted her head, her searching amethyst gaze meeting his tortured emerald green one. Her hand itched to stroke the sculpted jaw, to work free the tension knotting that firm, proud line. She hesitated, but in the end did not deny herself. " 'Tis proud you should be, Chase. Of that and a fine muckle more." His chin felt warm, the flesh slightly bristled as it scraped her palm. "I be thinking back to that first time I saw you. Not many would have gone against a mon like your father and Reubin. But you did. Ye saved me life. I knew then what a fine mon you be. And I saw the potential of you being finer still. Ye did not disappoint me."

Chase turned his cheek into her palm, inhaling deeply of the sweet scent of her skin. "Be careful what you say, vision." He nodded his head to the men who were still watching. The group was silent, hanging on every word. " 'Twould not be wise for them to hear you praising a Graham."

Marea had forgotten their presence. She chose to continue ignoring them. "Let them listen, for I speak the truth. There be no shame in that." Her amethyst eyes twinkled when her arms lifted, curling around the thick trunk of his neck. The golden curls at his nape tickled her fingers when she entwined them there. "Besides, ye be only half a Graham. The other half be of fine Armstrong stock" — she grinned teasingly — "no doubt the reason for any of the good qualities ye possess."

Chase's grin was crooked and quick as he tightened his hold on her. His hands trailed hotly down her spine, his palms searing her gently rounded bottom as he pulled her hard against him. "Leave it to a bloody Scot to toss a man's heritage in his face at a time like this," he said with a chuckle.

She smiled sweetly and wiggled against him. Though he tried to suppress it, she heard a groan rumble in his throat. The sound tingled up her spine, pleasing her immensely. "A time like what?" she asked, her voice thick. His hands were kneading her bottom. It was getting difficult to think, let alone talk.

"I was about to propose to you properly, wench," he informed her. His voice was lightly sarcastic, and heavily seductive. "But now . . ."

"Och! mon, we've done naught that is proper since we met," she said. Her breath caught when his palms seared a path down to the tops of her thighs. His fingers hooked around them, the tips nestling between. Even through the thick woolen plaid, his fingers

445

burned her quivering flesh. "Still," she continued breathlessly, "if ye feel the need, who be I to deny it?"

"Who be you?" he asked, his tone huskily serious as his gaze raked her upturned face. "Need you ask, vision? You are Marea MacKenzie of the Clan MacKenzie. You are the woman I love. You," he whispered, "are my life."

"Ah, Chase," she sighed, her arms tightening around his neck. His hair felt wonderful against her cheek as she buried her face in that soft hollow between shoulder and neck. "And you be mine. I could not face tomorrow if you were not there to share it, me feelings be that strong."

"Aaand . . . ?" he prodded. He was nuzzling her neck now, and his tongue was doing perfectly sinful things to her. Things that made her shiver. Things that made her burn.

"Aaand . . ." She gasped when his tongue slipped moistly over the curl of her ear, then dipped inside, "Bloody hell! Do you not know it already? I love you too."

"About time you admitted it," he whispered raggedly against her neck and at the same time bent to scoop her into his arms. She felt lighter than one of the kittens nestled snugly in that box. And much, much softer.

"Aye, past time, methinks," she agreed as she nibbled on his neck. "Long past time. Och! me kittens, mon!" she exclaimed, squirming in his arms when she caught sight of the crate as they passed it. "I canna leave them here. And there's still that wound in your hip to attend."

His long, confident strides carried them to the door.

"One of the men will fetch the kittens. And what wound is that?"

"You know what wound. And did you forget your brother? What will happen to Henry whilst ye satisfy your manly lusts?"

"I'll not keep you long," he said, kicking open the door with his foot and carrying her into the shadowy corridor. It was warm here, but not nearly as warm as the blood firing through her veins. "But I *will* keep you. And aye, I give you permission to tend my brother. After I'm through with you there will be time to work your magic on Henry. First"—his gaze raked her so hotly a blush kissed her cheeks—"you work your magic on me, witch."

Marea smiled and rested her head atop his warm, firm shoulder. She could feel the heat of his skin against her cheek even through his tunic. It felt delicious. "There will be advantages to sharing the keep o' a witch," she sighed. "Do you not agree, m'lord?"

"You're not a witch, you're a *healer*. And aye, vision, many advantages. I look forward to discovering each one. But first, you have to understand 'tis *my* keep we'll be sharing. Or did you forget, 'twas you who said our fight was unfair. That you had won unjustly."

She batted his shoulder with her fist, but smiled despite herself. "Aye, I said it, but—"

"Then 'tis my keep."

"Nay, 'tis mine!" she argued playfully as Chase shouldered his chamber door open and carried her over the threshold. "You said yourself a Graham admits defeat."

"When he sees it. But a Graham also never argues with a wench who's trying to gift him with a castle.

447

Methinks 'tis a Border law written somewhere. Remind me to show it to you."

"I'll not argue about this, Chase. Kinclearnon be mine."

"You'll have to argue, mistress. I'll not give it up."

She opened her mouth, only to have her words swallowed by his lips. Hot and hungry, he devoured every argument she had.

"I have to attend the next day of truce to get Godfrey back," he whispered raggedly against her lips. "You'll have a chance to air your views on who should own this keep then. The Wardens will delight in hearing it, I've no doubt. For now, I'd rather do what we do best. And it does *not* involve talking."

Marea sighed her agreement as Chase kicked the chamber door shut, then laid her atop his bed. Wrapped in each other's arms, their bodies straining into each other, they forgot for a little while that Kinclearnon Castle existed at all.